言語学、文学そしてその彼方へ

都留文科大学英文学科創設50周年記念研究論文集

Linguistics, Literature and Beyond:
A Collection of Research Papers Celebrating the 50th Anniversary
of the Foundation of the Department of English, Tsuru University

Edited by the Editorial Committee for the Research Papers Celebrating
the 50th Anniversary of the Foundation of the Department of English,
Tsuru University

ひつじ書房

都留文科大学英文学科創設50周年
記念研究論文集編集委員会［編］

A Japan Fantasy in Virginia Woolf's "Friendships Gallery"

Figure 1. The Japanese pattern used for Virginia and Leonard Woolf's *Two Stories* (p.245)

ハーレム・ルネサンスにおけるプリミティヴィズムとネグロフィリア

図 5　アーロン・ダグラス「ニグロの生の諸相―塔の歌」(1934 年) ニューヨーク公共図書館ショーンバーグ黒人文化研究センター所蔵。
Aaron Douglas, *Aspects of Negro Life: Song of the Towers*, 1934. Oil on canvas.©Art & Artifacts Division, Schomburg Center for Research in Black Culture, The New York Public Library.　　　　　　　　　　　(p.348)

ハーレム・ルネサンスにおけるプリミティヴィズムとネグロフィリア

図 8　アーロン・ダグラス「シカゴの創立」(1933 年) カンザス大学スペンサー美術館所蔵。
Aaron Douglas, *The Founding of Chicago*, 1933. Spencer Museum of Art, The University of Kansas, Museum purchase: R. Charles and Mary Margaret Clevenger Fund, 2006. 0027　　　　　　　　　　(p.349)

vi

Exploiting the Oncogenic MYC Pathway Activation in Targeting Triple-Negative Breast Cancer

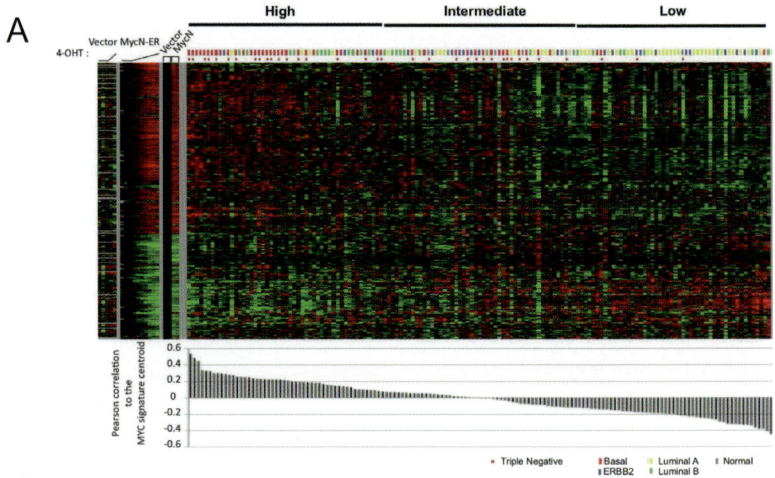

Figure 2. Elevated MYC signaling in human triple-negative breast cancers. (p.393)

英文学科創設 50 周年記念研究論文集
刊行にあたって

　都留文科大学英文学科は、1953 年に山梨県立臨時教員養成所として始まり、都留市立都留短期大学の時代を経て、1960 年には 4 年制の都留文科大学になった本学の 3 番目の学科として、1963 年 4 月 1 日に開設されました。当時は定員が 30 名、キャンパスが置かれていたのも、臨時教員養成所時代からの谷村町の旧キャンパスでした。そして、英文学科は、2013 年で開設 50 周年を迎えることができました。この場を借りて卒業生の皆さまならびに学科開設や運営に尽力された先人の皆さま、そして地元都留市の皆さまに、学科を代表してお祝いの言葉を述べさせていただきます。

　その後の英文学科は、1966 年に定員が 80 名、そして 1971 年には 100 名（現在 120 名）へと拡大し、また、1991 年には、本学文学専攻科の中に英文学専攻が置かれ、1998 年には、その専攻が発展して、大学院文学研究科修士課程の中に英語英米文学専攻が設置され現在に至っています。英文学科の開設当初から、本学の教員養成大学としての特性により、卒業生は全国各地の教員として活躍され、日本の中等教育において多大なる貢献を長期間にわたってしてきていることは周知の通りです。また、1998 年、本学と米国・カリフォルニア大学との学術交流協定締結以来、英文学科から多くの学生が留学生としてカリフォルニア大学の各キャンパスで学び、その国際化の一翼を担ってきました。近年は、民間企業において、また公務員や大学の教員として活躍される卒業生も多くなり、ますますその躍進には、目を見張るものがあります。

　英文学科が創設 50 周年を迎える 2013 年は、偶然にも、本学の記章

にもデザインされ、地元都留市にとってもかけがえのない存在である富士山が、世界文化遺産に登録されました。

　本年は、英文学科そして都留文科大学が、さらなる発展を遂げる歴史的とも言える節目の年として我々の記憶に長く残ることだと思います。

2013 年 10 月
英文学科長　竹島達也

まえがき

　本書は、都留文科大学文学部英文学科創設 50 周年記念行事の一環として出版されたもので、本学英文学科専任教員、名誉教授、本学英文学科卒業の研究者の論文、26 編が収められている。本書は、第Ⅰ部言語学、第Ⅱ部文学、第Ⅲ部その他の分野に分け、3 部構成にした。これらの分野順に論文を配し、各々の分野の中の掲載順序は英語論文、日本語論文の順で、筆者のアルファベット順（英語論文）および 50 音順（日本語論文）とした。

第Ⅰ部

　第Ⅰ部では、統語論、語用論、形態論、文字論、第二言語習得論、英語教育学、生物言語学、認知言語学を含む以下 15 編の論文が納められている。

Fukushima, Saeko（福島佐江子）"(In)directness and (In)formality in Japanese E-mail Requests" は語用論の論文で、日本人大学生の電子メールによる依頼を直接的―間接的及びフォーマル―インフォーマルという観点から分析している。依頼する側とされる側に力の差がない場合や親しい関係の場合には依頼の力を和らげる間接的―インフォーマルな依頼が頻繁に使用され、依頼される側に力がある関係では距離を置く間接的―フォーマルな依頼が多く使用されたと述べられている。

Imai, Takashi（今井隆）"Merge and Three Dimensional Structures" は、生物言語学の論文で、生物言語学において独特の操作（言語能力で3つの下位操作をする Merge）が存在すると提案し、樹形図が本当は平らな 2D ではなく、言語の多様性を説明する上で、樹形図は 3D であることを提唱している。また、世界の言語は、狭義の言語能力において、極めて均一であるとし、チョムスキーが最近言及している言語能力の外部にあるという第3の要因について検討している。

Matsuoka, Mikinari（松岡幹就）"Subjective Small Clause Predicates in English and Japanese" は、統語論の論文である。日本語の認識動詞の小節補部は、対応する英語の小節補部と異なり、名詞述語を持つことができないといくつかの先行研究では言われていることを踏まえ、問題の小節構造には、英語でも日本語でも、主観的命題内容を表すという意味的制限が課せられており、その条件を満たせば、日本語でも名詞述語が現れるという観察を提示している。

Okuwaki, Natsumi（奥脇奈津美）"Temporal Interpretation in L2 English by Japanese and Chinese Speakers" は、第二言語習得論の論文である。形態素の習得は SLA 研究で広く扱われてきたが、その多くは産出に関するものであり、意味解釈を調べた研究は少ないことを踏まえ、言語的に時制体系が異なる日本語と中国語に着目し、それぞれを母語とする英語学習者が、that 節補文と関係節内の時制をどの程度正確に解釈し、形式と意味の関係を習得しているのか調べ、その結果を第一言語の影響に言及しながら考察している。

Saito, Shinji（斎藤伸治）"Remarks on the English Writing System and its Logographic Nature" は文字論の論文で、英語の綴りに見られる表語的な性格について考察している。英語のようなアルファベット式書記体系を含めてすべての文字は、単に音を再現するというものではなく、それ自体の体系を持ち、場合によっては積極的に言語に働きかけるものであ

る。音と文字とは一緒になって言語の実体を構成していると考えなければならないということを論じている。

Sawasaki, Koichi（澤崎宏一）"The Role of Reading Experience in Construing Japanese Gapless Relative Clauses" は第二言語習得論の論文である。「ラーメンを食べたおつり」のような結果随伴物を伴う語用論的関係節文は、関係節内の動詞を非過去（食べる）に替えると不適格となる。アンケート調査の結果、読書経験が豊富なほど、「ラーメンを食べるおつり」の不自然さを敏感に察知できることがわかり、語用論的知識の個人差と読書経験の多寡との関係を示唆している。

Terakawa, Kaori（寺川かおり）"Textual Cohesion in the English as a Foreign Language (EFL) Classroom" は英語教育学の分野の論文である。結束性は、テキストを意味の通る文章にするために必要な要素の1つであり、長文読解の際、英語学習者は英語母語話者とは違い、文中の結束性の把握が困難である。そのため、結束性に学習者の注意を向けることで、読解力の向上が見込めることを踏まえ、結束性をどのように英語学習者に指導できるか、その方法を検討している。

Yamada, Masashi（山田昌史）"A Syntactic Approach to Language Variations of Aspectual Properties" は、統語論の論文である。日本語と英語に見られる結果性の標示に見られる形態的特徴の違いについて観察し、その違いが統語構造上の素性照合に関わる範疇の違いに帰すことを提案している。具体的には、統語構造に生じる［telic］素性を英語は XP 要素、日本語は X^0 要素が照合することで、日英語の違いが捉えられることを主張している。

Yasuhara, Kazuya（安原和也）"Jokes and Semantic Blinking: A Conceptual Blending Analysis" は、認知言語学の論文である。ジョークの意味は、複数の意味が相互にせめぎ合うことで、どちらとも解釈できないで揺ら

いでいる状況にその面白さの源泉があると言える。このようなジョークの性質を生み出す背景に、概念ブレンディングの認知プロセスが密接に関与していることを点滅圧縮（semantic blinking）という概念を中核に据えつつ示唆している。

上原義正「リメディアル教育における教員間のシナジー効果の検証―協働的 FD 活動を通じて―」は英語教育学の論文で、大学におけるリメディアル教育でのシナジー効果を検証した実践的研究である。大学生の学力低下が叫ばれるなか、補習プログラムの運営を行った。教育経営および英語教育の観点から、教育活動に焦点をあて、協働的な FD 活動を行った。結果として、シナジー効果が発生し補習プログラムは円滑に運営が行われたことが明らかとなった。

竹村雅史「SVT テストによる英文多読測定の試み」は英語教育学の論文である。英語多読授業では、学習者に読後レポートなどで読んだ内容を記録させて評価している。読みの向上に繋がったという報告は聞くが、しかし、実際にどの位理解しているかは、この方法ではわからない。本論文は SVT テスト（文章判読テスト）を用いて多読学習者の理解度測定が可能かを試みるものである。

内藤徹「英語教育における ICT 活用の効果―映画視聴時における１つの工夫―」は英語教育学の論文である。英語映画のリスニング中にタスクを用いた場合と用いない場合でどのように異なるのかを調べている。普通のリスニングとは異なり、映画の場合、大量に聴き取る extensive listening が可能だからである。今回の場合はタスクリスニングとした。今後の ICT を用いた英語教育への１つの提案をしている。

野中博雄「英語形容詞のカタカナ語の語彙範疇化について」は形態論の論文である。英語形容詞のカタカナ語が日本語文法の枠組みで何に語彙範疇化されるのかを解明しようとしたものである。日本語文中での英語

形容詞のカタカナ語の統語的特徴を名詞性・形容詞性の観点から考察し、それらは「形容動詞の語幹」として述語化、名詞化、形容詞化、副詞化されるのではないかと結んでいる。

松土清「学習指導要領の改訂と英語授業の構造改革―世界のグローバル化と日本の言語施策―」は英語教育学の論文である。近年の流通経済のグローバル化の加速やインターネット利用者の急増が拍車をかけ、広域コミュニケーション・ツールとしての英語のニーズが急騰していることを踏まえ、アジア諸国の英語教育施策等を概観し、高等学校新学習指導要領に特化して、時代に即した英語教育構造改革の推進のあり方について論じている。

宮岸哲也「シンハラ語における無意志他動詞構文の主語について」は統語論の分野の論文である。シンハラ語の無意志他動詞構文の主語としては、後置詞 atin を伴う名詞（atin 句名詞）、与格名詞、そして具格名詞の三つの形式が存在する。動詞によっては、主語標示交替が可能なものと不可能なものがあり、主語標示交替の点から無意志動詞を分類すると、atin 句主語のみ、与格主語のみ、具格主語のみ、atin 句主語と与格主語、atin 句主語と具格主語、atin 句主語と与格主語と具格主語の 6 タイプが存在し、これらの 6 タイプに分類される無意志他動詞がどのようなものなのかを明らかにしている。

第 II 部

　第 II 部では、英文学、米文学、英語文学、アメリカ文化論を含む 9 編の論文が収められている。

Kubota, Noriko（窪田憲子）"A Japan Fantasy in Virginia Woolf's "Friendships Gallery""は、英文学の論文である。ヴァージニア・ウルフの最も初期の作品の 1 つである『友情のギャラリー』(1907 年)の第 3 章

の舞台になっている日本について考察した。この時期のウルフの日本に対する関心がどのようなものであるのか、日本幻想とも言えるウルフの日本表象が、ウルフの「イングリッシュネス」批判と関連していることを検証した。

Ohira, Eiko（大平栄子）"A Quest for Identity and an Epiphany about Love：*About Daddy*, a Partition Novel" は、英語文学の論文である。M. A. Nayak の *About Daddy* が、祖国インドへの罪の意識を持つ父の娘（インド系ディアスポラ二世でアメリカ生まれの主人公）が、父の沈黙の物語を探求する中で成長するという独自の構成をもつ印パ分離独立小説であることを論じた。

Akaho, Eiichi（赤穂榮一）"An Analytical Study of *The Appeal* by John Grisham in Terms of Its Logic, Rationality, and Impact" は、米文学の論文である。ジョン・グリシャムは弁護士であり作家であった。かつてミシシッピー州議会議員に当選し、1990年まで務めた。グリシャム（内部から法律と政治に熟知している）は、しばしば、政治で法律陰謀の強力で、タイムリーで、衝撃的な作品を発表した。あまりにおなじみの策略を立てたこの小説について分析した。

髙橋愛「なぜ彼は引き金を引かなかったのか―『白鯨』第123章「マスケット銃」におけるスターバックの逡巡―」は、米文学の論文である。ハーマン・メルヴィルの『白鯨』においてスターバックは、白鯨への復讐というエイハブの腹案に唯一抵抗を示した人物である。本論文は、スターバックの人物像と彼の反乱の試みに注目し、『白鯨』の悲劇性について考察するものである。

瀧口美佳「ワシントン・アーヴィングとウォルター・スコット―『スケッチ・ブック』はどのようにして生まれたか―」は、米文学の論文である。アメリカ・ロマン派を代表するワシントン・アーヴィングは、

1817年敬愛するウォルター・スコットと面会の機会を得た。本論文ではその邂逅の経緯を検証し二人の語らいを通して、アーヴィング文学の根幹及び代表作『スケッチ・ブック』がスコットから授かった文学的知見や叡智に支えられていたという点について論じた。

竹島達也「「キャンプ的感覚」で探究する多元文化主義的ユートピア―『エンジェルズ・イン・アメリカ』とエイズ危機下のニューヨーク―」は、米文学の論文である。アメリカの同性愛の劇作家トニー・クシュナーによる『エンジェルズ・イン・アメリカ』について、その演劇的スタイル(ソンタグの「キャンプ的感覚」)と思想的背景(ベンヤミンの「歴史の廃墟」)を分析し、舞台となっているエイズ危機下の1980年代のニューヨークとの相関関係を解明したものである。

中地幸「ハーレム・ルネサンスにおけるプリミティヴィズムとネグロフィリア―『新しい黒人(ニューニグロ)』とアーロン・ダグラス―」は、アメリカ文化の論文である。アフリカ系アメリカ人によるモダニズム芸術運動であるハーレム・ルネサンスにおける〈ネグロフィリア〉と〈プリミティヴィズム〉が考察されるが、とりわけハーレムルネッサンスの金字塔ともいえる『新しい黒人』、および芸術家アーロン・ダグラスの絵画作品に焦点があてられ、論じている。

花田愛「サッコ゠ヴァンゼッティ事件を語る―シンクレアの『ボストン』とドス・パソスの『USA』―」は、米文学の論文である。サッコ゠ヴァンゼッティ事件を語る2つの作品、すなわち、因果的説明とフィクションを共存させたシンクレアの『ボストン』と因果律を手放し、無秩序を許容することで集合的な歴史を独自のスタイルで語ったドス・パソスの『USA』が共に挑んだ歴史の語り方に私たちが現在と過去を語るためのヒントを見出している。

依藤道夫「フォークナー世界と「過去」」は、米文学の論文である。ミ

シシッピー州は深南部色の濃い地方であり、同州の申し子たるウィリアム・フォークナーは、奴隷制に基づく農園体制の歴史（過去）を背景に、南北戦争や自身の家系も交えながら諸作品を創出した。過去への遡及性の強い独特のフォークナー世界も、実は、History（Histoire）の原義に即した、古典の王道を行っていた点について論じている。

第 III 部

第 III 部では、細胞生物学、物理学の 2 編の論文が納められている。

Horiuchi, Dai（堀内大）"Exploiting the Oncogenic MYC Pathway Activation in Targeting Triple-Negative Breast Cancer: Utility of CDK Inhibition Revisited" は、細胞生物学の論文である。エストロゲン、黄体ホルモンと HER2 レセプターネガティブ「トリプルネガティブ」乳癌は、最も臨床的に研究が急務なサブタイプ（現在、適切な治療方法が存在しない）を含む。プロ・アポトーシスの BCL-2 家族 BIM は、CDK 抑制の後、上方制御されて、この合成致死メカニズムに関与する。高い MYC 表現による悪性の胸腫瘍が CDK 抑制剤に唯一敏感なことを結果は示しており、治療への突破口になりうることを示した。

沢野伸浩「福島第一原子力発電所から放出されたセシウム 137 土壌沈着密度分布図の作成」は、物理学の論文である。福島第一原子力発電所事故により、広域に及ぶ放射能汚染が発生した。住民避難等に必要とされる汚染情報は米国により事故直後の段階で把握され、そのデータが一般公開されている。このデータを元にチェルノブイリ原発事故の際と同様の基準により汚染範囲推定したところ、福島はその半分程度であることが明らかとなった。

英文学科専任教員・名誉教授はもとより、英文学科 50 年の歴史の中で輩出した研究者による研究論文集が完成したことは、我々の喜びとす

る所である。本学英文学科卒業の研究者は内外で活躍され、その専門分野も多岐にわたるが、諸般の事情により執筆して頂けなかった方々もいらっしゃることも記しておく。

　本書を出版するにあたり、ひつじ書房松本功社長にはいろいろと便宜を図っていただいた。担当して下さった渡邉あゆみ氏には、様々な助言を頂いた。また、森脇尊志氏をはじめ編集スタッフの方々にもお世話になった。ここに御礼申し上げる。

　最後に、英文学科創設50周年記念研究論文集出版にあたり、助成していただいた都留文科大学に感謝申し上げる。

都留文科大学英文学科創設50周年記念
研究論文集編集委員会
委員長　　今井　隆
副委員長　福島佐江子

目次(Contents)

英文学科創設 50 周年記念研究論文集刊行にあたって
　竹島達也 ··· vii
まえがき
　今井　隆・福島佐江子 ··· ix

第 I 部 ··· 1

(In)directness and (In)formality in Japanese E-mail Requests
　Saeko Fukushima ·· 3

Merge and Three Dimensional Structures
　Takashi Imai ·· 29

Subjective Small Clause Predicates in English and Japanese
　Mikinari Matsuoka ·· 43

Temporal Interpretation in L2 English by Japanese and Chinese Speakers
　Natsumi Okuwaki ··· 55

Remarks on the English Writing System and its Logographic Nature
　　Shinji Saito ·· 73

The Role of Reading Experience in Construing Japanese Gapless Relative Clauses
　　Koichi Sawasaki ··· 81

Textual Cohesion in the English as a Foreign Language (EFL) Classroom
　　Kaori Terakawa ·· 111

A Syntactic Approach to Language Variations of Aspectual Properties
　　Masashi Yamada ··· 119

Jokes and Semantic Blinking:
　A Conceptual Blending Analysis
　　Kazuya Yasuhara ·· 141

リメディアル教育における教員間のシナジー効果の検証
　協働的 FD 活動を通じて
　　上原義正 ··· 159

SVT テストによる英文多読測定の試み
　　竹村雅史 ··· 167

英語教育における ICT 活用の効果
　映画視聴時における 1 つの工夫
　　内藤　徹 ··· 177

英語形容詞のカタカナ語の語彙範疇化について
　　野中博雄 ··· 189

学習指導要領の改訂と英語授業の構造改革
世界のグローバル化と日本の言語施策
松土　清 ·· 201

シンハラ語における無意志他動詞構文の主語について
宮岸哲也 ·· 219

第Ⅱ部 ··· 235

A Japan Fantasy in Virginia Woolf's "Friendships Gallery"
Noriko Kubota ··· 237

A Quest for Identity and an Epiphany about Love:
About Daddy, a Partition Novel
Eiko Ohira ··· 249

An Analytical Study of *The Appeal* by John Grisham in Terms of Its Logic, Rationality, and Impact
Eiichi Akaho ·· 261

なぜ彼は引き金を引かなかったのか
『白鯨』第123章「マスケット銃」におけるスターバックの逡巡
髙橋　愛 ·· 283

ワシントン・アーヴィングとウォルター・スコット
『スケッチ・ブック』はどのようにして生まれたか
瀧口美佳 ·· 299

「キャンプ的感覚」で探究する多元文化主義的ユートピア
『エンジェルズ・イン・アメリカ』とエイズ危機下のニューヨーク
竹島達也 ·· 313

ハーレム・ルネサンスにおけるプリミティヴィズムとネグロフィリア
『新しい黒人(ニューニグロ)』とアーロン・ダグラス
中地　幸 ………………………………………………………………… 329

サッコ＝ヴァンゼッティ事件を語る
シンクレアの『ボストン』とドス・パソスの『USA』
花田　愛 ………………………………………………………………… 351

フォークナー世界と「過去」
依藤道夫 ………………………………………………………………… 367

第Ⅲ部 ……………………………………………………………………… 375

Exploiting the Oncogenic MYC Pathway Activation in Targeting Triple-Negative Breast Cancer:
Utility of CDK Inhibition Revisited
Dai Horiuchi ……………………………………………………………… 377

福島第一原子力発電所から放出されたセシウム137土壌沈着密度分布図の作成
沢野伸浩 ………………………………………………………………… 411

執筆者一覧（A list of contributors）……………………………………… 423

第Ⅰ部

(In)directness and (In)formality in Japanese E-mail Requests

Saeko Fukushima

Abstract
This study attempts to investigate e-mail requests in Japanese by young Japanese people in contemporary Japan. (In)directness as well as (in)formality were taken into account in the investigation of requests. It was examined which request strategies young Japanese people would use when they make requests through e-mail. The data used in the present study were 1,080 e-mail requests by 83 Japanese female university students. The data were analyzed according to the classification of requests, which combined (in)directness and (in)formality. The results show that indirect & informal requests 1 (strategy 5) were frequently used among close equals, whereas indirect & formal requests 1 (strategy 7) were frequently used when there was a perceived power difference between S and H (P+: S<H). Moreover, direct and informal requests 1 (strategy 1) were frequently used when there was a power difference between S and H (P+: S>H). These results indicate that such classical variables as power and distance affect the request strategies in e-mail. This study is likely to contribute to filling the gap in request research and understanding of e-mail requests in Japanese by young Japanese people.

Keywords   requests, e-mail, Japanese, (in)directness, (in)formality

1. Introduction

The present study will look into Japanese requests through e-mails by young Japanese people. By young people, I mean those in their early twenties, and more specifically, those who attend university. The reason why this paper focuses on young Japanese people's requesting behavior is that there may be differences in requesting behavior according to generation (i.e., age). Indeed, Byon (2006: 270) argues that age is a crucial social variable affecting speech act behaviors. And empirical studies investigating request strategies through e-mails in contemporary Japan are still limited, especially those with focus on the requests by young Japanese people. Furthermore, many request studies so far have been conducted from the perspective of (in)directness. Therefore, (in)formality, which has not been paid as much attention as (in)directness in politeness research, and which is of great importance when considering requests, especially in Japanese which has a honorific system, is also taken into account in the present study.

In this study, e-mails were used in order to investigate Japanese computer-mediated communication (CMC), focusing on requests. E-mail data provide a potentially rich opportunity for gathering authentic data freed from the limitations of discourse completion tasks (DCTs). This paper sets out to explore request strategies by young Japanese people nowadays to draw more definite conclusions about the (in)directness and (in)formality of Japanese requests through e-mails. In the present study, only head acts, i.e., the minimal unit which can realize a request (Blum-Kulka et al., 1989: 275), are analyzed as in the study by Byon (2006). The research questions for the present study are as follows:

1. To what extent is the selection of request strategies (with different (in)directness and (in)formality levels) different according to different conditions (power, distance, imposition)?

2. What are the characteristics of e-mail requests made by young Japanese people?

The next section reviews literature, including Japanese communication style, (in)directness and (in)formality and Japanese honorifics. Section 3 presents the study; and the results and discussion follow.

2. Literature review

2.1 Japanese communication style

Japanese communication style has often been described as being indirect in previous studies (e.g., Clancy 1986; Lebra 1976; Nakane 1970; Okabe 1983; Yamada 1994; 1997). Some recent studies, however, do not support this claim. For example, Haugh (2003: 158) argues that the assumption that Japanese is more indirect and vague than English is questionable. Fukushima (1996) compared request strategies in British English and Japanese in two situations with different degrees of imposition by 16 British and 15 Japanese undergraduates. The results showed that more direct forms were used by the Japanese participants than by their British counterparts, while more politeness strategies were employed both in English and in Japanese when the degree of imposition increased. The results in Fukushima (2000), which compared British English and Japanese request strategies by 121 British and 133 Japanese undergraduates in eight situations with a combination of power difference, distance and degree of imposition, revealed that the Japanese participants selected more direct request strategies than their British counterparts in half of the situations investigated. Rose (1994) showed that the Japanese participants (89 undergraduates from four Japanese universities enrolled in summer programs at the University of Illinois) were more direct in making requests than the American participants (46 undergraduates enrolled in first-year composition courses at University of Illinois) on an open-ended discourse completion test, although the Japanese participants switched to hinting and opting out on a multiple choice questionnaire. Rose (1996), who collected data with an eavesdropping approach in a university copy shop, on an airplane, in an airport lobby, and on a crowded university bus, challenged the stereotypical notion of a difference between American English and Japanese, with the former frequently characterized as being explicit and direct, and the latter as being vague and indirect, showing that indirect requests in American English were common.

The results in Fukushima (2010), which investigated the evaluation of request situations and request strategies by the Japanese and British university students, show that such indirect requests as off-record requests were evaluated more negatively by the Japanese students than by the British students and that direct requests were more acceptable in Japanese than in English. This suggests that the young Japanese people may not always prefer indirect and vague ways of communication.

2.2 (In)directness & (in)formality

Politeness has been investigated mainly from the viewpoint of (in)directness and many studies have been conducted with request strategies being based on a direct-indirect scale. Leech (1983) and Brown and Levinson (1987) argue for a strong link between indirectness and politeness.

According to Leech (1983: 108), the use of more indirect illocutions will generally result in more politeness, because an indirect illocution gives the hearer more optionality and less force. This means that directness of request strategies has to do with the impact on a hearer (H), which can be the strongest with the direct requests. Since direct requests give H fewer options than indirect requests, they give H the impression that it is difficult to refuse the request. On the other hand, in case of indirect requests, which give H more options than direct requests, the impact on H, or the request force, is weaker than that of direct requests. The clarity of content can be also measured from the degree of directness. The more direct the request strategies are, the clearer the content (or the speaker's intention) is. According to Byon (2006: 259), the criteria for deciding the directness level is the length of the inferential process one needs to identify a token as a request.

While (in)directness has been focused on in previous politeness research, (in)formality has not been paid as much attention. Indeed, in many previous studies, (in)directness has been investigated in relation to politeness; and the three strategies (direct [bald-on-record] strategies, conventionally indirect [negative politeness] strategies and non-conventionally indirect [off-record] strategies), which are based on (in)directness, have been often used[1]. Direct (bald-on-record) strategies are the most direct; and non-conventionally indirect (off-record) strategies are the most indirect.

It is important to consider (in)formality level as well as (in)directness level when investigating politeness, as there are different levels of (in)formality within the same (in)directness level. Irvine (2001: 190) argues that there are three principal senses of formality; and that these different senses of formality have to do with whether the formality concerns properties of a communicative code, properties of the social setting in which a code is used, or properties of the analyst's description. According to Irvine (2001: 190–191), what formality means differ from authors to authors as follows: (1) an increased structuring and predictability of discourse, formality being an aspect of code, (2) a way of describing the characteristics of a formal social situation, which requires a display of seriousness, politeness and respect, and (3) a technical mode of description, in which the analyst's statement of the rules governing discourse is maximally explicit.

Formality in the present study is in the realm of the second sense above, the focus being on linguistic manifestation (i.e., realization of requests). (In)formality can be indexed by various factors. For example, settings such as university ceremonies, church services, and court hearings fall into the formal category (see examples in Atkinson 1982: 90–91). Not only in those multi-party settings, the following situations, where only two or three people may be present, may be regarded as more or less formal: between professional and lay persons, such as doctor and patient, lawyer and client, policeman and suspect, teacher and pupil, interviewer and interviewee, seller and buyer, etc. (Atkinson 1982: 110). Such formal situations as above can be considered as contextual variables, which include the relationship between S and H. In other words, (in)formality can be decided by the relationship between S and H, including the situations in which they are. These situational/contextual variables, which index (in)formality, influence linguistic manifestation; and one major way of expressing formality is the use of honorifics in the Japanese language.

Rinnert and Kobayashi (1999) considered formality level in analyzing requests in Japanese and English. Rinnert (1999) showed that formal and very formal levels in Japanese were rated as highly inappropriate with friends or acquaintances of the same age or status. Few other studies, however, have considered formality level in investigation of requests[2]. Byon (2006) investigated the link between politeness and indirectness of requests in the Korean language, which has honorifics. His findings showed that direct requests were used to a professor by a student, being marked by appropriate honorific elements to indicate politeness value. Byon (2006: 268) states that the use of direct strategies can be explained in terms of speech levels, and that the Korean direct speech act form can carry high honorific meaning through the use of the deferential speech level. Although Byon (2006) included formality level in his discussion, he included only directness level in the analysis, not having integrated formality level in his examination of requests.

In the present study, (in)formality is considered in addition to (in)directness to fill the gap in request research, as (in)formality has not been much investigated in previous research as stated above. Incorporating (in)formality into the investigation of request strategies means to take honorifics into account, which is important in analyzing Japanese data, as the Japanese language has an honorific system. Formality is expressed with honorifics. Rinnert and Kobayashi (1999: 1177–1178) argue that the formality level increases with the use of honorifics. They (1999: 1178) give the following example, how the honorific expression *itadaku* increases the level of formality:

Sono hon misete kuremasenka? (the book show receive-not Q ?)
'Wouldn't you show me the book?'

Sono hon misete itadakemasen ka? (the book show humble-receive-potentially-not Q ?)
'Couldn't I receive the favor of your showing me the book?'

A formal request in the present study contains honorifics. In the next subsection, a brief account of honorifics in the Japanese language is given.

2.3 Japanese honorifics

Japanese honorifics[3] have been traditionally divided into the following three types:

(1) *sonkeigo* 'respect forms'
(2) *kenjyogo* 'humble forms'(collectively referred to as referent honorifics); and
(3) *teineigo* 'polite forms' (addressee honorifics) (Barke 2010: 458)

According to guidelines issued by Bunka Shingikai [Japanese Council for Cultural Affairs] (2007), however, Japanese honorifics are divided into five categories: (1) *sonkeigo* 'respect forms,' (2) *kenjyogo* I 'humble forms I,' (3) *kenjyogo* II 'humble forms II,' (4) *teineigo* 'polite forms' and (5) *bikago* 'beautification'. *Sonkeigo* elevates the person referred. By lowering the speaker, *kenjyogo* I elevates the referent whereas *kenjyogo* II simply lowers the speaker's action. *Teineigo* are so-called *desu/-masu* forms. The formal forms of *desu* (i.e., *de gozaimasu*) are included in this category. *Bikago* are nouns that refer to things unrelated to the referent and to which the honorific prefixes *o-/go-* have been attached (Barke 2010: 459). Below are the examples from Bunka Shingikai (2007) for the five categories.

(1) *Sonkeigo*
irassharu ('go'); *ossharu* ('say')

Sensei   wa   raishu   kaigaie   irassharu
teacher NOMI next week abroad go (RESPECT)
'The teacher goes abroad next week.'

(2) *Kenjyogo* I
ukagau ('go' or 'visit'); *moushiageru* ('say')

Sensei	*no*	*tokoro*	*e*	<u>*ukagai*</u>	*tai*
teacher	POSS	place	to	go (HUMBLE)	want

'I want to go to (visit) the teacher.'

(3) *Kenjyogo* II
mairu ('go'); *mousu* ('say')

Asu	*kara*	*kaigaie*	<u>*mairi*</u>	*masu.*
tomorrow	from	abroad	go (HUMBLE)	(polite verbal ending)

'I will go abroad tomorrow.'

(4) *Teineigo*
desu (polite copula); *masu* (polite verbal ending)

Rokuji	*ni*	*oki*	<u>*masu.*</u>
six o'clock	at	get up	(polite verbal ending)

'I get up at six o'clock.'

(5) *Bikago*
Osake (*o* + *sake*)
'Japanese sake (liquor)'

3. The study

3.1 Participants

Eighty-three female Japanese university students (age range: 19–23; mean age: 20.96) served as the participants in this study. University students were chosen as the participants of this study in order to ensure as much homogeneity as possible in age range, educational background, occupation and social class. Age range was considered especially important, as this study focuses on young people's requesting behavior. The participants were confined only to female university students in order to exclude possible gender-based influence on the data. It was also because this study did not intend to investigate gender differences in e-mail requests.

3.2 Data collection

The participants assembled a corpus of the e-mail messages they sent and received. From the e-mail messages collected, the participants selected those containing requests, which they thought they could make public. The participants were asked to describe the relationship (power and distance) between the sender (S) and the receiver (H) of the e-mail messages and the degree of imposition of the requested act for each request. Specifically, in terms of the power relationship, the participants were asked to describe whether S had more power than H (P+: S>H); whether H had more power than S (P+: S<H); or whether S and H were equal (P-). As for distance, the participants were asked to describe whether S and H were close (D-) or not (D+). Regarding the degree of imposition, the participants were asked to describe whether the requests were with high degree of imposition (IH) or with low degree of imposition (IL).

3.3 Request strategies in this study

In this study, both (in)directness and (in)formality of request strategies are investigated. Investigating (in)directness in the present study, direct and indirect requests, which are further subcategorized, are used. Investigating (in)formality, there are two formality levels (formal and informal). Requests with the use of honorific forms are identified as formal and those with the non-use of honorific forms as informal. From a combination of (in)directness (direct-indirect) and (in)formality (formal-informal) arise four strategies, i.e., direct-informal, direct-formal, indirect-informal and indirect-formal requests. These four strategies are further divided into two, depending on the (in)directness or (in)formality level. Thus, requests in the present study are classified into the following eight strategies: strategy 1 (direct & informal requests 1), strategy 2 (direct & informal requests 2), strategy 3 (direct & formal requests 1), strategy 4 (direct & formal requests 2), strategy 5 (indirect & informal requests 1), strategy 6 (indirect & informal requests 2), strategy 7 (indirect & formal requests 1) and strategy 8 (indirect & formal requests 2). These request strategies are summarized in table 1. Explanation of these request strategies is given next.

Table 1. Request strategies in this study

Strategy	Form/Category	Example	English Gloss	Directness/Formality level
Strategy 1 (direct & informal requests 1)	Gerundive form	*noto kashite*	Lend me your notebook.	Strategy 1 is more direct than strategy 2.
Strategy 2 (direct & informal requests 2)	Gerundive form + a final particle *ne*	*noto kashite ne*	Lend me your notebook, will you?	
	Statement (informal) (Desire) (without Ellipsis)	*noto kashite hoshii*	I want you to lend me your notebook.	
Strategy 3 (direct & formal requests 1)	Gerundive form + *kudasai*	*noto kashite kudasai*	Lend me your notebook, please.	Strategy 4 is more formal than strategy 3.
Strategy 4 (direct & formal requests 2)	Statement (formal) (Desire) (without Ellipsis)	*noto kashite itadakitaku zonji masu*	I'd like you to lend me your notebook.	
Strategy 5 (indirect & informal requests 1)	Interrogative (informal)	*noto kashite kurenai?*	Can't you lend me your notebook?	
	Statement (informal) (Desire) (with Ellipsis)	*noto kashite hoshiindakedo…*	I want you to lend me your notebook, but….	Strategy 6 is more indirect than strategy 5.
Strategy 6 (indirect & informal requests 2)	Statement (informal) (Hint)	*kinou jyugyou yasunjatta*	I was absent from the class yesterday.	
Strategy 7 (indirect & formal requests 1)	Interrogative (formal)	*noto kashite itadake masenka?*	Couldn't you lend me your notebook?	
	Statement (formal) (Desire) (with Ellipsis)	*noto kashite itadakitai no desu ga…*	I'd like you to lend me your notebook, but ….	Strategy 8 is more indirect than strategy 7.
Strategy 8 (indirect & formal requests 2)	Statement (formal) (Hint)	*kinou jyugyou yasumi mashi ta*	I was absent from the class yesterday.	

3.3.1 Direct & informal requests (strategy 1 & strategy 2)

Direct & informal requests are further classified into two: direct & informal requests 1 (strategy 1) and direct & informal requests 2 (strategy 2), the former being more direct (having more request force) than the latter. According to Brown and Levinson (1987: 95), direct imperatives stand out as clear examples of bald-on-record usage, which is the most direct. Rinnert and Kobayashi (1999: 1179) categorize "*Sono hon misete*" ('Show me the book') as a direct and informal request. Such forms as "*… shite*"

('Do this') (Gerundive [*te* form]) (e.g., *Noto kashite* 'Lend me your notebook') are classified as direct & informal requests 1 (strategy 1).

The request force of direct & informal requests 2 (strategy 2) is softened by adding a final particle to a gerundive. The forms identified as direct & informal requests 2 (strategy 2) include gerundives with a final particle *ne* (e.g., *Noto kashite ne* 'Lend me your notebook, will you?') and such an informal statement without ellipsis as "... *shite hoshii*" ('I want you to do ...') (e.g., *Noto kashite hoshii* 'I want you to lend me your notebook').

According to Lee (2007: 384), the particle *ne* has the effect of softening the force of request and by the use of the particle *ne*, the speaker can also express the request unilaterally without indicating a recognition or willingness on the part of the speaker. There are also other views on *ne*: (1) an indexical which carries social meaning, i.e., affective common ground; (2) a turn-management device and (3) to advance a stance of weak or incomplete authority in relation to the other speaker (Morita 2002: 226). According to Zamborlin (2007: 45), this particle indicates the speaker's request for agreement about some presupposed shared knowledge and corresponds to an English tag question. Here in direct & informal requests 2 (strategy 2), too, the particle *ne* has the effect of softening the request force as well as seeking for agreement or compliance of requests, and it also shows familiarity between S and H when they are close, which is similar to affective common ground. Thus, direct & informal requests 2 (Gerundive [*te* form] + *ne*) (strategy 2) are less direct than direct & informal requests 1 (strategy 1).

3.3.2 Direct & formal requests (strategy 3 & strategy 4)

Direct & formal requests are further classified into two: direct & formal requests 1 (strategy 3) and direct & formal requests 2 (strategy 4). "... *shite kudasai*" ('Do this, please') (Gerundive forms + *kudasai*) (e.g., *Noto kashite kudasai* 'Lend me your notebook, please') is classified as direct and formal requests 1 (strategy 3), following Rinnert and Kobayashi (1999: 1179), who classify "*Sono hon misete kudasai*" ('Please show me the book') as a direct and formal request.

The declarative, indicating "desire" (e.g., "... *shite <u>itadaki taku zonji masu</u>*" 'I'd like you to do ...') (e.g., *Noto kashite <u>itadaki taku zonji masu</u>* 'I'd like you to lend me your notebook') is categorized as direct & formal requests 2 (strategy 4), as it has a strong request force; and it is formal with such honorific forms as *itadaku* (*Kenjyogo* I)[4], *zonzuru* ('think' *Kenjyogo* II) and *masu* (*Teineigo*). Therefore, direct & formal requests 2 (strategy 4) are more formal than direct & formal requests 1 (strategy 3).

3.3.3 Indirect & informal requests (strategy 5 & strategy 6)

Indirect & informal requests are further classified into two: indirect & informal requests 1 (strategy 5) and indirect & informal requests 2 (strategy 6). Such interrogative form as "... *shite kurenai?*" ('Can't you do …?') (e.g., *Noto kashite kurenai* 'Can't you lend me your notebook?) is categorized as indirect & informal requests 1 (strategy 5), as it is informal and more indirect than "... *shite ne*" (Gerundive [*te* form] + particle *ne*) (strategy 2) or "... *shite hoshii*" ('I want you to do …') (strategy 2). This is because the interrogative form gives an option for H to comply. Rinnert and Kobayashi (1999: 1179) categorize "*Sono hon misete kureru?*" ('Will you show me the book?') as an indirect informal request. Among the data, "... *kurenai?*" (*kureru* + negation) instead of "... *kureru?*" was found. As I believe the level of formality is the same between them, both "... *shite kurenai?*" and "... *shite kureru?*" were identified as indirect & informal requests 1 (strategy 5).

An informal statement with ellipsis ("... *shite hoshii* …" 'I want you to do … …' or "... *shite hoshiin dakedo* …" 'I want you to do …, but …') (e.g., *Noto kashite hoshiin dakedo*… 'I want you to lend me your notebook, but…') is also classified as strategy 5, because ellipsis indicates indirectness by avoiding the assertion or showing hesitation.

An informal statement with hints, i.e., off-record in Brown and Levinson's term (1987), is categorized as indirect & informal requests 2 (strategy 6) (e.g., *Kinou jyugyou yasunjatta* 'I was absent from the class yesterday,' hinting that a requester wants to borrow a notebook). According to Brown and Levinson (1987: 211), off-record strategies are indirect, as they do not attribute only one clear communicative intention, and the actor leaves himself an "out" by providing himself with a number of defensible interpretations. Therefore, the feature of off-record strategies is to state the request indirectly. In my view, not only can the actor avoid responsibility, but also can s/he show *enryo* or self-restraint with off-record strategies. In order for H to understand off-record strategies, S and H should share certain background knowledge and H should have the ability to infer S's desires. Off-record requests are sometimes called non-conventionally indirect requests (e.g. Rinnert and Kobayashi 1999) or requestive hints (e.g., Weizman 1993). According to Weizman (1993: 123), the category of requestive hints consists of the most nonconventional and indirect of all request strategies; and an example of requestive hints is "I have so much work to do (when used as a request to be left alone)." Indirect & informal requests 2 (strategy 6) are, therefore, more indirect than indirect & informal requests 1 (strategy 5).

3.3.4 Indirect & formal requests (strategy 7 & strategy 8)

Indirect & formal requests are further classified into two: indirect & formal requests 1 (strategy 7) and indirect & formal requests 2 (strategy 8). A formal interrogative form (e.g., "... *shite itadake masen ka*?" 'Couldn't you do ...?') (e.g., *Noto kashite itadake masen ka*? 'Couldn't you lend me your notebook?') and a formal statement with ellipsis (e.g., *Noto kashite itadaki taino desu ga* ... 'I'd like you to lend me your notebook, but ...') are categorized as indirect & formal requests 1 (strategy 7). Both forms are with such honorific forms as *itadaku* (*Kenjyogo* I) and *masu/desu* (*Teineigo*) and indicate indirectness, the former with an interrogative, which gives an option to H, and the latter with an ellipsis. According to Miyamoto et al. (2004: 134), with ellipsis, S leaves the judgment to H and tries to reduce the difference of opinions between S and H by reducing S's assertion.

A formal statement with hints, or off-record strategy, is categorized as indirect & formal requests 2 (strategy 8) (e.g., *Kinou jyugyou yasumi mashi ta* 'I was absent from the class yesterday,' hinting that a requester wants to borrow a notebook) (with *masu* (*Teineigo*)). Indirect & formal requests 2 (strategy 8) with hints are more indirect than indirect & formal requests 1 (strategy 7).

3.4 Data analysis

Before analyzing the data, the following constraints were applied to the data in order to limit the range of contexts in which the requests were made.

1. The e-mail messages which were sent from one person to many people were excluded, because of the following reasons: (1) It is complex to define the relationships between S and H in such situations; and (2) Request strategies may vary in the e-mails sent from one person to many people and those from one person to a single other person, the content and the relationship between a sender and a receiver/receivers being the same (e.g., between close friends). Requests to many people may be more formal than those to a single other person, because formal speech styles are used when addressing to many people or to the public. For example, when e-mail messages were sent from

one person to many people (e.g., announcing the change of an e-mail address and asking the receivers to register the new address), such a formal request as *"Toroku onegai shimasu"* 'Could you register my new address?' was used, whereas such an informal request as *"Toroku shite"* 'Register my new address' was used when e-mails were sent from one person to a single person. Consequently, only the e-mails sent from one person to a single other person were used.

2. There may be differences between requests which are made initially and requests made after compliance or refusal. Requests which are made after compliance may be more direct than the initial request, while requests which follow a refusal may be more indirect than the initial request. As there were only thirty-six requests which were made after compliance or refusal in the data, the analysis was confined to initial requests.

3. There were different kinds of requests: requests for information and requests for action. The requests for information (e.g., Is the English linguistics class in room 1301?), which occurred in the data, carried less imposition and were more direct than the requests for action. As these two differ in kind and only thirty-nine requests for information occurred, the requests for information were excluded from the data.

As a result of this sorting process, 1,080 requests were available for analysis. The data were analyzed as follows.

1. The 1,080 requests were classified into the eight request strategies described in 3.3.

2. The data were investigated on the basis of the relationship between S and H (power and distance) and the degree of imposition of the requested act. Power was classified into three: (1) S has more power than H (from a superior to a subordinate) (P+: S>H); (2) H has more power than S (from a subordinate to a superior) (P+: S<H) and (3) There is no power difference between S and H (P-). Distance was classified into two: (1) S and H are not close (D+) and (2) S and H are close (D-). The degree of imposition was classified into two: (1) high imposition (IH) and (2) low imposition (IL). All the requests were classified according to the combination of power, distance and

imposition, which resulted in a list of twelve conditions, summarized in table 2.

Table 2. Specification of twelve conditions

Condition	Power Difference between S and H	Distance between S and H	Degree of Imposition	Example contents of e-mails
1	+ (S>H)	+	High	A professor asks a student to talk about her experiences abroad in a class, which requires her a lot of time and effort for preparation. A student has to go all the way to a class, which she is not taking.
2	+ (S>H)	+	Low	A professor asks a student to erase the blackboard after class.
3	+ (S>H)	-	High	A senior club member, who has a fever, asks a junior club member to give a ride late at night to go to a doctor.
4	+ (S>H)	-	Low	A senior club member asks a junior club member to circulate an e-mail message to other club members.
5	+ (S<H)	+	High	A student asks a professor to extend the deadline of an assignment.
6	+ (S<H)	+	Low	A student asks a professor for a printed material from the last class, from which she was absent.
7	+ (S<H)	-	High	A student asks a seminar professor to visit a high school where a student is doing a practice teaching. A high school is far away (in a rural area) from the city where a professor lives.
8	+ (S<H)	-	Low	A student asks a seminar professor to make a photocopy of the professor's article.
9	-	+	High	An acquaintance, whom one met only once, asks another acquaintance to introduce her friend.
10	-	+	Low	There was something which one could not see very well on the blackboard in a class. She asks the person who happens to sit next to her to tell her what it was.
11	-	-	High	A student asks her classmate if she can make a photocopy of the classmate's notebook one day before a final exam.
12	-	-	Low	A student asks her classmate to take a printed material when she is absent from a class.

Power +: There is a power difference between S and H. S>H: S has more power than H. S<H: H has more power than H.
Power -: There is no power difference between S and H.
Distance+: S and H are not close. Distance -: S and H are close.

4. Results and discussion

The results of the first analysis (the classification of requests into the eight request strategies) reveal that indirect & informal requests 1 (strategy 5) (38.6%) were most frequently used, followed by direct & informal requests 1 (strategy 1) (16.1%) and indirect & formal requests 1 (strategy 7) (14.7%). Table 3 shows the distribution of request strategies.

Table 3. Distribution of request strategies overall

Strategy	Number of requests	%
Strategy 1 (direct & informal requests 1)	174	16.1
Strategy 2 (direct & informal requests 2)	129	11.9
Strategy 3 (direct & formal requests 1)	93	8.6
Strategy 4 (direct & formal requests 2)	83	7.7
Strategy 5 (indirect & informal requests 1)	417	**38.6**
Strategy 6 (indirect & informal requests 2)	20	1.9
Strategy 7 (indirect & formal requests 1)	159	14.7
Strategy 8 (indirect & formal requests 2)	5	0.5
Total	1,080	100

The results of the second analysis (the data analysis according to the combination of power, distance and imposition, i.e., twelve conditions in table 2) show that indirect & informal requests (strategy 5) were most frequently used under condition 11, followed by under conditions 3 and 12. Below are the examples.

Example 1 (indirect & informal requests 1 (strategy 5)) (under condition 11 (P-; D-; IH))
Ichigatsu tooka hima? Sono hi dake hitoga tarinakute komatte irundakedo moshi jikanga areba tetsudatte hoshiindakedo ...
'Are you free on the 10th January? We are in trouble, because we need more people who can work on that day. If you are free, I want you to help us out ...'

This mail was sent from a university student to another university student (they are close friends), asking to work part-time at a supermarket where the requester works part-time. H does not usually work part-time. As the request was made within a short notice, the degree of imposition was considered to be high.

Example 2 (indirect & informal requests 1 (strategy 5)) (under condition 12 (P-; D-; IL))
Sore kopii sasete moraeru?
'Can I make a photocopy of that?'

This mail was sent from a university student to another university student (they are close friends). Both of them look for a job after graduation. H has already written her resume. S asked to make a photocopy of H's resume so that S can consult that when she writes her own.

Both under conditions 11 and 12 (P-; D-), indirect & informal requests 1 (strategy 5) were used, as shown in examples 1 and 2. While S tried to compensate for a high degree of imposition by using indirect & informal requests 1 (strategy 5) in example 1, the use of indirect & informal requests 1 (strategy 5) in example 2 with a low degree of imposition can be considered as "softening," i.e., avoidance of a clear assertion or blurring the content, which Satake (2005a) argues. With the effect of "softening" S may try to gain compliance from H. The frequent use of indirect & informal requests 1 (strategy 5) among close equals may be because informality (characterized by non-honorific use, the use of spoken languages, the youth language, slangs, unfinished sentences, etc.) is a norm among close equals in the Japanese language.

Example 3 (indirect & informal requests 1 (strategy 5)) (under condition 3 (P+: S>H; D-; IH))
Nishi Kanto taikai ni kakaru hiyou tatekaete kurenai?
'Can't you pay the expenses for the west *Kanto* (the name of an area in Japan) tournament now?'

This mail was sent from a senior university club member to a junior club member, who is in charge of finance of a club, asking to pay the expenses for the tournament for now. As a junior club member lives far away from a bank, she felt that the imposition was high. She perceived that there was a power difference between a senior club member and a junior club member, the former having more power than the latter, although the age difference between them was only one year.

Direct & informal requests 1 (strategy 1) were next frequently used

(16.1%) after indirect & informal requests 1 (strategy 5). The results of the second analysis show that direct & informal requests 1 (strategy 1) were most frequently used under condition 4. Below is an example.

Example 4 (direct & informal requests 1 (strategy 1)) (under condition 4 (P+: S>H; D-; IL))
Shouhin narabete oite
'Display the goods.'

A student received this mail from an owner of a shop where she works part-time. She perceived that there was a power difference between a shop owner and herself, the shop owner having more power than her. The degree of imposition was considered to be low, as displaying the goods was within the duty of her part-time job.

The request strategy was more direct in example 4 than in example 3. The degree of imposition was lower in example 4 than in example 3, with the other conditions (i.e., power and distance) being the same. Moreover, there was a slight difference in the same power relationship (P+: S>H). When the participants reported that there was a power difference between S and H, there were two different cases: (1) Both S and H were students, who were a senior university club member and a junior club member, having only a slight age difference (one year or two) as in example 3 (This sense of age difference is the same line with Byon's (2006: 266) statement on Koreans, who are highly sensitive to relative age; and coincides with Mizutani and Mizutani (1987), who argue that age difference is still an important factor); and (2) S and H were a student and a professor (or a shop owner), having a considerable age difference and a status difference as in example 4. This difference may also have affected the request strategies, the request strategy in example 4 (the latter case) being more direct than in example 3 (the former case).

Indirect & formal requests 1 (strategy 7) were frequently used after indirect & informal requests 1 (strategy 5) and direct & informal requests 1 (strategy 1). The results of the second analysis show that they were most frequently used under conditions 5, 6, 7 and 8, in which H has more power than S. Below are the examples.

Example 5 (indirect & formal requests 1 (strategy 7)) (under condition 5 (P+: S<H; D+; IH))
Watashi no kadai o uketotte itadake nai deshouka?

'Couldn't you receive my assignment?'

This mail was sent from a student to a professor. A student takes a class for half a year only and has not talked to the professor outside the class. Therefore, the student perceived that there was a distance between her and a professor. She could not submit the final assignment by the deadline and asks the professor for an extension. The student thinks that the reason why she could not submit the assignment by the deadline was not legitimate (i.e., she could not concentrate on the assignment because of the troubles she had in the club activity). Therefore, the student perceived that the imposition was high.

Example 6 (indirect & formal requests 1 (strategy 7)) (under condition 6 (P+: S<H; D+; IL))
Honban ga owari shidai kuruma o deguchi ni tsukete itadake masuka?
'Could you park your car at the exit as soon as the concert finishes?'

This mail was sent from a university student to a high school teacher near the university. The teacher is an advisor to a brass band club at a high school. A student, who belongs to a brass band club, borrowed a musical instrument for a concert from the high school teacher and promised to return the instrument after the concert. The student asked the high school teacher to park her car at the exit after the concert. The student who sent this mail perceived that there was a distance between the teacher and her[5]. The teacher is obviously older than the student, but the age of the teacher was not identified.

Example 7 (indirect & formal requests 1 (strategy 7)) (under condition 7 (P+: S<H; D-; IH))
Saigo no zemi o kesseki shite shimatte kattena onegai nano desuga, sotsugyou ronbun ni taisuru goshiteki o itadaku tameni ojikan o itadaku koto wa kanou deshouka?
'I was absent from the last seminar. So, I know I am selfish to ask you, but would it be all possible to spare some time for me and give me your comments on my graduation thesis?'

This mail was sent from a student to her seminar professor. The student has been in the professor's seminar for three years. She was absent from the last class, in which the professor gave seminar students some comments on their graduation theses. She asks if the professor could spare extra time for her outside the class. She admits her fault (not having attended the last seminar). And it is not a professor's duty to spare extra time for her, because the reason that she could not attend the last seminar was not legitimate (i.e., she was in the U.S. to meet her friends). Therefore, the degree of imposition was considered to be high.

Example 8 (indirect & formal requests 1 (strategy 7)) (under condition 8 (P+: S<H; D-; IL))
Sensei no ronbun kopii sasete itadake masuka?
'Could I make a photocopy of your article?'

This mail was sent from a student to her seminar professor, asking to make a photocopy of the professor's article.

Examples 5, 6, 7 and 8 show that indirect & formal requests 1 (strategy 7) were used when H had more power than S, irrespective of degree of imposition and distance between S and H. In other words, indirect & formal requests 1 (strategy 7) were used both when the degree of imposition was high (example 7) and low (example 8), and both when S and H were close (under conditions 7 & 8) and not close (under conditions 5 & 6). Nishimura (2010) argues that honorifics are used to place a psychological distance between people, citing Takiura (2008). The results of this study, however, indicate that when honorifics are used in cases when S and H are close, there is also another function, i.e., to show deference, as examples 7 and 8 show. As noted in 2.1, a situation between professional and lay persons (e.g., a professor and a student) may be regarded as formal; and this has resulted in formal requests. Although indirect & formal requests 1 (strategy 7) were used both in examples 7 (with a high degree of imposition) & 8 (with a low degree of imposition), many more kinds of honorifics (e.g., *Bikago* (*goshiteki* and *ojikan*), *Kenjyogo* I (*itadaku*) and *Teineigo* (*desu*)) (they were underlined in example 7) were used in example 7 than in example 8. This may suggest that S tried to compensate for the high degree of imposition by the use of honorifics (both with high frequency and many different kinds).

The above results indicate that different request strategies were used, depending on the power (especially status and age) difference of S and H, and the degree of imposition. When requests were made between students with a power difference (e.g., from a junior club member to a senior club member), indirect & informal requests 1 (strategy 5) were frequently used (see example 3). When requests were made from a person who has more power to a person who has less power (e.g., from a shop owner to a student who works part-time) (see example 4), direct & informal requests 1 (strategy 1) were frequently used. When requests were made from a person who has less power to a person who has more power (e.g., from a student to a professor), indirect & formal requests 1 (strategy 7) (see examples 5, 6, 7 & 8) were frequently used. These results contradict Hori's (2000) results, i.e., a decline in concern with power difference among young Japanese people, and Suzuki's (2007) report, i.e., a less importance of the use of honorifics.

Although both indirect & informal requests 1 (strategy 5) and indirect & formal requests 1 (strategy 7) contain indirectness, it differs in quality. Indirectness in indirect & formal requests 1 (strategy 7), which were frequently used to superiors, places a distance between S and H and shows deference to H by the use of honorifics. Indirectness in previous studies, which were reviewed in 2.2, has been used in this sense. This can be called a classical sense of indirectness. On the other hand, indirectness in indirect & informal requests 1 (strategy 5) can be considered as "softening," which Satake (2005a) defined as one of the characteristics of young Japanese people's language use. Definite statements tend to be avoided by the use of indirectness. Therefore, the frequent use of indirect & informal requests 1 (strategy 5) among close equals does not mean that indirectness in the classical sense was employed.

The findings of this study, in which (in)formality was added to (in)directness in the examination of request strategies, indicate that the young Japanese participants use indirect and informal requests most frequently. This finding, which was perhaps somewhat unclear from the previous research investigated only from (in)directness, was tangible by incorporating (in)formality into the investigation of requests. This finding coincides with the studies by Hori (2000), i.e., informality of young people's speech, Rinnert (1999), i.e., formal and very formal levels in Japanese being rated as highly inappropriate with friends and acquaintances of the same age or status, Suzuki (2007), i.e., informal linguistic attitude, and Satake (2005b), i.e., an informal writing style by young people.

5. Summary and conclusion

The present study investigated request strategies by young Japanese people in contemporary Japan from the perspectives of (in)directness and (in)formality, using e-mail data. The major findings include that indirect & informal requests 1 (strategy 5) were frequently used among close equals, whereas indirect & formal requests 1 (strategy 7) were frequently used when there was a power difference between S and H (P+: S<H). These results indicate that informal requests were frequently used among close equals and that formal requests were frequently used to superiors, requests through e-mail also having been influenced by such classical variables as age and status. Indirectness in strategy 5 and that in strategy 7 differs in quality, the former having a function of softening requests and the latter of placing a distance between S and H or showing deference to H.

Request strategies in previous research have been often analyzed only from the perspective of (in)directness. Adding (in)formality to (in)directness in the examination of request strategies has increased the depth of investigation and has revealed a more detailed account than previous research dealing only with (in)directness. Using e-mail requests made it possible to collect authentic written request data, as many previous request studies had limitations by eliciting spoken data through written DCTs. It is hoped that this study can contribute to further understanding of requests in Japanese, especially those by young Japanese people.

Notes

1. For example, Rinnert and Kobayashi (1999: 1197) classified Japanese and American English requests into these three. Fukushima (2000) used the same three in comparing requests by British and Japanese university students. Hiraga and Turner (1996), who have also compared British English and Japanese, used those three request strategies, although they termed them direct requests, indirect requests and hints. Trosborg (1995) categorized requests into four, i.e., indirect requests (hints), conventionally indirect requests (hearer-oriented conditions), conventionally indirect requests (speaker-based conditions) and direct requests, but as she simply subcategorized conventionally indirect requests into two, it can be said that she also follows the above three choices. Economidou-Kogetsidis (2004; 2005) investigated the degree of directness of requests in Greek and British English by using bald-on-record, conventionally indirect and non-conventionally indirect strategies. Moreover, some other studies (e.g., Kasper 1994: 3208; Olshtain and Blum-Kulka 1985: 305) have also confirmed these three choices.
2. Felix-Brasdefer (2006) examined politeness strategies, focusing on degree of formality. The degree of formality in his study, however, is that of situations (e.g.,

situations of formal status, which means one makes refusals to a superior, or situations of informal status, which means one makes refusals to a friend). This is different from formality level in the present study.

3. There are different views on honorifics. Ide (1989) and Matsumoto (1988; 1989) maintain that honorifics in Japanese carry social information, and thus it is essential to choose an appropriate lexical/grammatical form according to the social context. That is, there is no neutral form that can be used without making known the speaker's relationship to the hearer. Ide and Matsumoto also claim that in FTA situations honorifics are used. However, Fukada and Asato (2004: 1997) argue that there is a use of honorifics in non-FTA situations, and they claim honorifics to be a negative politeness strategy according to Brown and Levinson's (1987) definition. Fukada and Asato's (2004) position seems to be valid, as honorifics can also be used in non-FTA situations (e.g., situations involving a high social status person). I side with Fukada and Asato (2004), in viewing honorifics as a negative politeness strategy, because both strategies express formality and/or deference, as Okamoto (1999: 69) also argues. According to Okamoto (1999: 70), the use of honorific and non-honorific expressions is a speech-style strategy based on a speaker's consideration of multiple contextual features as well as on his/her beliefs and attitudes concerning honorific uses. Pizziconi (2003) takes a similar perspective to this. According to Pizziconi (2003: 1471), the principles regulating the use of honorific devices in Japanese are not substantially different from those of English, both being similarly strategic. I also side with Nishimura (2010: 38), who argues that following a number of discursive theorists researching politeness phenomena (e.g., Locher and Watts 2005), no linguistic forms — including honorifics — are inherently polite or impolite.

4. Not only having the basic function of *Kenjyogo* I, this *itadaku* expresses the meaning of receiving a benefit/blessing (Bunka Shingikai 2007).

5. Although it was not required for the participants to report whether H was an in-group or out-group member, the student who sent this mail reported that she considered the high school teacher as an out-group member. From the fact that there was a distance between the student and the high school teacher, it can be assumed that H is an out-group member. In-group (*uchi*) (which must always include the speaker)/out-group (*soto*) boundaries, however, shift from moment to moment depending on the kinds of sociocultural factors, as Wetzel (1994: 75) argues. When S perceived that there was a psychological distance between S and H, it can be assumed that S regards H as an out-group member as this example shows. However, it is intricate where the in-group/out-group boundary lies, i.e., there may be a case in which S regards H as an in-group or an out-group member when S perceives that S and H are close (i.e., having no psychological distance). Therefore, the participants in this study were asked to report the power difference and closeness between S and H, and degree of imposition of the requested act, not the in-group/out-group relationship.

References

Atkinson, J. Maxwell (1982). Understanding Formality: the Categorization and Production of 'Formal' Interaction. *The British Journal of Sociology* 33 (1): 86–117.

Barke, Andrew (2010). Manipulating Honorifics in the Construction of Social Identities in Japanese Television Drama. *Journal of Sociolinguistics* 14 (4): 456–476.

Blum-Kulka, Shoshana, Juliane House and Gabriele Kasper (1989). *Cross-Cultural Pragmatics: Requests and Apologies.* Norwood, N.J.: Ablex Publishing Corporation.

Brown, Penelope and Stephen C. Levinson (1987). *Politeness: Some Universals in Language Usage.* Cambridge: Cambridge University Press.

Bunka Shingikai [Japanese Council for Cultural Affairs] (2007). Keigo no Shishin [A Guideline for Japanese Honorifics]. http://www.bunka.go.jp/1kokugo/pdf/keigo-toushin.pdf, accessed on the 24th November, 2010.

Byon, Andrew Sangpil (2006). The Role of Linguistic Indirectness and Honorifics in Achieving Linguistic Politeness in Korean Requests. *Journal of Politeness Research* 2 (2): 247–276.

Clancy, Patricia M. (1986). The Acquisition of Communicative Style in Japanese. In B. B. Shieffelin and E. Ochs (eds.), *Language Socialization across Cultures.* Cambridge: Cambridge University Press, pp. 213–250.

Economidous-Kogetsidis, Maria (2004). Requestive Directness in Intercultural Communication: Greek and English. In J. Leigh and E. Loo (eds.), *Outer Limits: A Reader in Communication and Behaviour across Cultures.* Melbourne: Language Australia, pp. 25–48.

Economidou-Kogetsidis, Maria (2005). "Yes, tell me please, what time is the midday flight from Athens arriving?": Telephone Service Encounters and Politeness. *Intercultural Pragmatics* 2 (3): 253–272.

Felix-Brasdefer, J. Cesar (2006). Linguistic Politeness in Mexico: Refusal Strategies among Speakers of Mexican Spanish. *Journal of Pragmatics* 38: 2158–2187.

Fukada, Atsushi and Noriko Asato (2004). Universal Politeness Theory: Application to the Use of Japanese Honorifics. *Journal of Pragmatics* 36: 1991–2002.

Fukushima, Saeko (1996). Request Strategies in British English and Japanese. *Language Sciences* 18 (3–4): 671–688.

Fukushima, Saeko (2000). *Requests and Culture: Politeness in British English and Japanese.* Bern: Peter Lang.

Fukushima, Saeko (2010). Hearer's Aspect in Politeness: The Case of Requests. In D. Shu and K. Turner (eds.), *Contrasting Meaning in Languages of the East and West.* Oxford: Peter Lang, pp. 103–135.

Haugh, Michael (2003). Japanese and Non-Japanese Perceptions of Japanese Communication. *New Zealand Journal of Asian Studies* 5 (1): 156–177.

Hiraga, Masako and Joan M. Turner (1996). Differing Perception of Face in British and Japanese Academic Settings. *Language Sciences* 18 (3–4): 605–627.

Hori, Motoko (2000). Language Change in Japanese Society. In M. Hori (ed.), *The Positive Politeness Trend in Recent Japanese.* Gifu: JACET Politeness Research Group, pp. 3–24.

Ide, Sachiko (1989). Formal Forms and Discernment: Two Neglected Aspects of Universals of Linguistic Politeness. *Multilingua* 2 (3): 223–248.
Irvine, Judith T. (2001). Formality and Informality in Communicative Events. In Alessandro Duranti (ed.), *Linguistic Anthropology: A Reader*. Oxford: Blackwell, pp. 189–207.
Kasper, Gabriele (1994). Politeness. In R. E. Asher and J.M. Y. Simpson (eds.), *The Encyclopedia of Language and Linguistics*. Oxford: Pergamon Press, pp. 3206–3211.
Lebra, Takie Sugiyama (1976). *Japanese Patterns of Behavior*. Honolulu: University of Hawaii Press.
Lee, Duck-Young (2007). Involvement and the Japanese Interactive Particles *ne* and *yo*. *Journal of Pragmatics* 39: 363–388.
Leech, Geoffrey (1983). *Principles of Pragmatics*. London: Longman.
Locher, Miriam A. and Richard J. Watts (2005). Politeness Theory and Relational Work. *Journal of Politeness Research* 1 (1): 9–33.
Matsumoto, Yoshiko (1988). Reexamination of the Universality of Face: Politeness Phenomena in Japanese. *Journal of Pragmatics* 12: 403–426.
Matsumoto, Yoshiko (1989). Politeness and Conversational Universals — Observations from Japanese. *Multilingua* 8 (2–3): 207–221.
Miyamoto, Setsuko, Mika Kotera and Mazda Kobe (2004). Gender Consciousness in the Mail Communication by Cellular Phone: From the Perspective of Politeness Strategies. *Himeji Kogyo University Kankyo Ningen Gakubu Kenkyu Hokoku* 6: 127–137.
Mizutani, Osamu and Nobuko Mizutani (1987). *How to Be Polite in Japanese*. Tokyo: The Japan Times.
Morita, Emi (2002). Stance Marking in the Collaborative Completion of Sentences: Final Particles as Epistemic Markers in Japanese. In N. M. Akatsuka and S. Strauss (eds.), *Japanese/Korean Linguistics*. Stanford: CSLI Publications, pp. 220–233.
Nakane, Chie (1970). *Japanese Society*. Berkley: University of California Press.
Nishimura, Yukiko (2010). Impoliteness in Japanese BBS Interactions: Observations from Message Exchanges in Two Online Communities. *Journal of Politeness Research* 6 (1): 33–55.
Okabe, Roichi (1983). Cultural Assumptions of East and West: Japan and the United States. In W. B. Gudykunst (ed.), *Intercultural Communication Theory: Current Perspectives*. Beverly Hills: Sage, pp. 21–44.
Okamoto, Shigeko (1999). Situated Politeness: Manipulating Honorific and Non-honorific Expressions in Japanese Conversations. *Pragmatics* 9 (1): 51–74.
Olshtain, Elite and Shoshana Blum-Kulka (1985). Degree of Approximation: Nonnative Reaction to Native Speech Act Behavior. In S. M. Gass and C. C. Madden (eds.), *Input and Second Language Acquisition*. Rowley: Newbury House, pp. 303–325.
Pizziconi, Barbara (2003). Re-examining Politeness, Face and the Japanese Language. *Journal of Pragmatics* 35: 1471–1506.
Rinnert, Carol (1999). Appropriate Requests in Japanese and English: A Preliminary

Study. *Hiroshima Journal of International Studies* 5: 163–176.
Rinnert, Carol and Hiroe Kobayashi (1999). Requestive Hints in Japanese and English. *Journal of Pragmatics* 31: 1173–1201.
Rose, Kenneth (1994). On the Validity of Discourse Completion Tests in Non-Western Contexts. *Applied Linguistics* 15 (1): 1–14.
Rose, Kenneth (1996). American English, Japanese, and Directness: More than Stereotypes. *JALT Journal* 18 (1): 67–80.
Satake, Hideo (2005a). Wakamono Kotoba to Sono Jidai [Youth Language and its Generation]. In A. Nakamura, M. Nomura, M. Sakuma and C. Komiya (eds.), *Hyogen to Buntai* [Expressions and Styles]. Tokyo: Meiji Shoin, pp. 416–424.
Satake, Hideo (2005b). Mail Buntai to Sore o Sasaeru Mono [Writing Styles in Mails and What Support Them]. In Y. Hashimoto (ed.), *Media*. Tokyo: Hituzi Syobo, pp. 56–68.
Suzuki, Toshihiko (2007). *A Pragmatic Approach to the Generation and Gender Gap in Japanese Politeness Strategies*. Tokyo: Hituzi Syobo.
Takiura, Masato (2008). Honorifics Seen from Politeness, Politeness Seen from Honorifics: An Overview of Focusing on Their Pragmatic Relativity. *The Japanese Journal of Language in Society* 11 (1): 23–38.
Trosborg, Anna (1995). *Interlanguage Pragmatics: Requests, Complaints and Apologies*. Berlin: Mouton de Gruyter.
Weizman, Elda (1993). Interlanguage Requestive Hints. In G. Kasper and S. Blum-Kulka (eds.), *Interlanguage Pragmatics*. Oxford: Oxford University Press, pp. 123–137.
Wetzel, Patricia J. (1994). A Movable Self: The Linguistic Indexing of *Uchi* and *Soto*. In J. M. Backnik and C. J. Quinn (eds.), *Situated Meaning: Inside and Outside in Japanese Self, Society, and Language*. Princeton, New Jersey: Princeton University Press, pp. 73–87.
Yamada, Haru (1994). Talk-distancing in Japanese Meetings. *Journal of Asian Pacific Communication* 5: 19–36.
Yamada, Haru (1997). *Different Games, Different Rules*. Oxford: Oxford University Press.
Zamborlin, Chiara (2007). Going beyond Pragmatic Failures: Dissonance in Intercultural Communication. *Intercultural Pragmatics* 4 (1): 21–50.

Merge and Three Dimensional Structures

Takashi Imai

Abstract
We live in the 3D world, and ultimately live in Time-Space dimensions in the universe. In the course from the earlier generative grammar to the faculty of language in biology, linguistics has been an interdisciplinary approach to the origin and evolution of language in corporations with biology, neuroscience, gene technology, and in order to investigate the faculty of language, one should consider the third factor (Chomsky 2005), which might be the case that physical laws and principles affect linguistic objects to generate sentences. This paper as a starting point, proposes some variations of the operation Merge in UG. Furthermore, at the initial stage of phrase construction, linguistic trees are formed three dimensionally and invariant across languages. In other word, the tree structure is underspecified until the Spell-Out. At the Spell-Out, the three dimensional structure is rendered into two dimensional structure by fixing the view point parameter-like mechanism, leading to linearization. The outcome is a superficial structure subject to word order variations. The consequence of the proposals here implies that the word order is trivial in the core syntax, but rather it is processed at Sensory-Motor system (PHON). This paper is an initial proposal for further investigation in biolinguistics.

Keywords   the faculty of language in narrow sense, merge, Merger and Acquisition, three-dimensional trees

1. Introduction

The nature of human language has profoundly been investigated since the advent of generative tradition by Noam Chomsky in 1950's. The linguistic research program initially called Generative Grammar, as Chomsky claims that linguistics is part of (human) biology in 1960's, has been well developed to be a super interdisciplinary field of sciences now called biolinguistics.

We will consider some issues here on the Faculty of Language (FL) in biolinguistics. We will observe what FL is, and its relation to the outside of human brain in section 2. Then, we will argue in section 3 that there exists a unique operation, Merge which has three sub-operations in FL. We will discern what was proposed in Imai (2000, 2013). In section 4, we will propose that tree diagrams are not really flat 2Ds, but 3Ds along the line of Klosek (2011) to account for language diversity, which seems to be superficial. Rather, languages in the world are trivially uniform in FLN (Faculty of Language in Narrow Sense). Section 5 concludes the present paper.

2. Biolinguistics: linguistics as natural science

Chomsky asserts that linguistics is part of (human) biology.[1] Thus, FL constitutes an organic system in the brain neural cells. Since we understand that FL is biologically endowed, linguistic operations and expressions involved in syntactic, semantic and phonological processes among others would be similar or paralleled to other biological processes in human body.[2]

Interdisciplinary approach to FL may reveal some unexpected outcomes as the discovery of spiral structures of DNA by biologist Watson and physicist Click in 1950's showed us an excellent example. The same thing is said for the Science of Language. There exist many questions and mysteries to be solved as to the origin and evolution of human language. Without cooperation with various fields of biology it is impossible for biolinguists to find answers to those questions and mysteries.

The ancestors of Homo Sapiens emerged in Africa some 2 million years ago, then according to Chomsky (2012a), probably some 60,000 years ago language was there though a complex symbolic system was there before 60,000—100,000 years ago. In the course of human evolution, the Faculty of Language was acquired in the sense of the Great Leap Forward, but not of gradual acquisition by Darwinian natural selection. At the time of FL acquisition, that language was uniquely one is obvious, let's call, the protolanguage. Then, a question arises. Why didn't language remain unique but rather it has proliferated in diversity? In the process of evolution and development (evo-devo), variations occurred across languages such as word order and speech sounds. Notice however that these variations would be found at Sensory-motor systems, just in the outside of human brain/mind, i.e. the Faculty of Language in Narrow Sense (FLN).[2] The investigation of FLN would shed light on the nature of human language, i.e. I-Language.

In the Biolinguistic Minimalist Program (BMP)[3], the goals of the linguistic theory would be eventually the goals of the scientific inquiry, which constitute the investigation of optimal solutions to the organic systems. It is attested that the operations may produce maximal outcomes with the minimal effort conforming with the economy principle.[4] The system exists of any form consisting of various contents independently. These contents self-organize at the point when the system itself activates. The self organization of the subsystems may form the higher and larger system.

Taking the biological foundation of language faculty in human beings for granted, the faculty of language (FL) constitutes part of the organic system in the brain neural cells. Assuming FL is biologically endowed, linguistic operations involved in syntactic, semantic, phonological processes among others would be similar to or parallel to other biological processes in human body.

Brown (1999) reports that Chinque and his research group investigated the biological characteristics of language faculty in such instances as word order, position of adverbs among others which are invariant across languages in the result of word orders in languages.

The importance of considering natural scientific approaches to linguistics is crucial for the sake of the advancement of the linguistic science.[5] Uriagereka (1998) mentions that the mobile model of Kayne's (1994) antisymmetry. This implies the linguistic structure (syntactic, semantic and phonological ones) is three dimensional. Baker (2001) also suggests that tree diagrams be three dimensional. Klosek (2011) explicitly argues that by representing syntactic structure three-dimensionally, it will be possible to eliminate much of the complexity inherent in two-dimensional syntactic structures, and proposes the potential for universal syntactic representation of synonymous propositions expressed in any language. The observation that the syntactic structure is three dimensional seems to be quite on the right track since as Klosek argues, we live in the three dimensional world, and our brain is part of the same world. Unifying the preceding work by those linguists, we will propose that the linguistic structure could be explained if we set the basic unit as a three dimensional structure in which the head X is always in the z-axis in the sense of the conventional mathematical axes of x, y, and z. It is posited that fixing the viewpoint angle is parametrized. By fixing the viewpoint angle, the particular word order for a language is trivially derived. We will return to this in detail in section 3. We have important consequences in that the uniqueness of the default structure could be attributed to the left-handedness of the solar system. The left-handedness could be a clue to explain why most of the movement operations are leftward and very few are rightward in classical generative grammar. This coincides that linguistic processing takes place from left to right, and is closely linked with the mental computation. The findings in physics and biology in a broad sense may well be useful for explanation in linguistics.

Note also that chemical structures, again three dimensional ones, could be a good model for associating linguistic structures. It follows that if the language processing in the brain is a case of molecular reaction at the cellular network in the brain, it is not so unnatural to assume that the linguistic structures could be somewhat similar to chemical structures. This could be important as to merging of categories and possibly the origin of word order variations.[6]

3. Merger and Acquisition (M&A)

In this section, we will observe the unique operation in FL, *Merge* and its application for how categories created by Merge get a label. Note that labels are relevant only at interface, assuming bare phrase structures in FLN (Chomsky 1995, Boeckx 2008).

FL would operate with the economy and optimal principles, then, operation *Merge* enters into the computational system, CHL. Imai (2000) argues that as is assumed by Chomsky, the most fundamental operation for language processing in broad language systems is the operation, *Merge*, which selects two syntactic objects (α, β) and form K (α, β) from them. Imai (2000) proposes that the relationship between the two elected objects (a merger and a mergee) can be specified as in (1):

(1) a. Suppose A is a merger and B is an mergee, then, A merges with B resulting in C in such a way that B is included in A. In this case, B is part of A retaining some characteristics of B. Hence, C is merger-oriented. → {C {A, B}}, C=A.

b. Suppose A is a merger and B is a mergee then, A merges with B resulting in C in such a way that A is included in B. In this case, A is a part of B retaining some characteristics of A. Hence, C is mergee-oriented. → {C {A, B}},C=B
c. Suppose A is a merger and B is a mergee, then A merges with B resulting in C in such a way that A and B are indistinctly amalgamated. In this case, C is an entirely new entity consisting of A and B. → {C {A, B}}, C = (A, B).
d. Suppose A is a merger and B is a mergee, then A merges with B resulting in C in such a way that A is not included in B and B is not included in A, either. In this case, C is neutral. → {C {A, B}}, C = Φ

The four types of *Merge* can be defined in terms of Acquisition.

(2) i. A acquires B and becomes C. (We call it the Progressive Merge.)
ii. B acquires A and becomes C. (We call it the Regressive Merge.)
iii. A and B acquire each other. The autonomy of each disappears. (We call it the Amalgamated Merge.)
iv. A does not acquire B and conversely B does not acquire A. The autonomy of each is respected. In other words, A and B are adjacent each other. (We call it the Neutralized Merge.)

The proposal mentioned above is a gist of Imai (2000).

It follows that the Operation, *Merge* is a universal operation with options mentioned above depending on a language to which the choice of items might be attributed. The consequence with (2 i–ii) is that we no longer need the head parameter any more.

Rizzi (2012) referring to an earlier version of Chomsky (2013), discusses labeling of the category created by Merge. Chomsky (2013) argues how categories created by Merge get a label by postulating the labeling algorithm as follows:

(3) The Labeling Algorithm:
The category created by Merge inherits the label of the closest head.

(4) Nodes must have a label to be properly interpreted: the interpretive systems must know what kind of object they are interpreting.

(4) is different from the previous model in which labeling was thought to be prerequisite for further applications of Merge. The new view makes Merge apply to unlabeled structures. Labeling is necessary only at interface.

We have three cases to be considered as to Merge:

(5) a. Head - Head Merge
 b. Head - Phrase Merge
 c. Phrase - Phrase Merge

Rizzi (2012) defines the closeness of a head in terms of c-command as follows:

(6) H_1 is the closest head to α iff
 i. α contains H_1, and
 ii. there is no H_2 such that i. α c-commands H_2 and
   ii. H_2 c-commands H_1.

We apply (2iii) for (5a) to account for the root and functional category. (2i-ii) account for (5b), which is subject to a natural language. We apply (2iv) for (5c) to form an unlabeled structure. As (2iii) is mysterious and somewhat complicated, we will put it aside here.

4. Three dimensional diagrams

When it comes to syntactic structures, we will deal with 3D structures rather than 2D ones, since we live in 3D world and process to interpret the world three dimensionally following Uriagereka (1998), Baker (2001), Klosek (2011) among others. We will propose the 3D tree diagrams at the level of Narrow Syntax. The syntactic structure is unspecified, but built by Merge. One cannot observe a firm structure until Spell-Out, but only can see the determined structure (i.e. word ordering) at SEM in a particular language, because one cannot pronounce words in a sentence simultaneously. This could be associated to Schrödinger's cat in Quantum Physics.[7] We have six cases consisting of Subject, Object and Verb in terms of word ordering. Let us observe the following six cases of the outcome.

(7) a. SVO[8]

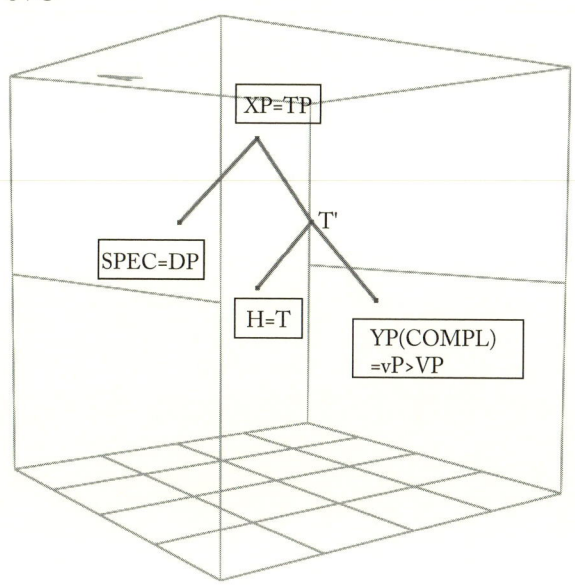

b. VSO

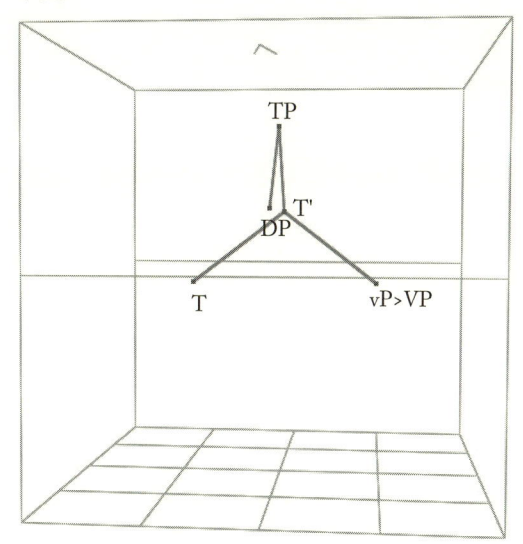

c. SOV

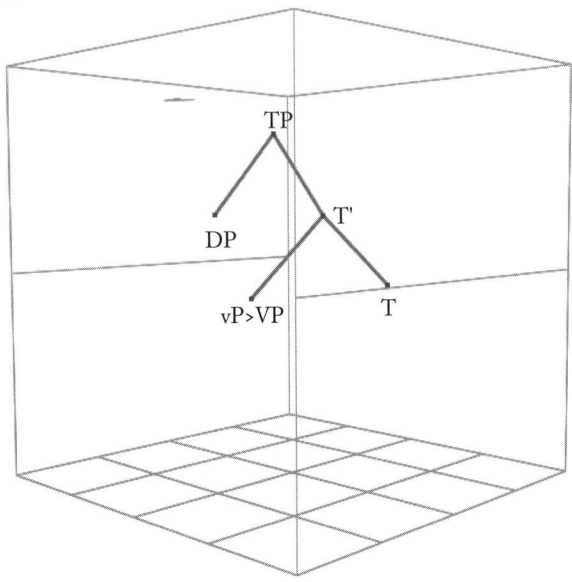

d. OVS

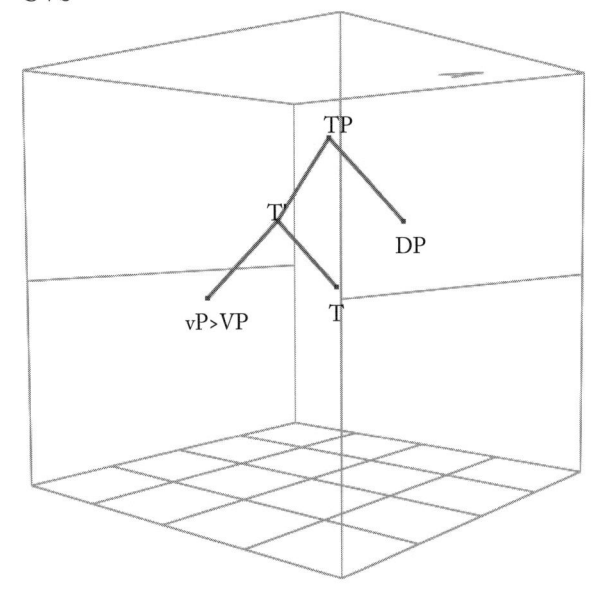

e. OSV

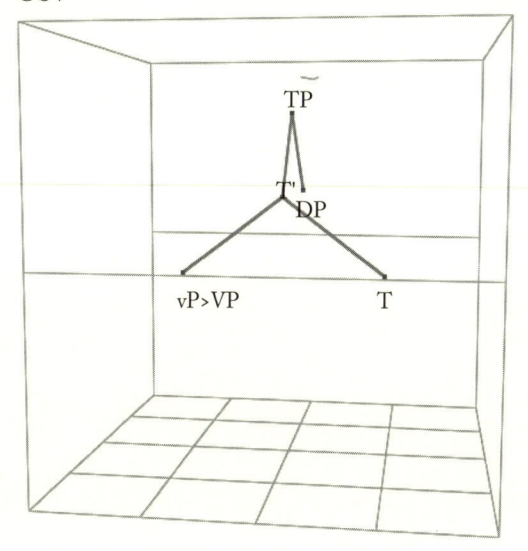

f. VOS

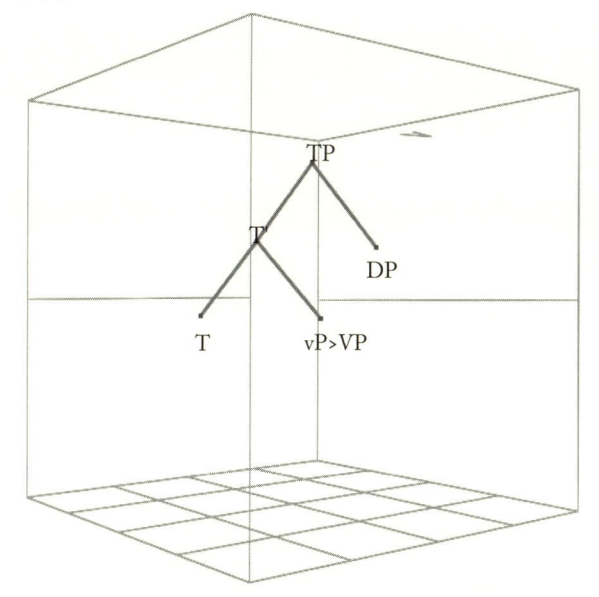

Up to the point of interface, the syntactic structure is underspecified, i.e., not determined. To rotate the viewpoint, we can fix the viewpoint to generate the syntactic structure of a specific language at the interface.

To determine the word order of a specific language is simple enough to set the viewpoint rendered at the interface of PHON and SEM. In the side of PHON, a parameterized rule: **Set the viewpoint of merged items** is fixed, then, we can obtain a structure in six combinations. Take for example, if the viewpoint of a sentence comprising of the subject, object and verb, i.e. a simplex sentence, is fixed at the angle of SVO, then, automatically the PHON-SEM rules activate to translate the three dimensional structure into the two dimensional structure as lineally ordered configuration. The viewpoint operation is proposed as in (8):

(8) Set the viewpoint of $\{\alpha^*\}$ at PHON (S-M system).

Next, the SEM ordering rule automatically activates the rule responsible for the order of merged items as follows:

(9) Pronounce $\{\alpha^*\}$ at the fixed structure of the two dimensional structure.

A natural computation of any sort is executed from left to right in the brain. When, the order of pronunciation of items, $\{\alpha^*\}$ is fixed, then, the outcome commences to pronounce from the leftmost item, second item, and so on up until the last item of $\{\alpha^*\}$, hence the operation is completed.

By setting the viewpoint of a simplex sentence, we can account for the six existent word orders. It is noteworthy that the word order of the opposite side exhibits a near perfect mirror image. For example, in Japanese the simplex sentence is a set of items comprising a subject noun, object noun and V-stem+Aspect/Tense such as sono otoko-no-ko-ga ringo-wo tabeta, which means "that boy-NOM apples-ACC eat-Tense (Past); The (That) boy ate apples. In Malagasy, the order of items is opposite of the Japanese counterpart, that is to say, Tense/Aspect-V-stem Acc-N Nom-N. This phenomenon is significant in that it proves the 3D model of sentences. Even in English, there are various word orders such as Topicalization, Object fronting among others. In sum, it could be best to assume that the viewpoint is movable globally as well as locally.

5. Concluding remarks

What we have observed so far is that we stress on the importance of correlation between linguistics and natural science. The concept of *Merge* is defined in the Merger and Mergee relation and three types of *Merge* are articulated in association with M&A with association to Chomsky (2013). The 3 D trees are proposed to describe syntactic structures at the initial stage to the interface point, S-O in FLN.[9]

Notes
This is an extensively revised version of Imai (2013).

1. In the early generative grammar model, Chomsky asserted that linguistics is a subfield of cognitive psychology. In 1960's, Chomsky said that linguistics is part of human biology, influenced by Lenneberg. See Lenneberg (1968) in which "biolinguistics" was first mentioned.
2. FLN is restricted to human language, while the Faculty of Language in Broad Sense (FLB) includes communication in other species. See Hauser, Chomsky and Fitch (2002).
3. The BMP is an extension of the Minimalist Program, thus, it is a core of syntax.
4. See Lemons (1997) for further details.
5. See Fukui (2012) for arguing for the importance of grasping linguistics as natural science. Kuroda's article originally appeared in *Sophia Linguistica* in 2008 as an appendix to Fukui (2012) argues that mathematics is a useful tool for exploring mysteries of generative grammar (biolinguistics).
6. Gunter Blobel, a cellular and molecular biologist, won the 1999 Nobel Prize in medicine for discovering that proteins carry certain signals that may act as ZIP codes, assisting them find to move to their correct locations within the cell. See Heemels (1999). This resembles the Operation *Agree* under matching, which is a relation that holds a Probe P and a Goal G in MP. See Chomsky (2000/2012b) for further details.
7. See Monroe, Meekhof, King, and Wineland (1996) for details.
8. For the sake of convenience, I use the conventional X-bar labeling, though bare phrase structures are assumed following Chomsky.
9. It is not so unreasonable to assume that structures in syntactic, phonological, and semantic domains are invariant as to the Spell-Out. Jackendof (2002) proposes this line of linguistic program, now we consider it as the Parallel Processing Model. For further research agenda, we should take generative musicology (Lerdahl and Jackendoff (1982), syntax of songbirds among others into account to investigate the nature of human language faculty.

References

Baker, M. C. (2001) *The Atoms of Language*, New York: Basic Books.
Boeckx, C. (2008) *Bare Syntax*, Oxford: Oxford University Press.
Brown, K. (1999) Grammar's Secret Skeleton. *Science*, 283, 774–775.
Chomsky, N. (1995) *The Minimalist Program*, Cambridge, Mass: The MIT Press.
Chomsky, N. (2000) Minimalist Inquiries: the Framework. In Martin, R. D., R. D. Michaels and Uriagereka, J. eds. *Step by Step: Essays on Minimalist Syntax in Honor of Howard Lasnik*, Cambridge: The MIT Press. Also in Chomsky (2012b) Chapter 7, *Chomsky's Linguistics*, edited by Peter Graff and Coppe van Urk, Cambridge, Mass: the MIT Press, 393–471.
Chomsky, N. (2005) Three Factors in Language Design. *Linguistic Inquiry* 36, 1–22.
Chomsky, N. (2012a) *The Science of Language*, Cambridge: Cambridge University Press.
Chomsky, N. (2012b) *Chomsky's Linguistics*, edited by Peter Graff and Coppe van Urk, Cambridge, Mass: the MIT Press.
Chomsky, N. (2013) The Problems of Projection. *Lingua* 130, 33–49.
Fukui, N. (2012) *Shin-Shizen Kagaku toshiteno Gengogaku (Linguistics as Natural Science: New Version)*, Tokyo: Chikuma Shobo.
Hauser, M., N. Chomsky, and T. Fitch (2002) The Faculty of Language: What Is It, Who Has It, and How Did It Evolve? *Science*, 298, 1569–1579.
Heemels, M-T. (1999) Medicine Nobel Goes to Pionieer of Protin Guidance Mechanisms. *Nature*, 401, 625.
Imai, T. (2000) Some Considerations on Optimal Derivations. *Tsuru Studies in English Linguistics and Literature*, 28, 26–37.
Imai, T. (2013) Some Thoughts on the Biolinguistic Program. *Tsuru Studies in English Linguistics and Literature*, 41, 1–12.
Jackendoff, R. (2002) *Foundations of Language: Brain, Meaning, Grammar, Evolution.* Oxford: Oxford University Press.
Kayne, R. (1994) *The Antisymmetry of Syntax*, Cambridge, Mass: The MIT Press.
Klosek, J. (2011) Three-Dimensional Syntax. LingBuzz. http://ling.auf.net/lingbuzz/001327
Kuroda, S-Y. (2008) Sugaku to Seisei Bumpo (Mathematics and Generative Grammar). in Fukui 2012.
Lemon, D. S. (1997) *Perfect Form*, Princeton, NJ: Princeton University Press.
Lerdahl, F. and R. Jackendoff (1982) *A Generative Theory of Tonal Music*, Cambridge, Mass: MIT Press.
Lenneberg, E. (1968) *Biological Foundation of Language.* New Yorsk: John Wiley and Son.
Monroe, C., D. M. Meekhof, B. E. King, and D. J. Wineland, (1996) A "Schrödinger Cat" Superposition State of an Atom. *Science*, 272, 1131–1136.
Rizzi, R. (2012) Cartography, Criteria, and Labeling: III. Labeling and Criteria. Handout, Blaise Pascal Lectures, Ealing 2012, September 11–13, 2012.
Uriagereka, J. (1998) *Rhyme and Reason: An Introduction to Minimalist Syntax*,

Cambridge, Mass: The MIT Press.

Subjective Small Clause Predicates in English and Japanese

Mikinari Matsuoka

Abstract

It is claimed in some previous studies that small clause constructions involving epistemic verbs in Japanese, unlike corresponding constructions in English, cannot have nominal predicates in their complements. It is argued in this study that the problem is not concerned with syntactic category but with semantics. In particular, examples are presented to show that the complements of those small clause constructions in both English and Japanese must represent subjectively viewed propositions rather than objectively viewed ones. It is noted that if these semantic requirements are met, nominal predicates do occur in the small clause complements in Japanese as well as in English.

Keywords small clause, complement, proposition, subjective, objective

1. Introduction

It is known that so-called small clause (henceforth, SC) constructions in English involving epistemic verbs can have either adjectival or nominal predicates in their complements, as shown in (1):

(1) a. Mary considers John foolish.
 b. John considers Mary a liar.

On the other hand, it is suggested in some previous studies that comparable SC constructions in Japanese can involve adjectival predicates, as shown in (2a), but not nominal counterparts, as shown in (2b) (Kawai 2006, Hoshi and Sugioka 2009, Matsuoka 2009):[1]

(2) a. Taroo-wa   Hanako-o   tanomosi-ku   omotte-i-ru.
       Taro-Top   Hanako-Acc   reliable-Aff   think-Asp-Pres
       'Taro considers Hanako reliable.'
    b. *Karera-wa   Tanaka   sensei-o   gakusya-ni
        they-Top   Tanaka   professor-Acc   scholar-Pred
        omotte-i-ru.
        think-Asp-Pres
        'They consider Professor Tanaka to be a scholar.'

In this study, I will claim that the problem with examples like (2b) is not concerned with syntactic category but with semantics. It is argued by Borkin (1984) that the complements of the SC constructions in English must describe propositions about someone's personal experience or judgment rather than about empirically verifiable matters of fact. I will provide examples indicating that the same constraints are imposed on the SC complements in Japanese irrespective of whether they involve adjectival or nominal predicates. It will be shown that if the semantic requirements are filled, nominal predicates do occur in the SC constructions in Japanese as well as in English.

Note that there has been controversy over the syntactic structure of these constructions in both English and Japanese. Some claim that the object (accusative) NP and the adjectival or nominal predicate constitute a clausal complement, that is, an SC. However, others contend that the adjectival or nominal predicate forms a complex predicate with the verb in the underlying structure. In this study, I will not commit myself on this issue and call the constructions in both (1) and (2) SC constructions given that the object NP and the adjectival or nominal predicate are interpreted as constituting propositions.[2]

The following discussion proceeds as follows. In section 2, we consider the semantic properties of the complements in SC constructions in English, comparing them with those of the complements in other constructions involving epistemic verbs. In section 3, we turn to the semantic properties of the SC complements in Japanese. Finally, concluding remarks are given in section 4.

2. SC complements in English

In English, propositions conveying the same cognitive message can often be expressed by finite clauses introduced by *that* or nonfinite clauses in so-called Exceptional Case Marking (henceforth, ECM) constructions and SC constructions, as shown in (3):

(3) a. I find that this chair is uncomfortable.
    b. I find this chair to be uncomfortable.   (ECM)
    c. I find this chair uncomfortable.   (SC)

However, Borkin (1984: 79) argues that these three constructions are distinguished by some semantic properties concerning whether the propositions are regarded as matters of human judgment or empirically verifiable matters of fact, which is virtually equivalent to the distinction between *subjective* vs. *objective* in Bolinger (1973). In particular, Borkin observes that *that* clauses are most appropriate to propositions about empirically verifiable matters of fact, whereas SCs are most suitable for propositions about someone's personal experience or judgment, ECMs being intermediate between these. Thus, according to Borkin, the *that* clause complement in (3a) denotes a proposition viewed as based on evidence, whereas the SC complement in (3c) describes the report of an experience. For example, she notes that she might use (3a) but not (3c) as a statement about consumer reaction tests, while she would use (3c) and not (3a) as a statement about how the chair feels to her. On the other hand, (3b) might be used in either circumstance.[3]

Another trio of examples in (4) involves propositions that are usually viewed as being about empirically verifiable matters of fact, which are most appropriate in *that* clauses and least in SC complements (Borkin 1984: 56, 76):

(4) a. When I looked in the files, I found that she was Mexican.
    b. ? When I looked in the files, I found her to be Mexican.
    c. * When I looked in the files, I found her Mexican.

Thus, these examples are also consistent with Borkin's generalization.

Although the examples we saw in (3) and (4) all involve the verb *find*, Borkin (1984) indicates that the same tendency holds with other epistemic verbs selecting propositions. If we focus on ECM and SC constructions, the following examples involving the verbs *believe* and *prove* indicate that propositions about empirically verifiable matters of fact are more appropriate in ECM complements in (5a) and (6a) than in SC complements in (5b) and (6b) (Borkin 1984: 76):

(5) a. ? Why, I believe Tom to be Italian after all.
    b. * Why, I believe Tom Italian after all.

(6) a. ? June's birth certificate proved her to be a doctor of veterinary medicine.
    b. * June's birth certificate proved her a doctor of veterinary medicine.

On the other hand, the SC examples in (7) are much better than those in (5b) and (6b) (Borkin 1984: 76–77):

(7) a. I believe Tom capable, if not astoundingly competent.
    b. June's track performance proved her agile enough for the big time.

As noted by Borkin, the complements in (7), unlike those in (5) and (6), are viewed as matters of judgment.

Moreover, Borkin suggests that though the verb *consider* has an orientation toward describing a subjective judgment rather than a state of belief concerning a matter of fact, the ECM counterpart is more appropriate than the SC in (8) when the proposition is understood from the viewpoint of truth or falsity (Borkin 1984: 77):[4]

(8) I just found out that Sally isn't related to me at all, and it surprises me because I always considered her
    a. to be my sister.
    b. ? my sister.

In contrast, the SC counterpart is more appropriate in (9) because the verb describes the speaker's feelings toward another person and the proposition is not concerned with a literal matter of fact (Borkin 1984: 77):

(9) I always considered him part of the furniture.

Thus, the difference between ECM and SC complements seems to hold to some degree across verbs.

Given these observations made by Borkin, we can understand the contrast between the two examples in (10), which is noted in Endo (1991: 65):[5]

(10) a. John considers Mary a liar.
b. *John considers Mary an attorney.

Since the statement that someone is a liar is usually understood as a matter of personal judgment, we can expect that the SC example describing it in the complement in (10a) is acceptable. However, the proposition that someone is an attorney usually represents a matter of fact, which accounts for why the SC example involving it in (10b) is not appropriate.

Note that the example in (10b) seems to sound better if the nominal predicate in the complement is modified by an adjective, as shown in (11), according to Endo (1991: 71, fn. 12):

(11) John considers Mary a good attorney.

This is also understandable given that degree words contribute to making the truth of a proposition not absolute but subject to one's view of things, as noted by Borkin (1984) (see also Bolinger 1973). In the following ECM example provided by Borkin (1984: 57), a degree adverb and an adjective modify the predicate in the complement and yield a proposition of the subjective or judgmental type:

(12) I consider Fran to be a very able translator.

Then, the adjective *good* in (11) seems to have the same function as the adverb and the adjective in (12), contributing to converting a proposition about a matter of fact to one about personal judgment.

3. SC complements in Japanese

Now let us consider propositional complements of epistemic verbs in Japanese. Those complements appear in three different syntactic frames, which are comparable to the three in English we saw in (3). The first one, shown in (13a), is equivalent to the *that* clause construction in English: it involves the complementizer *to* 'that', the subject of the complement is marked by nominative Case, and the embedded predicate bears a finite inflectional marker. The second one, shown in (13b), is often called an ECM construction in the Japanese literature: though it also involves the complementizer and an embedded predicate in a finite form, the subject of the complement is marked by accusative Case. The third one, shown in

(13c), is the SC counterpart having a non-finite embedded predicate, which was introduced in section 1:

(13) a. Taroo-wa   Hanako-ga   tanomosi-i   to
       Taro-Top   Hanako-Nom   reliable-Pred.Pres   Comp
       omotte-i-ru.
       think-Asp-Pres
       'Taro thinks that Hanako is reliable.'
    b. Taroo-wa   Hanako-o   tanomosi-i   to
       Taro-Top   Hanako-Acc   reliable-Pred.Pres   Comp
       omotte-i-ru.   [ECM]
       think-Asp-Pres
       'Taro thinks that Hanako is reliable.'
    c. Taroo-wa Hanako-o   tanomosi-ku omotte-i-ru.   [SC]
       Taro-Top Hanako-Acc reliable-Aff think-Asp-Pres
       'Taro considers Hanako reliable.'

Comparing examples of these three frames involving *omou* 'think' and *kanziru* 'feel' as the main verbs and adjectives as the embedded predicates, Morita (1981: 84–89) observes that the construction in (13a), that is, the *that* clause counterpart, and the ECM in (13b) are generally objective and analytic expressions, whereas the SC in (13c) is subjective and nonanalytic. In particular, he notes that those adjectives occurring in the SC frame describe subjective emotions (see also Masuoka 1984). These observations are remarkable given that Borkin points out a similar difference between *that* clauses and SC complements in English, as discussed above.

The difference noted by Morita also seems to hold when the complements have nominal predicates. The following examples involve a noun referring to a nationality as the embedded predicate, which yields a proposition about an empirically verifiable matter of fact (see (4), (5)). The *that* clause and the ECM counterparts are appropriate, as shown in (14a,b), whereas the SC counterpart is not, as shown in (14c):

(14) a. John-wa   Mary-ga   nihonzin-da   to
       John-Top   Mary-Nom   Japanese-Pred.Pres   Comp
       omotte-i-ta.
       think-Asp-Past
       'John thought that Mary was Japanese.'

   b. John-wa　　　Mary-o　　　nihonzin-da　　　　to
      John-Top　　 Mary-Acc　 Japanese-Pred.Pres　Comp
      omotte-i-ta.
      think-Asp-Past
      'John thought that Mary was Japanese.'
   c. *John-wa　　　Mary-o　　　nihonzin-ni　　omotte-i-ta.
      John-Top　　 Mary-Acc　 Japanese-Pred　think-Asp-Past
      'John considered Mary Japanese.'

It seems that the objectively viewed proposition does not fit in with the subjective nature of the SC frame in (14c).

With these points in mind, let us consider SC complements involving nominal predicates that are discussed in previous studies. Hoshi and Sugioka (2009: 183) suggest that nominal predicates in general cannot occur in SC complements except for a few expressing emotions on the basis of the following examples:

(15) a. *Mary-ga　　 John-o　　　satuzinhan-ni　　omot-ta.
       Mary-Nom　John-Acc　 murderer-Pred　 think-Past
       'Mary considered John to be the murderer.'
    b. Mary-ga　　　hurusato-o　　　hokori-ni　　omot-ta.
       Mary-Nom　 hometown-Acc　pride-Pred　 think-Past
       'Mary considered her hometown to be a source of her pride.'

Now we can understand why these sentences are different in acceptability. The complement in (15a), involving the nominal predicate *satuzinhan* 'murderer', is viewed as being about an empirically verifiable matter of fact, which is not appropriately described in SC frames. On the other hand, the complement in (15b), containing the predicate *hokori* 'pride', is about a matter of personal judgment, which is suitable for SC. Hoshi and Sugioka (2009) note that other nouns such as *yorokobi* 'joy', *kyoohu* 'fear', and *hazi* 'shame' can also occur as the predicates in SC complements. This is also understandable because they are concerned with personal experience or judgment rather than matters of fact.

Next, the following example given by Matsuoka (2009: 68) seems to be accounted for on the same grounds:

(16) * Karera-wa   Tanaka   sensei-o   gakusya-ni
      they-Top   Tanaka   professor-Acc   scholar-Pred
      omotte-i-ru.
      think-Asp-Pres
      'They consider Professor Tanaka to be a scholar.'

The SC complement in (16), involving the nominal predicate *gakusya* 'scholar', is viewed as a matter of fact rather than one of personal judgment, in particular, if the noun is interpreted as referring to an occupation, which does not fit in with the SC frame. It is notable that the acceptability of this kind of example seems to improve for some speakers if the nominal predicate is modified by an adjective, as shown in (17) (see Matsuoka 2009: 67, fn. 6):[6]

(17) ?? Karera-wa   Tanaka   sensei-o   rippa-na
        they-Top   Tanaka   professor-Acc   honorable-Aff
        gakusya-ni   omotte-i-ru.
        scholar-Pred   think-Asp-Pres
        'They consider Professor Tanaka to be an honorable scholar.'

As discussed in section 2, degree words typically occur with judgments rather than with neutral descriptions of facts. Then, the adjective *rippa* 'honorable' in (17) seems to have the function of turning a proposition about a matter of fact to one about personal judgment in the same way as the adjectives in (11) and (12).

Finally, the following example given by Masuoka (1984: 95) also seems to be in line with the present discussion. Note that a formal noun *mono* 'thing' modified by an adjective occurs as the predicate of the SC complement:

(18) Kare-wa   tabun   watasi-no   kansee-ya   rikairyoku-o
     he-Top   probably   I-Gen   sensibility-or   understanding-Acc
     usankusai   mono-ni   omotte-i-ru-ni   tigaina-i.
     questionable   thing-Pred   think-Asp-Pres-Pred   certain-Pred.Pres
     'It is certain that he considers my sensibility and understanding questionable.'

The adjective *usankusai* 'questionable' in (18) as well as that in (17) appears to contribute to yielding a proposition about a matter of personal judgment.

4. Concluding remarks

It is claimed in some previous studies that small clause constructions involving epistemic verbs in Japanese, unlike corresponding constructions in English, cannot have nominal predicates in their complements. However, I have argued in this study that the problem is not concerned with syntactic category but with semantics. In particular, I have presented examples indicating that the complements of those small clause constructions in both English and Japanese must represent propositions about matters of personal experience or judgment rather than about empirically verifiable matters of fact. We have seen that if these semantic requirements are met, nominal predicates do occur in the small clause complements in Japanese as well as in English.

If the observations made in this study are correct, the question arises as to why the small clause complements have the particular interpretations. Given that the characteristic meanings are found with small clause constructions involving epistemic verbs in both English and Japanese, distinguished from the meanings of finite clauses, there is a possibility that the interpretations are linked to the syntactic structure of the constructions. I leave investigation into this matter for future research.

Acknowledgements

I would like to thank students at the University of Yamanashi for kindly acting as consultants for some of the Japanese examples provided here. My thanks also go to Gerry Allen for editorial improvement. This research is supported in part by JSPS KAKENHI Grant Number 23520459. All remaining errors and inadequacies are my own.

Notes

1. Following abbreviations are used in the glosses: Acc (accusative case), Aff (inflectional affix), Asp (aspect), Comp (complementizer), Gen (genitive case), Nom (nominative case), Pred (predication), Pres (present), Top (topic).
2. As regards the English constructions in (1), see Chomsky (1975), Bach (1979), and Larson (1988) for the complex predicate analysis, Bowers (1993), Rothstein (2004), and Den Dikken (2006) for the small clause analysis, and Stowell (1991) for a hybrid analysis. On the other hand, as regards the Japanese constructions in

(2), see Takezawa (1987) and Kikuchi and Takahashi (1991) for the small clause analysis, and Hoshi and Sugioka (2009) for the complex predicate analysis.
3. Noting that any proposition in practice can be viewed as a matter of fact or a matter of judgment in a suitable context, Borkin (1984: 55) suggests that the distinction between the two kinds of propositions depends on pragmatic conditions.
4. Borkin (1984: 57) suggests that the fact that *consider* occurs with *that* clauses less regularly than with infinitives is related to the fact that the complement of the verb is usually about a matter of judgment.
5. Endo (1991: 65) indicates that since *consider* expresses subjective judgment, the example in (10b) may sound better in a pragmatically elaborated situation where someone's attorneyhood is debated (see note 3). However, he notes that there is a clear difference between the two examples in (10) when they are uttered out of the blue. Endo (1991: 66) also observes that the ECM counterparts to the two examples are both acceptable.
6. Masaki Sano (p.c.) and Yuji Takano (p.c.) independently informed me that nouns modified by adjectives are more likely to occur as SC predicates than bare nouns, for which I am grateful to them.

References

Bach, Emmon. (1979) Control in Montague Grammar. *Linguistic Inquiry* 10: 515–531.

Bolinger, Dwight. (1973) Objective and Subjective: Sentences without Performatives. *Linguistic Inquiry* 4: 414–417.

Borkin, Ann. (1984) *Problems in Form and Function*. New Jersey: Ablex Publishing Corporation.

Bowers, John. (1993) The Syntax of Predication. *Linguistic Inquiry* 24: 591–656.

Chomsky, Noam. (1975) *The Logical Structure of Linguistic Theory*. New York: Plenum. (Drawn from an unpublished 1955–56 manuscript)

Dikken, Marcel den. (2006) *Relators and Linkers: The Syntax of Predication, Predicate Inversion, and Copulas*. Cambridge, Mass.: MIT Press.

Endo, Yoshio. (1991) The Syntax and Semantics of Small Clauses. In *Topics in Small Clauses*, ed. Heizo Nakajima and Shigeo Tonoike, 59–74. Tokyo: Kurosio Publishers.

Hoshi, Hiroto, and Yoko Sugioka. (2009) Agree, Control and Complex Predicates. In *The Dynamics of the Language Faculty: Perspectives from Linguistics and Cognitive Neuroscience*, ed. Hiroto Hoshi, 177–202. Tokyo: Kurosio Publishers.

Kawai, Michiya. (2006) Raising to Object in Japanese: A Small Clause Analysis. *Linguistic Inquiry* 37: 329–339.

Kikuchi, Akira, and Daiko Takahashi. (1991) Agreement and Small Clauses. In *Topics in Small Clauses*, ed. Heizo Nakajima and Shigeo Tonoike, 75–105. Tokyo: Kurosio Publishers.

Larson, Richard. (1988) On the Double Object Construction. *Linguistic Inquiry* 19: 335–391.

Masuoka, Takashi. (1984) Jojutsuseihosokugo-to Ninshikidohshikohbun [Predicative Complements and Epistemic Verb Constructions]. *Nihongogaku* [Japanese Linguistics] 3: 88–98.

Matsuoka, Mikinari. (2009) On Secondary Adjectival Predicates Selected by Epistemic Verbs in Japanese. In *Tsukuba English Studies vol. 27*, ed. Hiroyuki Iwasaki and Mai Osawa, 63–78, University of Tsukuba.

Morita, Yoshiyuki. (1981) *Nihongo-no Hassoh* [Conceptions in Japanese]. Tokyo: Tohjusha.

Rothstein, Susan. (2004) *Predicates and Their Subjects*. Dordrecht: Kluwer.

Stowell, Timothy. (1991) Small Clause Restructuring. In *Principles and Parameters in Comparative Grammar*, ed. Robert Freiden, 182–218. Cambridge, Mass.: MIT Press.

Takezawa, Koichi. (1987) *A Configurational Approach to Case-Marking in Japanese*. Ph.D. dissertation, University of Washington.

Temporal Interpretation in L2 English by Japanese and Chinese Speakers

Natsumi Okuwaki

Abstract
A wide body of production data on L2 morphology collected so far has provided an informative insight into the process of L2 acquisition. Recent work, however, shows that L2 speakers may still not have acquired the subtle semantics of the morphology even if they are able to produce the form. The present study examines the acquisition of L2 tense morphology by Japanese-L1 and Chinese-L1 speakers learning English to see if they are able to correctly interpret the form that encodes temporal relations in embedded sentences. An interpretation test conducted in the study reveals how Japanese and Chinese learners interpret temporal expressions in English, which are morphosyntactically different from their L1. The results indicate that L2 speakers, to some degree, were able to acquire the properties based on positive evidence in the L2, but at the same time it suggests L1 plays a significant role in the acquisition of the temporal system in L2.

Keywords tense, interpretation, morphosyntax, L1 effects, the form-meaning relation

1. Introduction

Temporality is a universal property in languages, but there is variation in how morphosyntactic properties realise tense. All languages have their own ways expressing a temporal ordering of events in very different ways (Giorgi, 2008). The task for L2 speakers is to establish the nature of the temporal system in the L2 involving the morphological and syntactic properties associated with it. Given that tense is a complex property which also involves the lexicon, the interpretive component, and the interfaces between them, the syntax of tense is taken as a starting point to consider how these components are involved in L2 grammar.

The present study examines whether Japanese-L1 speakers learning English are successful in acquiring the properties of the complex English tense system and argues for the effect of L1 in the acquisition of tense. In addition to Japanese-L1 speakers, L2 knowledge of Chinese-L1 speakers will be investigated. Chinese is well known as a language which does not mark temporal situations with a morphosyntactic device. Comparing the performances of Japanese and Chinese learners whose L1s have different ways interpreting the temporal location of events, the role of L1 will be discussed. It will be argued that there are some differences in the representation of tense between English, Japanese, and Chinese, and that L1 plays a significant role in the acquisition of the temporal system in L2.

As Gabriele & Martohardjono (2005) suggest in their study on L2 aspectual morphology, although a wide body of production data on L2 morphology collected so far is informative, it has been observed that learners who are able to produce aspectual morphology may still not have acquired the subtle semantics of the morphology; in other words, learners may acquire the form before the meaning (Bardovi-Harlig 1995; Montrul & Slabakova 2002). The same can be applied to the study on L2 tense morphology. Taking views from these studies, the present study investigates how learners *interpret* forms that encode temporal relations in a sentence using an interpretation task.

This article proceeds as follows: It first outlines the temporal systems encoded in English, Japanese, and Chinese in terms of syntax and morphology. Based on this discussion, the following sections examine the temporal interpretations yielded by temporal forms in embedded sentences in each language including so called sequence-of-tense (SOT) phenomena. The article suggests potential difficulties for Japanese-L1 speakers in the acquisition of the temporal system in English.

2. Tense in languages

Tense is used in languages to indicate the time at which an action or event described in sentences take place. Traditionally 'tense' has been used to refer to the temporal inflection assigned to finite verb forms, which in English is represented in either form: present (nonpast) or past. In addition, in the research tradition of generative grammar, 'tense' is used to refer to the head of the abstract syntactic functional category, TP, introduced by Pollock (1989), which plays a role in the theory of phrase structure. According to Comrie (1985), the concept of time can be linguistically expressed in two ways. Firstly, a temporal situation is expressed lexically using temporal adverbs which indicate the time of the event or express the duration of the event. The other way is to deploy a grammatical device associated with the verb. It is the second way that is traditionally called 'tense', which is considered a grammaticalised expression of location in time.

Typologically, languages differ widely as to the way of expressing temporal relations (Giorgi 2008). Some languages such as Italian and Romanian have a rich and complex morphological system encoding relations in time. Other languages such as English have a simpler system encoding only a subset of the distinctions made available in Italian or Romanian. There is another type of languages like Chinese which do not morphosyntactically realise tense in a sentence. It should be noted, however, that in all languages sentences express a temporal location of events, be the language Italian, Romanian, English, or Chinese.

In inflectional languages like English and French, tense is usually expressed by verb inflections. It can be argued that English grammaticalises tense, since it distinguishes past events from present situations by making a form change in the verb in a systematic way, assigning the past tense affix *-ed* to verb stems or changing the stem. Similarly, Japanese also grammaticalises tense, since a past event is normally distinguished from a nonpast situation through affix-type morphology; *V-ta* for past vs. *V-(r)u* for nonpast. These are illustrated in (1).

(1) a. John walked (*walk) to the station yesterday.
    b. John-wa   kino   eki   made arui-ta (*aruk-u).
       John-TOP yesterday station to   walk-PAST (*walk-NPST)
       "John walked to the station yesterday."

(1) refers to an event which has taken place prior to the time of utterance, as is signalled by the temporal adverbial *yesterday*. In both English and Japanese, it is not grammatical to use the nonpast form in past contexts. Thus, the presence of tense in the grammar of a language is verified if the time reference is expressed by a specific grammatical form in an obligatory and systematic way.

In contrast, Chinese is well known as a language without tense morphology; its verbs are not inflected for overt morphological tense markers. Temporal interpretation is not determined by tense markers in Chinese; instead, there are at least four factors which influence the temporal interpretation of a simple clause (Lin 2006: 2): (i) temporal adverbials, (ii) default viewpoint aspect, (iii) aspectual markers, and (iv) modal verbs. Although some researchers claim for the presence of finite-nonfinite distinction in terms of INFL and suggest a possibly empty Infection node in Chinese (Huang 1998; Li 1990), others suggest Chinese lacks morphological tense and semantic features of tense at all (Lin 2003, 2006; Smith & Erbaugh 2005).

In the Reichenbach tradition, as in many traditional descriptions of English grammar, three time coordinates, ordered relative to each other, are used to specify the temporal location of the event or situation associated with the thematic verb. In this tradition, the tense of a sentence is generally considered as the temporal relation between the event time (ET) of the thematic verb and the moment of speech time (ST). Roughly speaking, tenses can be represented as in (2) which shows three types of relative temporal location of ET and ST in a clause.

(2) a. ET — ST
    b. ST, ET
    c. ST — ET

In (2a), the ET is prior to the ST, and in (2b) the ET and ST share the same interval, representing the past and present tense, respectively. (2c) refers to the situation where the ET is posterior to the ST, representing the future tense.

Time coordinates also include the reference time (RT) which mediates the ST and ET. The RT is the time to which the situation refers, whose role becomes important when tense becomes temporally complex. In a sentence *I had cooked dinner yesterday*, all three time coordinates are involved. The event [I cook] had taken place before the RT [yesterday], which itself precedes the ST. In the order of temporal location, the RT mediates the ET and ST (ET—RT—ST), representing the past perfect construction. Thus, in Reichenbach's view the semantics of tense involves three time coordinates arranged in various ways.

3. The interpretation of tense in a complement clause in languages

In this section, I describe and compare the temporal interpretation in a complement clause in English, Japanese, and Chinese, and specify how these languages differ. It is shown that a language has its own way to encode temporal relations in the grammar in terms of syntax and morphology. Although on the surface English and Japanese seem to express a reference to the past time in a similar way, some differences are present, suggesting underlying differences in the syntax of tense, and this is exactly what makes a study of tense interesting for many researchers.

3.1 One form with multiple meanings

The past tense forms in Japanese and English are not the same kind of inflection: *-ed* in English is an affix, whereas *-ta* in Japanese is an auxiliary which cliticises onto a verbal/adjectival/negative host (Okuwaki 2005). This might be reflected in the difference between relative tense (Japanese) and absolute-relative tense (English) in Comrie's terms (1985).

The Japanese nonpast form *V-(r)u* expresses multiple temporal meanings; it refers to present situations, future events, and past posterior events, as shown in (3).

(3) a. John-ga   ki-no   sita-ni   i-ru.
       John-NOM   tree-GEN   under-LOC   be-NPST
       "John is under the tree."
    b. John-wa   raigetu   kekkonnsu-ru.
       John-TOP   next month   get-married-NPST.
       "John will get married next month."
    c. John-wa   Mary-ga   ku-ru   to   it-ta.
       John-TOP   Mary-NOM   come-NPST   COMP   say-PST.
       "John said Mary would come."

In (3a), the nonpast form *-(r)u* refers to the present stative situation. This nonpast form also refers to the future event in (3b). In (3c) the same form in the complement clause refers to the event posterior to the one in the matrix clause. In English, however, distinct forms must be used in each case, as shown in the counterpart sentences. The difference between Japanese and English then seems to involve the temporal reference of the form itself and the temporal relation between a complement and matrix clause. Next, compare (4a) with (4b).

(4) a. Taro-wa   Mary-ga   hasi-te-i-ru   to
       Taro-TOP   Mary-NOM   run-ASP-**NPST**   COMP
       sit-te-i-ta
       know-ASP-PST
       "Taro knew that Mary was running."
   b. Taro-wa   Mary-ga   hasi-ta   to   sit-te-i-ta
       Taro-TOP   Mary-NOM   run-**PST**   COMP   know-ASP-PST
       "Taro knew that Mary had run."

In (4a), -*te i-* and -*(r)u* in the embedded clause denote an event simultaneous with the event of the matrix clauses, whereas in (4b) -*ta* in the embedded clause denotes the event anterior to that of the matrix clause (Soga 1983; Machida 1989). This suggests that the relative time of an embedded event to a matrix event-time is a determinant of the tense of an embedded clause in Japanese. Roughly speaking, the value of T of a complement clause is determined via T of a matrix clause; what matters is whether the complement event-time precedes, follows or is simultaneous with the matrix event-time.

In contrast, the English counterparts of (4) suggest that the embedded event-time is valued to the speech time (ST). In particular, (4a) in English represents the so-called SOT phenomenon, which refers to the specific temporal interpretation in which the past form of the embedded clause is treated as simultaneous with the matrix event.

3.2 The sequence-of-tense phenomenon

In English, Dutch, Spanish, and a number of other languages, sentences with a past tense embedded under another past tense are ambiguous. The past tense morphology of an embedded clause can have two different interpretations, as illustrated in (5) below.

(5) John said that Mary was pregnant.
   a. John said at time X that Mary had been pregnant at some time before X, Y.
   b. John said at time X that Mary was pregnant at the moment, X.

The first interpretation, paraphrased in (5a), is referred to as the backward-shifted reading. The situation described in the embedded clause

(Mary's being pregnant) is in the past with respect to the situation in the main clause (John's saying). The second interpretation, paraphrased in (5b), is often referred to as the simultaneous reading. The situation descried in the embedded clause (Mary's being pregnant) and the situation described in the matrix clause (John's saying) hold at the same moment. Under the simultaneous reading, the embedded past tense behaves as if it were absent; the embedded past tense does not contribute anything in terms of 'pastness' to the interpretation. The ambiguity seen in sentences like (5) is considered as an effect referred to as the SOT phenomenon (Enç 1987; Hornstein 1990; Ogihara 1989; Stowell 1995; Zagona 1995).

The SOT phenomenon is not seen in Japanese. The Japanese counterpart of (5) only denotes the backward-shifted reading, as illustrated in (6), where John says at a past time that Mary is pregnant which is prior to the time of John's saying (Ogihara 1989). 'Past' in the embedded clause precedes the event-time in the matrix clause. To obtain a simultaneous reading, tense in the embedded clause must be nonpast as in (7). The situation described in the embedded clause (Mary's being pregnant) includes the matrix event-time of John's saying about it. It seems *-(r)u* in the embedded clause denotes an event simultaneous with the event of the matrix clause.

(6) John-wa   Mary-ga   ninnsinsi-te-i-ta   to
    John-TOP   Mary-NOM   be-pregnant-ASP-**PST**   COMP
    it-ta
    say-PST
    "John said that Mary had been pregnant."
(7) John-wa   Mary-ga   ninnsinsi-te-i-ru   to
    John-TOP   Mary-NOM   be-pregnant-ASP-**NPST**   COMP
    it-ta
    say-PST
    "John said that Mary was pregnant."

Similarly, Mandarin Chinese does not show the SOT phonenon (Lin 2006). However, it does not mean that the temporal interpretation of tense in Chinese is the same with Japanese. Consider (8).

(8) Zhangsan   shu   Lisi   hen   jinzhang.
    Zhangsan   say   Lisi   very   nervous
    "Zhangsan said that Lisi was nervous."

According to Lin (2006), the Chinese sentence in (8) assumes the simultaneous reading as the default reading. The time of the embedded clause is identified as the time of the speaking event in the matrix clause, yielding the simultaneous reading.

To sum up, the temporal interpretations available in English, Japanese, and Chinese are shown in Table 1. To avoid complexity, the present study only deals with the case when tenses in both matrix and embedded clauses are past.

Table 1. Temporal interpretations of past in a complement clause

	English	Japanese	Chinese
backward-shifted reading	✓	✓	✗
simultaneous reading	✓	✗	✓

4. The present study

4.1 Hypotheses for the study

Languages vary widely in the way of expressing temporal relations in a sentence. The variation among languages seen in the interpretation of tense in an embedded clause makes the matter more complex. The task for L2 speakers is to understand how the temporal system in L2 works and establish the associations between the morphology and syntactic properties in L2 which might be different from L1. The question is how L2 speakers establish the complicated form-meaning relations of tense based on positive evidence they obtain during the course of L2 development, which comprises the first hypothesis.

The second hypothesis concerns the effect of L1. Although English and Japanese seem to possess similar ways of expressing temporality, it was implied that they are different in underlying syntax. If one assumes any theory of 'transfer of L1 properties' into L2 initial-state grammars (e.g., Schwartz & Sprouse 1996; Housen 2000) and that Japanese-L1 speakers learning English start L2 acquisition with the specification for tense, it is predicted they would have a specific problem in acquiring tense in an embedded clause. To see the effect of L1 further, the behaviours of Japanese and Chinese speakers are compared and examined, as the influence of L1 should be observed in a different way if there is some.

The following hypotheses are raised for the present study:

1) If positive evidence works on the acquisition of temporal interpretation in L2, both L2 groups (Japanese and Chinese) would know the correct interpretation of *past* in an embedded clause like English native speakers do.
2) If there is any influence of L1 in the acquisition of tense, Japanese and Chinese learners would behave differently as their L1s express temporal relations in a very different way.

4.2 Participants

There were three groups of participants: 32 Japanese-L1 speakers learning English, 32 Chinese-L1 speakers learning English, and 7 English native speakers. L2 speakers were Japanese and Taiwanese undergraduates tested at a university in Japan and Taiwan. They were divided into two proficiency levels on the basis of their scores on the Quick Placement test (QPT) (2001). QPT is an exam that consists of listening and grammar parts. Japanese learners in the Upper group (n = 16) scored between 30–35 on the test and learners in the Lower group (n = 16) scored between 18–28. Chinese learners in the Upper group (n = 16) scored between 30–36 on the test and learners in the Lower group (n = 16) scored between 23–26.

Table 2. Participants' QPT scores

	Group	N	QPT mean	QPT range
Japanese	Upper	16	32.38	30–35
	Lower	16	26.95	18–28
Chinese	Upper	16	32.00	30–36
	Lower	16	24.50	23–26

4.3 Interpretation Acceptability Test

Interpretation Acceptability Test was designed to see whether the L2 groups could assign the same interpretation, hence the semantic features, to temporal morphology as the native group. Each item consisted of an opening context followed by two sentences involving past/nonpast forms in an embedded clause. The participants judged the appropriateness of pairs of sentences in contexts which privileged one interpretation over others. For example, in (9), the simultaneous situation described in the context favours the past tense form in (a) rather than the nonpast form in (b).

(9) Linda likes taking a walk along the river in the evening. Yesterday when her husband came back early from work, she was not at home.

    a. He thought she was taking a walk along the river.   -2 -1 0 +1 +2
    b. He thought she is taking a walk along the river.   -2 -1 0 +1 +2

It should be noted that all the sentences tested were grammatical, meaning that Interpretation Acceptability Test was not a test of intuition of grammaticality; rather, it was intended to reveal the interpretation the participants assign to verb forms by asking them to decide the appropriateness of the form to the context.

Test items consisted of 36 pairs of sentences containing 6 target pairs and other 32 pairs (distractors). The target pairs were randomised, and next to each sentence there was a 5-point scale: -2, -1, 0, +1, +2, where +2 represented the maximum score accepting the sentence, and -2 represented the maximum score rejecting the sentence. In the instruction part of the test, the participants were told that +2 means that the sentence was 'fully OK' to the context, -2 means that it was 'very odd'. They could also choose -1, 0, and +1 as gradations between the two extremes if they thought the sentence was more or less appropriate to the context. Three practice items were conducted before the actual test to make sure that they understood the procedure of the test.

5. Results of Interpretation Acceptability Test

5.1 Japanese participants

The scores of Interpretation Acceptability Test were analysed with a two-way repeated-measures ANOVA with Group (NS, Upper, and Lower) as a between-participants factor and Form (*past* vs. *nonpast*) as a within-participants factor. The main effect of Form was significant, $F(1,36)=50.934$, $p<.001$, and the main effect of Group was not significant, $F(2,36)=2.198$, $p=.126$, but the Form x Group interaction was significant, $F(2,36) = 16.890$, $p<.001$. Given the significant interaction between Form and Group, their simple effects are analysed.

The results showed that the simple effect of Form was significant for NS group, $F(1, 36)=51.815$, $p<.001$, and for Upper group, $F(1,36)=12.564$, $p<.01$, but not for Lower group, $F(1,36)=0.121$, $p=.730$, suggesting that Upper group noticed the difference between past-nonpast forms and distinguished them in a similar way to NS group. However, Lower group did not distinguish the two forms and treated them as if they were the same. Next, let us look at the simple effect of Group which was analysed in each form. The results showed the it was significant in the case of *past*, $F(2, 36)=9.353$, $p<.01$, and also in the case of *nonpast*, $F(2, 36)=17.43$, $p<.001$. Bonferroni post-hoc tests were conducted to reveal between which groups the difference lied. In the case of *past*, the results showed that the performance of Upper group was not significantly different from NS group ($p=.060$), but Lower group behaved differently from NS group ($p<.001$). In the case of *nonpast*, the post-hoc test revealed that both L2 groups behaved differently from NS at the same level ($p<.01$).

Table 3. Mean scores and Standard Deviation (SD) of Japanese participants

Group	Form			
	past		*nonpast*	
	Mean	SD	Mean	SD
NS	1.714	0.488	-1.548	0.448
Upper	0.937	0.827	***-0.125	0.820
Lower	***0.354	0.641	***0.250	0.580

Significant difference from NS group: ***$p < .001$

5.2 Chinese participants

The same analysis was employed for Chinese participants. The analysis showed that the main effect of Form was significant, $F(1,36)=49.690$, $p<.001$, and the main effect of Group was not significant, $F(2,36)=1.220$, $p=.307$, but the Form x Group interaction was significant, $F(2,36) = 9.012$, $p < .01$. Therefore, the simple effect of Form and Group is analysed.

The results showed that the simple effect of Form was significant for NS, $F(1, 36)=38.189$, $p<.001$, and for Lower group,: $F(1,36)=12.817$, $p<.01$, but not significant for Upper group, $F(1, 36)=2.789$, $p=.104$, suggesting that only Lower group knew the difference between *past* and *nonpast* and distinguished the two in a similar way to NS group. However, Upper group did not distinguish the two forms. The simple effect of Group was analysed in terms of each form. It was found that the simple effect of Group was significant both in *past* and *nonpast* (*past*: $F(2,36)=7.283$, $p<.01$, *nonpast*: $F(2,36)=7.683$, $p<.01$). To found out where the difference lied, Bonferroni post-hoc tests were conducted. In the case of *past*, the performance of Lower group was not significantly different

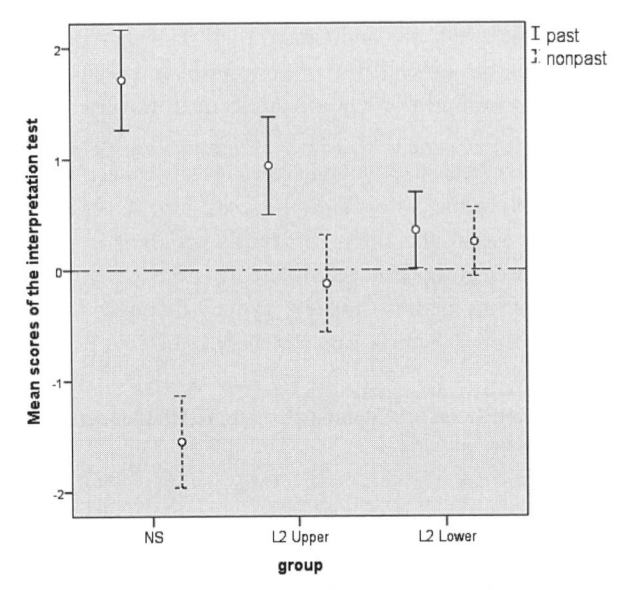

Figure 1. Mean scores of Japanese participants

from NS group (*p*=.053), but Upper group behaved differently from NS group (*p*<.01). In the case of *nonpast*, the post-hoc test revealed that both L2 groups behaved differently from NS group at the same level (*p*<.01).

Table 4. Mean scores and SD of Chinese participants

Group	Form			
	past		non-past	
	Mean	*SD*	*Mean*	*SD*
NS	1.714	0.488	-1.548	0.448
Upper	**0.542	0.734	**-0.042	1.067
Lower	0.948	0.688	**-0.302	0.751

Significant difference from NS group: **p< .01

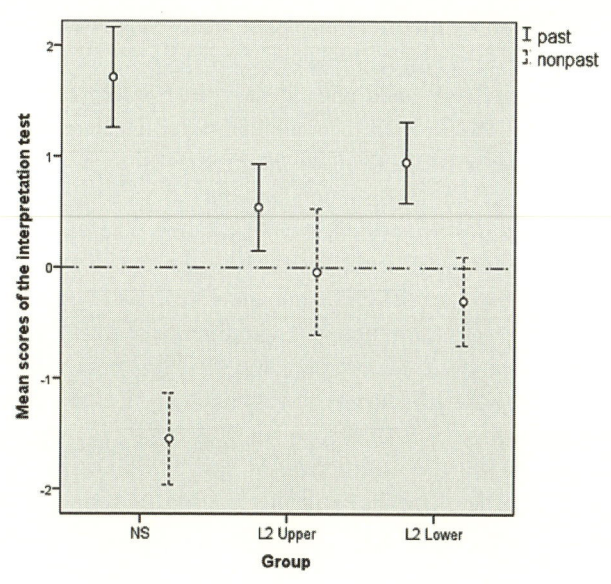

Figure 2. Mean scores of Chinese participants

6. Discussion of results

The present study examined how Japanese-L1 and Chinese-L1 speakers learning English interpret a morphological form encoding a temporal relation in an embedded clause and compared their performance from that of native speakers. Remember the two hypotheses raised for the present study (written again):

1) If positive evidence works on the acquisition of temporal interpretation in L2, both L2 groups (Japanese and Chinese) would know the correct interpretation of *past* in an embedded clause like English native speakers do.
2) If there is any influence of L1 in the acquisition of tense, Japanese and Chinese learners would behave differently as their L1s express temporal relations in a very different way.

The first hypothesis was partially supported; Upper group of Japanese and Lower group of Chinese knew the correct interpretation of *past* in an embedded clause like native speakers. Based on the positive evidence they obtain in the course of L2 development, those L2 leaners have acquired the relevant temporal interpretation associated with the morphological form in an embedded clause. However, Lower group of Japanese and Upper group of Chinese could not tell the correct interpretation. Upper group of Japanese was shown to have a much better understanding of correct temporal interpretation than Lower group. It should be natural for upper-level learners to have a better understanding about L2, but the point here is that positive evidence alone did not seem enough for the lower-level learners to acquire the correct interpretation of a morphological form. In order to acquire the same amount of L2 knowledge, more positive evidence will be required, or more time to restructure L2 grammar will be needed. In either way, the lower-level learners are expected to be able to develop the L2 knowledge in the long run, as the upper-level learners have done.

What was puzzling, however, was the case of Chinese-L1 speakers; the L2 proficiency level was not a predictor of the performance given by L2 learners; Lower group surprisingly showed a better performance over Upper group. How could this be interpreted? Assuming any parameter theory of a language in L2 acquisition, it has been argued that acquiring some parameter settings in L2 grammars would lead to the acquisition of their values and their associated syntactic properties[1] (Smith & Tsimpli, 1995). Considered in terms of tense in syntax, by extension, knowing the syntactic features of tense should lead to the acquisition of associated temporal properties, including its correct interpretation. If this is on the right track, it can be argued that the L2 proficiency level did not explain the knowledge of tense for Chinese learners, simply because their L2 grammar does not possess the basis to accommodate syntactic tense as there is no tense morphology in L1, and as a result the solid L2 knowledge of tense cannot be developed in the L2.

The second hypothesis was supported; Japanese and Chinese speakers behaved differently in Interpretation Acceptability Test, and the effect of L1 could be traced in their performance to a great extent. L1 effect explains the Chinese learners' performance in Interpretation Acceptability Test, where the result was in inverse proportion to the L2 proficiency level. Due to the absence of syntactic tense in the L1, the incremental acquisition of the tense property in L2, which should normally be expected, could have been interfered. As the Failed Functional Features Hypothesis of Hawkins & Chan (1997) suggests, syntactic features which are not represented in the L1 cannot be acquired in the L2.

Let's move on to the result that L2 groups invariantly failed to interpret *nonpast* in an embedded clause. This can be attributed to the effect of L1 solely, especially in the case of Japanese learners. The data showed that Japanese learners had a persistent difficulty rejecting *nonpast* in the context where the simultaneous construal was a correct reading. This problem can easily be explained if the Japanese counterpart sentence was taken into consideration. As discussed in the earlier section, Japanese *nonpast* is always used in a complement clause to encode a simultaneous reading. Japanese learners did not reject *nonpast* in the simultaneous reading context simply because it was the right form in the L1. Let me refer to another study which investigated the temporal interpretation in an embedded clause for more advanced Japanese-L1 speakers learning English. Okuwaki (2012) showed that advanced Japanese learners were able to interpret *past* in a complement clause just like native controls, but they still had problem rejecting *nonpast* in the same context. They cannot interpret *nonpast* correctly even in a later stage of L2 development. It would generally be less difficult for L2 speakers to judge the correctness of a correct item than declaring the incorrectness of an incorrect item, but if the L2 knowledge is solid enough, declaring the implausibility would not be impossible at all. Rather, in this case it is more likely that the interpretation encoded by the L1 form influences the interpretation in L2.

Now let us go back to the question why Lower group of Japanese (and Upper group of Chinese) failed to distinguish *past* vs. *nonpast* in a complement clause, given the obvious difference present on the form. One of the possibilities is the failure in processing; tense in a matrix clause is salient on the surface for L2 learners and is an element necessary to calculate the meaning of a whole sentence, whereas tense in an embedded clause, less salient in a sentence, might pass through without being processed for the sentence to be interpreted. It can thus be argued that Lower group might not be able to afford to process tense morphology in an embedded clause and just pass through without processing the element. Shibuya & Wakabayashi (2008) investigated Japanese learners' sensitivity to the overuse and omission of 3rd person –*s*. They found that Japanese learners were sensitive to the overuse of 3rd person –*s* when a plural subject was syntactically expressed by conjunction or by free morphemes, whereas they were not sensitive to overuse when the plural subject was marked only by a plural –*s*, a bound morpheme. This implies, the way in which a plural feature on subjects is marked influences learners' sensitivity to the overuse of 3rd person –*s*; some plural subjects (*these two* secretaries) are more salient for Japanese learners than others (*the chefs*), which are necessarily processed for the sentences to be correctly interpreted. If this is on the right track, it is plausible to argue by extension that L2 learners in the present study were not sensitive to a tense in an embedded clause and did not process it for the sentence to be correctly interpreted, simply because a threshold level of L2 proficiency has not been achieved. As a result, less proficient learners were not able to detect the difference between *past* vs. *nonpast* in an embedded clause.

7. Conclusion

Based on the differences in the representation of tense between English, Japanese, and Chinese, the present study investigated how L2 speakers interpret temporal expressions of L2 which are different from L1. It turned out that L2 speakers were able to acquire the properties based on positive evidence to some degree, but at the same time L1 plays a significant role in the acquisition of the temporal system in L2.

The Bottleneck Hypothesis proposed in Slabakova (2006, 2008) assumes that the acquisition of syntax and semantics flows smoothly once inflectional morphologies are successfully acquired. If the morphology encoding temporal relations are acquired in L2 as the L2 proficiency increases, the interpretive properties should also be acquired as the L2 developmental stage proceeds. Although the data in the study only provide partial evidence, if this is on the right track, it would fully be possible for L2 speakers to acquire semantic properties of L2 eventually. Future research would benefit from collecting data from more advanced learners with various L1 backgrounds to see if L2 speakers get over the effect of L1 and could ultimately attain form-meaning relations in L2.

Acknowledgements

I appreciate the help received from Yang, Hsiu-Ju, at Tung Hai University in Taiwan, who collected data from Chinese-L1 speakers learning English. This research was partially supported by the Ministry of Education, Science, Sports and Culture, Grant-in-Aid for Young Scientists (B), 19720139, 2007–2011.

Note

1. For example, if L2 speakers know the value of the null-subject parameter in a language, they should also show knowledge of the grammaticality of *that*-trace structures, as this correlates with the availability of null subjects. They should allow

postverbal subjects and subject extraction from the postverbal position, as it is considered to be an associated property of the null-subject parameter (Smith & Tsimpli, 1995).

References

Bardovi-Harlig, K. (1995) A narrative perspective on the development of the tense/aspect system in second language acquisition. *Studies in Second Language Acquisition*, 17: 263–291.

Comrie, A. (1985) *Tense*. Cambridge/New York: Cambridge University Press.

Enç, M. (1987) Anchoring conditions for tense. *Linguistic Inquiry*, 18: 633–657.

Gabriele, A., & Martohardjono, G. (2005) Investigating the role of transfer in the L2 acquisition of aspect. In L. Dekydtspotter, R. A. Sprouse, & A. Liljestrand (eds.), *Proceedings of the 7th Generative Approaches to Second Language Acquisition Conference* (pp. 96–110). Somerville, Mass: Cascadilla Press.

Giorgi, A. (2008) Crosslinguistic variation and the syntax of tense. *Working Papers in Linguistics*, 18: 145–147. University of Venice.

Hawkins, R., & Chan, C. (1997) The partial availability of Universal Grammar in second language acquisition: the 'failed functional features hypothesis'. *Second Language Research*, 13: 187–226.

Hornstein, N. (1990) *As Time Goes By: Tense and Universal Grammar*. Cambridge, Mass: MIT Press.

Housen, A. (2000) Verb semantics and the acquisition of tense-aspect in L2 English. *Studia Linguistica*, 54: 249–259.

Huang, C.-T. James. (1998) *Logical Relations in Chinese and the Theory of Grammar*. New York: Garland.

Li Yen Hui, A. (1990) *Order and Constituency in Mandarin Chinese*. Dordrecht: Kluwer.

Lin, Jo-wang. (2003) Selectional restrictions of tenses and temporal references of Chinese bare sentences. *Lingua*, 113: 271–302.

Lin, Jo-wang. (2006) Time in a language without tense: The case of Chinese. *Journal of Semantics*, 23(1): 1–53.

Machida, K. (1989) *Nihongo no Jisei to Asupekuto [Tense and Aspect in Japanese]*. Tokyo: Aruku.

Montrul, S., & Slabakova, R. (2002) On aspectual shifts in L2 Spanish. In B. Skarabela, S. Fish, & A. H.-J. Do (eds.), *Proceedings of the 26th Annual Boston University Conference on Language Development* (pp. 631–642). Somerville, Mass: Cascadilla Press.

Ogihara, T. (1989) *Temporal Reference in English and Japanese*. Unpublished doctoral dissertation. University of Texas, Austin.

Okuwaki, N. (2005) *Acquisition of Tense and Aspect in L2 English*. Unpublished doctoral dissertation. University of Essex.

Okuwaki, N. (2012) The temporal interpretations of complement and relative clauses by Japanese speakers learning English. Paper presented at the Chubu English Language Education Society, 42, 4–5 August 2012, Aichi Gakuin University, Aichi,

Japan.
Oxford University Press & University of Cambridge Local Examinations Syndicate. (2001) *Quick Placement Test*. Oxford University Press.
Pollock, J.-Y. (1989) Verb movement, Universal Grammar, and the structure of IP. *Linguistic Inquiry*, 20: 365–424.
Schwartz, B., & Sprouse, R. (1996) L2 cognitive states and the 'full transfer/full access model. *Second Language Research*, 12: 40–72.
Shibuya, M., & Wakabayashi, S. (2008) Why are L2 learners not sensitive to subject-verb agreement? In L. Roberts, F. Myles, & A. David (eds.), *EUROSLA Yearbook, Volume 8* (pp.235–258). Amsterdam: John Benjamins.
Slabakova, R. (2008) *Meaning in the Second Language*. Berlin: Mouton de Gruyter.
Slabakova, R. (2006) Learnability in the L2 acquisition of semantics: A bidirectional study of a semantic parameter. *Second Language Research*, 22: 1–26.
Smith, C. S. & Erbaugh, M. (2005) Temporal interpretation in Mandarin Chinese. *Linguistics*, 42: 713–756.
Smith, N., & Tsimpli, I. M. (1995) *The Mind of a Savant: Language Learning and Modularity*. Oxford: Blackwell.
Soga, M. (1983) *Tense and Aspect in Modern Colloquial Japanese*. Vancouver: University of British Columbia Press.
Stowell, T. (1995) What do the present and past tenses mean? In P. Bertinetto, V. Bianchi, J. Higginbotham, & M. Squartini (eds.), *Temporal Reference, Aspect, and Actionality, vol. 1: Semantics and Syntactic Perspective* (pp. 381–396). Torino: Rosenberg and Sellier.
Zagona, K. (1995) Temporal argument structure: Configurational elements of construal. In P. Bertinetto, V. Bianchi, J. Higginbotham, & M. Squartini (eds.), *Temporal Reference, Aspect, and Actionality, vol. 1: Semantics and Syntactic Perspective* (pp. 397–410). Torino: Rosenberg and Sellier.

Remarks on the English Writing System and its Logographic Nature

Shinji Saito

Abstract
In this paper, we are concerned with the logographic aspect of the English writing system. We show that written language differs from spoken language in English in significant ways, most of which are of logographic nature and argue that all writing systems, including alphabetic writing systems like English, are logographic to a varying degree.

Keywords   alphabet, Chinese characters, logograms, homophones, writing systems

1. Introduction

This paper is intended as an investigation of the English writing system, with a special reference to its logographic nature. In Western linguistics, it has been generally accepted that writing has nothing to do with language and that letters or graphemes are mere representations of the spoken language. For example, in their seminal books, Ferdinand de Saussure and Leonard Bloomfield declare as in (1) and (2), respectively.

(1) Language and writing are two distinct systems of signs; the second exists for the sole purpose of representing the first. The linguistic object is not both the written and the spoken forms of words; the spoken forms alone constitute the object.   (Saussure 1959: 23)
(2) Writing is not language, but merely a way of recording language by means of visible marks.... A language is the same no matter what system of writing may be used to record it, just as a person is the same no matter how you take his picture.   (Bloomfield 1933: 21)

If the only purpose of writing is to represent speech, their statements are sensible. But apparently this is not the case, as will be shown in the following sections. Written language and spoken language differ in significant ways and we must consider writing to be a linguistic subsystem to be studied in its own right. English orthography has many features having no correlate in the speech, most of which are of logographic nature.

The point I would like to make in this paper is that the English writing system, and for that matter, any alphabetic writing systems in the world, are logographic to a varying degree and that we can find logographic features in the English writing system similar to Chinese characters used in Japanese, which are considered to be an exemplary logographic writing system. Actually, logographic features of the English writing system have already been pointed out in various studies (see Bradley 1913, Venezky 1970, Carney 1994, Coulmas 2003, Cook 2004, among others), some of which will be reviewed in the next section.

2. Logographic nature of the English spelling

In the Western world, where a phonetically based alphabet is used to record language, writings have tended to be regarded as mere representations of the spoken language. On close examination, however, we find that written language and spoken language differ in significant ways, and all writing systems, even the English writing system, which has been intensively researched and written about in recent decades (see, for example, Venezky 1970, Carney 1994 and Cook 2003), are not redundant systems of the spoken counterparts. Writings carry more information than is contained in the sound. The following features of English orthography, for example, have no correlate in the spoken language.

(3) a. The use of word spaces (word separation)
　　b. The use of capital letters
　　c. The three-letter rule

In English and other modern European languages written in Roman or Cyrillic, words are divided by spaces, as pointed out in (3a). This introduces structural organization in alphabetic writing that has nothing to do with the spoken language. With regard to (3b), English orthography uses capitalization to distinguish between proper nouns and common nouns or adjectives that are spelled the same; 'Smith' /'smith', 'Frank' /'frank'. In addition, proper names are often distinguished from common nouns or adjectives by having a final<e> (e.g. 'Browne' / 'brown'), by doubling the final consonant (e.g. 'Kidd' /'kid'), and by having <y> rather than <i> (e.g. 'Smythe' /'smith') (Cook 2003: 58). The three-letter rule in (3c) states that content words must have more than two letters (Cook 2003: 57). Two-letter words are likely to be function words, whereas homophonous content words add a consonant or vowel letter. Hence, we have pairs such as 'be'/'bee', 'by'/'buy', 'in'/'inn'. This rule suggests that function words and lexical homophones are held orthographically distinct.

These features of the English orthography are phonetically useless and convey no information relating to sound. We can say that these features make the word more distinct and exemplify a logographic component in the English writing system[1]. As argued by, for example, Kōno (1994), there seems to be logographic aspects to all writing systems, regardless of whether they are logograms (or ideograms), like Chinese characters, or phonograms like alphabets in English[2]. This is probably because we read not to intone, but to understand the meaning and the ultimate end of written language is to convey meaning. Even in alphabetic writing, the representation of sounds is only a means to represent a word or a morpheme and, through this, convey meaning.

As noted above, however, it has been a widely accepted notion among Western linguists that writings are mere representations of sounds uttered of a language. If so, in alphabetic writing as in English, there should ideally be a one-to-one correspondence between sounds and their written representation. But actually, as is well known, there are numerous discrepancies between letters and sounds in the English orthography, which has been one of the driving forces behind the perennial movement to reform English spelling.

The <a> in 'nature', for example, corresponds to /eɪ/, while the <a> in 'natural' to / æ/. So, the one-to-one principle between sounds and their written representation is breached here, since <a> corresponds to two sounds. But, by preserving the same written vowel <a>, the link between the two related words is shown which are lost in the actual speech. Similarly, the semantic relatedness of the following word pairs would be obscured if the spelling were adapted to the pronunciation: 'critic '/' criticize' (<c> − /k/, /s/), 'elect' /'election' (<t> − /t/, /ʃ/), 'autumn'/'autumnal'(<n> −/φ/, /n/). Thus, in English spelling, word or morpheme constancy is often given priority over phoneme constancy (cf. Coulmas 2003: 184). And many other irregularities in English spelling should be explained in terms of its logographic nature.

At the same time, there are many homophones in English—that is, words with different spellings (and meanings), but the same pronunciation. So much so that Henry Bradley (1913: 29) laments that partly because of the abundance of homophones in the language, English is far more unsuited than other European tongues to be written phonetically. The following are common examples of homophones in English: 'for'/'four', 'horse'/'hoarse', 'knight'/'night', 'morning'/'mourning', 'son'/'sun', 'to sow'/'to sew', 'to rain'/'to reign'. This graphic differentiation of homophones also weakens the unequivocal sound-letter link, which obviously is helpful to word recognition and rapid apprehension of the import of the word.

In 1913 in the midst of the English spelling reform movement in Britain, Bradley, arguing convincingly against any radical spelling reform based on purely phonetic principles, points out that writing systems that were originally phonetic tend to become ideographic or logographic with regard to their function. He says that homophones were once pronounced differently and written phonetically, but have come to be alike in sound and that" because to the ordinary people it is more important that a written word should quickly and surely suggest its meaning than it should express its sound, the old spelling has been allowed to remain unaltered" (Bradley 1913: 11). Thus, we can say that numerous discrepancies between letters and sounds in the English orthography, including the case of homophones, can also be ascribed to, and should be explained by, the logographic nature of English alphabetics.

In the next section, we will show that a spoken word is accompanied by a flow of graphic imagery through the mind when it is not so clear in a given context which of the two homonyms is being used and that differences in spelling are helpful to the disambiguation of homophonous words not only on the level of written language but also on the level of spoken language, based on the study of Suzuki (1987) on homophonous words abundant in Japanese.

3. Writing and homophones

Modern Japanese is most commonly written utilizing the mixture of Chinese characters and kana (Japanese phonetic characters). Written using only kana characters, Japanese sentences would be extremely difficult to read. One of the reasons is that in the Japanese orthography, unlike in the English one, words are not divided by spaces, so in the texts written in only kana characters, it is hard to recognize words or other meaningful units. Chinese characters, on the other hand, being signs of a word or a morpheme (logograms), signify meanings independently of sounds. So including Chinese characters in Japanese texts facilitates reading. Kana, Japanese phonetic alphabet, lacks other logographic features as observed in the Roman alphabet in English orthography (i.e., the use of capital letters and the three-letter rule) discussed in the previous section, and hence without Chinese characters, Japanese texts are extremely hard to read because of word recognition difficulty.

Furthermore, there are a large number of homophonous words in Japanese because of the extreme simplicity of the phonetic system, but they are written using different Chinese characters. The only way to distinguish between homophonous words is through the Chinese characters. So although homophones may occasionally cause confusion in the spoken language, they are easily distinguished in the written language, in the same manner as many English homophones discussed in the preceding section.

Suzuki (1987) argues that writing and language are so tightly connected with each other in Japanese that we must regard some part of writing as an essential component of language. He also says that in Japanese "a lot of linguistic information is often carried jointly by the written and spoken forms in much the same way as in television, where we get information as a combination of visual and auditory impressions" (Suzuki 1987: 5). Let us consider how homophones are processed in the Japanese communication. As noted above, because of the extreme simplicity of the phonetic system, it is inevitable that there are plenty of homonyms in Japanese, which are made up of Chinese characters. For example, *kagaku* can mean both 'science' (科学) and 'chemistry' (化学). Another example is *shiritsu*, which can mean both 'private' (私立) and 'municipal' (市立). Thus in Japanese, 'science' and 'chemistry'or'private' and 'municipal', as well as many other similar homonyms, cannot be distinguished by sound alone and it is often difficult for us to understand what is said unless we know how the word is written with Chinese characters. So Suzuki (1987) contends that in their speech, the Japanese are heavily dependent on the graphic image of the word that is stored in their minds and that in Japanese one's ability to talk well and understand well depends so much on one's knowledge of writing (Suzuki 1987: 16).

On the other hand, according to Suzuki (1987), in English, as well as other European languages where a phonetically based script is used, language is essentially sound, and writing does not add any new information to the language. This claim, however, is untenable, as discussed in section 2. Some logographic features which have no correlate in the speech can also be found in the English writing system. Rather, we should say that all writing systems have logographic aspects in varying degrees, regardless of the type of writing systems.

Then, we can expect that the fact holds true in English as well that in their speech the Japanese are heavily dependent on the graphic image of the word that is stored in their minds. Bradley, whom we mentioned earlier, gives some examples of English homophones, saying that it quite often also in English that words are used in writing without any fear of misunderstanding, but if the passage were read aloud the hearer would be puzzled. "A newspaper says that somebody has invented a new sowing-machine; the reader understands at once, but the hearer does not, that it is an agricultural implement. I once heard quoted the statement that Trafalgar Square is the finest sight (or site) in London. Whether the word meant 'spectacle' or 'situation' I cannot guess." (Bradley 1913: 11–2) Then, when British or American people hear "Trafalgar Square is the finest sight (or site) in London", for example, and it is not clear to them whether 'sight' or 'site' is intended, is the utterance of the word not accompanied by spelling or the graphic image of the word that is stored in their minds? Probably it is. Bradley states like this: "With educated people, the utterance of a word is usually accompanied by some obscure reminiscence of its spelling; their notion of the word is a blend of its audible and its visible form. Hence, when two words of the same sound happen to be distinguished in spelling, we are often imperfectly conscious of their identity to the ear."(Bradley 1913: 23–4) In short, also in English, writing must be considered to be intertwined with language and constitute an essential component of it, though it may not be as much as in Japanese.

4. Conclusion

In conclusion, we have observed that English alphabetic writing system has a number of logographic features having no correlate in the speech, which shows that even in alphabetic writing like English, the representation of sounds is only a means to represent a word or a morpheme and that the ultimate end of writing is to convey meaning by representing a word or a morpheme. Furthermore, we have argued that a spoken word is accompanied by a flow of graphic imagery through the mind when it is not so clear in a given context which of the two homonyms is being used not only in Japanese but also in English. Writing, thus, does not exist only to represent sound, as claimed in (1) and (2), and must be considered to be intertwined with language and constitute a substantial component of it in both languages to a lesser or greater degree.

Notes

1. The use of capital letters, for example, is reminiscent of the use of "determinatives" common in such logographic writing systems as Sumerian and Egyptian writing systems (see Gnanadesikan 2009: 18).
2. For the argument that all writing systems are logographic, see Chapter 1 of Kōno (1994)

References

Bloomfield, L. (1933) *Language*. London: George Allen and Unwin.
Bradley, H. (1913) *On the Relations between Spoken and Written Language with Special Reference to English*. Oxford: Clarendon Press.
Carney, E. (1994) *A Survey of English Spelling*. London: Routledge.
Cook, V. J. (2003) *The English Writing System*. London: Routledge.
Coulmas, F. (2003) *Writing Systems: An Introduction to Their Linguistic Analysis*. Cambridge: Cambridge University Press.
Gnanadesikan, A. E. (2009) *The Writing Revolution : Cuneiform to the Internet*. Oxford: Wiley-Blackwell.
Kōno, R. (1994) *Mojiron* (Writings on Writing). Tokyo: Sanseidō.
Saussure, F. de. (1959) *Course in General Linguistics*. Translated by Wade Baskin. New York: The Philosophical Library.
Suzuki, T. (1987) *Reflections on Japanese Language and Culture*. Tokyo: Keio University Institute of Cultural and Linguistic Studies.
Venezky, R. L. (1970) *The Structure of English Orthography*. The Hague: Mouton.

The Role of Reading Experience in Construing Japanese Gapless Relative Clauses

Koichi Sawasaki

Abstract
This study is a quantitative analysis of the relationship between individual differences in reading experience and the construal of Japanese "gapless" relative clauses with resultative head nouns. Gapless relative clauses are a cross-linguistically uncommon structure that differs from that of typical "gapped" relative clauses. Imperfective verbal aspect can render such gapless structures implausible, and some have suggested that pragmatic knowledge may play an important role in their construal. In this study, reading experience is taken as one indicator of pragmatic knowledge. Participants responded to a questionnaire on reading experience, and also rated the naturalness of gapped and gapless relative clauses. We predicted that readers with rich reading experience would find it easier to construe gapless relative clauses and would accept implausible sentences more readily than lower-level readers would. However, the results revealed that experienced readers were more sensitive to the degree of plausibility in different gapless relative clauses. In contrast, less experienced readers were not consistent in distinguishing degrees of plausibility in different gapless relative clauses. The findings suggest that individuals' reading experience is indeed related to their construal of gapless relative clauses.

Keywords   gapless relative clauses, pragmatic relative clauses, sentence comprehension, reading experience, pragmatic knowledge

1. Introduction

Japanese relative clauses display both gapped structures, in which "gaps" are coindexed with head nouns, and gapless ones, in which no such gap appears.

(1) a. (*gap$_i$*) Toire-ni   ikenai   kodomo$_i$ (gapped relative clause)
        restroom-to cannot go child
        'the child that cannot go to the restroom'
    b. Kodomo-ga   toire-ni   ikenai
        child-NOM[1] restroom-to cannot go
        terebi (gapless relative clause)
        TV
        Lit: *the TV that the child cannot go to the restroom
        'the TV that makes the child unable go to the restroom'

Example (1a) is called a gapped relative clause, in which a gap is coindexed with the head noun *kodomo* 'child.' In (1b), however, the gap coindexed with the head noun *terebi* 'TV' is absent. Literal translations of gapless structures make no sense when rendered into English and other European languages, which permit only gapped relative clauses.

In the absence of structural co-indexing, the construal of gapless relative clauses is largely dependent on one's pragmatic knowledge: speakers must rely on long-term memory, world-view, word association, and so on (e.g., Kato 2003; Matsumoto 1988; 1990; Teramura 1992). For example, interpretation of (1b) requires pragmatic knowledge involving both cultural and situational information: a familiar cultural trope in Japan is that restrooms at midnight are spooky places; and perhaps the child in question has watched a scary ghost story on TV. Native speakers of Japanese can thus draw on broad as well as specific pragmatic awareness in order to comprehend gapless relative clause like (1b).

A second example appears below, in which the two phrases are identical except for the head noun.

(2) a. (*gap$_i$*) Kookoo nyuushi-ni   zettai   ukaru hito$_i$
        high school entrance exam-DAT absolutely pass person
        Lit: the person who surely passes the high school entrance exam
        'the person who can surely pass the high school entrance exam'
    b. (*pro*)[2] Kookoo nyuushi-ni   zettai   ukaru
        high school entrance exam-DAT absolutely pass
        katei kyooshi
        tutor
        Lit: *the tutor who (someone) surely passes the high school entrance exam
        'the tutor with whose assistance one can surely pass the high

school entrance exam' (Matsumoto 1990:122)

In spite of the surface similarity between the two sentences, (2a) is best understood as a gapped relative clause and (2b) as a gapless relative clause. That is, the head noun *hito* 'person' in (2a) is the person who will pass the exam, but the head noun *katei kyooshi* 'tutor' in (2b) is the person who helps someone else pass the examination. This difference stems from shared real-world knowledge about the role of the tutor in Japanese high school entrance examinations.

While general pragmatic knowledge is assumed to play an important role in comprehension of gapless relative clauses, studies have not yet investigated how individual variation in pragmatic knowledge can affect speakers' construal of such structures. This study sets out to address that gap. In particular we ask whether speakers' individual reading experience—a quantifiable aspect of their pragmatic knowledge—influences their interpretations of gapless relative clauses whose head noun denotes a result.

This chapter is organized as follows. Section 2 presents some general background on Japanese gapless relative clauses with a resultative head noun in particular. Section 3 describes the design of the experiment, and sections 4 and 5 present results and discussion, respectively. Finally, section 6 provides concluding remarks.

2. Background

2.1 Gapless relative clauses with resultative head nouns

Of the many types of gapless relative clauses in Japanese, the one we are concerned with here involves a head noun that denotes a result of some kind (Kato 2003). Examples in (3) are of this type

(3) a. Raamen-o   tabeta   otsuri
       noodles-ACC eat-PER   change
       Lit: *the change that (I) ate noodles
       'the change that I received as a result of having eaten noodles'
    b. # Raamen-o taberu   otsuri
       noodles-ACC eat-IMP   change
       Lit: *the change that (I) eat noodles
       'the change that I will use to eat noodles'

In the gapless structure (3a), *otsuri* 'change' is the consequence of the eating activity. Unlike the word *change* in English, *otsuri* in Japanese cannot refer to small coins—it always refers to the amount of money returned to a costumer after a purchase. In order for *otsuri* to be construed as a result of the eating event, then, the relative verb must be expressed with a perfective form, i.e., *tabeta* 'ate' (Kato 2003). Example (3b) illustrates the constraints on these structures: when the imperfective *taberu* 'eat' appears, *otsuri* can no longer be construed as money returned to a costumer after purchasing noodles. Instead, it may refer to money received *before* eating; perhaps the speaker has change from some prior shopping activity and intends to use it to purchase noodles. Such an interpretation is possible, but the sentence is less plausible than (3a) and its construal requires active imagination. This contrast between perfective and imperfective verbal forms emerges when the head noun denotes the result of the event described in the relative clause.

Throughout the remainder of this discussion, we shall use the term "gapless relative clauses" to refer specifically to those with resultative head nouns. We shall use the term "non-gapped relative clauses" to refer to those not specifically containing resultative head nouns.

2.2 The processing of Japanese relative clauses

Many studies have examined how Japanese relative clauses are processed, but most of them focus only on gapped relative clauses (Kahraman 2011; Miyamoto and Nakamura 2003; Sato 2011; Ueno and Garnsey 2007, for the processing asymmetry of subject relatives and object relatives; Hirose 2002; Hirose and Inoue 1998; Mazuka and Itoh 1995, for the processing asymmetry of subject reanalysis and subject-object reanalysis constructions; Miyamoto, Gibson, Pearlmutter, Aikawa and Miyagawa 1999, for the processing preference of the relative clause with the "NP-of-NP" head).

Those studies that have compared gapped and non-gapped relative clauses show that non-gapped relative clauses are more difficult to understand than gapped relative clauses (Currah 2002; Yamashita, Stowe and Nakayama 1993; but Venditti and Yamashita 1994). For example, in a self-paced reading experiment that measured online reading times, Yamashita, Stowe and Nakayama (1993) found that non-gapped relative clauses were read more slowly than gapped relative clauses (object relatives). Currah (2002) employed a naturalness rating task, a self-paced reading task, and a probe recognition task, and her findings from all three showed that non-gapped relative clauses were felt to be more unnatural and were processed more slowly than gapped relative clauses.

To date, however, studies concerning non-gapped relative clauses have failed to take individual differences into consideration. As we mentioned above, understanding of non-gapped relative clauses is dependent on one's pragmatic knowledge, which includes long-term memory, world-view, word association, and so on (e.g., Kato 2003; Matsumoto 1988; 1990; Teramura 1992). Such knowledge is of course shared among speakers to a large extent, but there are also many individual differences; indeed, as Matsumoto (1990: 118) notes, "some speakers in some contexts may draw on a world-view quite different from what would be described as usual."

2.3 Reading experience and individual pragmatic knowledge

Previous studies have shown that individual differences stemming from reading experience influence one's knowledge about the world (Stanovitch and Cunningham 1992; 1993; West and Stanovitch 1991). Stanovitch and Cunningham (1993) found that American university students with greater exposure to paper media such as books, newspapers, and magazines tend to have a broader knowledge of history, culture, sciences, health, cooking, etc. However, the same was not observed among students with a greater exposure to TV programs. In a similar study, West and Stanovitch (1991) claims that exposure to the paper media leads to richer knowledge about culture and history, but it does not influence school grades. In other words, reading experience does not necessarily influence academic performance, but it is a profound source of world knowledge, or what we know about our everyday life. In considering individual differences in pragmatic knowledge, reading experience could be a promising basis on which to measure such differences.

The present study is a first attempt to use quantitative measures to examine whether individual differences in pragmatic knowledge influence the construal of Japanese gapless relative clauses. Measuring pragmatic knowledge is difficult, since it is accumulated through an individual's lifelong experiences in conversation, education, entertainment, books and other media, and of course through basic sensory experiences. Any measure of pragmatic knowledge is therefore necessarily partial and approximate.

In this study, we take individuals' summative reading experience—that is, how much, how often, and how they read—as one indicator of pragmatic knowledge. As we have seen above, though reading is by no means the sole contributor to pragmatic understanding, it is certainly a profound one; and we can reasonably expect that rich reading experience also enriches pragmatic knowledge. Reading experience in this study is understood to comprise individuals' reading habits and abilities in general, which we set out to measure through a questionnaire explained in the following section.

3. Methods

This quantitative study examines whether reading experience plays a role in the construal of gapless relative clauses with resultative head nouns.

3.1 Participants

Fifty-two native speakers of Japanese participated in this study. All were undergraduate students at a public university in the Shizuoka area (mean age: 18.96, *SD*: 1.17).

3.2 Tasks and test materials

There were two tasks in this study: a judgment rating task and a questionnaire. The judgment task asked the participants to rate the relative naturalness/unnaturalness of 28 unrelated sentences. The questionnaire asked about their reading experience from elementary school to the present, and also asked how well and quickly they could understand reading materials. (See the Appendix for the full contents of the questionnaire.)

3.2.1 Naturalness rating task

The naturalness rating task is designed to examine how native speakers of Japanese would comprehend gapless relative clauses in terms of semantic plausibility. Test materials consisted of four sets of three sentences (a total of 12 sentences) like those in (4) below. All sentences were grammatical, but they differed from each other in their degree of semantic plausibility.

(4) a. Raamen-o tabeta otsuri-ga moo
noodles-ACC eat-PER change-NOM already
nakunatta. (GaplessP)
gone
Lit: *The change that (I) ate noodles is already gone.
'The change that I received as a result of having eaten noodles is already gone.'

b. # Raamen-o taberu otsuri-ga moo
   noodles-ACC eat-IMP change-NOM already
   nakunatta. (GaplessIP)
   gone
   Lit: *The change that (I) eat noodles is already gone.
   'The change that I will use to eat noodles is already gone.'
c. Raamen'ya-de moratta otsuri-ga moo
   noodle shop-at receive-PER change-NOM already
   nakunatta. (Gapped)
   gone
   'The change that I received at the noodle shop is already gone.'

The first sentence contains a gapless relative clause, and the aspect of the verb *tabeta* 'ate' is perfective. In our subsequent discussion, this structure will be referred to as the GaplessP type. A resultative construal of the head noun is possible only if the verbal aspect of the relative clause is perfective.

The second sentence contains a gapless relative clause with imperfective verbal aspect, *taberu* 'eat,' which will be referred to as the GaplessIP type. The GaplessP and GaplessIP types are identical except for verbal aspect of the relative clause. As we have already seen, sentence (4b) is not plausible without very active imagination.

The last sentence contains a gapped relative clause, which will be referred to as the Gapped type. The relative head *otsuri* 'change' is coindexed with the gap created by the missing argument (direct object) of the verb *moratta* 'received.' This sentence was included to establish a baseline for the data.

In addition to the four sets of three test sentences (12 sentences), another 65 Japanese sentences were prepared as fillers and practice sentences. In order to avoid priming effects, the sentences were divided into three lists so that the participants would not read more than one sentence from the same set of three. As a result, each list contained a total of 35 sentences, with no duplication of phrases in the set: 7 practice items, 4 test sentences, and 24 fillers.

Each participant read one of the three sentence lists, which were all presented in Japanese, and rated the naturalness of each sentence. Typical grammaticality or acceptability judgments that require respondents to classify sentences as simply "acceptable" or "unacceptable" can be problematic, since these choices can obscure subtle differences between these ends of the spectrum. In order to more closely capture each participant's relative judgments of the stimuli, we employed a rating method known as *Magnitude Estimation* (Brad, Robertson and Sorace 1996), in which participants were instructed to assign any number they wished to each item, but to give lower scores for plausible sentences and higher scores for implausible sentences.

In the task, the participants were first presented with a reference sentence (5) below, and they were asked to rate its naturalness (or unnaturalness) with any number they wish except for negative numbers. They were instructed to give a higher number if (5) was felt implausible.

(5) Shachoo-wa honshabiru-no arubaito-ni banana-o
    president-TOP headquater-of part-timer-from banana-ACC
    karita.
    borrow-PER
    'The president borrowed the banana from the part-timer at the headquarter office.'

The plausibility level of the reference sentence was set relatively low, prompting participants to start with a relatively high number and thereby avoiding a floor effect. All subsequent sentences were to be rated based on their relative naturalness (or unnaturalness) compared to the reference sentence. For example, participants were asked to assign a score twice that given for (5) if the test sentence was perceived to be twice as unnatural as (5).

3.2.2 Questionnaire on reading experience

The questionnaire is a modified version of Sawasaki (2012a), consisting of 23 questions regarding participants' reading habits and abilities. Each question is followed by a 1–7 rating scale, and the participants were asked to choose one out of the seven choices. They were all presented in Japanese.

The 23 questionnaire items comprise three subcategories: (i) questions about their current reading habits (11 questions), (ii) questions asking about their current and previous reading habits (8 questions), (iii) questions asking about their general reading abilities (4 questions). Sample questions from each subcategory are translated below. (See the Appendix for the complete questionnaire.)

(6) Sample questions about current reading habits
   a. Do you like to read in Japanese?
      Scale: hate it--------kind of hate it-------kind of love it----------love it
            1   2   3   4   5   6   7
   b. How often do you read Japanese books such as novels?
      Scale: seldom---------sometimes-------once in a few days--------every day
            1   2   3   4   5   6   7

(7) Sample questions about current and previous reading habits
   a. How often do you read Japanese books now?
   b. How often did you read Japanese books in high school?
   c. How often did you read Japanese books in junior high school?
   d. How often did you read Japanese books in elementary school?
   Scale: seldom---------not much---------relatively often---------every day
         1   2   3   4   5   6   7

(8) Sample questions about reading abilities
   a. How fast do you think you can read Japanese? For example, how long would it take to read a 200-page-long book?
   Scale: more than---------in a half---------------in a few-----------in 1–2 hours
        1 day   day   hours
        1   2   3   4   5   6   7
   b. How did you usually score in Japanese at mock tests for college entrance examination (excluding classical Japanese)?
   Scale: 30%------40%------50%-------60%------70%-------80%------90%
      or less   or more
       1   2   3   4   5   6   7

The questionnaire basically consists of introspective questions. Ratings closer to 7 indicate relatively rich reading experience, and ratings closer to 1 indicate relatively poor reading experience.

3.3 Procedure

The two tasks were administered in one sitting using pencil and paper. Participants first completed the naturalness rating task, then filled out the reading experience questionnaire. It took approximately 20 minutes for participants to finish the tasks.

3.4 Analysis and predictions

The ratings obtained from the naturalness rating task were converted into z-scores for each participant for later statistical comparison. The z-scores are the converted data such that the mean is set zero and the standard deviation (*SD*) is set one. The formula for obtaining the z-scores is:

(9) z-score = (rating − mean rating) / *SD*

The ratings from the questionnaire task were treated as numerical data. Furthermore, the "total scores for current and previous reading habits (Total Habits)" were calculated by summing the ratings of the following four questions, which are also shown in (7) above.

(10) Total scores for current and previous reading habits (Total Habits):
   a. How often do you read Japanese books now?
   b. How often did you read Japanese books in high school?
   c. How often did you read Japanese books in junior high school?
   d. How often did you read Japanese books in elementary school?

In previous studies by Sawasaki (2012a; 2012b), the "total scores for current and previous reading habits (Total Habits)" was found to be significantly related to other areas of reading. The same was true with the "current reading habits for novels (Novel Habits)," which is question (6b), restated below as (11).

(11) Current reading habits for novels (Novel Habits):
   How often do you read Japanese books such as novels?

Statistical analysis of the data relied upon two tests. First, Pearson's Correlation tests were conducted between ratings for reading experience and naturalness ratings for each sentence type (GaplessP, GaplessIP, and Gapped). Next, ratings for Total Habits and Novel Habits were used to divide the participant pool into two groups, HIGH group and LOW group (see section 4.2 below). Taking these HIGH and LOW groups as between-group independent variables and the three sentence types as within-group independent variables, 2 x 3 Analysis of Variance (ANOVA) was performed using naturalness ratings as dependent variables.

3.5 Predictions

We posited two general sets of predictions for the present experiment, as stated below. Prediction I suggests that reading experience and construal of the gapless relative clauses would be in some way related. Furthermore, Prediction II suggests that rich reading experience would increase the ease of understanding gapless relative clauses.

(12) Prediction I
If the construal of gapless relative clauses is influenced by one's reading experience,
 a. The ratings for reading experience should show some correlation with naturalness ratings for the gapless relative clauses.
 b. This would be especially true for the gapless relative clauses with imperfective verbal aspect (GaplessIP), because these structures rely more heavily on pragmatic knowledge for their interpretation.
 c. Rating experience would show a lesser correlation with the naturalness ratings for gapped relative clauses (Gapped) because the gapped relative clauses are construed based on their straightforward structure rather than on pragmatic knowledge.

(13) Prediction II
If reading experience aids in the construal of gapless relative clauses,
 a. Readers with rich reading experience would perceive the gapless relative clauses as more natural than readers with poor reading experience would.
 b. Such an effect would be more evident in gapless relative clauses with imperfect verbal aspect (GaplessIP).

We expected Prediction I be borne out if significant correlations could be found between the two ratings, and if the naturalness ratings of the HIGH and LOW groups were significantly different from each other. On the other hand, Prediction II would be borne out if negative correlations were observed, and also if the HIGH group assigned significantly lower scores (that is, reported a relatively greater level of naturalness) than the LOW group.

4. Results

4.1 Correlation between naturalness ratings and reading experience

The results of the Pearson's Correlation analyses are shown below in Table 1, which indicates the correlation between reading experience and naturalness ratings for the three relative clause types. The numbers in the table indicate the number of questions that revealed significant (or marginally significant) correlations with the naturalness ratings. (Positive and negative correlations are represented by + and -, respectively.)

Table 1. Correlations between naturalness ratings and reading experience

Sentence Type	Reading Habits		Reading Abilities	
	$p < .05$	$.05 \leq p < .01$	$p < .05$	$.05 \leq p < .01$
GaplessP	none	none	1 (+)	1 (+)
GaplessIP	1 (+)	2 (+), 1 (−)	none	none
Gapped	none	none	none	none

Correlations between the two ratings were observed only in the GaplessP type and the GaplessIP type. The strengths of correlations were all weak ($.2 < |r|s < .3$). On the other hand, not a single correlation was found in the Gapped type. These results seem to accord with Prediction I, stated in (12) above. However, correlations were found in fewer than five out of the 23 total reading questions for each gapless relative clause type. It is not clear whether these results are robust enough to support the prediction that the construal of gapless relative clauses is influenced by one's reading experience.

4.2 HIGH and LOW reading groups and their naturalness ratings

Next, in order to perform ANOVA, the 52 participants were divided into two groups (HIGH and LOW) based on their "total scores for current and previous reading habits (Total Habits)" in (10) and also based on "current reading habits for novels (Novel Habits)" in (11). These criteria resulted in 24 participants in the HIGH group and 28 in the LOW group based on Total Habits, and 28 HIGH and 24 LOW participants based on Novel Habits. The ANOVA based on Total Habits revealed a significant main effect on sentence type ($F(2,202)=39.386, p<.001$), but there was no main effect on group ($p>.1$), and no interaction was observed ($p>.1$). Similar results were found in the ANOVA based on Novel Habits: for sentence type, $(F(2,202)=40.075, p<.001)$; for group and interaction, ps>.1. Bonferroni's pairwise comparisons showed that the ratings of the three sentence types were significantly different from each other, both for Total Habits and for Novel Habits groupings. The Gapped type was perceived to be the most natural, the GaplessIP type the least natural, and the GaplessP type fell between the other two types (regardless of whether HIGH group or LOW group). These results indicate no specific effect of reading experience on the construal of gapless relative clauses. Therefore, Predictions I and II were not supported.

4.3 Further analyses: Analyses for each test item

The initial results failed to reveal expected relationships between reading experience and the construal of gapless relative clauses. It is possible that the naturalness ratings varied among test sentences, and this variation may have obscured our results when composite scores were calculated for all test sentences. In order to examine whether the plausibility ratings varied among test sentences, each set of three relative clauses was analyzed separately.

The four sets of three relative clauses are listed below. The first one is identical to (4) shown earlier. For the sake of convenience, these sets will be referred to as Triplexes I, II, III and IV.

(14) Triplex I
    a. Raamen-o   tabeta   otsuri-ga   moo
        noodles-ACC eat-PER change-NOM already
        nakunatta. (GaplessP)
        gone
        Lit: *The change that (I) ate noodles is already gone.
        'The change that I received as a result of having eaten noodles is already gone.'
    b. # Raamen-o   taberu   otsuri-ga   moo
        noodles-ACC eat-IMP change-NOM already
        nakunatta. (GaplessIP)
        gone
        Lit: *The change that (I) eat noodles is already gone.
        'The change that I will use to eat noodles is already gone.'
    c. Raamen'ya-de moratta   otsuri-ga   moo
        noodle shop-at receive-PER change-NOM already
        nakunatta. (Gapped)

gone
'The change that I received at the noodle shop is already gone.'

(15) Triplex II
    a. Heya-o sooji-shita gomi-o doko-ni suteru
       room-ACC clean-PER trash-ACC where throw away
       ka mayotta.
       whether wondered
       Lit: *(I) wondered where (I) throw away the trash that (I) had cleaned the room.
       'I wondered where I should throw away the trash that I got as a result of having cleaned the room'
    b. # Heya-o sooji-suru gomi-o doko-ni suteru
       room-ACC clean-IMP trash-ACC where throw away
       ka mayotta.
       whether wondered
       Lit: *(I) wondered where (I) throw away the trash that (I) clean the room.
       'I wondered where I should throw away the trash that I will use to clean the room'
    c. Heya-de mitsuketa gomi-o doko-ni suteru
       room-at find-PER trash-ACC where throw away
       ka mayotta.
       whether wondered
       'I wondered where I should throw away the trash that I found in the room'

(16) Triplex III
    a. Endaka-ga susunda kekka-o
       yen-appreciation-NOM continue-PER results-ACC
       moo ichido bunseki shinakereba naranai.
       once again analysis have to do
       Lit: *Once again, (we) have to analyze the results that the yen has kept becoming strong."
       'Once again, we have to analyze the results of the yen having become strong.'
    b. # Endaka-ga susumu kekka-o
       yen-appreciation-NOM continue-IMP results-ACC
       moo ichido bunseki shinakereba naranai.

once again   analysis   have to do
Lit: *Once again, (we) have to analyze the results that the yen keeps becoming strong."
'Once again, we have to analyze the results of the yen becoming strong.'

c. Endaka-ga   maneita   kekka-o
   yen-appreciation-NOM   bring-PER   results-ACC
   moo ichido   bunseki   shinakereba naranai.
   Once again   analysis   have to do
   'Once again, we have to analyze the results that the strong yen has brought.'

(17) Triplex IV
   a. Jugyoo-o   kiita   chishiki-wa   itsuka
      class-ACC   listen-PER   knowledge-TOP   someday
      yaku ni tatsu   daroo.
      become useful   will
      Lit: *The knowledge that (I) listened to the lecture will become useful someday.
      'The knowledge that I received as a result of having listened to the lecture will become useful someday.'

   b. # Jugyoo-o   kiku   chishiki-wa   itsuka
      class-ACC   listen-IMP   knowledge-TOP   someday
      yaku ni tatsu   daroo.
      become useful   will
      Lit: *The knowledge that (I) listen to the lecture will become useful someday.
      'The knowledge that I need to listen to the lecture will become useful someday.'

   c. Jugyoo-de   eta   chishiki-wa   itsuka
      class-at   gain-PER   knowledge-TOP   someday
      yaku ni tatsu   daroo.
      become useful   will
      'The knowledge that I gained at the lecture will become useful someday.'

4.3.1 Correlation between naturalness ratings and reading experience

For each triplex, Pearson's Correlation analyses were performed between naturalness ratings and the ratings of the 23 questions in the reading experience questionnaire. The results are shown below in Tables 2, 3, 4 and 5.

Table 2. Triplex I: Correlations between naturalness ratings and reading experience

Sentence Type	Reading Habits		Reading Abilities	
	p < .05	.05 ≤ p <.01	p < .05	.05 ≤ p <.01
GaplessP	none	none	none	none
GaplessIP	1 (+)	1 (+)	none	1 (-)
Gapped	3 (+)	none	1 (+)	none

Table 3. Triplex II: Correlations between naturalness ratings and reading experience

Sentence Type	Reading Habits		Reading Abilities	
	p < .05	.05 ≤ p <.01	p < .05	.05 ≤ p <.01
GaplessP	1 (+), 1 (-)	none	1 (+)	none
GaplessIP	none	none	none	none
Gapped	none	1 (-)	1 (-)	none

Table 4. Triplex III: Correlations between naturalness ratings and reading experience

Sentence Type	Reading Habits		Reading Abilities	
	p < .05	.05 ≤ p <.01	p < .05	.05 ≤ p <.01
GaplessP	1 (+), 1 (-)	none	1 (+)	none
GaplessIP	4 (+)	5 (+)	1 (+)	none
Gapped	none	none	none	none

Table 5. Triplex IV: Correlations between naturalness ratings and reading experience

Sentence Type	Reading Habits		Reading Abilities	
	p < .05	.05 ≤ p <.01	p < .05	.05 ≤ p <.01
GaplessP	1 (-)	1 (-)	1 (+)	none
GaplessIP	1 (-)	2 (-)	none	2 (-)
Gapped	3 (-)	none	none	none

The tables above show that the degree of correlation varies among sentences. For example, Triplex III revealed relatively many significant (and marginally significant) correlations for the GaplessIP type, whereas fewer correlations were found for the GaplessP type and no correlations were observed for the Gapped type. These results are congruous with Prediction I, but other triplexes do not exemplify the similar results. Triplexes I and possibly IV yielded more significant correlations for the Gapped type than the GaplessP and GaplessIP types. Triplex II showed strong counterevidence against Prediction I because it revealed no correlations for the GaplessIP type.

The reason why Triplex III was congruous with Prediction I and Triplex II was not may be obvious when we compare their particular GaplessIP sentences.

(18) Triplex II: GaplessIP
#Heya-o   sooji-suru   gomi-o   doko-ni   suteru
room-ACC   clean-IMP   trash-ACC   where   throw away
ka   mayotta.
whether   wondered
Lit: *(I) wondered where (I) should throw away the trash I that clean the room.
'I wondered where I should throw away the trash that I will use to clean the room'

(19) Triplex III: GaplessIP
#Endaka-ga   susumu   kekka-o
yen-appreciation-NOM   continue-IMP   results-ACC
moo ichido   bunseki   shinakereba naranai.
once again   analysis   have to do
Lit: *Once again, (we) have to analyze the results that the yen keeps becoming strong."
'Once again, we have to analyze the results of the yen becoming strong.'

A previous study claims that the GaplessIP type is implausible when the head noun denotes a consequence of the event described in the relative clause (Kato 2003). In this regard, both GaplessIP sentences in Triplexes II and III above should be implausible. However, the comparison of (18) and (19) above clearly shows that the intended meaning of (18) for Triplex II is extremely difficult to imagine, but the intended meaning of (19) for Triplex III is quite possible. In (18), "using the trash to clean the room" could be possible as an innovative metaphor, but it is extremely unusual as a real life event. In (19), the imperfective verb *susumu* 'continue' should take a perfective form because *kekka* 'results' always follow the event of yen-appreciation (Kato 2003). However, many native speakers may in fact accept this sentence, and some may not be able to find huge differences in meaning between (19) and (16a), where *susumu* 'continue' is expressed with a perfective form; i.e., 'Once again, we have to analyze the results of the yen having become strong.' Put another way, the degree of naturalness varies among the GaplessIP sentences, and Prediction I was rejected when the intended meaning of the GaplessIP sentence was especially difficult (Triplex II). On the other hand, the same prediction was accepted when the intended meaning of the GaplessIP sentence was relatively plausible (Triplex III). Thus, it appears that the relation between naturalness ratings and reading experience depends on the plausibility of the GaplessIP sentences. This is exemplified even more clearly in the following section.

4.3.2 HIGH and LOW reading groups and naturalness ratings

Figures 1, 2, 3, and 4 below show the naturalness ratings in HIGH and LOW groups according to Novel Habits. (A comparison between the two groups according to Total Habits is not shown here due to space limitations, but its results pattern similarly to those discussed here.) In these figures, negative z-scores indicate that the sentence is felt to be natural, while positive scores indicate perceived unnaturalness.

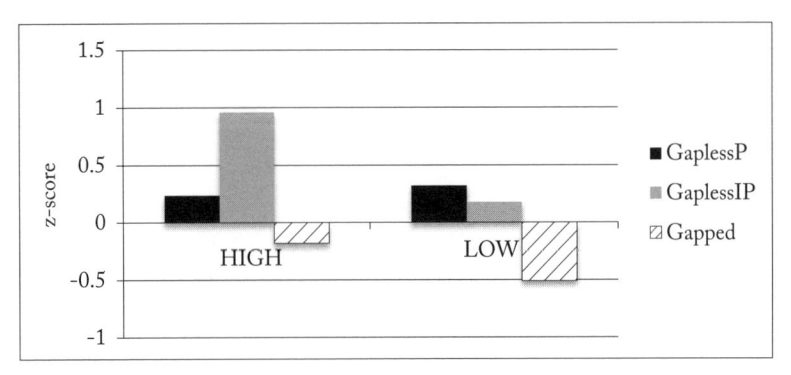

Figure 1. Triplex I: Naturalness ratings and novel habits (HIGH&LOW)

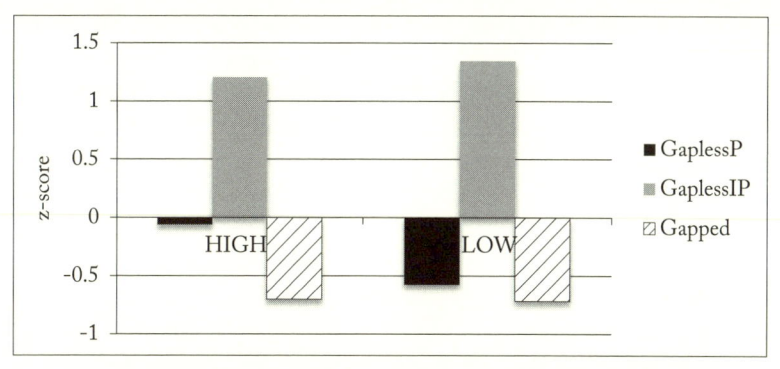

Figure 2. Triplex II: Naturalness ratings and novel habits (HIGH&LOW)

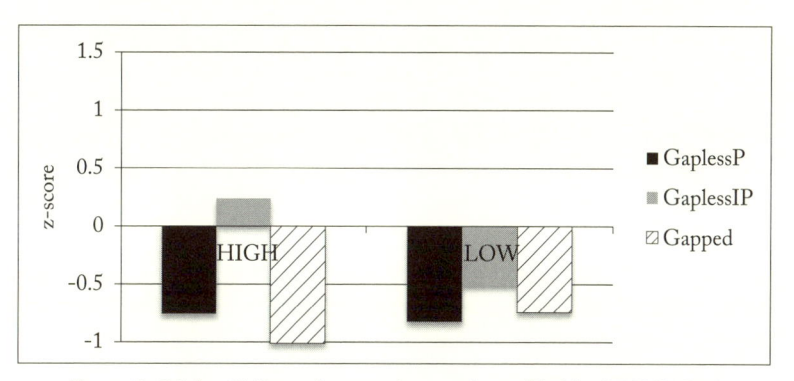

Figure 3. Triplex III: Naturalness ratings and novel habits (HIGH&LOW)

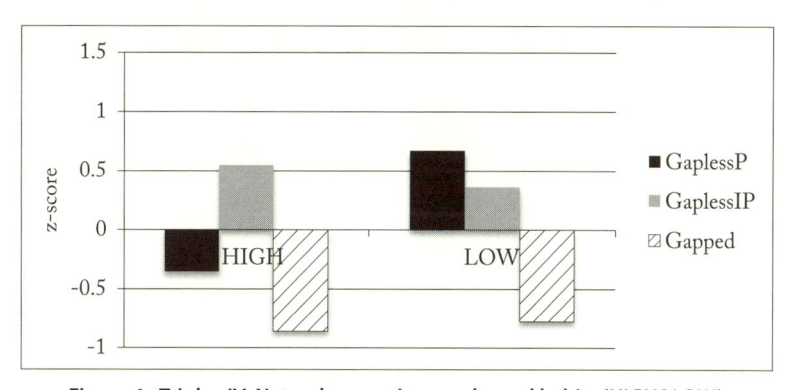

Figure 4. Triplex IV: Naturalness ratings and novel habits (HIGH&LOW)

Figure 2 indicates that the GaplessIP type in Triplex II is perceived to be very unnatural by both the HIGH and the LOW groups. Among the four triplexes, Triplex II is the only one in which the rating of GaplessIP exceeds a z-score of 1.0 in both groups (i.e., outside the range of the "mean rating + one standard deviation"). In contrast, as Figure 3 shows, the GaplessIP type in Triplex III is perceived differently by HIGH and LOW groups: LOW experience readers found this type to be relatively natural (negative z-score), while HIGH experience readers found it relatively unnatural (positive z-score). Therefore, Triplex II and Triplex III are very different from each other in terms of the ratings for the GaplessIP sentences, and these points suggest that the degree of naturalness does indeed vary among the four triplexes.

However, the four triplexes seem to share the following commonalities:

(20) a. Among HIGH readers, the GaplessIP type is always rated most unnatural, which is not the case among LOW readers.
 b. Among HIGH readers, the GaplessP type and the Gapped type show similar ratings whereas LOW readers do not always rate these the same.

In other words, the HIGH group exhibits consistent commonalities, but such consistency is not found among the LOW group. In the following, we will examine whether such consistency is statistically confirmed.

A 2x3 ANOVA was conducted for each triplex using group and sentence type as the independent variables and naturalness rating as the dependent variables. Simple main effects (i.e., pairwise comparisons between sentence types in each group) are conventionally examined after the interaction between group and sentence type has been found significant. However, because our purpose in this analysis is specifically to investigate whether the observation stated in (20) is supported, we will discuss the simple main effects regardless of the significance of the interaction.

First, in Triplex I, ANOVA revealed no significant interaction ($p=.150$). However, simple main effects were significant. Among the HIGH group, GaplessIP was rated most unnatural: i.e., it was significantly more unnatural than Gapped ($p=.004$) and also than GaplessP ($p=.078$), though its effect was marginal. Moreover, GaplessP and Gapped were found not to be significantly different from each other ($p>.1$). Among the LOW group, GaplessP was only numerically more unnatural than GaplessIP ($p>.1$) and more significantly unnatural than Gapped ($p=.012$). These results were congruous with the expected results in (20); i.e., GaplessIP is most unnatural and the other two are similar to each other in the HIGH group, but the same is not true of the LOW group.

In Triplex II, no significant interaction ($p>.1$) was evident, but simple main effects were found. Among the HIGH group, GaplessIP was rated most unnatural; i.e., it was more unnatural than GaplessP ($p<.001$) and Gapped ($p<.001$). Moreover, GaplessP and Gapped were not different from each other ($p>.1$). Among the LOW group, GaplessIP was rated more unnatural than both GaplessP ($p<.001$) and Gapped ($p<.001$). No difference between GaplessP and Gapped was observed ($p>.1$). Thus, in Triplex II, too, the expected results were observed among the HIGH group; i.e., GaplessIP was most unnatural, while GaplessP and Gapped scores were similar to each other. The LOW group showed identical results to those from the HIGH group.

In Triplex III, significant interaction was observed, although it was marginal ($F(2,46)=3.097$, $p=.055$), and significant simple main effects were also found. Among the HIGH group, GaplessIP was rated most unnatural: it was significantly more implausible than GaplessP ($p=.005$) and Gapped ($p=.001$). Moreover, GaplessP and Gapped exhibited no significant differences ($p>.1$). Among the LOW group, however, all three sentences were perceived to be natural. GaplessIP was rated as natural as GaplessP ($p>.1$) and Gapped ($p>.1$). These results in Triplex III are congruous with the expected results presented in (20).

Finally, in Triplex IV, there was no significant interaction ($p>.1$), but significant simple main effects were found. Among the HIGH group, GaplessIP was significantly more unnatural than Gapped (p=.009) and numerically more unnatural than GaplessP ($p>.1$). There was no significant difference between GaplessP and Gapped ($p>.1$). Among the LOW group, on the other hand, GaplessP was numerically more unnatural than GaplessIP ($p>.1$) and significantly more unnatural than Gapped ($p=.001$). These results in Triplex IV are also almost congruous with the expected results in (20).

In summation, the ANOVA results in each triplex strongly support the observation stated in (20) above. Among the HIGH group, GaplessIP was always the most unnatural sentence of the three, and GaplessP and Gapped were rated similarly to each other. This was consistently observed only in the HIGH group but not in the LOW group.

5. Discussion

The aim of this study was to investigate how individual differences in pragmatic knowledge would influence understanding of gapless relative clauses. Because it is not easy to measure pragmatic knowledge as a whole, this study took reading experience as an indicator of rich or poor pragmatic knowledge. Our predictions held that readers with richer reading experience would find it easier to construe gapless relative clauses— that is, HIGH readers would tend to accept less plausible sentences more readily than LOW readers would.

The predictions were not supported when the four triplex test sentences were analyzed as composite data. The results from a correlational study did not show a strong indication of correlation between the construal of the pragmatic relative clauses and reading experience. Nor did the results from ANOVA reveal significant differences between HIGH and LOW reading groups.

However, when the test sentences were analyzed for each triplex, different results emerged. As shown below, the HIGH reading group and the LOW reading group did exhibit differences in terms of how they construed pragmatic relative clauses.

(21) a. Among HIGH readers, the GaplessIP type is always rated most unnatural, which is not the case among LOW readers.
 b. Among HIGH readers, the GaplessP type and the Gapped type show similar ratings, which is not always so among LOW readers.

These results lead us to a claim somewhat different from the one this study originally anticipated. Our original prediction was that the pragmatic awareness of readers with rich reading experience would make it easier for them to understand gapless relative clauses, and we predicted that these readers would find the sentences less unnatural. However, (21) indicates that the readers with richer reading experience were better at identifying the unnatural sentences; furthermore, they seem to distinguish different plausibility levels (i.e., degrees of unnaturalness). On the other hand, the readers with poor reading experience were less sensitive to different plausibility levels and they tended to perceive different types of relative clauses in a similar way. This may indicate a connection between individuals' reading experience and their pragmatic sensitivity to degrees of plausibility in gapless relative clauses.

The plausibility differences in question are attributed to the verbal aspect; i.e., whether the verb in the structure appears in its perfective form or imperfective form. The current findings suggest that readers with rich experience are more sensitive to the perfective/imperfective distinction, as in (22) of Triplex III. As Figure 3 above illustrates, only the HIGH group discerned (22b), GaplessIP, as most unnatural, and they did the same in Triplexes I and IV. The LOW group exhibited quite different construal patterns.

(22) a. Endaka-ga susunda kekka-o
yen-appreciation-NOM continue-PER results-ACC
moo ichido bunseki shinakereba naranai.
once again analysis have to do
Lit: *Once again, (we) have to analyze the results that the yen has kept becoming strong."
'Once again, we have to analyze the results of the yen having become strong.'
b. # Endaka-ga susumu kekka-o
yen-appreciation-NOM continue-IMP results-ACC
moo ichido bunseki shinakereba naranai.
once again analysis have to do
Lit: *Once again, (we) have to analyze the results that the yen keeps becoming strong."
'Once again, we have to analyze the results of the yen becoming strong.'

However, the sensitivity to the perfective/imperfective verbal form was robust in Triplex II, not only among the HIGH group but also among the LOW group. The GaplessIP sentence in Triplex II, (23b) below, was extremely difficult to imagine in real life, and the difference between (23a) and (23b) was obvious.

(23) a. Heya-o sooji-shita gomi-o doko-ni suteru
room-ACC clean-PER trash-ACC where throw away
ka mayotta.
whether wondered
Lit: *(I) wondered where (I) should throw away the trash that I had cleaned the room.

'I wondered where I should throw away the trash that I got as a result of having cleaned the room'

b. # Heya-o   sooji-suru   gomi-o   doko-ni   suteru
    room-ACC clean-IMP trash-ACC   where   throw away
    ka   mayotta.
    whether wondered

Lit: *(I) wondered where (I) should throw away the trash that I clean the room.

'I wondered where I should throw away the trash that I will use to clean the room'

As exemplified in Figure 2, both HIGH and LOW groups perceived the GaplessIP sentence to be unnatural. This seems to show that the difference in pragmatic sensitivity between HIGH and LOW groups is typically observed when the relationship between the gapless relative clauses and their resultative head nouns has at least some degree of comprehensibility.

This study has offered some insights into the relationship between reading experience and the construal of gapless relative clauses, although the results did not pattern according to our original predictions in (12) and (13) above. Our findings showed that the readers with richer reading experience were more sensitive to the differences created by verbal aspect in gapless relative clauses. Previous studies have claimed that the construal of gapless relative clauses is deeply related to one's pragmatic knowledge. Insofar as reading experience may be viewed as one measurable dimension of pragmatic knowledge, this study offers demonstrable, quantitative support for these claims.

6. Conclusion

This study offers evidence that reading experience may indeed influence the construal of gapless relative clauses. Our original prediction was that more experienced readers would interpret implausible sentences as more natural. However, analysis of the naturalness and questionnaire ratings for each test sentence type revealed different patterns. In fact, experienced readers were consistently sensitive to distinctions in the degree of plausibility of different gapless relative clauses. On the other hand, less experienced readers tended to construe different gapless relative clauses in a similar manner and did not distinguish degree of plausibility.

Certain limitations are evident in this study. We have assumed that reading experience is a major factor in pragmatic awareness, but it is certainly not the only one. The degree to which reading experience offers a reliable picture of "pragmatic knowledge" remains to be seen. Other factors could influence the construal of gapless relative clauses. In addition, our focus so far has been on the relatively narrow domain of gapless relative structures containing resultative head nouns. Other types of non-gapped relative clauses exist, and whether these findings can be generalized to other types is a matter for further research. These are preliminary steps toward understanding the relationship between gapless (non-gapped) relative clauses and pragmatic knowledge, and future studies will be needed to address these issues from broad and diverse points of view.

If reading experience can be said to be one valid indicator of pragmatic knowledge, these results confirm that the construal of the gapless relative clauses is related to pragmatic knowledge. The relationship between gapless relative clauses and pragmatic knowledge has long been postulated in the literature of syntax and pragmatics, but so far as we know, this claim had never been investigated quantitatively or psycholinguistically. In this regard, this study offers a first step forward, confirming a long-suspected relationship, suggesting some important dimensions of individual variation, and adding new insights into readers' varying pragmatic sensitivities.

Acknowledgements

A part of this study was presented at the Autumnal J-SLA (Japan Second Language Association) Seminar, 2012, and at the 23rd JASLA (Japanese Association of Second Language Acquisition) Annual Conference, 2012. I would like to thank the audience for their helpful comments. Of course, any shortcomings are mine.

Notes

1. The following abbreviations are used in the glosses throughout this chapter.
   NOM: nominative   ACC: accusative   DAT: dative   TOP: topic
   PER: perfective   IMP: imperfective
2. *Pro* is an empty pronoun whose antecedent can be found in the prior context. Explicit subjects and objects are not required in Japanese if they are understood from the context. For the sake of simplicity, indication of *gap* and *pro* will be omitted in the rest of the examples.

References

Brad, Ellen G., Dan Robertson and Antonella Sorace. (1996). Magnitude Estimation of Linguistics Acceptability. *Language* 72: 32–68.

Currah, Satomi. (2002). *Processing Japanese Adnominal Structures: An Empirical Study of Native and Non-native Speakers' Strategies*. Ph.D. Dissertation, University of Alberta, Canada.

Hirose, Yuki. (2002). Resolution of Reanalysis Ambiguity in Japanese Relative Clauses. In Mineharu Nakayama (ed.) *Sentence Processing in East Asian Languages*, pp. 31–52. Stanford, CA: CSLI Publications.

Hirose, Yuki and Atsu Inoue. (1998). Ambiguity of Reanalysis in Parsing Complex Sentences in Japanese. In Hillert Dieter (ed.) *Syntax and Semantics 31: A Crosslinguistic Perspective*, pp. 71–93. New York: Academic Press.

Kahraman, Barış. (2011). *Nihongo Oyobi Torukogo ni Okeru "Kuusho to Maigo no Izon Kankei" no Shori: Bunshori no Chikujisei o Megutte*. Ph.D. Dissertation, Hiroshima University, Japan.

Kato, Shigehiro. (2003). *Nihongo Shuushoku Koozoo no Goyooronteki Kenkyuu*. Hituzi Publishers.

Matsumoto, Yoshiko. (1988). Semantics and Pragmatics of Noun-modifying Constructions in Japanese. *Proceedings of the Fourteenth Annual Meeting of the Berkeley Linguistics Society*: 166–175.

Matsumoto, Yoshiko. (1990). The Role of Pragmatics in Japanese Relative Clause Constructions. *Lingua* 82: 111–129.

Mazuka, Reiko and Kenji Itoh. (1995). Can Japanese Speakers Be Led Down the Garden Path? In Reiko Mazuka and Noriko Nagai (eds.) *Japanese Sentence Processing*, pp. 295–329. Hillsdale, NJ: Lawrence Erlbaum Associates.

Miyamoto, Edson T., Edward Gibson, Neal J. Pearlmutter, Takako Aikawa and Shigeru Miyagawa. (1999). A U-shaped Relative Clause Attachment Preference in Japanese. *Language and Cognitive Processes*, 14: 663–686.

Miyamoto, Edson T. and Machiko Nakamura. (2003). Subject/object Asymmetries in the Processing of Relative Clause in Japanese. In Gina Garding and Mimu Tsujimura (eds.) *WCCFL33 Proceedings*, pp. 342–355. Somerville, Mass: Cascadilla Press.

Sato, Atsushi. (2011). *Nihongo Kankeisetsu no Shorifuka o Kettei Suru Yooin no Kentoo: Koopasu ni Okeru Shiyoohindo no Eikyoo o Chuushin ni*. Ph.D. Dissertation, Hiroshima University, Japan.

Sawasaki, Koichi. (2012a). The Relationship between University Students' Reading Experiences and Reading Comprehension (Daigakusei no Dokusho Keiken to Bunshoo Rikairyoku no Kankei). *Journal of International Relations and Comparative Culture* 10(2): 23–41.

Sawasaki, Koichi. (2012b). The Effect of Reading Experiences and Working Memory on Sentence Comprehension: Using Difficulty Rating Studies with Multiple "*Ga*" Marked NP Sentences and Multiple Animate NP Sentences (Dokusho Keiken to

Sadoo Kioku ga Bunrikai ni Oyobosu Eikyoo: "Ga" Kaku/Yuusei Meishi Renzokubun no Nanido Hantei yori). *Ars Linguistica* 19: 21–40.

Stanovich, Keith E. and Anne E. Cunningham. (1992). Studying the Consequences of Literacy within a Literate Society: The Cognitive Correlates of Print Exposure. *Memory & Cognition*, 20(1): 51–68.

Stanovich, Keith E. and Anne E. Cunningham. (1993). Where Does Knowledge Come from?: Specific Associations between Print Exposure and Information Acquisition. *Journal of Educational Psychology*, 85(2): 211–229.

Teramura, Hideo. (1992). *Teramura Hideo Ronbunshuu I*. Kurosio Publishers.

Ueno, Mieko and Susan M. Garnsey. (2007). Gap-filling vs. Filling Gaps: Event-related Brain Indices of Subject and Object Relative Clauses in Japanese. In Naomi Hanaoka McGloin and Junko Mori (eds.) *Proceedings of the 15th Japanese-Korean Linguistics Conference*, pp. 286–298. Stanford, CA: CSLI Publications.

Venditti, Jennifer J. and Hiroko Yamashita. (1994). Prosodic Information and Processing of Complex NPs in Japanese. *MIT Working Paper in Linguistics* 24: 375–391.

West, Richard F. and Keith E. Stanovich. (1991). The Incidental Acquisition of Information from Reading. *Psychological Science*, 2(5): 325–330.

Yamashita, Hiroko, Laurie Stowe and Mineharu Nakayama. (1993). Processing of Japanese Relative Clause Constructions. *Japanese/Korean Linguistics*, 2: 248–263.

Appendix: Reading Experience Questionnaire (Translated from Japanese)

(1) Questions about current reading habits (11 questions)
   (Preferences)
   a. Do you like to read in Japanese?

   Scale: hate it--------kind of hate it-------kind of love it----------love it
           1   2   3   4   5   6   7

   (Frequency)
   b. How often do you read books, newspapers, magazines, and Internet articles in Japanese?
   c. How often do you read Japanese books such as novels?
   d. How often do you read Japanese Internet articles and blogs?
   e. How often do you read Japanese newspapers?
   f. How often do you read Japanese magazines?
   g. How often do you read Japanese textbooks?

   Scale: seldom--------sometimes-------once in a few days--------every day
           1   2   3   4   5   6   7

   (Quantity)
   h. How much do you read Japanese books such as novels?

   Scale: 1–2 books---------1 book---------------1 book-------------1 book in
        in a year   in a month   in 1–2 weeks   1–3 days
           1   2   3   4   5   6   7

   (Attitude)
   i. How carefully do you read Japanese Internet articles and blogs?
   j. How carefully do you read Japanese newspapers?
   k. How carefully do you read Japanese textbooks?

   Scale: headlines-----------skim------------carefully read--------carefully read
        only   some articles   some articles   them all
           1   2   3   4   5   6   7

(2) Questions asking about current and previous reading habits (8 questions)
   (Frequency)
   a. How often do you read Japanese books now?
   b. How often did you read Japanese books in high school?
   c. How often did you read Japanese books in junior high school?
   d. How often did you read Japanese books in elementary school?
   e. How often did you read Japanese newspapers in high school?
   f. How often did you read Japanese textbooks in high school?

   Scale: seldom---------not much---------relatively often---------every day
           1   2   3   4   5   6   7

The Role of Reading Experience in Construing Japanese Gapless Relative Clauses 109

(Attitude)
g. How carefully did you read Japanese newspapers in high school?
h. How carefully did your read Japanese textbooks in high school?
Scale: headlines-----------skim------------carefully read-------carefully read
only   some articles   some articles   them all
1   2   3   4   5   6   7

(3) Questions asking about reading abilities (4 questions)
(Speed)
a. How fast do you think you can read Japanese? For example, how long would it take to read a 200-page-long book?
Scale: more than---------in a half--------------in a few----------in 1–2 hours
1 day   day   hours
1   2   3   4   5   6   7

(Understanding)
b. How well do you think you can understand when reading Japanese in books, newspapers, and magazines?
Scale: sometimes-----often need to-------sometimes need---------usually
need to   reread when   to reread when   no need
reread   complicated   complicated   to reread
1   2   3   4   5   6   7

(Test score)
c. How did you score in Japanese (excluding classical Japanese) on the Center Test [a nation-wide entrance examination tests for college administered by the government]?
d. How did you usually score in Japanese on mock tests* for the college entrance examination (excluding classical Japanese)?
*The tests are called *mogi shiken*, practice exams usually administered by a nation-wide private company.
Scale: 30%------40%------50%-------60%------70%-------80%------90%
or less   or more
1   2   3   4   5   6   7

Textual Cohesion in the English as a Foreign Language (EFL) Classroom

Kaori Terakawa

Abstract
This paper[1] investigates English as a foreign language (EFL) learners' perception of textual cohesion. Cohesion is considered to be one of the elements that create texture, a feature that makes a text meaningful. However, previous studies have suggested that EFL learners find it difficult to perceive cohesive relationships between words or clauses in English texts. The purposes of this study are as follows: first, to clarify the concepts of cohesion and texture, and second, to emphasize the importance of cohesion in the teaching of reading. At the end of the paper, suggestions are given for teaching reading to EFL learners, taking cohesion into consideration.

Keywords   cohesion, texture, EFL, reading comprehension

1. Introduction

Systemic Functional Linguistics (SFL) provides useful frameworks for unpacking the underlying meanings of texts. Moreover, theories and research in the fields of SFL and Discourse Analysis provide concepts that serve particularly well to describe how readers comprehend the overall messages of English texts. One of these concepts is called cohesion. A number of researchers have stated that cohesion helps readers to understand the overall message of a text (Cohen, Glasman, Rosenbaum-Cohen, Ferrara, & Fine 1979; Chapman 1983; McCarthy 1991; Thornbury 2005; Grabe 2009). This paper, therefore, aims to explore ways to stress the importance of cohesion in reading and to direct EFL students' attention to textual cohesion. The paper is structured as follows: first, the concepts of cohesion and texture are explained in order to provide a theoretical background for the discussion. Next, a previous study is described. Lastly, sample analyses of magazine articles, which focus on cohesive devices, are presented.

2. Cohesion and texture

Textual cohesion refers to the semantic relationship between different parts of a text. Cohesion is objective in the sense that cohesive elements are identifiable at the surface level of sentences. Halliday and Hasan (1976: 4) explain the notion as follows:

> The concept of cohesion is a semantic one; it refers to relations of meaning that exist within the text, and that define it as a text. ... Cohesion occurs where the INTERPRETATION of some element in the discourse is dependent on that of another. The one PRESUPPOSED the other, in the sense that it cannot be effectively decoded except by recourse to it. When this happens, a relation of cohesion is set up, and the two elements, the presupposing and the presupposed, are thereby at least potentially integrated into a text.

They argue that cohesion gives a text "texture." Texture can be defined as a feature that enables a text to be a meaningful whole. They describe texture as follows (1976: 2):

> The concept of TEXTURE is entirely appropriate to express the property of "being a text." A text has a texture, and this is what distinguishes it from something that is not a text. It derives this texture from the fact that it functions as a unity with respect to its environment.

Here is an example of a non-text, taken from Nuttal (2005: 24):

> There was no possibility of a walk that day. Income tax rates for next year have been announced. What is the defining characteristic of the ungulates? Surely you did not tell her how it happened?

At first sight, the above collection of sentences may look like a text, but when one attempts to connect the message of each sentence to that of the next sentence, it becomes clear that the overall meaning is non-sense.

Therefore, the sentences are not considered as a text because they lack texture, a necessary component of a text.

Messages are embedded in texts. By looking at cohesive devices, one can see how meanings are constructed beyond clauses, sentences, and paragraphs, and how a particular idea is expanded into the next clause, sentence, or paragraph. Cohesion helps readers to read at the discourse level, not just the sentence level. Therefore, it is assumed that cohesion can be a useful tool for the EFL learners to better understand texts as a whole and become more fluent readers.

3. Cohesive devices

Cohesion is made up of various cohesive devices: "reference," "substitution," "ellipsis," "conjunction," and "lexical cohesion." As mentioned above, cohesive resources can be perceived at the sentence surface level. These are all devices that enable one or more words to adhere in meaning.

Among the five cohesive devices mentioned above, reference, substitution, and ellipsis are grammatical devices because they have to do with syntax. However, conjunction and lexical cohesion are slightly different in that, first, conjunctions do not have any referred items, as they show how the message is related between different sentences or clauses, and second, lexical cohesion is not grammatical but shows the chain of words, that is, how a certain meaning is expressed in the same or different words.

In terms of lexical cohesion, Nuttal (2005: 91) notes that "the most obvious problem occurs when a writer uses different lexical items to refer to one and the same thing. This is common in English, where the preference is for 'elegant variation', that is, avoiding repetition by using a different expression with similar meaning". McCarthy (1991: 66) argues the reasoning for choosing a synonym rather than repetition as follows:

> Discourse analysts have not yet given us any convincing rules or guidelines as to when or why a writer or speaker might choose a synonym for reiteration rather than repetition, though some research suggests a link between reiteration using synonyms and the idea of "re-entering" important topic words into the discourse at a later stage, that is to say bringing them back into focus, or foregrounding them again.

Therefore, it should be pointed out here that lexical chains express the topic of the text, and non-natives tend to regard synonyms as completely different because the word forms are different. Therefore, it is recommended that EFL learners become familiar with the phenomenon of lexical cohesion.

4. Background

A study conducted in Israel in the 1970s (Cohen, Glasman, Rosenbaum-Cohen, Ferrara, & Fine 1979, cited in Carrell, Devine, & Eskey 1998) is particularly important to note in this study. Cohen et al. (1979) investigated problematic areas for non-native readers of English, asking, What makes a text difficult to understand for non-natives? The study participants were native Hebrew-speaking university students and native English-speaking (American) students who were studying in Israel for a year. The participants were first asked to read articles and were later asked to answer "micro" and "macro" questions about the texts. Micro questions were those concerned with the small units of the text, such as the meaning of vocabulary and antecedents of reference. Macro questions were those pertaining to the overall comprehension or topic of the text. The researchers found that the non-native students did well on answering the micro questions but had poor comprehension at the macro level. They note that non-native speakers read more "locally" than native speakers, and because of this tendency, they were unable to see the whole picture.

Cohen et al. (1979) conclude that the following three areas are the ones that non-native students found difficult: (1) heavy noun phrases (i.e., long phrases that function as nouns), (2) syntactic markers of cohesion (i.e., conjunctions), and (3) nontechnical vocabulary in technical texts. They note that students' lack of ability to grasp the overall message of the text resulted from their poor understanding of conjunctions or paying little attention to such connective markers between sentences. They point out that "learners were not picking up on the conjunctive words signaling cohesion, not even the more basic ones like 'however' and 'thus'" (Cohen et al. 1979 reprinted in Carrel 1998: 160). Therefore, it seems that EFL learners tend to be distracted by smaller units such as unknown words and phrases, which leads to their failure to grasp the overall message.

5. Magazine articles

Two articles are analyzed in this paper to suggest ideas to direct EFL learners' attention to cohesive devices. The articles are as follows: "'Human nature' is often a product of nurture," taken from *WIRED UK edition* magazine, April 12, 2012 (see Figure 1), and "Morals and the machine," taken from *The Economist*, June 2, 2012 (see Figure 2). Each article was analyzed with a focus on the cohesive devices of conjunctions and lexical cohesion. Arrows and underlines were added to the text to clearly indicate the relationship between words. Both articles show significant uses of cohesive devices. The first article repeatedly uses conjunctions to show a clear contrast between two ideas, and the second shows cohesive ties realized by lexical cohesion. The features of each article are discussed in greater detail below.

In "'Human nature' is a product of nurture," one can immediately notice the uses of conjunctions to contrast two different concepts. The conjunctions are highlighted in gray (see Figure 1); each paragraph has two of them. The writer makes a contrast between what he calls "thing technology" and "idea technology." The single underlined words and phrases are related to "thing technology," and the double underlined parts to "idea technology." Note that each idea is paraphrased to explain the concepts. For example, to describe "idea technology," the writer says, "science creates concepts, ways of understanding the world." Then, "thing technology" is, "technological objects and processes."

> When we think about the technological impact of science, we tend to think of the things science has produced. But there is another kind of technology produced by science that has just as big an effect on us as thing technology. We might call it idea technology. In addition to creating things, science creates concepts, ways of understanding the world that have an enormous influence on how we think and act.
>
> However, there is something about "idea technology" that differentiates it from most of "thing technology". Whereas technological objects and processes generally don't affect our lives unless they work, idea technology can have profound effects on people even if the ideas are false. Let's call idea technology based on false ideas "ideology"...[2]

Figure 1. "'Human nature' is often a product of nurture," *WIRED*

The second article, "Morals and the machine," is taken from *The Economist*, June 2, 2012 (see Figure 2). This article uses many references and synonyms. Readers should be able to see that some of the different words mean the same thing. In this article, the topic "ethical decisions" is restated in several different forms: "moral judgments," "moral agency," "machine ethics," "the ethics of the robotics," and "robo-ethics." This suggests that the writer continues to convey that the important concept is "moral agency." Additionally, the word "robot" and its synonyms are repeated many times. Given that it is typical in English for repeated words to express the topic of the article or paragraph, it can be concluded that

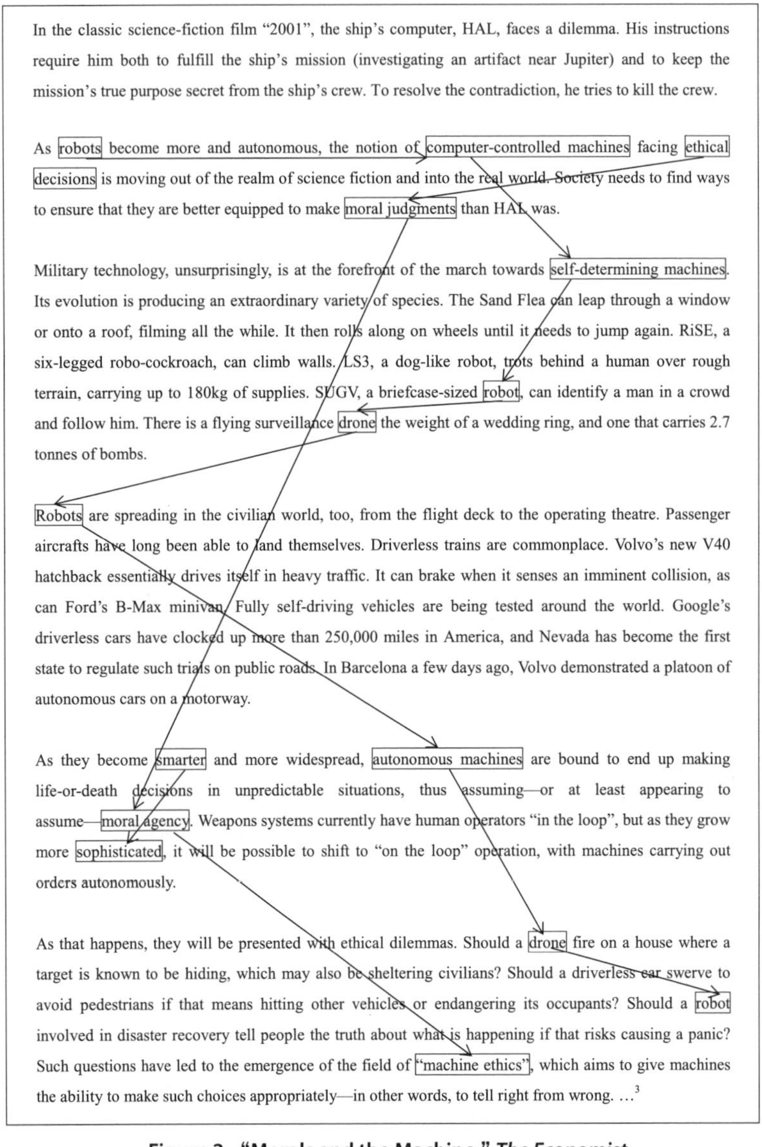

> In the classic science-fiction film "2001", the ship's computer, HAL, faces a dilemma. His instructions require him both to fulfill the ship's mission (investigating an artifact near Jupiter) and to keep the mission's true purpose secret from the ship's crew. To resolve the contradiction, he tries to kill the crew.
>
> As robots become more and autonomous, the notion of computer-controlled machines facing ethical decisions is moving out of the realm of science fiction and into the real world. Society needs to find ways to ensure that they are better equipped to make moral judgments than HAL was.
>
> Military technology, unsurprisingly, is at the forefront of the march towards self-determining machines. Its evolution is producing an extraordinary variety of species. The Sand Flea can leap through a window or onto a roof, filming all the while. It then rolls along on wheels until it needs to jump again. RiSE, a six-legged robo-cockroach, can climb walls. LS3, a dog-like robot, trots behind a human over rough terrain, carrying up to 180kg of supplies. SUGV, a briefcase-sized robot, can identify a man in a crowd and follow him. There is a flying surveillance drone the weight of a wedding ring, and one that carries 2.7 tonnes of bombs.
>
> Robots are spreading in the civilian world, too, from the flight deck to the operating theatre. Passenger aircrafts have long been able to land themselves. Driverless trains are commonplace. Volvo's new V40 hatchback essentially drives itself in heavy traffic. It can brake when it senses an imminent collision, as can Ford's B-Max minivan. Fully self-driving vehicles are being tested around the world. Google's driverless cars have clocked up more than 250,000 miles in America, and Nevada has become the first state to regulate such trials on public roads. In Barcelona a few days ago, Volvo demonstrated a platoon of autonomous cars on a motorway.
>
> As they become smarter and more widespread, autonomous machines are bound to end up making life-or-death decisions in unpredictable situations, thus assuming—or at least appearing to assume—moral agency. Weapons systems currently have human operators "in the loop", but as they grow more sophisticated, it will be possible to shift to "on the loop" operation, with machines carrying out orders autonomously.
>
> As that happens, they will be presented with ethical dilemmas. Should a drone fire on a house where a target is known to be hiding, which may also be sheltering civilians? Should a driverless car swerve to avoid pedestrians if that means hitting other vehicles or endangering its occupants? Should a robot involved in disaster recovery tell people the truth about what is happening if that risks causing a panic? Such questions have led to the emergence of the field of "machine ethics", which aims to give machines the ability to make such choices appropriately—in other words, to tell right from wrong. …[3]

Figure 2. "Morals and the Machine," *The Economist*

this article is about "robots" and "morals."

As shown above, it is beneficial to pay attention to cohesive devices when reading to find the topic of the text. Important messages are usually repeated throughout the text in the form of repetition, synonyms, or other categories such as hyponyms and collocation.

6. Conclusion

The first part of this paper reviewed cohesion and cohesive devices. The second part showed how cohesion is realized in authentic texts, specifically, magazine articles. This study aimed to highlight the importance of cohesion in EFL learning/teaching. As previous studies showed, non-native speakers of English can find it difficult to comprehend the overall message of a text because they do not pay enough attention to cohesion, especially conjunction and lexical cohesion. Therefore, the elements of cohesion should not be neglected but rather focused on in the EFL classroom.

A number of areas should be investigated in future studies. First, other cohesive elements, that is, ellipsis and substitution, should be taken into account for a more detailed analysis. Second, as a number of researchers claim (Thornbury 2005; Bloor & Bloor 2004), there are concepts other than cohesion that create texture. Bloor and Bloor (2004), for example, argue that "Given and New structure," or information structure, and "Theme and Rheme," or thematic structure, are other components of texture.

Notes
1. A different version of this article first appeared in *JALT2012 Conference Proceedings* published by the Japan Association of Language Teaching (reproduced with permission from the Japan Association of Language Teaching).
2. Only the first two paragraphs are reproduced here.
3. Only the first six paragraphs are reproduced here.

References
Bloor, Thomas and Meriel Bloor. (2004) *The Functional Analysis of English: A Hallidayan Approach (2nd edition)*. London: Arnold.

Chapman, John. (1983) *Reading Development and Cohesion*. London: Heinemann.

Cohen, Andrew, Hilary Glasman, Phyllis R. Rosenbaum-Cohen, Jonathan Ferrara, and Jonathan Fine. (1979) 'Reading English for specialized purposes: discourse analysis and the use of student informants'. *TESOL Quarterly* 13: pp. 551–564. [Reprinted in. Carrell et al. (1998) *Interactive Approaches to Second Language Reading*. pp. 152–167. Cambridge: Cambridge University Press.]

Grabe, William. (2009) *Reading in a Second Language: Moving from Theory to Practice*. Cambridge: Cambridge University Press.

Halliday, Michael A.K. and Ruqaiya Hasan. (1976) *Cohesion in English*. London: Longman.

McCarthy, Michael. (1991) *Discourse Analysis for Language Teachers*. Cambridge: Cambridge University Press.

Nuttal, Christine. (2005) *Teaching Reading Skills in a Foreign Language*. Oxford: Macmillan.

Terakawa, Kaori. (2013) Aspects of Cohesion and Their Application to English Teaching in Japan. In Nozomu Sonda and Aleda Krause. (eds.), *JALT2012 Conference Proceedings*. pp. 597–602. Tokyo: JALT.

Thornbury, Scott. (2005) *Beyond the Sentence: Introducing Discourse Analysis*. Oxford: Macmillan.

A Syntactic Approach to Language Variations of Aspectual Properties

Masashi Yamada

Abstract
This paper argues that the aspectual properties of predicates should be captured in Syntax and claims that observing different aspectual realizations between English and Japanese, the difference can be captured in the syntactic structure. In English, XP elements are responsible for conversion of an activity verb into a telic predicate, whereas in Japanese, X^0 ones are. This paper proposes Aspectual Parameter; a telic predicate can be constructed either by (i) XP or (ii) X^0. Each language has to select one of the two options. English selects (i), whereas Japanese (ii). I also propose a syntactic structure which accommodates a functional projection called 'Aspectual Phrase (=AspP)' whose head is specified as [+telic], following Borer (1994) and Travis (2003). The difference between English and Japanese can be accounted for by the different feature-checking mechanism, extending Alexiadou & Anagnostopoulou (1998). The proposal in this paper can account for (i) why an activity verb in English can be converted into a telic predicate only by attachment of AP or PP, and (ii) why Japanese needs a complex predicate to encode an activity verb into a telic predicate.

Keywords   aspectuality of predicates, feature checking, functional categories, parameter, complex predicates,

1. Introduction

This paper will discuss morphological differences between English and Japanese with respect to aspectual realizations. As observed in some studies (Kageyama 1996, Washio 1997), these two languages behave differently in the resultative construction or sentences containing a motion verb or a directed motion verb.

(1) a. John ran to the station.
    b. John hammered the metal flat.
    c. John kicked a ball into the goal.
(2) a. Taro-ga   eki-e   hasi-ttei-tta.
       Taro-NOM   a station-to run-go-PAST
       'Taro ran to the station.'
    b. John-ga   kinzoku-o   petyanko-ni tataki-tubusi-ta.
       John-NOM   the metal-ACC flat   pound-smash-PAST
       'John pounded the metal flat.'
    c. Taro-ga   booru-o   gooru-ni   keri-kon-da.
       Taro-NOM   ball-ACC   the goal-into kick-put into-PAST
       'Taro kicked a ball into the goal.'

In English these sentences can be relatively freely constructed if they contain an Adjectival Phrase (=AP) referring to the resultant state or a Prepositional Phrase (=PP) denoting a goal. In Japanese, on the other hand, in order to generate the sentences which have the same meaning as English examples in (1), we need to add to a main verb an additional verb which denotes a resultant state or a goal, such as (2). These language differences have been observed and analyzed in the semantic framework, but have not been accounted for in the syntactic field except Hasegawa (1998) for the resultative construction. It is crucial to notice that in the sentences in (1) and (2), the activity verbs are converted to be telic predicates. This suggests that these languages can be morphologically differentiated with respect to how to express a change of state or location. This paper will claim that the difference between (1) and (2) should be captured in the syntactic structure. I would like to propose a syntactic structure which accommodates a functional category inducing the aspectual properties, following Travis (2003). In the structure, the head of the functional category has a syntactic feature [+telic] which has to be licensed in Syntax. Alexiadou & Anagnostopoulou (1998) claim that the syntactic feature would be licensed either by XP or by X^0. Extending their proposal, I will assume that the [+telic] can be checked either by XP or X^0. I will claim that the choice of either XP or X^0 for checking [+telic] can capture the language differences of the aspectual properties of predicates. The morphological difference between (1) and (2) can be captured by the proposed syntactic structure and a feature checking mechanism.

This paper is composed of as follows. Section 2 reviews some studies on verb's classification (cf. Vendler 1967, Dowty 1979), on aspectual properties of predicates (Dowty 1991, Tenny 1988) and on the syntactic structure to capture aspectuality of predicates (Borer 1994). And then, based on Talmy's (1985) language typology of motion verbs, we will observe some English and Japanese constructions like (1) and (2) and propose an aspectual parameter. In Section 3, I will review Travis (2003) where a syntactic structure is proposed to deal with the aspectual properties of predicates and Alexiadou & Anagnostopoulou (1998) which propose that feature-checking is not only mediated by a Spec-Head relation but also by a Head-Head relation. In Section 4, I would like to propose a syntactic structure extending Travis (2003) and claim that the difference observed in (1) and (2) can be accounted for by means of the different feature-checking mechanism selected by each language. Section 5 concludes this paper and points out some extensions.

2. A short history of verb's classification and an aspectual parameter

This section provides us a short history of the verb's classification and language variations in terms of aspectual properties of predicates. Since Vendler's (1967) classification of verbs, many studies (cf. Vendler 1967, Dowty 1979, Dowty 1991, and Tenny 1988) have argued the nature of verbs and classified verbs by means of their properties. It is also shown that aspectuality is crucial to classify verbs or predicates. It has been discussed in Borer (1994) and Ritter & Rosen (1993) that aspectuality can be captured in Syntax. In this section, considering these studies, I will argue that aspectuality is a syntactic object and that it should be captured in Syntax. As I pointed out in (1) and (2), there exists a difference of morphological realization between English and Japanese. I will scrutinize some constructions in Japanese and English based on Talmy's (1985) typology and claim an aspectual parameter, which defines that a telic predicate is constructed by two options.

2.1 A short history of verb's classification

In this section, I will discuss the verb's classification and aspectuality of predicates, reviewing some crucial studies on the verbal or predicative aspect (cf. Vendler 1967, Dowty 1979) and show that telicity is the best way to account for the aspectuality of predicates (cf. Tenny 1988). And then, I will argue that the it can be captured in Syntax (cf. Borer 1994).

In the traditional literature of studies on verb's classification, Vendler (1967) points out that verbs can be classified based on a meaning of verbs. He claims that the verbs can be splited into four types; activity, state, achievement, and accomplishment. The activity verbs express an on-going event, whereas the state verbs denote the permanent or temporal state of individuals. The achievement verbs express an instantaneous event which is over as soon as it has begun, and the accomplishment verbs have a natural endpoint.

Dowty (1979) clarifies Vendler's classification with respect to logical entailments of verbs and interaction with temporal modifiers.

(3) a. activity : run, walk, swim, push a cart, drive a car, …
 b. state : know, believe, have, desire, love, understand, …
 c. achievement : recognize, spot, notice, find, reach, die, …
 d. accomplishment : paint a picture, make a chair, deliver a salmon, …

Each types of verbs behave differently, when being attached a progressive morpheme, *-ing*. The activity can occur with the *-ing*, but the state and the achievement cannot.

(4) a. *John is believing in the afterlife. (state)
 b. *Mary is recognizing John. (achievement)
 c. Mary is running. (activity)   (Rothstein 2004: 11)

(4c) means an on-going event of running and shows a progressive aspect. On the other hand, (4a) and (4b) are ungrammatical; thus, they do not have a progressive aspect. Only in some cases, state and achievement verbs can take a progressive aspect, like *The stocks are lying on the bed*, or *Our pizza is arriving*. But, these examples do not entail an ongoing event like activity verbs. This suggests that verbs are semantically classified in terms of whether each verb can take a progressive aspect.

The four-way classification, however, has some problems. First, it is not clearly apparent that verbs are classified either by properties of verbs or those of predicates. Scrutinizing (3), we notice that the activity in (3a) contains verbs and a predicate, *drive a car*. The members of the accomplishment, on the other hand, are all predicates. Therefore, the classification above is not so clear in terms of what type of categories is a criterion for classification. Second, this is merely a classification. Therefore, we need to explore its semantically higher-order theoretical basis.

Developing the four-way classification, verbs are classified into a two-way classification in terms of whether verbs contain an endpoint of the event described by a predicate. This is known as 'telicity' or 'delimitedness.' Instead of the four-way classification, this criterion of verb's classification is regarded as a semantically higher-order principle since it is developed on a highly abstract semantic concept like 'telicity' or 'delimitedness'. The accomplishment and the achievement have a clear endpoint of the event described by the predicate, while the activity and the stative do not. This suggests that the four types of verbs are integrated into the two-way classification, based on the telicity of verbs.

Telicity, however, is not within the verb's classification. Dowty (1991) claims that it can be specified by predicates, as well as by verbs. The telicity of predicates is determined, relying on the properties of their internal argument.

(5) a. John ate an apple { in ten minutes / *for ten minutes }.
    b. John ate apples { *in ten minutes / for ten minutes }.

In (5a) the predicate has a telic meaning since the sentence can occur with a time adverbial, *in ten minutes*, which can modify an eventuality within a temporal period of time, but cannot with the durative time adverbial, *for ten minutes*. In (5b), on the other hand, the predicate, *ate apples*, is atelic, since it can occur with *for ten minutes*. (5) leads us to conclude that aspectuality depends on the predicate composed of a main verb and its complement.

The question arises: Where the aspectual properties of predicates come from? Are they specified in the lexicon, in the argument structure, or in Syntax? Tenny (1988) proposes the Aspectual Interface Hypothesis to show that aspectuality has to be treated in Syntax.

(6) Aspectual Interface Hypothesis
    The mapping between cognitive (thematic) structure and syntactic argument structure is governed by aspectual properties. The aspectual properties associated with internal (direct), external and oblique (internal indirect) arguments constrain the kinds of event participants that can occupy these positions. Only the aspectual part of cognitive or thematic structure is visible to the syntax.   (Tenny 1988: 3)

Tenny says that telicity is a syntactic object and that it shoud be captured in Syntax.

Borer (1994) explores Tenny's hypothesis and proposes a syntactic structure which can capture the predicative aspect as a syntactic object. She assumes a functional category encoding the predicative aspect. She names it the Aspectual Phrase (= AspP) which is located between TP and VP.

(7) a. John ate three apples { in ten minutes / *for ten minutes. }
  b. [$_{TP}$ John [$_{AspP}$ Asp [$_{VP}$ eats three apples]
              [+telic]   [+telic]

Borer (1994) assumes that the head of AspP has a [+telic] feature and it has to be checked in the syntax through a Spec-Head relation, following Chomsky's (1995) feature checking mechanism. In (7b), a Theme DP covertly raises to [Spec, AspP] in order to check the [+telic] specified on Asp. This feature checking ensures that (7a) has a telic interpretation.

In sum, the Vendler's (1967) classification is subsumed under telicity of predicates. This semantic property, moreover, has to be captured in the syntactic structure, as Borer (1994) proposed. This paper stands for the analyses that aspectuality should be captured in the syntactic structure. I will discuss the syntactic structure for the aspectual property of predicates in Section 4.

In the next subsection, I will argue that the aspectual property of predicates appears differently in different languages. This paper will mainly observe different morphological realization between English and Japanese with respect to a telic aspect.

2.2 Aspectual Parameter

This section will observe aspectual differences between English and Japanese and propose a parameter that holds the difference, extending Talmy's (1985) typology of languages.

Talmy (1985) claims that languages can be classified into two types in terms of how motion verbs are constructed. According to Talmy, the motion verbs are differently composed by fusing the meaning of 'Motion' either with 'Manner' or with 'Path.' One type of the languages is called a 'Verb frame' language. Romance languages such as Italian, Spanish, and French belong to this group, in which motion verbs are constructed by integrating 'Move' with 'Path,' not with 'Manner.'

(8) a. La botella entro   a la   cueva (flatando).
       the bottle MOVE-in to the cave foating.
       'The boat floated into the cave.'
    b. Meti   el barril a la   bodega   rodandolo.
       I-MOVE-in the keg   to the storeroom rolling.
       'I rolled the keg into the storeroom.'   (Talmy 1985: 69–70)

In Italian motion verbs, *entro* and *Meti* in (8), 'Path' is fused with 'Motion.' 'Manner' is externalized out of the verb as modifiers.

Another type of the languages is called a 'Satellite frame' language. Germanic languages like English and German are members of this type. In this type, 'Motion' is fused with 'Manner,' rather than 'Path.'

(9) a. The rock slid / rolled / bounced down the hill.
    b. I ran / jumped / stumbled / rushed / groped / my way down the stairs.   (Talmy 1985: 63)

In English, 'Motion' is tied up with 'Manner,' but 'Path' is externalized.

Talmy's (1985) typology can nicely account for language variations on motion verbs in terms of which element 'Motion' can easily accept, 'Manner' or 'Path.'

Which type does Japanese belong to? Tanaka and Matsumoto (1997) mention that Japanese belongs to the 'verb frame' language, observing the following data.

(10) a. iku 'go,' kuru 'come,' noboru 'climb,' oriru 'descend,' otiru 'fall,' kaeru 'go back,' koeru 'go across,' wataru 'go across,' tassuru 'reach,' …
     b. aruku 'walk,' hasiru 'run,' hau 'crawl,' korogaru 'roll,' …
                                   (Tanaka and Matsumoto 1997: 141–143)

In Japanese, motion verbs fused with 'Path' in (10a) are more frequently observed than the verbs with 'Manner' in (10b); therefore, Japanese is in the same slot as Romance languages. This means that Japanese is different from English in terms of how to construct motion verbs. In addition to this difference, these two languages have another difference in motion verbs.

These languages have a different flavor when a motion verb appears with a directional phrase. As is well known, the motion verbs are inherently atelic, but they would turn to be telic, if they take a goal phrase.

(11) a. John ran { for an hour / *in an hour }.
　　b. John ran to the station { *for an hour / in an hour }.

In (11a) the verb, *run*, is atelic since it is modified by a durative time adverbial, *for an hour*, but not by *in an hour*. In (11b), on the other hand, the reverse can be true. The goal phrase, *to the station*, converts an atelic predicate into a telic one. This suggests that attaching a goal phrase changes the aspectual property of the predicate.

The same is not observed in Japanese.

(12) a. Taro-ga　　{ itizikan　　/ *itizikan-de } hasi-tta.
　　　　Taro-NOM　{ for an hour /　in an hour } run-PAST
　　b. ?*Taro-ga　　eki-e　　{ itizikan　　/ itizikan-de } hasi-tta.
　　　　Taro-NOM　a station-to　{ for an hour / in an hour } run-PAST

As in English, the Japanese motion verb is also atelic in nature. The sentence with a goal phrase in (12b), however, is at most marginal. If it would be acceptable, it does not denote runner's arrival to the station. This indicates that the presence of a goal PP does not affect aspectuality of the predicate. The sentence is, however, ameliorated if the predicate takes an additional verb which means change of location, *-iku*.

(13) Taro-ga　　eki-e　　　{*itizikan　　/ itizikan-de} hasi-ttei-tta.
　　　Taro-NOM　a station-to　{ for an hour / in an hour} run-go-PAST
　　'Taro ran to the station.'

In (13), the sentence is telic, because it can be with a time-span modifier, *itizikan-de* 'in an hour.' The formation of a complex predicate makes a Japanese motion predicate telic. In this respect, Japanese has more complex morphological process than English.

The same is also observed in sentences containing a directional motion verb. In English, the sentences below express the event that an affected object moves to a goal indicated by a PP.

(14) a. John pushed the cart into the shop.
　　b. John kicked a ball into the goal.

(14a) means that the cart was moved into the shop after John's pushing the cart. (14b) means that the ball kicked by John also flied into the goal, and John got a point. These facts suggest that in English the activity verb with a goal phrase can express the event of change of location. In Japanese, on the other hand, an activity verb with a goal phrase cannot express the event of reaching to a goal.

(15) a. Taro-ga   booru-o   gooru-ni   ket-ta.
       Taro-NOM   ball-ACC   the goal-into kick-PAST
    b. Taro-ga   kaato-o   omise-ni   osi-ta.
       Taro-NOM   the cart-ACC the shop-into push-PAST

These sentences can only express the event of Taro's intentional motion. They do not express the event that affected objects get into intended goals. These sentences, however, would make grammatically perfect and have a meaning of change of location, when they take an additional verb to the main verb to construct complex predicates.

(16) a. Taro-ga   booru-o   gooru-ni   keri-kon-da.
       Taro-NOM   ball-ACC   the goal-into kick-put into-PAST
    b. Taro-ga   kaato-o   omise-ni   osi-tei-tta.
       Taro-NOM   the cart-ACC the shop-into pushed-go into-PAST

These sentences have the same meaning as the English ones in (14). Like motion verbs, the formation of the complex predicate is obligatory to have the same meaning as English even in a predicate containing a directional motion verb.

Moreover, the aspectual difference between English and Japanese goes beyond these two types of verbs. The resultative construction also shows the same syntactic and morphological behavior.

Washio (1997) and Kageyama (1996) notice that the resultative construction has two variations. One is called 'Strong Resultative' which is derived from activity verbs. In this type of the resultatives, an atelic predicate is made telic only by being attached a resultative AP such as (17a). The other type of the resultatives is named 'Weak Resultative' that is derived from accomplishment or achievement verbs, like (17b). The verbs in this type of the resultatives have a resultant state in nature. The resultative phrase makes explicit the resultant state which the verb originally contains.

(17)a. John hammered the metal flat.
   b. Mary dyed the dress pink. (Washio 1997: 5)

In English, both types of the resultative construction can be relatively freely constructed, while in Japanese, the 'Weak Resultatives' can be easily formed such as (18b), but the 'Strong Resultative' cannot, like (18a).

(18)a.?? John-ga   kinzoku-o   petyanko-ni   tatai-ta.
       John-NOM   the metal-ACC   flat   pound-PAST
       'John pounded the metal flat.'
   b. Mary-ga   doresu-o   pinku-ni   some-ta.
       Mary-NOM   the dress-ACC   pink   dye-PAST
       'Mary dyed the dress pink.'   (Washio 1997: 5)

These data suggest that Japanese resultatives are restricted by the type of main verbs.

Japanese, however, permits 'Strong Resultative' in a certain condition.

(19) John-ga   kinzoku-o   petyanko-ni   tataki-tubusi-ta.
      John-NOM   the metal-ACC   flat   pound-smash-PAST
      'John pounded the metal flat.'

Different from (18a), (19) has a complex predicate, in which the main verb is amalgamated with the secondary verb which expresses the resultant state of the affected object. The forming a complex predicate, therefore, enables us to make a grammatical resultative sentence.

As we have observed three constructions above, we notice that there exists a difference between Japanese and English in terms of encoding an activity verb into a telic predicate. In English, DP, AP and PP are responsible for making telic predicates, whereas in Japanese, the formation of the complex predicate is a crucial factor for making them. Considering the observations above, we can conclude that in English phrasal-level elements contribute to producing telic predicates, whereas in Japanese head-level elements, especially a complex predicate formation, do. Therefore, it may be said that we have two options to encode an atelic predicate into a telic one and each language selects one of the two options. I, thus, propose the following parameter concerning aspectual properties of predicates.

(20) Aspectual Parameter
 The telic predicate can be constructed either by (i) XP elements or by (ii) X^0 elements. Each language selects either (i) or (ii).

In this parameter, English selects (i), whereas Japanese (ii). This parameter setting can account for why the complex predicate formation is obligatory to convert an activity verb to a telic predicate in Japanese.

This paper will propose in Section 4 that this parameter can be captured by the feature checking mechanism in Syntax[1].

3. Syntactic structures and feature checking mechanism

In the above section, I proposed the aspectual parameter, observing some constructions of English and Japanese. In English, the XP takes to licensing of the aspectual properties, whereas in Japanese the X^0 does.

In this section, before proposing my syntactic analysis in Section 4, I would like to review some analyses concerning a syntactic structure to capture the aspectual properties of predicates (cf. Travis 2003) and feature checking mechanism in the syntactic structure (cf. Alexiadou & Anagnostopoulou 1998).

3.1 Travis (2003)

As I mentioned above, Tenny (1988) proposes Aspectual Interface Hypothesis that the aspectual properties of predicates can be a syntactic object, and they should be captured in the syntactic structure. Extending her proposal, Borer (1994), Ritter and Rosen (1993) and cited therein claim that there exists a functional projection encoding the predicative aspect in a syntactic tree. It has been called the Aspectual Phrase (= AspP). In this projection an aspectual feature is licensed in order to ensure that the predicate encodes a telic meaning. The sentence in (21a) has the syntactic structure in (21b).

(21) a. John ate three apples { in ten minutes / *for ten minutes. }
  b. [$_{TP}$ John [$_{AspP}$ Asp [$_{VP}$ eats three apples]
             [+telic]   [+telic]

In (21b), a Theme DP with a [+telic] feature covertly raises to [Spec, AspP] in order to check the [+telic] specified on Asp, following feature-checking mechanism proposed by Chomsky (1995). This feature-checking ensures that (21a) has a telic interpretation.

In the flow of the studies on how we treat aspectuality of predicates with respect to the syntactic structure, Travis's (2003) proposal seems to be the most remarkable syntactic structure which can deal with the language variations. I will review her proposal below.

Travis (2003) claims that the locus of aspectual licensing is not only in the AspP, but also at other two syntactic positions, that is a little v and an X in the head of XP projected as a complement of V. Aspectuality can be marked in different positions in different languages. The structure proposed by Travis is in the following.

(22) [$_{vP}$ v [$_{AspP}$ DP Asp [$_{VP}$ V [$_{XP}$ X]

The Bulgarian facts illustrate that aspectualiy is produced in the head of vP. In this language, telicity is in tandem with agentivity of verbs, as shown in (23).

(23) a. Kounot   raz-smja / raz-plaka   bebeto.
      Clown   pv-laugh / pv-laugh   baby
     'The clown laughed/cried the baby.
   b. Toj na-pis-a   pisma   *3 casa   / za 3 casa
     he   pv-write   letters   for three hours / in three hours
     'He wrote the letters in three hours.'   (Travis 2003: 319–320)

In (23a), the preverbal morpheme, *raz-*, adds an agent to the root verb and has the verb phrase express the causative event. In (23b), in addition to a causative meaning, *na-* creates a telic predicate. Travis (2003) claims that this morpheme appears in the head of vP and marks causality and telicity of the predicate. The element in v, therefore, is responsibile for telicity of the Bulgarian predicates.

The aspectuality of predicates is also determined in AspP, as I mentioned above. In English, an internal argument contributes to producing a telic meaning. In (24), the definiteness of an internal argument affects aspectuality of the predicate.

(24) a. The children ate the muffin { in three minutes / *for three minutes }.
   b. The children are muffins {*in three minutes / for three minutes }.

As proposed by Borer (1994), Travis (2003) also claims that aspectuality is licensed in AspP.

As for telicity in XP, it is realized as an AP or a PP. As I mentioned above, in the resultative construction and directed motion predicates, the resultative phrase or the goal phrase convert an atelic predicate into a telic one.

(25) a. John hammered the metal thin.
b. John kicked a ball into the goal.

Chinese is a language which uses the XP in order to make a telic predicate, as shown in the following:

(26) a. wo zuootian xie-le yifeng xin, keshi mei xie-wan
I yesterday write-LE one-CL letter but not write-finish
? 'I wrote a letter yesterday, but I didn't finish it.'
b. *wo zuotian xie-wan-le yi-feng xin, keshi mei
I yesterday write-finish-LE one-CL letter but not
xie-wan.
write-finish
? 'I wrote a letter yesterday, but I didn't finish it.'
(Travis 2003: 316–317)

In (26) without a special marker, -*wan*, the verb does not entail a telic event. To ensure a telic meaning, the marker appears in X and fuses with the main verb.

In sum, Travis (2003) proposes the three-layered syntactic structure for producing a telic meaning. Each language selects the positions where the aspectuality of predicates is licensed. This paper basically follows her analysis in that the languages differ in how aspectuality of predicates is licensed in the syntactic structure. I will, however, propose a simpler syntactic structure to account for the aspectuality of predicates in Syntax and their language differences in Section 4.

3.2 Alexiadou & Anagnostopoulou (1998)

In the previous subsection, I have reviewed the study which claims that the aspectual properties can be captured in the syntactic structure. Travis (2003) claims that the aspectual properties are induced in three syntactic positions. In this section, I would like to sum up Alexiadou &

Anagnostopoulou (1998) (hereafter A&A 1998), which propose a parameter that the Extended Projection Principle (=EPP) feature may be checked either by move/merge XP or by merge/move X^0, observing the cross-linguistic variations of word order and expletive constructions.

In the literature in the Minimalist Program, Chomsky (1995) claims that T has a [+EPP] feature which has to be checked through a Spec-Head agreement in TP. As for English, a DP with a [D] feature is raised from its base-generated position, [Spec, vP], to the [Spec, TP] in order to check the [EPP] on T. In VSO languages, however, the subject is not in [Spec, TP], as in the following.

(27) a. efige   o Petros.
      left   Peter
      'Peter left.'
   b. ektise   I Maria   to spiti.
      built   Mary   house
      'Mary built the house.'   (A&A 1998: 495)

It is well known that an English inverted subject is restricted to an indefinite noun. In VSO languages, on the other hand, the restriction is not observed; therefore, a strong quantified NP can be in a subject position in the inverted construction.

(28) irthe   to   kathe   pedi.
      arrived   the   every   children   (A&A 1998: 496)

It is suggested that the subject in VSO languages is different from the subject in SVO languages in the syntactic status. A&A (1998) point out that the way of EPP-feature checking is not universal. They note that in VSO languages verbal agreement has the same categorical status as a DP in English. The following facts illustrate that VSO languages have rich verbal morphemes.

(29) a. I love   we love   b. agap**o**   agap**ame**
      you love you love   agap**as**   agap**ate**
      he loves   they love   agap**a**   agap**ane**
                                                     (A&A 1998: 517)

In this language, the EPP in T does not have to be checked by the subject

DP. A&A (1998) claim that instead of DP, the agreement morpheme has an ability to check EPP. The EPP in this language may be checked by the agreement morpheme via V-raising to T. This suggests that the EPP feature can be checked not only by a DP, but by an agreement morpheme. A&A (1998) claim that the element for EPP checking is parameterized. It has to be checked by a XP in some languages, or by an X^0 element in other languages. Each language selects either of the two options.

A&A (1998)'s claim on the mechanism of EPP-feature checking suggests that the way of feature checking in the functional categories can be parameterized and it may be checked by either by XP or X^0. Extending this, I would like to propose in the next section that a [+telic] feature specified in the head of AspP can be checked either by XP or X^0 in the syntactic structure.

4. Proposal

In this section, adopting Travis (2003) and A&A (1998), which I have reviewed in the previous section, I would like to consider how the aspectual licensing can be captured in Syntax, and how the language variation of aspectual realization can be accounted for.

I assume the following syntactic structure, basically following Travis (2003).

(30) [$_{vP}$ v [$_{AspP}$ Asp [$_{VP}$ V DP]]]
            [+telic]

As I have reviewed in Section 2.1 and Section 3.1, the aspectual phrase is the locus of producing aspectuality of a predicate. This functional category is projected between vP and VP. This category is independently motivated from vP, where the agentivity and the objective Case are marked. Travis (2003) assumes that aspectuality is marked in three syntactic positions. This paper, however, assumes that only the head of the AspP is responsible for the aspectual properties in the syntactic structure. The language difference is not captured by syntactic positions, but by feature checking mechanism in the syntactic structure in (30).

If the Asp takes as its complement a VP which contains any element denoting definiteness, resultant state or a final location, it would be specified as [+telic]; otherwise, it won't. When the feature can be properly checked in the syntactic structure, the sentence is ensured to have a telic meaning. Following A&A (1998), I propose that the [+telic] specified in the head of AspP has to be licensed either by XP or X⁰ in Syntax. Each language selects out of XP or X⁰, following the Aspectual Parameter in (20). English selects XP, while Japanese picks X⁰ out.

In English, the XP is responsible for inducing a telic meaning. Especially, definiteness of a DP is responsible for the aspectuality of the predicate. In (31a) the definite noun phrase, *three apples*, affects the telicity of the predicate, *ate three apples*. The Asp selects the VP containing DP$_{[telic]}$. This selection activates the [+telic] feature on Asp. The feature is specified on Asp, and then, it has to be checked in Syntax.

(31) a. John ate three apples in ten minutes.
   b. [$_{vP}$ v [$_{AspP}$ Asp [$_{VP}$ V DP$_{[+telic]}$]]]
               [+telic] ←   Agree   →|

[+telic] can be checked by the DP through Agree, which is proposed by Chomsky (2000). The feature on the head of AspP is checked without any movement of the DP.

The same analysis is applied to the resultative construction and the sentence containing a directional motion verb.

(32) a. John ran the pavement thin.
   b. John kicked the ball into the goal.
   c. [$_{vP}$ v [$_{AspP}$ Asp [$_{VP}$ V AP/PP$_{[+telic]}$]]]
               [+telic] ←   Agree   →|

In (32), the PP and the AP work as a delimiter; thus, the [+telic] is specified on Asp since the head of the AspP takes a complement the VP containing an element with [+telic]. The [+telic] feature on Asp can be properly checked through an Agree relation with the feature on the AP or the PP. It can be correctly predicted in the syntactic structure in (32c) that these sentences have a meaning of change of state or location.

(33), however, the AP/PP cannot play any role for a delimiter. In these sentences, VP does not contain any element with [+telic]. The Asp, thus, is deactivated and is not projected in Syntax like (33c).

(33) a. John danced in the room.
   b. John kicked the ball in the park.
   c. [$_{vP}$ v [$_{VP}$ V AP/PP$_{[-telic]}$]]]

If AspP is not projected in the syntactic structure, these sentences do not have a telic meaning. This suggests that telicity of the predicate can be differentiated by whether the AspP is projected in the syntactic structure or not.

This analysis in this paper can nicely account for the fact that English can relatively freely form the resultative construction and make a sentence denoting change of state or location.

In Japanese, on the other hand, an XP element does not matter in terms of the aspectual properties of predicates. Instead of XP, an X^0 element is crucially responsible for the property, as suggested in Section 2.2.

(34) a. Taro-ga   eki-e   {*itizikan   / itizikan-de } hasi-ttei-tta.
         Taro-NOM a station-to { for an hour / in an hour } run-go-PAST
         'Taro run to the station.'
     b. [$_{vP}$ v [$_{AspP}$ Asp [$_{VP}$ V PP$_{[+telic]}$]]]
         [+telic] ← Morphologically realized as '-iku'

The formation of the complex verb makes (34a) grammatical. (34a) has the syntactic structure in (34b) where a PP is a goal phrase and the Asp is activated by the VP which has a PP with [+telic]. Japanese takes an X^0 from the aspectual parameter; thus, PP$_{[+telic]}$ cannot work as a checker for the [+telic] in the head of AspP. It only activates the [+telic] feature in the head of AspP. In order to check the activated [+telic] feature on Asp, the [+telic] realizes as a verbal morpheme, -iku and forms the complex predicate.

This analysis also extends to Japanese resultative constructions.

(35) a. Mary-ga   doresu-o   pinku-ni   some-ta.
         Mary-NOM   the dress-ACC   pink   dye-PAST
         'Mary dyed the dress pink.'
     b. ??John-ga   kinzoku-o   petyanko-ni   tatai-ta.
         John-NOM   the metal-ACC   flat   pound-PAST
     c. John-ga   kinzoku-o   petyanko-ni   tataki-tubusi-ta.
         John-NOM   the metal-ACC   flat   pound-smash-PAST
         'John pounded the metal flat.'

(35a) and (35c) respectively have the following syntactic structures.

(36) a. [$_{vP}$ v [$_{AspP}$ Asp [$_{VP}$ V AP$_{[+telic]}$]]]
    [+telic] ← [+telic]
 b. [$_{vP}$ v [$_{AspP}$ Asp [$_{VP}$ V AP$_{[+telic]}$]]]
    [+telic] ← Morphologically realized as '-*someru*'

In (36), AP$_{[+telic]}$ activates [+telic] on Asp. In (36a), the change of state verb, *some-ru*, is a main verb, which inherently has a [+telic] feature. The feature licenses the [+telic] on Asp through Agree relation with the main verb. (36b), however, has a activity verb as a main verb, which does not have [+telic]. In this case, the [+telic] on Asp cannot be checked by an X^0 element in its complement. In order to check [+telic] on Asp, the main verb, *tataku*, calls on another verb for aid. The [+telic] feature on Asp realizes as the verb, which means a resultant state, *tubu-su*, forming the complex predicate, *tataki-tubusu*. This syntactic operation ameliorates the sentence in (35b). This analysis can account for the fact that Japanese can form 'Weak Resultatives,' but cannot form 'Strong Resultative,' with a single verb, and the latter type of the resultative construction is forced to form a complex predicate.

In this section, I have proposed a syntactic structure which can easily account for the morphological difference of aspectuality in English and Japanese. The proposed syntactic structure accommodates a functional category, AspP, whose head is specified as [+telic] when the Asp takes as a complement a VP containing the item denoting change of state or location. The feature on Asp can be licensed by XP or X^0. The choice is determined by the Aspectual Parameter in (20). English selects XP, whereas Japanese X^0. In English the [+telic] should be checked by DP, AP, or PP with [+telic]. Therefore, English can easily convert an atelic predicate to be a telic one only by attachment of AP or PP. In Japanese, however, the [+telic] should be licensed by a verb. The feature needs to be checked by the verb denoting change of state or location in nature or to realize as an additional verb to form a complex predicate. This proposal can account for why Japanese needs a complex predicate to encode an activity verb into a telic predicate.

I will summarize this paper and discuss some extensions of my proposal in Section 5.

5. Concluding remarks

This paper has discussed the differences of aspectual realization in English and Japanese and proposed (i) the aspectual parameter where selection of XP or X^0 is responsible for encoding a telic predicate and (ii) the syntactic structure which can capture (i). In the proposed syntactic structure, the head of AspP has a [+telic] feature if it takes as an its complement a VP which contains an item denoting a telic aspect. In English, the [+telic] on Asp should be checked by XP elements in a VP through Agree. In Japanese, on the other hand, it has to be realized as a morphological element since Japanese selects a X^0 element to induce a telic meaning. These proposals provide a theoretical basis for the language differences in (1) and (2).

The different aspectual realization in English and Japanese is beyond verbal predicates. It is also observed in noun phrases.

(37) a. bark   b. bite
(38) a. hoe*(-goe)   b. kami*(-kizu)
     bark-voice   bite-hurt

English has a so-called zero-derivation: thus, verbs can be converted into deverbal nouns without any morphological elements like (37). In Japanese, on the other hand, deverbal nouns are not simply derived from verbs. In (38), the verbs, *hoe-ru* and *kam-u*, are nominalized like *hoe-* and *kami-*. These morphemes do not independently work as words. They have to appear together with head nouns like *-koe* and *-kizu*, which express the items changed or produced after the event denoted by an original verb. This means that Japanese deverbal nouns have to come out with the item denoting change of state.

The difference, moreover, is seen in adjectival morphemes.

(39) a. yaki-tate-no   pan   b. nomi-kake-no   wain
        bake-TATE-GEN bread   drink-KAKE- GEN wine
        'the bread which has jus baked' 'the wine which has half drunk'

-tate means that an event has just finished, while *-kake* denotes an event which has been done on the way or has partly finished. English does not have adjectival morphemes corresponding to these morphemes in Japanese; therefore, it can be said that Japanese adjectival morphemes are more sensitive to verbal aspect and that they have to be morphologically realized.

The remaining of issues in this paper is that we should consider how to extend the proposal in this paper to the peculiar morphological facts seen in (38) and (39).

Note
1. Snyder (2001) observes language variations of resultatives, verb-particle constructions, *make*-causative constructions and other four syntactic patterns, and then proposes the following parameter.

   (i) Compounding Parameter
   The grammar { disallow*, allows } formation of endocentric compounds during syntactic variation. [+unmarked value]

   In Snyder's analysis, English has the same parametric value as Japanese, since both of them have a N-N compounding. As I argued in the text, English is clearly different from Japanese in terms of formation of a V-V compounding to compose a telic predicate. I, therefore, do not adopt his parameter and propose the parameter in (20).

References

Alexiadou, Artemis & Elena Anagnostopoulou (1998) Parameterzing AGR: Word Order, V-movement and EPP-checking. *Natural Language and Linguistic Theory* 16, 491–539.

Borer, Hagit (1994) The Projection of Arguments. Benedicto, E. Elena & Jeffrey T. Runer (eds.), *Functional Projections. University of Massachusetts Occasional Papers in Linguistics* 17, 19–47.

Chomsky, Noam (1995) *The Minimalist Program*. Cambridge, Mass.: MIT Press.

Chomsky, Noam (2000) Minimalist Inquiries: The Framework. In Roger Martin, David Michels, and Jua Uriagereka (eds.), *Step by Step: Essays on Minimalist Syntax in Honor of Howard Lasnik*. 89–156. Cambridge, Mass.: MIT Press.

Dowty, David (1979) *Word Meaning and Montague Grammar*. Dordrecht: Kluwer.

Dowty, David (1991) Thematic Proto-roles and Argument Selection. *Language* 67, 546–619.

Hasegawa, Nobuko (1998) Syntax of Resultatives. In Kazuko, Inoue (ed.), *Researching and Verifying an Advanced Theory of Human Language* 2-(A), 31–58. Kanda University of International Studies.

Kageyama, Taro (1996) *Doo-shi Imi-ron (Semantics of Verbs)*. Tokyo: Kuroshio Publisher.

Ritter, Elizabeth & Sara Thomas Rosen (1993) Deriving Causation. *Natural Language and Linguistic Theory* 11, 519–556.

Rothstein, Susan (2004) *Structuring Events: A Study in the Semantics of Lexical Aspect*. Maiden, Mass.: Blackwell Publishing.

Snyder, William (2001) On the Nature of Syntactic Variation: Evidence from Complex Predicates and Complex Word-formation. *Language* 77(2), 324–342.

Talmy, Leonard (1985) Lexicalization Pattern: Semantic Structure in Lexical Forms. In Tim Shopen (ed.), *Language Typology and Syntactic Description (vol. 3): Grammatical categories and the Lexicon*, 57–149. Cambridge, Mass.: Cambridge University Press.

Tanaka, Shigenori & Yo Matsumoto (1997) *Kuukan-to Idoo-no Hyogen (Expressions of Space and Movement)*, Tokyo: Kenkyu-sya.

Tenny, Carol (1988) The Aspectual Interface Hypothesis: The Connection between Syntax and Lexical Semantics. In Carol Tenny (ed), *Studies in Generative Approaches to Aspect. Lexicon Project Working Papers* 24. Cambridge, Mass.: MIT Press.

Travis, Lisa (2003) Lexical Items and Zero Morphology. In Liceras, M. Junna, et al (eds.), *Proceedings of the 6th Generative Approaches to Second Language Acquisition Conference*, 315–330. Somerville, Mass.: Cascadilla Proceedings Project.

Vendler, Zeno (1967) *Linguistics in Philosophy*. Ithaca, NY: Cornell.

Washio, Ryuichi (1997) Resultatives, Compositionality and Language Variation. *Journal of East Asian Linguistics* 6, 1–49.

Jokes and Semantic Blinking: A Conceptual Blending Analysis

Kazuya Yasuhara

Abstract
This paper analyzes how the humorous (or comical) effect of jokes is constructed within the theoretical framework of Conceptual Blending Theory (cf. Fauconnier & Turner 1994, 1998, 2002, 2006), with its special focus on two types of Japanese jokes (more specifically, Construal Jokes and Framing Jokes). In so doing, the paper reveals that the general cognitive process widely known as Conceptual Blending is deeply involved in the meaning construction of jokes. In addition, it suggests that the humorous effect of jokes can occur as a result of *Semantic Blinking* in the blended space: (i) Blinking Compression leads to Semantic Blinking, and (ii) Semantic Blinking invokes the humorous (or comical) effect of jokes (i.e. laughter). Generally speaking, this adds further supportive evidence to the theoretical framework of Conceptual Blending, especially within the domains of literary studies and humor research.

Keywords   joke, humor, conceptual blending, profiling, frame

1. Introduction

While it can be an interesting research topic, the study of language play has hardly received attention in the literature of traditional linguistics. In fact, such a shadowy relationship can also be easily understood from the following Crystal's (1998) observation:

(1) Ludic language has traditionally been a badly neglected subject of linguistic enquiry — at best treated as a topic of marginal interest, at worst never mentioned at all.   (Crystal 1998 : 1)

With this kind of situation in mind, this paper provides an opportunity to examine how linguistics and the study of language play are closely related to each other.

More specifically, the purpose of this paper is to analyze how the humorous (or comical) effect of jokes is constructed within the theoretical framework of Conceptual Blending Theory (cf. Fauconnier & Turner 1994, 1998, 2002, 2006), with its special focus on two types of Japanese jokes. In so doing, the paper reveals that the general cognitive process widely known as Conceptual Blending is deeply involved in the meaning construction of jokes. In addition, it suggests that the humorous effect of jokes can occur as a result of *Semantic Blinking* in the blended space. Generally speaking, this adds further supportive evidence to the theoretical framework of Conceptual Blending, especially within the domains of literary studies and humor research.

2. Conceptual Blending Theory

In the research context of cognitive linguistics (or cognitive semantics), the framework of Conceptual Blending has been proposed and developed by Fauconnier & Turner (1994, 1998, 2002, 2006). Conceptual Blending is a general cognitive operation for online meaning construction, and it is routinely employed in a variety of cognitive domains as a foundation for the creativity of human thought. The constitutive principles of Conceptual Blending are basically quite simple, and they are summarized as follows [see Figure 1]:

(2) A. *Partial Cross-Space Mappings* mean partial mappings of counterparts between the Input Spaces I_1 and I_2.
 B. *Generic Space* contains some common (usually more abstract) structure and organization shared by the Inputs I_1 and I_2.
 C. *Selective Projection to the Blend* stands for the partial projection of the Inputs I_1 and I_2 onto the Blended Space. Hence, all the elements and relations in the Inputs are not necessarily transferred into the Blend.
 D. *Development of Emergent Structure*: The Blended Space has emergent structure not provided by the Inputs, via the following three interrelated ways (for convenience, the box in the Blend represents emergent structure here).
   a. *Composition* that means projections of elements and relations

from the Inputs
b. *Completion* that recruits frames and scenarios from our long-term memory on the basis of pattern agreement
c. *Elaboration* through "running the blend" imaginatively according to its own emergent logic (i.e. mental simulation or mental imaging)

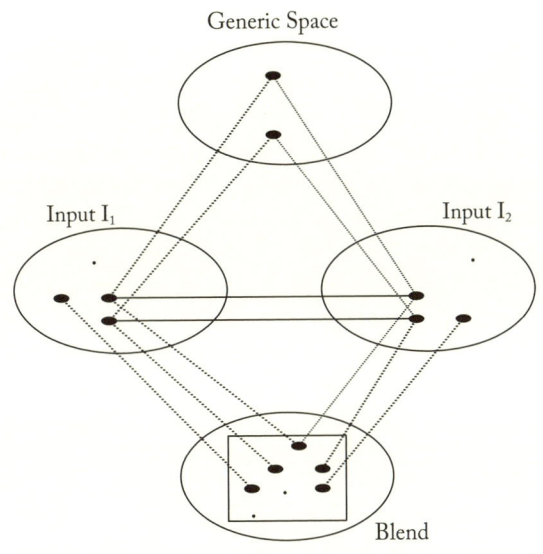

Figure 1. Basic Diagram (Fauconnier & Turner 2002: 46)

In previous research, as convergent evidence for the existence of Conceptual Blending, a number of researchers have revealed the workings of this general cognitive process within a wide range of cognitive domains. To the best of my knowledge, research areas related to this range from language in general to literary works and signed language, and even to mathematics and music (for more details, see the blending website *http://blending.stanford.edu/*):

(3) a. *Language:* Turner & Fauconnier (1995), Fauconnier & Turner (1996), Mandelblit (1997), Sweetser (1999), Grady, et al. (1999), Coulson (2001), Yasuhara (2012)
   b. *Literary Works:* Turner (1996), Freeman (2005), Hiraga (2005)
   c. *Signed Language:* Liddell (2003), Dudis (2004)
   d. *Mathematics:* Robert (1998), Lakoff & Núñez (2000)

e. *Music:* Zbikowski (2001), Sayrs (2003)

To arrive at a deeper understanding of Conceptual Blending Theory, let us here consider the following metaphorical example discussed in Grady, et al. (1999):

(4) This surgeon is a butcher.   (Grady, et al. 1999: 103)

Since Lakoff & Johnson's (1980) discussion of Conceptual Metaphor Theory, the research topic of metaphors has been widely recognized as a prime object of investigation in the field of cognitive linguistics (or cognitive semantics). In Conceptual Metaphor Theory, metaphorical phenomena are generally described and explained by a simple cognitive model such as unidirectional mapping relations from Source Domain to Target Domain [see Figure 2]. However, Conceptual Blending Theory takes a negative position toward this kind of cognitive model, pointing out that there are metaphorical examples that cannot be explained by Lakoff & Johnson's (1980, 1999) two-domain model of metaphors.[1] One representative example of this is indeed the above example (4).

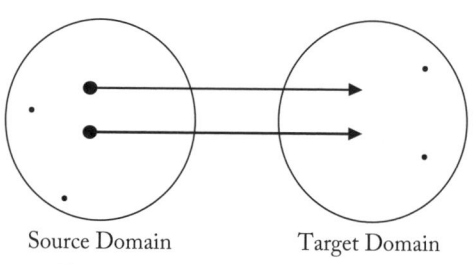

Source Domain   Target Domain
Figure 2. Conceptual Metaphor Theory

According to Grady, et al. (1999), it is claimed that the metaphorical example (4) can be understood as a statement about "an incompetent surgeon". When this example is analyzed in terms of Lakoff & Johnson's (1980, 1999) two-domain model, the metaphorical structure may be explained as unidirectional mappings from the source domain of Butchery to the target domain of Surgery: i.e. "by a series of fixed counterpart mappings: "butcher" onto "surgeon"; "animal" (cow) maps onto "human being"; "commodity" onto "patient"; "cleaver" onto "scalpel"; and so forth" (Grady, et al. 1999: 103). However, what is problematic here is that this kind of analysis cannot offer an important implication of this statement: "the surgeon is incompetent". As Grady, et al. (1999) observe, this is because "A butcher, though less prestigious than a surgeon, is typically competent at what he does and may be highly respected." (Grady, et al. 1999: 103). Hence, it is important to note that the notion of incompetence cannot be established via the traditional two-domain model of metaphors (i.e. direct projection from Source Domain to Target Domain). Intuitively speaking, this notion of incompetence can be conceived as resulting from the partial fusion of Surgeon and Butcher. However, Lakoff & Johnson's (1980, 1999) two-domain model fails to achieve this kind of inference, because the model does not assume any cognitive mechanism for dealing with this kind of partial fusion.

In contrast, Conceptual Blending Theory can explain this notion of incompetence in a straightforward way. The reason is that Conceptual Blending Theory adopts a cognitive model that makes it possible to construct emergent structure (or emergent contexts), assuming four spaces such as two input spaces, a generic space and a blended space. To analyze the metaphorical example (4) in terms of Conceptual Blending Theory, the metaphorical structure is easily explainable as in (5), including the emergence of the notion "incompetence" [see Figure 3]:

(5) a. *Input Spaces:* Input 1 (that serves as a target input) is structured by the domain of Surgery: i.e. a surgeon is performing the operation of a patient in the operating room. Input 2 (that functions as a source input) is set up on the basis of the domain of Butchery: i.e. a butcher is severing an animal's flesh in the abattoir.
  b. *Cross-Space Mappings:* Counterpart mappings are established between the two Inputs: e.g. Surgeon—Butcher, Patient—Animal, Scalpel—Cleaver, Operating Room—Abattoir, etc.
  c. *Generic Space:* Generic Space stores some common structure shared by the two Inputs. In this case, the following abstract structure is projected to the Generic Space: "a person uses a sharp instrument to perform a procedure on some other being" (Grady, et al. 1999: 104).
  d. *Selective Projection to the Blend:* The Blend is constructed by inheriting some structure from the two Inputs. In the case of the example (4), the following elements from each Input are projected to the Blend: [Input 1] "the identity of a particular person being operated on (i.e. the speaker), the identity of another individual who is performing the operation, and perhaps details of

the operating room setting" (Grady, et al. 1999: 104), [Input 2] "the role "butcher" and associated activities" (Grady, et al. 1999: 104). What should be noted here is that the surgeon in the Input 1 and the butcher in the Input 2 are conceptually compressed to become a unitary (or blended) and emergent entity "Surgeon as Butcher". This process of conceptual compression therefore leads to the central inference of "an incompetent surgeon", because "the BUTCHERY space projects a means-end relationship incompatible with the means-end relationship in the SURGERY space" (Grady, et al. 1999: 104). In the Butchery space, the goal is "to kill the animal and then sever its flesh from its bones" (Grady, et al. 1999: 105), whereas in the Surgery space, the goal is "to heal the patient" (Grady, et al. 1999: 105). In the Blend, however, the combination of the butcher's means with the surgeon's ends evokes an emergent property of incongruity, which consequently draws the inference of the butcher's incompetence. In general, this kind of emergence cannot be explicitly captured within the framework of Conceptual Metaphor Theory.

e. *Emergent Structure:*
[Composition] Through the selective projection of some structure from the two Inputs, the following structure is established in the Blend: the hybrid element "Surgeon as Butcher" is performing the operation of the patient in the operating room.
[Completion] To make sense of the scene in the Blend, the projection of a butcher into an operating room results in the recruitment of the notions "incompetence" and "malice" from our longterm memory to the Blend. Hence, this process of completion leads to the situation where the surgeon is recognized as incompetent and malicious.
[Elaboration] The mental simulation of the event in the Blend can be performed to produce various possible images indefinitely. For instance, the following images can be developed via this process: "the image of a butcher carving a patient" (Grady, et al. 1999: 107), "the even more grotesque image of a butcher packaging the patient's tissue as cold cuts" (Grady, et al. 1999: 107), etc.

```
                        GENERIC SPACE
                    ----Agent----
                    --Undergoer--
                   /Sharp instrument\
                   / Work Space \
                    Procedure
                    (Goal/Means)

INPUT SPACE 1                              INPUT SPACE 2
   Role: Surgeon                              Role: Butcher
   Identity of surgeon
   Role: Patient (Person)                     Role: Commodity (Animal)
   Identity of patient
   Scalpel                                    Cleaver
   Operating room                             Abattoir
   Goal: healing                              Goal: severing flesh
   Means: Surgery                             Means: butchery

              Identity of surgeon ——— Role: Butcher
              Identity of patient ——— Role: Patient (Person)
              Cleaver? Scalpel? (Unspecified)
              Operating Room
              Goal: healing    Means: butchery
                      Incompetence
                                              BLENDED SPACE
```

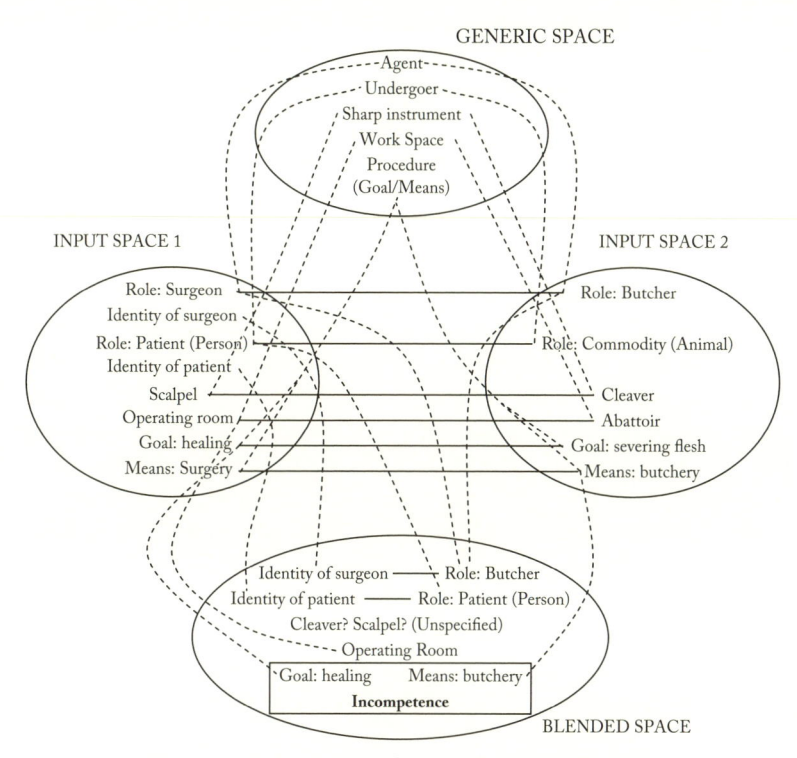

Figure 3. Surgeon as Butcher (Grady, et al. 1999: 105)

Of particular interest in a series of conceptual blending processes is that the inference of "an incompetent surgeon" does not exist in individual spaces such as the Input 1 and the Input 2, but it takes place as a result of the development of emergent structure in the Blend. This reflects the very nature of emergent structure provided by neither of the Inputs, which is a central claim of Conceptual Blending Theory.

3. Semantic Blinking and Japanese Jokes

Jokes are one of the language plays that frequently appear in our everyday communication. Yamanashi (2004: 85–99) claims that the meaning of jokes or the humorous effect of jokes resides in the situation where multiple meanings compete with each other. Likewise, traditional studies of humor (e.g. Koestler 1964, Norrick 1986, Raskin 1985, etc.) argue that the meaning peculiar to humor is established by virtue of the conflict between more than two different schemas. In this section, bearing these observations in mind, the understanding process of jokes is reanalyzed from the viewpoint of Conceptual Blending Theory, focusing especially on two types of Japanese jokes (more specifically, Construal Jokes and Framing Jokes). In so doing, the section shows the importance of Conceptual Blending and Semantic Blinking in the meaning construction of jokes.

3.1 Construal Jokes

The research field of cognitive linguistics (or cognitive semantics), especially Langacker's (1987, 1990, 1991, 2000, 2008, 2009) framework of Cognitive Grammar, has widely accepted the importance of *construal*. Generally speaking, this notion means "our capacity for construing the same conceived situation in alternate ways" (Langacker 1995: 364), which includes *profiling, figure/ground configuration, the level of specificity, viewpoint, scope*, etc. For example, in the case of profiling, the word *knuckle* "evokes as its base the conception of a finger, within which it profiles (designates) a certain subpart (any joint)" (Langacker 2000: 7) [see Figure 4 (profiling is shown in bold)]. However, when the profiled part changes, a different conceptualization is achieved. For example, the word *nail* also evokes the conception of a finger, but it is different in profiled portion from the word *knuckle* [see Figure 5].

Figure 4. Knuckle (Langacker 2000: 7)    Figure 5. Nail

This section is concerned with jokes based on *construal* (henceforth construal jokes) and discusses the meaning construction process of construal jokes from the perspective of Conceptual Blending Theory. The following is a representative example of construal jokes from Japanese:

(6) A: 「昨日、そうめんを一本ゆでて、食べたんです」
Kinou, somen-wo ippon yudete, tabetan-desu.
(I ate a packet of *somen* yesterday.)[2]

B: 「たった一本ですか?」
Tatta ippon desu-ka? (Only one strand?)

A: 「ええ」
Ee. (Yes.)

B: 「それで足りましたか?」
Sore-de tarimashita-ka? (Was it enough?)

A: 「ええ」
Ee. (Yes.)

B: 「僕は細身ですが、一本は一本でも、せめてそうめん一束は欲しいですね」
Boku-wa hosomi desu-ga, ippon-wa ippon-demo, semete somen hitotaba-wa hoshii-desu-ne.
(I'm skinny, but I want to eat at least one packet of *somen*.)[3]

As a general point, the comical effect of this joke lies in the semantic contrast between two interpretations given by the expression "somen ippon" (そうめん一本) [i.e. a packet of *somen* or a strand of *somen*]. Within the framework of Conceptual Blending, the emergent process of this comical effect can be analyzed as in (7) [see also Figure 6]:

(7) a. *Input Spaces:* Input 1 contains the conventional interpretation of the expression "somen ippon" (そうめん一本), i.e. a packet of *somen*. The space therefore profiles a packet of *somen* as a whole. In contrast, Input 2 has the non-conventional interpretation of the expression, i.e. a strand of *somen*. Hence, the space confines its profiling to only a strand of *somen*.

b. *Cross-Space Mappings and Generic Space:* Along with cross-space mappings between the two Inputs, the common structure between them is projected to Generic Space.

c. *Conceptual Blending and Emergent Structure:*
[Composition] The conceptual structures of the two Inputs are projected to the Blend to serve as a unitary entity. In other words, two individual entities at the Input level are established as a single entity in the Blend (In Fauconnier & Turner (2002), this type of composition is generally called *conceptual compression*. Note that the box with rounded corners in the Blend of Figure 6 stands for

this conceptual compression).

[Completion] Through the process of composition, the Blend has one emergent entity constructed from the two Inputs. However, in actuality, the compressed entity leads to the inference that the two input entities are inconsistent with each other. As a result, based on this inferential pattern, the images of tightness and struggle are recruited from our long-term memory to the Blend.

[Elaboration] The images of tightness and struggle bring about some motion in the compressed entity of the Blend: i.e. the profiled portions of the two Inputs interchange, which is shown by a double-headed arrow in the Blend of Figure 6. Consequently, the motion leads to the humorous (or comical) effect of the joke (6).

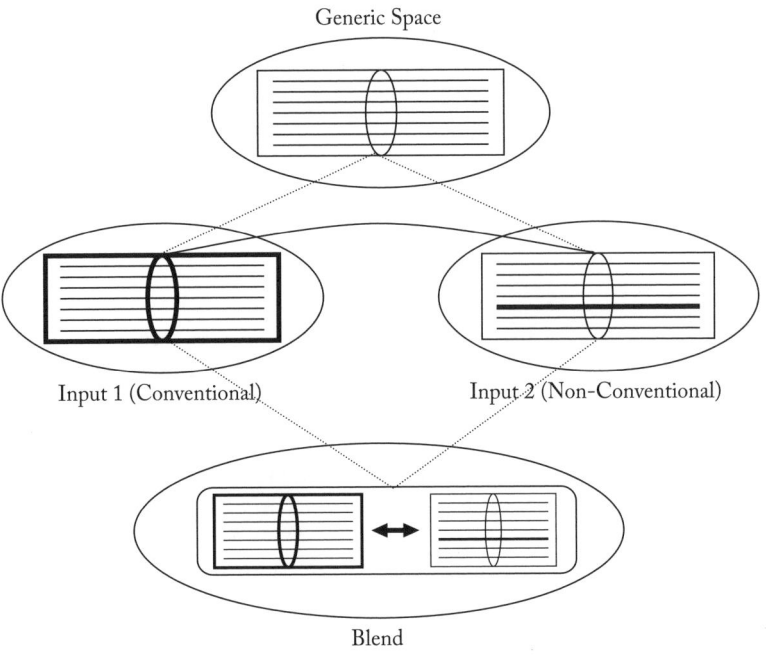

Figure 6. Construal Joke

Generally speaking, the interchange between two interpretations in the elaboration process can be understood as reflecting the notions "semantic competition" in Yamanashi (2004) and "schema conflict" in traditional humor research (cf. Koestler 1964, Norrick 1986, Raskin 1985, etc.).

For convenience, this kind of interchanging phenomenon might be termed Semantic Blinking, which functions as the direct source of the comical effect of construal jokes. In that sense, the conceptual compression (or conceptual blending) for Semantic Blinking could be called (Semantic) Blinking Compression or (Semantic) Blinking Blending.

3.2 Framing Jokes

The previous section has discussed the meaning construction process of construal jokes, whose humorous effect is derived through construing the same frame in alternate ways.[4] In contrast, this section focuses mainly on another type of joke as shown in (8)–(10), where the comical effect of jokes is created on the basis of two different frames (for the sake of convenience, this type of joke is termed Framing Jokes):

(8) A: 「ちょっとテレビ消しといて！」
　　　Chotto terebi keshitoite! (Turn off the TV, please.)
　　B: 「マジシャンじゃないから、よー消しません」
　　　Mazishan-ja nai kara, yo keshimasen.
　　　(I can't, because I'm not a magician.)[5]
(9) A: 「先に洗濯機をまわしたら？」
　　　Saki-ni sentakki-wo mawashitara?
　　　(You should first turn on the washing machine.)
　　B: 「そんなバカな！　危なすぎますよ！」
　　　Sonna baka-na! Abunasugimasu-yo!
　　　(Unbelievable! It's too dangerous!)[6]
(10) A: 「こたつを抜いとかないと！」
　　　Kotatsu-wo nuitokanaito!
　　　(I should pull out the plug to disconnect the *kotatsu*.)[7]
　　B: 「こたつを抜くの？　大根じゃあるまいし」
　　　Kotatsu-wo nuku-no? Daikon-ja arumai-shi!
　　　(Really, pull it out? But it isn't a Japanese radish.)[8]

In what follows, the meaning construction process of Framing Jokes is analyzed from the viewpoint of Conceptual Blending Theory.

As an example, let us here consider the emergent process of the comical effect of (8) [see also Figure 7]. In this case, the comical effect resides in the semantic contrast between two different frames given by the expression "terebi-wo kesu" (テレビを消す):

(11) a. *Input Spaces:* Input 1 includes the "Watching TV" frame, where the expression "terebi-wo kesu" (テレビを消す) is interpreted. As a result, the space obtains the interpretation "the TV turns off". In contrast, Input 2 contains the "Magic" frame, in which the expression "terebi-wo kesu" (テレビを消す) is construed. As a consequence, the space gets the interpretation "the TV disappears".
  b. *Cross-Space Mappings and Generic Space:* Through cross-space mappings between the two Inputs, Generic Space stores the structure they share: [at the formal level] the expression "terebi-wo kesu" (テレビを消す), [at the conceptual level] "the TV changes states in a certain way".
  c. *Conceptual Blending and Emergent Structure:*
  [Composition] The conceptual structures of the two Inputs are projected to the Blend, and as a result, they work as a single entity in the Blend (by way of conceptual compression).
  [Completion] On the basis of the inferential pattern that the two entities in the Inputs are out of harmony with each other in the Blend, the images of tightness and struggle are recruited from our long-term memory to the Blend.
  [Elaboration] The completion process (i.e. recruiting the images of tightness and struggle) results in the Semantic Blinking Effect in the compressed entity of the Blend (i.e. the interchanging effect in the Blend between the profiled portions of the two Inputs). As a consequence, the Semantic Blinking Effect triggers the humorous effect of the joke (8).

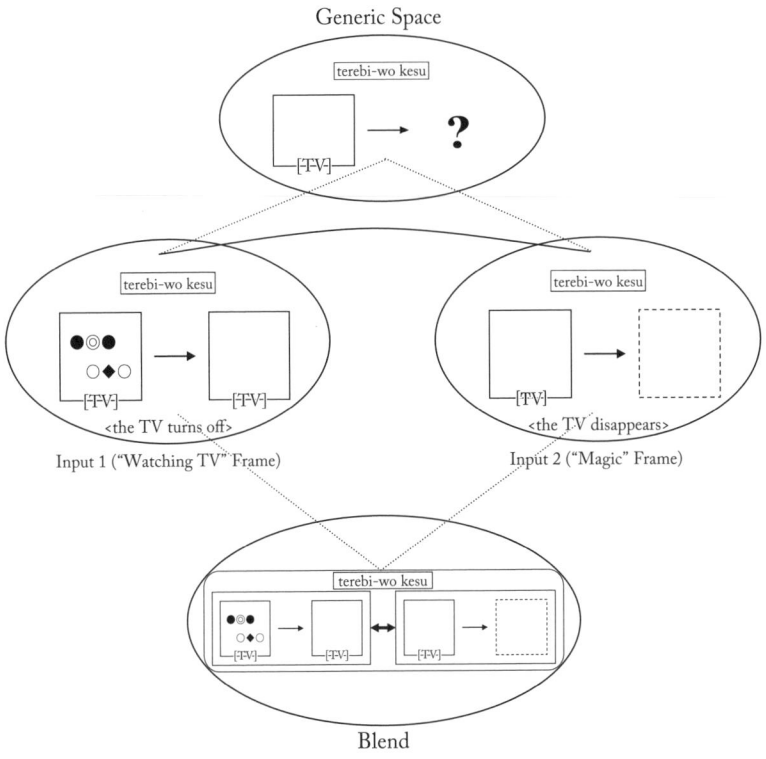

Figure 7. Framing Joke

4. Conclusion

What needs to be noted in the above-mentioned meaning construction process of jokes is that the Blend ultimately contains emergent structure of its own, which is not provided by the two Inputs. To put it more specifically, the Semantic Blinking Effect and the humorous (or comical) effect do not occur in the two Inputs, whereas these effects arise in the Blend by dint of a series of emergent processes (composition, completion, and elaboration). This is the very nature of conceptual emergence in Conceptual Blending Theory.

From the discussion above, it is quite obvious that the general cognitive process of Conceptual Blending is deeply involved in the meaning construction of jokes. In particular, the following two points are worth emphasizing here: (i) Blinking Compression leads to Semantic Blinking, and (ii) Semantic Blinking invokes the comical effect of jokes (i.e. laughter). In addition, it cannot be overlooked that construal (cf. Langacker 1987, 1990, 1991, 2000, 2008, 2009) and the evocative power of frames (cf. Fillmore 1982, 1985) are closely related to the comprehension process of jokes.

In general terms, the pattern of emergence discussed in this paper (i.e. Blinking Compression → Semantic Blinking → Comical Effect) may also be widely observed in the meaning construction process of language plays other than jokes. If so, the relationship between Semantic Blinking and language play in general should be further explored in future research.

Acknowledgements

This paper is a revised version of Yasuhara (2006), which was presented at the 23rd Annual Meeting of the Japanese Cognitive Science Society. I would like to thank Professor Takashi Imai (Tsuru University) for giving me an opportunity to complete this paper. I am also grateful to Yasutaka Aoyama (a colleague and native speaker of English) for his suggestive comments on the earlier manuscripts of this paper.

Notes

1. In recent works on Conceptual Metaphor Theory (e.g. Lakoff & Johnson 1999, Lakoff & Núñez 2000), the conceptual blending model of metaphors has also been playing an important role in the comprehension of metaphorical phenomena, as well as the traditional two-domain model. This can be easily understood, given the fact that the recent literature above proposes the term *Metaphorical Blends*, where three spaces *Source Input*, *Target Input*, and *Blend* are used.
2. *Somen* (a kind of Japanese noodles; そうめん) are "thin[fine] wheat noodles" (Yamaguchi & Bates 2010: 252).
3. The expression "somen ippon" (そうめん一本) can be interpreted in two ways: one is "a packet of *somen*", and the other is "a strand of *somen*".
4. Depending on Coulson (2001), the term *frame* is employed here as a cover term for a whole set of related knowledge-bases, including *frame* (Minsky 1980; Fillmore 1982, 1985), *script* (Schank & Abelson 1977), *idealized cognitive model* (Lakoff 1987), *cognitive domain* (Langacker 1987, 1990, 1991, 2000, 2008, 2009), and *scenario* (Sanford & Garrod 1981).
5. The Japanese verb "kesu" (消す) can be interpreted in two ways: [in the Watching TV Frame] "turn off", or [in the Magic Frame] "disappear".
6. The Japanese verb "mawasu" (まわす) can be interpreted in two ways: [in the Washing Frame] "turn on the washing machine", or [in the Acrobatics Frame] "turn".

7. *Kotatsu* (こたつ) is "a Japanese traditional heating device made of a low table which has a square latticed wooden frame covered with a coverlet" (Yamaguchi & Bates 2010: 161).
8. The Japanese verb "nuku" (抜く) can be interpreted in two ways: [in the *Kotatsu* Frame] "pull out the plug to disconnect the *kotatsu*", or [in the Harvest Frame] "pull something out of the ground".

References

Coulson, Seana. (2001) *Semantic Leaps: Frame-Shifting and Conceptual Blending in Meaning Construction*. Cambridge: Cambridge University Press.

Crystal, David. (1998) *Language Play*. Chicago: The University of Chicago Press.

Dudis, Paul G. (2004) Body Partitioning and Real-Space Blends. *Cognitive Linguistics* 15 (2): 223–238.

Fauconnier, Gilles, and Mark Turner. (1994) Conceptual Projection and Middle Spaces. Technical Report no.9401, Department of Cognitive Science, University of California, San Diego.

Fauconnier, Gilles, and Mark Turner. (1996) Blending as a Central Process of Grammar. In Adele E. Goldberg (ed.), *Conceptual Structure, Discourse, and Language*, pp. 113–130. Stanford: CSLI Publications.

Fauconnier, Gilles, and Mark Turner. (1998) Conceptual Integration Networks. *Cognitive Science* 22 (2): 133–187.

Fauconnier, Gilles, and Mark Turner. (2002) *The Way We Think: Conceptual Blending and the Mind's Hidden Complexities*. New York: Basic Books.

Fauconnier, Gilles, and Mark Turner. (2006) Mental Spaces: Conceptual Integration Networks. In Dirk Geeraerts (ed.), *Cognitive Linguistics: Basic Readings*, pp. 303–371. Berlin/New York: Mouton de Gruyter.

Fillmore, Charles J. (1982) Frame Semantics. In The Linguistic Society of Korea (ed.), *Linguistics in the Morning Calm*, pp. 111–137. Seoul: Hanshin Publishing Co.

Fillmore, Charles J. (1985) Frames and the Semantics of Understanding. *Quaderni di Semantica* 6 (2): 222–254.

Freeman, Margaret H. (2005) The Poem as Complex Blend: Conceptual Mappings of Metaphor in Sylvia Plath's 'The Applicant'. *Language and Literature* 14 (1): 25–44.

Grady, Joseph E., Todd Oakley, and Seana Coulson. (1999) Blending and Metaphor. In Raymond W. Gibbs, JR. and Gerard J. Steen (eds.), *Metaphor in Cognitive Linguistics*, pp. 101–124. Amsterdam: John Benjamins.

Hiraga, Masako K. (2005) *Metaphor and Iconicity: A Cognitive Approach to Analyzing Texts*. New York: Palgrave Macmillan.

Koestler, Arthur. (1964) *The Act of Creation*. New York: Macmillan.

Lakoff, George. (1987) *Women, Fire, and Dangerous Things: What Categories Reveal about the Mind*. Chicago: The University of Chicago Press.

Lakoff, George, and Mark Johnson. (1980) *Metaphors We Live By*. Chicago: The University of Chicago Press.

Lakoff, George, and Mark Johnson. (1999) *Philosophy in the Flesh: The Embodied Mind*

and its Challenge to Western Thought. New York: Basic Books.
Lakoff, George, and Rafael E. Núñez. (2000) *Where Mathematics Comes From: How the Embodied Mind Brings Mathematics into Being.* New York: Basic Books.
Langacker, Ronald W. (1987) *Foundations of Cognitive Grammar, Vol.1: Theoretical Prerequisites.* Stanford: Stanford University Press.
Langacker, Ronald W. (1990) *Concept, Image, and Symbol: The Cognitive Basis of Grammar.* Berlin/New York: Mouton de Gruyter.
Langacker, Ronald W. (1991) *Foundations of Cognitive Grammar, Vol. 2: Descriptive Application.* Stanford: Stanford University Press.
Langacker, Ronald W. (1995) Cognitive Grammar. In E. F. K. Koerner and R.E. Asher (eds.), *Concise History of the Language Sciences: From the Sumerians to the Cognitivists*, pp. 364–368. Oxford: Pergamon.
Langacker, Ronald W. (2000) *Grammar and Conceptualization.* Berlin/New York: Mouton de Gruyter.
Langacker, Ronald W. (2008) *Cognitive Grammar: A Basic Introduction.* Oxford: Oxford University Press.
Langacker, Ronald W. (2009) *Investigations in Cognitive Grammar.* Berlin/New York: Mouton de Gruyter.
Liddell, Scott K. (2003) *Grammar, Gesture, Meaning in American Sign Language.* Cambridge: Cambridge University Press.
Mandelblit, Nili. (1997) *Grammatical Blending: Creative and Schematic Aspects in Sentence Processing and Translation.* Ph.D Dissertation, University of California, San Diego.
Minsky, Marvin. (1980) A Framework for Representing Knowledge. In Dieter Metzing (ed.), *Frame Conceptions and Text Understanding*, pp. 1–25. Berlin/New York: Walter de Gruyter.
Norrick, Neal R. (1986) A Frame-Theoretical Analysis of Verbal Humor: Bisociation as Schema Conflict. *Semiotica* 60 (3/4): 225–245.
Raskin, Victor. (1985) *Semantic Mechanisms of Humor.* Dordrecht: D. Reidel.
Robert, Adrian. (1998) Blending and Other Conceptual Operations in the Interpretation of Mathematical Proofs. In Jean-Pierre Koenig (ed.), *Discourse and Cognition: Bridging the Gap*, pp. 337–350. Stanford: CSLI Publications.
Sanford, Anthony J., and Simon C. Garrod. (1981) *Understanding Written Language: Explorations of Comprehension beyond the Sentence.* New York: John Wiley & Sons.
Sayrs, Elizabeth P. (2003) Narrative, Metaphor, and Conceptual Blending in The Hanging Tree. *Music Theory Online* 9 (1). [Available at *http://www.societymusictheory.org/mto/issues/mto.03.9.1/ mto.03.9.1.sayrs.html*]
Schank, Roger C., and Robert P. Abelson. (1977) *Scripts, Plans, Goals, and Understanding: An Inquiry into Human Understanding.* Hillsdale, N.J.: Lawrence Erlbaum.
Sweetser, Eve E. (1999) Compositionality and Blending: Semantic Composition in a Cognitively Realistic Framework. In Theo Janssen and Gisela Redeker (eds.), *Cognitive Linguistics: Foundations, Scope, and Methodology*, pp. 129–162. Berlin/New

York: Mouton de Gruyter.

Turner, Mark. (1996) *The Literary Mind: The Origins of Thought and Language*. Oxford: Oxford University Press.

Turner, Mark, and Gilles Fauconnier. (1995) Conceptual Integration and Formal Expression. *Journal of Metaphor and Symbolic Activity* 10 (3): 183–204.

Yamaguchi, Momoo, and Steven Bates. (2010) *Wa-Ei: Nihon-no Bunka Kanko Rekishi Jiten (A Japanese-English Dictionary of Culture, Tourism and History of Japan)*. Tokyo: Sanshusha.

Yamanashi, Masa-aki. (2004) *Kotoba no Ninchi Kukan [The Cognitive Space of Language]*. Tokyo: Kaitakusha.

Yasuhara, Kazuya. (2006) Semantic Blinking: A Conceptual Blending Analysis of Jokes. *Proceedings of the 23rd Annual Meeting of the Japanese Cognitive Science Society*, pp. 48–53.

Yasuhara, Kazuya. (2012) *Conceptual Blending and Anaphoric Phenomena: A Cognitive Semantics Approach*. Tokyo: Kaitakusha.

Zbikowski, Lawrence. (2001) *Conceptualizing Music: Cognitive Structure, Theory, and Analysis*. Oxford: Oxford University Press.

リメディアル教育における教員間の
シナジー効果の検証
協働的 FD 活動を通じて

上原義正

要旨

　本論文は大学におけるリメディアル教育でのシナジー効果を検証した実践的研究である。大学生の学力低下が叫ばれるなか、補習プログラムの運営を行った。教育経営および英語教育の観点から、教育活動に焦点をあて、協働的な FD 活動を行った。結果として、シナジー効果が発生し、補習プログラムは円滑に運営が行われたことが明らかとなった。

キーワード　大学英語教育、リメディアル教育、シナジー効果、補習プログラム、協働的 FD

1. はじめに

　ここ数年、大学生の学力低下が叫ばれてから久しい。学力低下を補完するためのリメディアル教育[1]における学習方法やモチベーションの研究などが盛んに行われている他方で、リメディアル教育での教員間のシナジー効果の研究はほとんど行われてこなかった。

　学生主体の学習の研究も必要ではあるが、学習者を牽引する教員の活動の検証も看過できないであろう。特に教員を教育する教師教育も課題となっている。

　この課題に対して、reflection cycle[2] によって教師教育が強調され続けている(秋田・ルイス編、2008)。ただし、大学における教師教育は、Faculty Development(以下、FD 活動)である。大塚(2007: 123)によれ

ば、「FDの目指すところは、まずは個々の授業を変えていくことであり、そのためには、個々人の改善・向上行動が引き出されなければならない。」と端的にFD活動の要領が明記されている。これはリメディアル教育にも当てはまるであろう。

そこで、本論文では、FD活動がどのように補習プログラム(リメディアル教育)のプロジェクトで行われ、どのようにシナジー効果が発生してきたのかについて2007年度のA校の事例を中心に検証の俎上に乗せることとしたい。

2. 英語履修制限の実施

補習クラスの設置と運営に関する検討の前に、英語履修制限について述べておきたい。ここで述べる英語履修制限とは、選択必修科目としての英語の最終科目を受講する以前に、各種英語検定試験により、その最終科目を履修可能であるかどうかについての診断をする、という意味である。

実際の学生の動向を見てみると、2005年度から英語履修制限がA校に導入され、以下のように英語履修制限にかかるテスト等を受験する率が上がっている。たとえば、TOEIC、英検の導入前と導入後のテスト受験者の概数は、若干、変動があるものの、2倍に伸びていた(表1参照)。

表1　各種英語検定試験の年度ごとの受験者数の変動

テスト名 年度	TOEIC -IP	英検	TOEFL -ITP
2004年度	107	103	32
履修制限の導入			
2005年度	266	265	236
2006年度	197	269	159
2007年度	254	167	114

他方で、この制限をなかなかクリアすることが出来ない学生の学習支援をするために、補習クラスが用意された。

3. 補習クラスの設置

質保証、すなわち数値で英語力を示す場合、2005年度に設定された英語履修制限のスコアまたは級での合格率が50%前後であったため、2006年度から補習クラスが設置された経緯がある。

大学での補習クラスの全国的情勢をみてみると、『大学における教育内容の改革状況について』(文部科学省、2007)の「補習授業の実施」では、2004年度では160校(私学は96校)に対し、2005年度ではおよそ1.3倍にあたる210校(私学は135校)と増加傾向にある。こういった状況のなかで、この事例で挙げる補習クラスは、学習支援の方策として開講された。

設置の当初は自由参加であったが、2007年度より、ポイントシステムを導入し、積極的参加が促進された。ポイントシステムとは、出席(80%以上)と試験(60%以上獲得)のポイントを学生に明示し、10ポイントを獲得するまで補習クラスで英語能力を強化し、学習支援を行うシステムであった。

4. 補習プログラムにおいて協働的スタイルを形成するには？

このような補習プログラムにおいて、担当教員は、年2回実施(4月と9月)される英語教員ワークショップで、補習クラスを担当することをその場で再度承認していた。ワークショップでは、補習クラスの学生に対する指導方法として以下の図1のような提案を行った。

Realistic Study Preview (RSP)
- Remark their low motivation toward English
- Reveal or Show the Learners' English Proficiency
- Suggest the optimal way of Learning
- Encourage the learners
- Focus on their Process bench marking

図1 補習クラスの学生に対する指導方法

　ポイント制度が発生する前の制度では、学生の自主性を重んじていたため僅少の学生の参加しか見られなかった。しかし、ポイント制度が導入された後に、80％以上の出席の上に、プロジェクトリーダーの筆者（以下プロジェクトリーダー）により、小テスト・統一テストの受験が各補習クラスに参加する学生を対象に義務として提案され、方向性が一旦出来た。
　この方向性の背景には、各教員との連携と各教員が有する知識資源（knowledge resource）を共同運営するというねらいがあった。野中（1999）によれば、知識は財である。また、コミュニティー・ラーニング[3]（吉田、2008）が求められていたとも解釈できよう。ただし、あくまでも学生の英語力の向上のための施策であった。
　各教員がすでに有している知識資源を引出し、個々人の授業改善を目標としたFD活動を以下のように行った。
　まず、協働的な作業を行った。80％以上の出席率を維持させるため

に出席管理が常日頃できているのかを知るため、E-mail、または、口頭で直に出席状況を尋ねた。次に、各補習クラスの教員に統一テキストの内容に準拠した小テストを分担作業で実施するように促し、作った小テストを一旦補習クラス担当者であるプロジェクトリーダーに提出してもらい、プロジェクトリーダーが確認をし、それを各補習クラスの教員に配分した。小テスト作成は2007年度前期の期間に行った。

統一テストは2007年度に英語教育プログラムディレクターの下で作成された。つまり、

1)　小テストをつくる
2)　小テストから統一テストを作成する
3)　80%以上の出席を学生に伝える

これらの業務[4]について英語教育プログラムディレクターをトップの管理者としたMOODLEを頻繁にコミュニケーション・ツールとして稼働させていた(図2参照)。

このシステムでは、「親記事」が補習クラス担当教員の全員のメールアドレスに配信され、その「親記事」に返信できる「フォーラム型」となっている。このサイトでは、プロジェクトリーダーが授業の進捗状況を確認し、授業の方法論についてのトピックが挙げられていた。このことからも教員間の協働的なFD活動が行われていたといえよう。新たな教育方法論が模索されていたともいえる。

また、ミーティング等で各教員と話し合いを行い、そこから補習プログラムの新たな方向性が生み出されていた。新たな方向性とは、ポイントシステムの見直しであり、ポイントシステムを改正する契機となった。

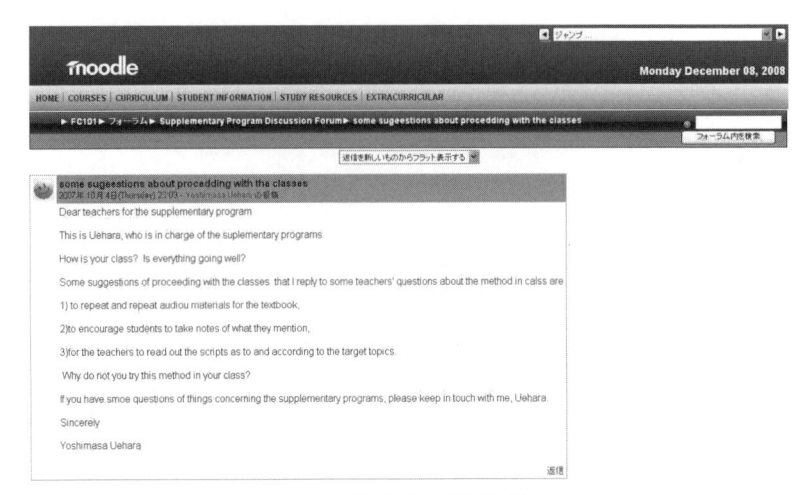

図2　MOODLE の活用例

5.　むすびにかえて

　このような現象、教員間に発生した事柄は、次の2点である。職能の力量(出席管理、小テストの作成など)を確実にするための知識資源の共同運営。いま1つは、教員間での共通認識と協働。これらの2点が組み合わさり教育活動に功を奏していると言え、シナジーを産出しているとこの事例から謳うことができる。

　さらに、補習プログラムのプロジェクトリーダーと各教員との協働的な FD 活動、MOODLE を用いての情報の共有、ミーティング等から、各教員が補習プログラムでの新たな教育方法論を模索し、新たな方向性を創造するといったリメディアル教育おけるシナジー効果はあった。また、円滑に補習プログラムが運営されたといえよう。

　これは、プロジェクトの代表者の力だけで行ったものではなくチームとしての一定の産物であった、と reflection cycle からいえよう。また、孤立無援となりがちな、大学教育のなかで、知識資源の共同運営と協働作業のシナジーにより、一致団結した「ユニフォーム効果」を得られたといってよい。

補習クラスの授業の方法と内容については、また別の機会に発表することとする。

注
1. 広義でのリメディアル教育は、基礎学力が低下し学習支援を必要とする大学生を教育することである。
2. reflection cycle とは教育の現場での出来事を振り返る作業のことである。
3. コミュニティーにおいて知識をマネジメントし、普及させる学習スタイルをコミュニティー・ラーニングと呼ぶ。
4. テキストすべて完了することを前提にスケジュールを立て、期日内に小テストを作成し、提出してもらった。

参考文献
秋田喜代美、キャサリン・ルイス編(2008)『授業の研究　教師の学習レッスンスタディーへのいざない』明石書店.
文部科学省(2007)『大学における教育内容等の改革状況について』
　　(http://www.mext.go.jp/b_menu/houdou/19/04/07041710.htm)
野中郁次郎(1999)『知識経営のすすめ―ナレッジマネジメントとその時代』筑摩書房.
大塚雄作(2007)「高等教育の個別的実践と普遍的理論化の狭間で―大学評価・FD実践の体験を通して」『高等教育研究』第10集、日本高等教育学会、玉川大学出版部.
渡辺　深(2007)『組織社会学』ミネルヴァ書房.
吉田孟史(2008)「コミュニティー・ラーニングとは」吉田孟史編『コミュニティー・ラーニング　組織学習論の新展開』ナカニシヤ出版.

SVT テストによる英文多読測定の試み

竹村雅史

要旨

　伝統的に精読に代表される訳読授業は日本の中等教育の英語授業の中心に位置づけられてきた。しかし、その中にあって学習者が選んだ Graded Readers（語彙制限のあるテキスト）を自分のペースで大量に、易しめのテキストを読み進めていく多読授業がこの 10 年で全国的な広がりを見せている。背景に学習者の動機付けの観点から、学習者の読みの向上につながっていると報告されている。本来、英文多読授業では、学習者に対して読後の評価測定は本来の読む行為を阻害するものとして馴染まないとされ、読みの伸張度を測ることは難しい。更に、外部試験のテキストは実際に読んだテキストと異なっているので、どのくらい理解できたかを測定する上で、必ずしも理想とは言えない。本論文は、読んだテキストを理解できたかをみる SVT Test（文章判読テスト）を用いて、学習者のテキストの理解測定が可能かを試みるものである。

キーワード　英文多読、SVT テスト、EPER、Graded Readers、多読評価

1. はじめに

　高瀬（2010）によると、英文多読授業は 2003 年頃から全国に普及し始めたとされている。ここで言う多読とは、酒井邦秀氏が提唱した多読 3 原則（1. 辞書は引かない、2. わからない部分は飛ばす、3. 合わない

本、素材はやめる）に則った授業を指す。導入された学校種は公立・私立の中学校、高等学校、高等専門学校、大学、私塾に至るまで広範囲にまたがっている。この背景には、これまでの訳読を支えていた授業者中心の授業から学習者中心の授業へ変わることで、学習者のやる気や自信といった英語学習における情意面での効果が大きいと思われる。竹村(2006)によれば、これが本来の読む行為によって得られる読書の楽しみにつながっていき、自律的な学習者へ成長させるきっかけとなると言われている。

ただ、学習者への評価という観点からみると様々な問題点も指摘されている。その1つとして、Nuttall (2000) は、学習者が同じテキストを読んでいないため、統一した試験を行うことができず、評価に馴染まない活動であることが大きな原因となっていると指摘している。学習者がどこまでテキストを理解できたかを確かめる方法として、読後のレポート提出があるが、あくまでも学習者自身の判断での報告であり、授業者側からの判断はできない。このことから読んだテキストを理解できたかどうかを測定する方法が求められる。

2. EPER Test とは

EPER とは、Edinburgh Project on Extensive Reading の略でエジンバラ大学応用言語学研究所の David R Hill が中心となって1970年代から進められてきた Graded Readers の普及を進める事業である。この事業を始めるに当たって2つのテストが開発された。1つは Placement/Progress Test であり、もう1つは Extensive Reading Test である。前者は、学習者の能力の伸張を測る目的と EPER プログラムの学習者のレベルを測るプレースメント・テストの役割があり、それぞれ70語からなる12の文章で構成され、初級からネイティブ・スピーカーに至るレベルに対応できるクローズ形式のテストである。後者は、学習者の主に読みの流暢さを測る目的があり、約1000語からなる8つの文章で構成され、8段階の難易に分けられている内容理解テストである。

本論文では、伸張度を測る前者の Placement Test の Test Pack E (complete) の 10 の文章 (A〜J) の難易順に 3 つ選択 (B, E, H) し使用した。以下が一番易しい B の文章例である。(　) にはそれぞれ 1 単語が入り正解となる。

Billy is American. He is a teacher (1) works in a big (2) in New York. But Billy is not (3) New York. (4) father and mother live (5) a small town a long (6) away from there. Billy (7) not see his parents (8) often, but every year, (9) Christmas, he takes the train (10) the town where his (11) live and stays with them (12) a week. Then he (13) also see his little sister, Cathy, (14) still lives (15) her mother and father.

3. SVT Test とは

　SVT Test は、The Sentence Verification Technique Test の略で、Royer et al. (1979) によって初めて「読む・聴く行為」の受容的な理解力を測るための心理学分野で開発されたテストである。これは一種の文章判読技術(筆者訳)テストである。
　このテスト方法の概略を述べると、被験者は、まず初めに原文(テキスト)を読み、その後、原文(テキスト)を基に作られた 4 種類(Originals, Paraphrases, Meaning changes, Distractors) の文を読んで原文と一致しているか否かを答えるものである。ただし、一旦、原文を読んだら元の原文には戻れない。
　4 種類の文とは、以下のものである。
 (1)　Original：原文中に出ている文と全く同じ文である。(原文の意味と同じ)
 (2)　Paraphrase：原文中に出ている文の意味は変えないが、単語を出来るだけ替えてある。(原文の意味と同じ)
 (3)　Meaning change：原文中の構造と出来る限り同じようにしなが

ら、単語を入れ替えることによって元の文の意味を変えてある。（原文の意味と異なっている）

（4） Distractor：原文中の文とは話題は同じようにしてあるが、意味と表現は文と異なっている。

　Original と Paraphrase は原文と意味が同じなので、答えは 'Yes' になり、逆に Meaning change と Distractor は 'No' になる。(Royer は原文と同じであれば、前に出てきたので 'Old' という表現を使い、原文と違っている場合は、新たに出てきた意味と考え 'New' という表現を使用している。)

3.1　SVT Test の理論

　SVT Test は次の理論的仮定から形成されている。

> "... comprehension is a 'constructive' process, one that entails an interaction between context, the linguistic message, and the knowledge base of the listeners or readers."　　　　　　(Royer et al. 1987: 417).

ここでの読解力とは文章理解力と定義づける。文章理解とは、文脈、言語的意味、そして読み手の知識の間の相互作用を伴う構造的過程である。更に、Royer et al. (1987: 417) は、

> "This interaction results in a construction that preserves the meaning, but not the precise words of a message."

と述べ、この作用は結果的にメッセージを表す正確な単語ではなく、その意味を保持する構造に生じるものであるとしている。つまり、読み手は読んだ言語的な表層上の構造（文字）に意味を見い出しているのではなく、言語的メッセージの意味を記憶表出しているのである。更に、この作用は難しい（理解できない）箇所になった場合以外はほぼ無意識的に自動的に行われている。

もし読み手がテキストを理解し、しかもその意味を記憶の中に保持できたならば、originals と paraphrases は原文と意味が同じであるので、正しいと判断でき、逆に meaning changes と distractors は記憶の中で異なっている意味であると認識した場合、間違いであると判断するのである。

　Royer et al. (1987)によると、このテストは、記憶力の良し悪しで理解の程度が変わるものではないと言われている。記憶力が良くても理解されない場合は意味の保持がされておらず、原文と比較した場合、4種類の文の識別は曖昧なものになると述べている。

3.2　SVT Test の得点

　実験はペーパーテストで実施され、採点も手作業によって行われた。平均値がおよそ75％（50％は偶然であることも忘れてはならない）であれば、その文章は難までとはいわないが、被験者が挑む（読む）に値するレベルである。65％を下ると、その文章はおそらく難しすぎる。85％を超えると、おそらく易し過ぎると判断できる（Royer et al. 1987: 420）。

3.3　SVT Test の具体例

　以下は、2. EPER Test で示した Placement Test の同一文章を用いて、本実験に用いるために作られた SVT Test の一部である。

（テスト用紙の表面）

次の英文をよく読み、意味内容をしっかり把握して下さい。読み終わったら裏返しにし、読んだ文章に関した質問に答えて下さい。尚、一旦裏返しにしたら元に戻ってはいけません。

Billy is American. He is a teacher who works in a big school in New York. But Billy is not from New York. His father and mother live in a small town a long way away from there. Billy cannot see his parents very often, but every year, at Christmas, he takes the train to the town where his parents live and stays with them for a week. Then he can also see his little sister, Cathy, who still lives with her mother and father.

(テスト用紙の裏面)

よく注意して各文を読んで下さい。もし各文が前に読んだ文章と同じ意味であれば Yes に○をし、もし意味が違っているなら No に○をして下さい。

Yes/No　　Billy is Mexican.
Yes/No　　He works as a teacher in a big school in New York.
Yes/No　　Billy cannot see his parents very often, but every year, at Christmas, he takes the train to the town where his parents live and stays with them for a week.
Yes/No　　Then he also loves a little dog, Candy, who still lives with her mother and father.
Yes/No　　But Billy is from New York.
Yes/No　　His parents live in a small town far away from New York.

4. 実験

4.1 目的

本論文の目的は、EPER の Placement/Progress Test と同じ文章を用いて SVT Test に変えて、SVT Test の多読理解のテストとしての有効性を検証するものである。また、それが可能ならば、学習者の読んだテキストを用いて読みの理解テストとしての活用も期待できる。

4.2 仮説

EPER の Placement/Progress Test は、学習者の多読の伸張度を測定するために作られている。これまで多読の実証研究でも利用され、信頼

性、妥当性も高い。このクローズ・テストと文章判読テスト (SVT Test) を比較し、相関を求めることは意味がある。もし相関があれば、文章理解の伸張度を測るテストとしての有効性が確認できる。よって、本論文では、下記に仮説を設定した。

　「多読で用いられている EPER Test と SVT Test にはある程度有意な相関がある」

4.3　実験参加者

　本論文は 2012 年 4 月、短期大学生 1 年生 120 名（男子 6 名、女子 114 名）を対象に授業時間内に実験が行われた。授業第 1 週目の EPER Test、第 2 週目の SVT Test 両方を受けた者の数を実験参加者数とした。

4.4　実験方法

　EPER で開発されたクローズ・テスト形式の Placement/Progress Test E の 3 つのテキスト (B, E, H) を、SVT Test (B, E, H) にして作成する。授業時間内での実施のため全てのテキストは使えず、難易順に 3 つのテキストを抽出して作成した。同じ文章の記憶が残らないように実験参加者には何も予告せずに、授業第 1 週目に EPER Test を、授業第 2 週目に SVT Test を受けてもらった。解答時間は各テキスト 5 分の合計 15 分で時間を区切って指示した。（　）1 つを 1 点とし採点した。SVT Test の方は、表面の読みが各自に任せられているので、時間制限は特に設けなかったが、終了はほぼ同じくして試験答案を回収できた。Yes/No のどちらかが合っていれば、1 点として採点した。

5. 結果と考察

表1はEPER TestとSVT Testの平均(Mean)と標準偏差(SD)を示したものである。

表1　EPER Placement Test と SVT Test の平均と標準偏差（N = 120）

	Mean	SD
EPER B (15)	7.00	2.19
EPER E (15)	2.63	1.88
EPER H (15)	0.93	1.14
SVT B (6)	5.77	0.51
SVT E (8)	6.95	0.99
SVT H (8)	6.50	1.16

（　）は満点を示す

EPER Test の方は、平均点をみると、B, E, H の順に平均点が低くなり難化していることが伺える。SVT Test の方は、B だけがテキストのセンテンス数が6なので設問数も6となり、他の E, H の8と揃っていないので、単純に平均点で比較はできない。また、SVT の B, E は標準偏差も B が0.51、E が0.99と実験参加者間のばらつきがないので、高得点に集まっていることが伺える。

表2は、実験参加者の各テストの正答率を表したものである。

表2　EPER Placement Test と SVT Test の正答率（%）

EPER B (15)	46.6
EPER E (15)	17.5
EPER H (15)	0.06
SVT B (6)	96.1
SVT E (8)	86.8
SVT H (8)	81.2

SVT の B のみ6点満点なので、表2から、各テキストの難易さが、より鮮明になった。EPER Test も SVT Test も共に B, E, H の順に難化

している。しかし、SVT Test の方は3つとも80%を超えており、SVT Test は EPER Test ほど弁別力が高くはないと言える。また、SVT Test の各設問数が6〜8と少ないことも一因ではないかと思われる。

表3は EPER Test と SVT Test の各 B, E, H の3種類のテキストの合計点を Pearson の相関係数で算出したものである。

表3　EPER Test と SVT Test の各合計の相関　　　　　　　　（N=120）

	1. EPER	2. SVT	Mean	SD
1. EPER	―	.423**	10.56(45)	3.95
2. SVT		―	19.23(22)	1.82

（　）は満点　**$p<.01$

3つのテキストの EPER Test の合計点数と SVT Test の合計点数間には有意な中程度の相関（$r=.423, p<.01$）があることがわかった。仮説の「多読で用いられている EPER Test と SVT Test にはある程度有意な相関がある」が支持され、多読の理解度を測るテストとしての可能性があることが判明した。

6. まとめ

SVT Test は読んだテキストをそのまま使えることは、利点として挙げられる。ただ、今回の実験では、各テキストのセンテンス数に設問を合わせるため、設問数が少ない場合、その弁別力が効かないこともわかった。しかも、解答が Yes/No の二者択一のため、易しめのテキストは高得点になり、多読テキストのレベルを知る上で有効であるが、理解度テストとしては、まだまだ改善の余地が多くあるように思われた。実験は、授業時間内での実験であったので実施時間に限界があり、どうしてもテスト作成はそれに合わせたものに作らざるをえなかった。対象のサンプル量も少なくなるので、SVT Test の改善と同時に、時間を十分にかけての実施が今後の課題として残った。

参考文献

Day, R. R., & Bamford, J. (1998). *Extensive Reading in the Second Language Classroom.* USA: Cambridge University Press.

Day, R (Eds.). (2011). *Bringing Extensive Reading into the Classroom.* China: Oxford University Press.

Grabe, W & Stoller, F. L. (2011). *Teaching and Researching Reading.* Malaysia: Peason.

門田修平・野呂忠司(2001)『英語リーディングの認知メカニズム』くろしお出版

Nuttall, C. (2000). *Teaching Reading Skills in a Foreign Language.* Thailand: Macmillan.

Royer, J. M., Green, B. A., and Sinatra, G. M. (1987). The sentence Verification Technique: A practical procedure for testing comprehension. *Journal of Reading Behavior* 30. 414–423.

Royer, J. M., Hastings, C. N., and Hook, C. (1979). A sentence verification technique as a measure of listening and reading comprehension. *Journal of Reading Behavior* 11. 355–363.

酒井邦秀・神田みなみ(2005)『教室で読む英語100万語［多読授業のすすめ］』大修館書店

高瀬敦子(2010)『英語多読・多聴指導マニュアル』大修館書店

竹村雅史(2006)「函館高専に於ける英語多読指導の試み―最終報告」『函館高専紀要41号』113–118.

英語教育における ICT 活用の効果
映画視聴時における 1 つの工夫

内藤　徹

要旨
　本論文は ICT を活用した英語教育の一部を扱う。コンピュータや視聴覚機器等を使うと、聴覚のみならず視覚にも訴えるので、映像等が助けになって理解がし易くなる。また、注意力を喚起するので、学習者の集中力は増し、理解が深まり、動機づけも高まる。学生に行ったアンケートでも、肯定的な結果が出ている。今回、DVD 映画のリスニング中にタスクを用いた場合と用いない場合でどのように異なるのかを調べた。映画は Disney の *Cinderella* である。これを用いたのは、大量に聴き取るリスニング（extensive listening）が可能だからである。そして、ただ聴くだけではなく、タスクを与えて大きなストーリーの中で聴き取る作業を行うタスクリスニングとした。今回、この方法が extensive listening に、より効果が大きいことが支持された。これからの ICT を用いた英語教育への 1 つの示唆になれば幸いである。

キーワード　ICT、タスク、リスニング、映画、動機づけ

1. はじめに

　近年 ICT を活用した英語教育が盛んになってきている。インターネットに接続したコンピュータや視聴覚機器を使うといろいろな利点がある。素早い検索だけでなく、辞書として、百科事典として調べることが容易である。そして、DVD や CD などを用いた教材の場合でも、聴覚

のみならず視覚にも訴えるので、映像（や画像）が助けになって理解がし易くなる。また、そのような教材は注意力を喚起するので、学習者の集中力は増し、理解が深まる。そして、その結果動機づけも高まると考えられる（内藤 1987, 1988）。

　DVDで映画を見せる場合、タスクを用いると理解力や集中力が増し、内容把握に効果的であると考えた。今回、DVD映画のリスニング中にタスクを用いた場合と用いない場合でどのように異なるのかを調べてみた。タスクを用いたリスニングとは、予め与えられた課題に対する答えを探すようにして聴く方法であるが、この方法がこれからのICTを用いた英語教育の1つの示唆になれば幸いである。

2.　実証研究

2.1　文献および目的

　Listening task の利点等について Rod Ellis (2003) は次のように述べている。

> Listening tasks provide an excellent means for measuring whether learners have acquired the feature in question. Further, listening tasks can be devised to facilitate the acquisition of the targeted feature. For example, the input can be 'modified' to enable learner to process the feature and thereby create the conditions for acquisition. Listening tasks, then, provide a means of investigating the effect of different kinds of input modification. For teachers, listening tasks provide the obvious starting point for a task-based course designed for low-proficiency learners. Simple listening tasks can be devised that can be performed with zero competence in the L2 and that thus cater to the 'silent period', which characterizes the early stages of acquisition for some learners (Krashen 1981). They provide a non-threatening way of engaging beginner learners in meaning-centered activity and, thereby, of

developing the proficiency that, later on, can be used in production tasks. Also, of course, like researchers, teachers can use listening tasks to present the students with input enriched with specific features they wish to target.

今回用いた DVD の映画は Disney の *Cinderella* である。この映画を用いたのは、普通の精緻に聴き取る能力を向上させるためのリスニング (intensive listening) とは異なり、大量に聴き取るリスニング (extensive listening) が可能 (Field 2008、Hinkel 2005) だからである。そして、ただ聴くだけの授業ではなく、タスクを与えて大きなストーリーの中で聴き取る作業を行うタスクリスニングとした。

2.2 仮説
映画などの大量に聴き取るリスニングの場合、聴き取る流れの中にタスクを組み込むことによって集中力が増し、内容理解はより深まる。

2.3 被験者内訳
J大学　A組54名　B組19名　計73名（ほとんど女子）
F大学　C組28名　D組32名　計60名（ほとんど男子）

2.4 分析方法 [**Hatch and Farhady（1982）、内藤（1996）**]
平均 (MEAN)、標準偏差 (STANDARD DEVIATION = SD)
t-test［平均点の有意差検定］
χ^2-test［アンケート項目間の有意差検定］
両検定とも、有意水準は 5%(*)、1%(**)、0.1%(***)

2.5 結果および考察
☆映画視聴前の英語の学力 (TOEIC 模試：100点満点に換算)

表1　J大学　総合(Listening + Reading)

	A組	B組	t-test
mean	36.3	40.0	t=1.726
sd	8.1	7.4	df=71
n	54	19	p＜0.09　有意差なし

表2　F大学　総合(Listening + Reading)

	C組	D組	t-test
mean	46.2	45.9	t=0.125
sd	8.5	9.9	df=58
n	28	32	p＜1.0　有意差なし

表3　J大学 Listening

	A組	B組	t-test
mean	39.6	41.1	t=0.513
sd	10.6	11.4	df=71
N	54	19	p＜0.7　有意差なし

表4　J大学 Reading

	A組	B組	t-test
mean	33.2	37.8	t=1.731
sd	9.8	9.9	df=71
n	54	19	p＜0.1　有意差なし

表5　F大学 Listening

	C組	D組	t-test
mean	42.9	47.2	t=1.409
sd	10.6	12.4	df=58
n	28	32	p＜0.2　有意差なし

表6　F大学 Reading

	C組	D組	t-test
mean	49.5	44.5	t=1.527
sd	12.6	12.3	df=58
n	28	32	p＜0.2　有意差なし

A組とC組は1枚目のタスクシートで、映画を視聴しながら課題を行う。B組とD組は視聴後に課題を行う。

☆映画視聴時

①は1枚目のタスクシート、②は2枚目のタスクシート：①と②は視聴している教材(映画)内容は同じであるが、設問は異なる。

表7　J大学　①

	A組	B組	t-test
mean	61.2	33.5	$t = 5.955$
sd	18.4	13.2	$df = 71$
n	54	19	*** $p < 0.001$　　0.1%水準で有意差あり

表8　J大学　②

	A組	B組	t-test
mean	24.3	16.3	$t = 2.012$
sd	16.4	8.1	$df = 71$
n	54	19	* $p < 0.05$　　5%水準で有意差あり

表9　F大学　①

	C組	D組	t-test
mean	57.2	36.7	$t = 4.816$
sd	15.3	16.9	$df = 58$
n	28	32	*** $p < 0.001$　　0.1%水準で有意差あり

表10　F大学　②

	C組	D組	t-test
mean	25.2	17.8	$t = 2.314$
sd	14.8	8.1	$df = 58$
n	28	32	* $p < 0.03$　　5%水準で有意差あり

表11　学習者へのアンケート

視聴覚機器やパソコン等を用いた授業について答えて下さい。
項目：楽しい、動機づけられる、分かり易い
a＝強く思う、b＝思う、c＝普通、d＝思わない、e＝全く思わない

上記の内容でアンケートを行った。表12から表15の各段階における数字はパーセントである。

J大学は教員のみならず、学習者もネットに接続してあるパソコンを使用し、教材はDVDやCDを使って動画などをプロジェクターやモニターテレビで視聴できる環境の授業である。F大学は、学習者はパソコンは使えないが、その他はJ大学と同じである。

第1回アンケート：6回目の授業／15回

表12　J大学 n＝73

	a	b	c	d	e	χ^2-test
楽しい	10	46	43	1	0	各項目とも
動機づけられる	11	26	55	7	1	*** p＜0.001
分かり易い	13	25	54	8	0	0.1％水準で有意差あり

表13　F大学 n＝60

	a	b	c	d	e	χ^2-test
楽しい	10	29	58	3	0	各項目とも
動機づけられる	3	28	52	14	3	*** p＜0.001
分かり易い	6	33	49	12	0	0.1％水準で有意差あり

第2回アンケート：15回目の授業／15回

表14　J大学 n＝72

	a	b	c	d	e	χ^2-test
楽しい	56	38	6	0	0	各項目とも
動機づけられる	49	43	8	0	0	*** p＜0.001
分かり易い	92	4	0	0	0	0.1％水準で有意差あり

表15　F大学 n＝59

	a	b	c	d	e	χ^2-test
楽しい	47	42	11	0	0	各項目とも
動機づけられる	35	48	17	0	0	*** p＜0.001
分かり易い	56	35	9	0	0	0.1％水準で有意差あり

被験者はJ大学生とF大学生である。A組とB組はJ大学、C組とD組はF大学である。A組とC組は1枚目のタスクシート①を渡し

て、映画を視聴しながらそのシートの課題を行った。B組とD組は1枚目において映画を視聴している間にはシートを渡さず、映画の視聴後にシートの課題を行った。これは、1枚目のタスクを行いながら視聴するグループと、タスクをしないで視聴するグループの(点)差を見るためである。2枚目②においては、全クラスにおいて、映画を視聴している間にはシートを渡さず、視聴後にシートを渡しその課題を行った。これは、1枚目の視聴中にタスクがあったグループと視聴中にタスクがないグループで2枚目に(点)差がでるかどうかを見るためである。すなわち、1枚目の視聴中にタスクをするという前向きな姿勢が2枚目に影響があるかどうかを調べるためである。2枚目のチェックによって、どれだけ理解が深まっているかがわかる。

まず、実践をする前に比較検討をするクラス間に成績上の有意差があるかどうかを調べた。学力差をみるためにTOEIC模試(Listening + Readingの総合)(100点満点に換算)を用いた。J大学の場合ではA組(n = 54)がmean 36.3、sd 8.1、B組(n = 19)はmean 40.0、sd 7.4で有意差はない($p<0.09$)[表1]。F大学ではC組(n = 28)がmean 46.2、sd 8.5、D組(n = 32)はmean 45.9、sd 9.9で有意差はない($p<1.0$)[表2]。また、総合が2つのパートに分かれているのでListeningとReadingについても調べた。これは、技能の学力バランスが均衡に保たれているとは限らないからである。J大学のListeningは、A組がmean 39.6、sd 10.6、B組はmean 41.1、sd 11.4で有意差なし($p<0.7$)[表3]。J大学のReadingは、A組がmean 33.2、sd 9.8、B組はmean 37.8、sd 9.9で有意差なし($p<0.1$)[表4]。F大学のListeningは、C組がmean 42.9、sd 10.6、D組はmean 47.2、sd 12.4で有意差なし($p<0.2$)[表5]。F大学のReadingは、C組がmean 49.5、sd 12.6、D組はmean 44.5、sd 12.3で有意差なし($p<0.2$)[表6]。従って、全ての比較するクラス間には点数上の有意差はなかった。

さて、実証研究データである。J大学①の場合である。A組(n = 54)がmean 61.2、sd 18.4、B組(n = 19)はmean 33.5、sd 13.2で両クラス間には0.1%水準で有意差がある(*** $p<0.001$)[表7]。J大学②の場合、A

組が mean 24.3、sd 16.4、B 組は mean 16.3、sd 8.1 で両クラス間に 5% 水準で有意差がある（* p＜0.05）［表 8］。F 大学①の場合、C 組（n＝28）が mean 57.2、sd 15.3、D 組（n＝32）は mean 36.7、sd 16.9 で両クラス間には 0.1% 水準で有意差がある（*** p＜0.001）［表 9］。F 大学②の場合、C 組が mean 25.2、sd14.8、D 組は mean 17.8、sd 8.1 で両クラス間に 5% 水準で有意差がある（* p＜0.03）［表 10］。まとめると、J・F の両大学において、①の場合の映画を視聴しながらタスクを行う方が断然成績が良く、その後の②においても①のタスクをしながら視聴した方が内容理解は深まっているといえる。従って、仮説は支持された。

　最後に ICT の効果を調べるため、参考に学習者にアンケートをとってみた。J 大学、F 大学とも 15 回の授業において 6 回目と 15 回目の 2 回アンケートを行った。第 1 回アンケート（6 回目の授業時）、J 大学は a と b をまとめて「楽しい」が 56% で、「動機づけられる（やる気がでる）」が 37%、「分かり易い」は 38% であった［表 12］。F 大学も傾向は似ていて「楽しい」が 39%、「動機づけられる」が 31%、「分かり易い」は 39% であった［表 13］。「思わない」は d と e をまとめても少ない。第 2 回アンケート（15 回目の授業時）、J 大学は a と b をまとめて「楽しい」が 94% で、「動機づけられる（やる気がでる）」が 92%、「分かり易い」は 96% であった［表 14］。F 大学も傾向は同じで「楽しい」が 89%、「動機づけられる」が 83%、「分かり易い」は 91% であった［表 15］。両大学とも「思わない」は d と e をまとめてゼロとなった。これらのアンケートでは a・b とも第 2 回アンケート（15 回目の授業時）の数値がかなり大きく伸びている。付け加えると、F 大学は学習者がパソコンを使える環境にはなかったので、J 大学と比べると若干 a・b が少ないという影響があったのだろう。さて、総合的にみると、学習者は視聴覚機器などを用いた授業が「楽しく」「やる気が出て」「より分かり易い」と感じているといえる。χ^2 検定でも項目間に 0.1% 水準での有意差がみられる（*** p＜0.001）。なお、学習者のコメントでは「英語が身につく」「楽しい」「（こういう英語が）分かり易くていい」「音声だけよりもいい」「動画が分かり易い」などがあった。

3. おわりに

リスニングにはいろいろな方法がある。映画を見せる場合、全体の中の1つの場面だけを取り出してきて、クローズ式のチェックをしたり、その場面の全文や部分を書き取らせたりすることはよくある。また、120分以上の映画を全部見せることもあるが、そうすると時間もかかりチェックがしづらくなる。それ故に、視聴させるだけで終わってしまうことがしばしばある。今回、比較的短いDisneyの *Cinderella*（73mins.）を選び、90分の授業時間内に視聴して、タスクも完成させるものとした。タスクリスニングは、前述のとおり「予め与えられた課題に対する答えを探すようにして聴く方法」で、今回、この方法が大量に聞き取るリスニング（extensive listening）により効果が大きいことが支持された。Mackey and Gass（2005）も述べているようにICTを活用した英語教育が盛んになる中、いろいろな方法が検討されるべきである。そして、Rost（2002）が主張している「学習者がより積極的に学んでいくActive Learning」をさらに推進していきたい。

参考文献

Ellis, Rod. (2003) *Task-based Language Learning and Teaching*. Oxford University Press, p.37.

Field, John. (2008) *Listening in the Language Classroom*. Cambridge University Press, pp.14–17

Hatch, Evelyn and Farhady, Hossein. (1982) *Research Design and Statistics for Applied Linguistics*. Newbury House Publishers, Inc., pp.192–214

Hinkel, Eli. (2005) *Handbook of Research in Second Language Teaching and Learning*. Routledg Taylor & Francis Group, pp.12–23

Mackey, Alison and Gass, Susan M. (2005) *Second Language Research*, Lawrence Erlbaum Associates, Inc., pp.185–220

内藤 徹 (1987) A Study on the Correlation between Listening and Reading. *Journal of the Chubu English Language Education Society*. No. 17, pp.7–12

内藤　徹(1988)「VTR の効果とその限界―「音声」と「音声＋映像」の有意差より」『中部地区英語教育学会紀要』第 18 号 235–240 頁

内藤　徹(1996)『新しい　英語教育ハンドブック』リーベル出版 17–37 頁

Rost, Michael. (2002) *Teaching and Researching Listening.* Pearson Education Limited, p.158

参考資料

(タスクシート①):
Cinderella (73 min)

　　　　　　　　　　No._____Name_____

Cinderella を鑑賞しながら設問に答えなさい。
1. 義母(継母)のことを英語ではどう言っていますか？
 　(　　　　　)
2. 「夢はきっと叶う」という歌の一節を英語で埋めなさい。
 　The (　　　　　) that I wish will come (　　　　　).
3. 「朝ごはん」とは英語で何ですか？(　　　　　)
4. 「今、行きます」は英語で "I'm (　　　　　)."
5. 「はいはい　ただいま(持って行きます)」は短くして
 　"In a (　　　　　)."
6. 「舞踏会」は英語で(　　　　　)
7. 「王子様」は英語で(　　　　　)
8. 「馬車」は英語で(　　　　　)または(　　　　　)の２つ出てきます。
9. 「奇跡」は英語で(　　　　　)
10. 「カボチャ(南瓜)」は英語で(　　　　　)。そして、このカボチャが馬車に変わった。
11. 「魔法の言葉」は英語で(　　　　　)(　　　　　)
12. 「ガラスの靴」は英語で(　　　　　)(　　　　　)
13. 「以前には見たことがない」の意味になるように英語で埋めなさい。
 　I've (　　　　　)(　　　　　) her (　　　　　).
14. 「これが愛(恋)」とは英語で　So this is (　　　　　).
15. 「待って！」は英語で "Please (　　　　　)!"
16. 「王様からの通達」は英語でどう書いてありましたか。
 　"(　　　　　)(　　　　　)(　　　　　) A Proclamation."
17. 「もう片方(の靴)がここに」の英語は
 　"I have the (　　　　　) slipper."
　　　　　　　　　　　　　　　　　　　　ここまで聴き取りテスト↑
18. "Cinderella story" と言うと、その意味は次のどれですか？
 　1) 突然の成功話　　　2) 美しい女性の話
 　3) 不遇な女性の話　　4) 心温まる話

19. Cinderella とはどういう意味か語源も含めて書きなさい。

20. あなたが知っている Cinderella と違うところがあれば書きなさい。

21. 面白かった（または印象に残った）ことを書きなさい。
    また、変だと思われることがあれば書きなさい。

［18〜21 は調べ学習］

英語形容詞のカタカナ語の語彙範疇化について

野中博雄

要旨

　本論文は英語形容詞のカタカナ語（外来語として日本語に借用された語）が日本語文法の枠組みで何に語彙範疇化されるのかを解明しようとしたものである。日本語では「綺麗」「健康」「元気」など漢語から借入した語が「形容動詞」とも「形容名詞」とも呼ばれており、英語形容詞のカタカナ語と似た振る舞いをする。それらの概念を第2節で捉え、英語形容詞のカタカナ語の名詞性を第3節で、その形容詞性を第4節で考察した。そして英語形容詞のカタカナ語には名詞性はないと予測され、「形容動詞の語幹」として述語化、名詞化、形容詞化、副詞化されるのではないかと結んだ。

　例文用のカタカナ語サンプルは『コンサイスカタカナ語辞典第2版』（三省堂編修所 2000）より英語形容詞を使い「な」が付加される語を639語選択した。さらに語選択の恣意性を排除するためにエクセルの RAND 関数を使って抽出した。

キーワード　英語形容詞のカタカナ語、形容動詞、形容名詞、名詞性、形容詞性

1. はじめに

　『コンサイスカタカナ語辞典第2版』（三省堂編修所 2000）によると英語より借用され、語尾に「な」を付加し、形容詞的な語となる語が 648

語ある。その中で639語は英語形容詞から借用されており、残りの9語が名詞、動詞、副詞、副詞句から借用されている。その凡例ページ（ix）では『「な」をつけて形容動詞として使われることを示した』と説明している。すなわち英語からの借用語に「な」を付加された語は日本語では「形容動詞」として語彙範疇化されるというのである。「形容動詞」の概念は国語学者諸家の見解であるが、その類の語を「形容動詞」ではなく「形容名詞」としてみるべきだという中島(1987)や影山(1993)の考えもある。本論文での疑問は『果して「な」を付加されたカタカナ語は日本語において「形容動詞」として語彙範疇化するのが妥当か。もしくは「形容名詞」として語彙範疇化するのが妥当か』である。特に英語形容詞のカタカナ語の名詞性、形容詞性に焦点を当てて考察する。

　第2節では「形容動詞」「形容名詞」の概念についての先行研究を概観する。第3節では英語形容詞のカタカナ語について名詞性の観点から考察する。第4節では英語形容詞のカタカナ語の形容詞性の観点から形態的・統語的特徴を捉え、本論文での疑問についての考察を試みたい。

2. 「形容動詞」「形容名詞」の概念

　本論文のテーマは「形容動詞」の概念や、「形容名詞」の概念と関係する。従ってこの順序で先行研究を追ってみる。

　大野(1999: 96-97)は「形容動詞」の成立についてこう説明している。

> 形容動詞の発達は、奈良時代から平安時代にかけて、知識階級の人々が、必ず学んだ漢文の膨大な語彙を日本語で訓読し、日本語の文章の中に取り込むためには、ぜひ必要な工夫であった。(中略)形容動詞は形容詞が足りなかったところを、<u>形容詞の語幹の部分にはほかの体言をもってきて据え、それの語尾に、ニ・ニアリ・ニアル・ニアレを加えて形容詞と同じ役目をさせたものである</u>。漢語を語幹にして形容動詞とするには、現在では「堂々たり」のようにタ

リが付くと決まっている。しかし、平安時代のはじめには漢語の下にも、ニアリとかナリとかがついた。(中略)漢文脈を主とする文章語では形容詞はふえず、多く増加したのは形容動詞だった。そして漢語を語幹にする方法が古く感じられると、今日では「グロッキーだ」とか「ラッキーな」とか「ナウな」とか、カタカナ語を語幹にして「……ニ」「……ダ」「……ナ」をつけるという方法で形容語をふやしている。
（下線は筆者による）

上記下線部に見るように、平安時代のはじめに漢語の体言(名詞)に「ニ・ニアリ・ニアル・ニアレ」を付けて形容詞と同じ働きをする言葉を作り、今日ではカタカナ語を語幹にして「に」「だ」「な」をつける方法で「形容語」を増やしている。従って「グロッキー」「ラッキー」「ナウ」は形容詞性を持った語と説明されている。

「にてあり」が「だ」になった経緯や「だ」の扱いについて、中島(1987: 140)は次のように述べている。

> この語形は文語の「にてあり」が口語で「である」となり、これが「ぢゃ」を経て「だ」になったものと説明される。文語で名詞や形容名詞につく「なり」(例「静かなり」)は「にあり」に由来するが、「なり」となってからは、もとの「あり」のもつ存在の意味がうすれて、「にてあり」と同じように、単に承認判断を表す形式動詞となった。普通「だ」は助動詞といわれているが、名詞や形容名詞に直接接続する語であるから、助動詞というのはおかしい。本書では「だ」を名詞や形容名詞を述語とする形式動詞として扱ってきた。
> （下線は筆者による）

下線部1箇所目が「にてあり」が「だ」になった経緯であり、下線部2箇所目で「だ」の助動詞説の否定をしている。さらに下線部3箇所目は「だ」を「名詞や形容名詞を述語とする形式動詞」として扱う中島の

見解となっている。ここでは従来の「形容動詞」という品詞の概念とは違う「形容名詞」という品詞の概念がたてられているが、このことについては影山(1993)の論と併せて後述する。

上田(2004: 86)は国語学者諸家の「形容動詞」に対する概念を簡潔に説明している。

表1 「静的属性概念表現」諸説

静詞	和語		漢語		外来語	
語例	美しい	静か	綺麗	立派	エレガント	スマート
橋本文法	形容詞	形 容 動 詞 の 語 幹					
時枝文法	形容詞	体 言				
宮田文法	活用形容詞	無 活 用 形 容 詞				
三浦文法	形容詞	活 用 の な い 静 詞				
	静 詞					
山浦文法	静用詞		静 体 詞			
	静 的 属 性 詞 ＝ 静 詞					

（出典） 上田博和「無活用動詞論―漢語外来語の属性概念表現」、『言語過程説の探求第1巻』明石書店 2004：86.

表1においては、和語、漢語、外来語に「だ」がついた場合の捉え方に違いが現れている。「形容動詞」について国語学者諸家の概念を整理すると、橋本文法では「静か」「綺麗」「立派」「エレガント」「スマート」を「形容動詞の語幹」とし、それらに「だ」がついたのを1語とみなしている。一方時枝文法では、それらを体言（名詞）であるとし、「だ」を指定の助動詞と認定している。宮田文法の「無活用形容詞」は「形容動詞の語幹」のことであり、三浦文法や山浦文法も「形容動詞の語幹」説を唱えている。

従来の「形容動詞」を「形容名詞」とする説について中島(1987)と影山(1993)の説を紹介する。中島(1987: 82-83)が「形容動詞」を「形容名詞」とする理由は以下のようである。

「静か」の類の語は、「だ」をとって述語になり、「な」をとって連

体修飾語になり、「に」をとって連用修飾語になる。これは普通の名詞とよく似ている用法である。これを形容名詞として扱ったほうが、「静かだ」という形容動詞を立て、連体形が「静かな」、連用形が「静かに」と活用すると考えるよりも、日本語の名詞的性格に合っていると思われる。形容動詞をたてると、たとえば「貧乏だ」は「貧乏な人」というときは「貧乏な」が連体形であるといえるが、「貧乏のつらさ」というときは「の」がでる。この時の「貧乏」は名詞だということになる。このちがいは<u>「貧乏」が貧しい状態を意味するときは形容名詞として「な」をとり、貧しい状態そのものの名称として用いられるときは名詞として「の」をとると説明したほうが、形容動詞と名詞の違いというよりも分かりやすいと思う。「静か」は静かな状態を意味するから形容名詞であり、その状態そのものの名称となるときは「静かさ」という名詞となる。</u>
（下線は筆者による）

中島(1987: 82)は「貧乏な人」の表現における「貧乏な」の形容詞的性格を「貧乏(形容名詞)」に「な」がついて形容詞となり、「貧乏のつらさ」の「貧乏」が名詞として「の(形式名詞)」をとると説明したほうが、「形容動詞」と名詞の違いというよりも分かりやすいと思うと述べている。「貧乏」に形容詞的機能と名詞的機能が備わっているために形容名詞という品詞をたてている。

影山(1993: 24)は「形容動詞を巡る論争が、それを名詞か形容詞かに割り振ろうとするところに原因があることを指摘しておきたい。むしろ形容動詞(本書で言う形容名詞)は、名詞と形容詞の両方の特徴を兼ね備えた、独立の存在である。(中略)smart, realなどの形容詞を借入する場合はそのまま形容詞(＊リアルい　＊スマートい)として活用させるのではなく名詞性を持った形容詞すなわち形容名詞(リアルな　スマートな)として使用している」と述べている。つまり「美しい」や「悲しい」などのように語尾に「い」の付く形容詞とはならない点を指摘している。さらに「形容名詞」の特性として「名詞」や「形容詞」との相違

点、共通点を以下のように指摘している。

① 統語的な観点からは、形容名詞基体がそのままの形で主語や目的語として機能することからその名詞性を示唆している。
② 形態論的観点から、否定を意味する「不一」が名詞と形容名詞には付くが純粋な形容詞と動詞には付かない。
③ 形容名詞は接尾辞「一さ」によって名詞化することができるが、この特徴は名詞にはなく、形容詞と平行する。
④ 動詞化接辞「一がる」が形容名詞と形容詞を選択する。
⑤ 純粋な名詞や形容詞には普通付かない「一な」の屈折語尾を持つ。
(影山 1993: 24-25)

野中(1999: 117-123)は英語形容詞のカタカナ語(ここではカタカナ語を日本語借入語と表現している)について、影山(1993)の指摘した「形容名詞」の特徴を考察し、以下の点を指摘した。

① 英語形容詞の日本語借入語には、影山の言う日本語形容名詞の持つ特徴は見られない。本稿では、動詞化接辞「一になる」、名詞化接辞「一さ」「一み」「一げ」の結合において、「ナ形容詞」と同様の統語的特徴を持つことが示された。
② 英語形容詞の日本語借入語には名詞性がない。これは日本語形容詞や日本語動詞と同様の機能である。

3. 英語形容詞のカタカナ語の名詞性

　野中(1999: 122)は「英語形容詞の日本語借入語(カタカナ語)には名詞性はない」としたが、本論文では選択した語例の恣意性を排除するために、『コンサイスカタカナ語辞典第2版』(三省堂編修所 2000)より抽出した「な」付加の可能な英語形容詞のカタカナ語639語をエクセル表に入力し、RAND関数で抽出した語(RAND関数で並べ替えた後、

1–5行目に現れる語を選択する)を使って検証することとした。

　影山 (1993: 24) の「統語的な観点からは、形容名詞基体がそのままの形で主語や目的語として機能することからその名詞性を示唆している」という指摘が、英語形容詞のカタカナ語にあてはまるかどうかから検証する。RAND関数で抽出した語で意味の通る「だ」文を作ってみる。以下に示す。

（1）a.　このウイルスは人間にとってハームレスだ。
　　　b.　彼の好みはパティキュラーだ。
　　　c.　彼の言い方はスノビッシュだ。
　　　d.　この状態に私たちはアンコンシャスだ。
　　　e.　彼の行為はリーガルだ。

上記の英語形容詞のカタカナ語が名詞性を持つとするならば、主語にして言い換える事ができるはずであるが、そうはならない。

（2）a.　*ハームレスは人間にとってのこのウイルスだ。
　　　b.　*パティキュラーは彼の好みだ。
　　　c.　*スノビッシュは彼の言い方だ。
　　　d.　*アンコンシャスはこの状態の私たちだ。
　　　e.　*リーガルは彼の行為だ。

また (1a–e) のカタカナ語を目的語にした場合も同様に非文となる。

（3）a.　*このウイルスは人間にとってハームレスを与える。
　　　b.　*彼の好みはパティキュラーを表す。
　　　c.　*彼の言い方はスノビッシュを含む。
　　　d.　*この状態に私たちはアンコンシャスを感じる。
　　　e.　*彼の行為はリーガルを示す。

時枝(1950: 132)は『「親切」「健康」は「大変」「非常に」などの連用修飾語を加えることができる』と指摘している。連用修飾語はおもに動詞、形容詞、形容動詞などを修飾するものであるから名詞は基本的に修飾しない。(1a–e)の文中のカタカナ語が名詞である場合、副詞の使用ができないはずだが、副詞の使用は可能である。従ってそれらは名詞ではないことを示す。

(4) a. このウイルスは人間にとってとてもハームレスだ。
　　b. 彼の好みはすこぶるパティキュラーだ。
　　c. 彼の言い方はたいへんスノビッシュだ。
　　d. この状態に私たちはまったくアンコンシャスだ。
　　e. 彼の行為はきわめてリーガルだ。

奥津(1974: 119)は「形容動詞」が名詞とは考えられない根拠として他の副詞と同様に連体修飾文を受けることができないことを下記の例によって指摘している。

(5) a. 川ガ　静かニ　流レル　→
　　　　*川ガ　流レル　静カ
　　b. 華やかニ　万博の幕ガ　開イタ　→
　　　　*万博ノ幕ガ　開イタ　華ヤカ
　　c. 水車ノ音ガ　単調ニ　響ク　→
　　　　*水車ノ音ガ　響ク　単調
　　d. パーティーハ　ナゴヤカニ　進行シテイル　→
　　　　*パーティーハ　進行シテイル　ナゴヤカ

奥津(1974: 120)は「名詞とは、叙述文中にある要素でそれぞれの文末に転位して被修飾語たり得るものと定義できるものである。つまり、上例のように文末に転位した時に非文となる場合は、その要素は名詞として定義できない要素である」としている。このことが英語形容詞のカ

タカナ語についてはどうか、RAND 関数で抽出した前例とは別の語を使って検証してみる。

(6) a.　球が　イレギュラーに　跳ねる
　　　　*球が　跳ねる　イレギュラー
　　b.　彼が　スポンテーニアスに　反応した
　　　　*彼が　反応した　スポンテーニアス
　　c.　その計画が　ワーカブルに　進行した
　　　　*その計画が　進行した　ワーカブル
　　d.　彼が　マクロスコピックに　発表した
　　　　*彼が　発表した　マクロスコピック
　　e.　彼が　インタレスティングに　述べた
　　　　*彼が　述べた　インタレスティング

英語形容詞のカタカナ語も日本語形容動詞と同様に連体修飾文を受けることができないのである。従って名詞性がないことを意味する。

4.　英語形容詞のカタカナ語の形容詞性

　本節では英語形容詞のカタカナ語の形容詞性について考察する。影山 (1993: 25) は『形容名詞は接尾辞「―さ」によって名詞化することができるが、この特徴は名詞にはなく、形容詞と平行する』と指摘しているが、英語形容詞のカタカナ語についてはどうであろうか。RAND 関数で抽出した語を使って検証してみる。抽出語に「さ」を付けてインターネットで検索した。

(7) a.　アグレッシブさが足りない。
　　b.　日本はクレージーさをアメリカから学ぶべき。
　　c.　梅雨らしいヒューミッドさが、あつあつの夏を予感させる。
　　d.　インテリアのスポーティーさに注目。

e.　ロイヤルさが欠片もない。

　上記の例は「美しさ」や「やさしさ」などの様に「さ」を付けて名詞化する形容詞と同様の形態的特徴を示している。
　「な」が付加される英語形容詞のカタカナ語は今回の研究データとして639語を数えたが、その類の語の名詞修飾機能（形容詞的機能）と「に」を付加して副詞化された場合について検証する。例によってRAND関数で抽出した語を使い、インターネットで検索した。

（8）a.　ビジュアルな履歴書を作ってくれる。
　　　b.　ヘッドライン要素に使えるボールドなフォント集です。
　　　c.　マイルドな味でした。
　　　d.　センシャスな香り。
　　　e.　フォトジェニックな女性になる。

（9）a.　自分の能力をフルに（*フルく）生かす。
　　　b.　想いをイモータルに（*イモータルく）刻む。
　　　c.　自然とともにエコロジカルに（*エコロジカルく）暮らす。
　　　d.　こんなにダルに（*ダルく）過ごすのは生まれて初めてである。
　　　e.　普通に就職をして、それからフリーに（*フリーく）なる。

　(7a–e) より英語形容詞のカタカナ語は日本語形容詞と同様に「さ」によって名詞化でき（日本語形容詞や形容動詞の場合は語幹に「さ」を付加することで名詞化できる）、(8a–e) より名詞修飾機能を持ち（日本語形容詞・日本語形容動詞の場合も同様）、(9a–e) より「に」を付加することで副詞化できる（日本語形容詞の場合は形容詞基体に「く」を付加することで副詞化でき、また日本語形容動詞は「に」を付加することで副詞化できるが、英語形容詞のカタカナ語は「に」のみで副詞化されるようである）。上記の観察により、英語形容詞のカタカナ語は日本語形容動詞と平行した形態的特徴・統語的特徴を有していると言える。

5. おわりに

　本論文は英語形容詞のカタカナ語が日本語文法の枠組みで何に語彙範疇化されるのかを疑問とし、形態的・統語的特徴から名詞性、形容詞性を考察した。

　第2節では和語、漢語、外来語に「だ」がついた場合の捉え方について概観した。「形容動詞の語幹」に「だ」が付いたとする国語学者諸家の説と、それが名詞性と形容詞性を持つゆえに「形容名詞」とする中島 (1987) や影山 (1993) の説、または英語形容詞のカタカナ語には名詞性がないのではないかとする野中 (1999) の指摘などの先行研究を概観した。

　第3節では英語形容詞のカタカナ語の名詞性について考察した。『コンサイスカタカナ語辞典第2版』(三省堂編修所 2000) より抽出した「な」付加の可能な英語形容詞のカタカナ語 639 語からランダムに語を選び、文中での統語的特徴について観察した。それらは主語や目的語になり得ず、副詞によって修飾されることができる。また連帯修飾文を受けることができない。これらの特徴により、英語形容詞のカタカナ語には名詞性がないと考えられる。

　第4節では英語形容詞のカタカナ語の形容詞性について考察した。「さ」を付けて名詞化できること、「な」を付けて名詞修飾できること、「に」を付けて副詞化できることなどは日本語形容詞と平行した形態的特徴・統語的特徴を持つことを指摘した。

　確かに「貧乏」「空腹」「健康」「元気」などは「形容動詞の語幹」として形容詞的機能を有すると同時に主語や目的語となり名詞的機能も有する。このことにより「形容名詞」説が提唱されているが、その語数は名詞的機能を持たない語より少なく、英語形容詞のカタカナ語と併せて名詞性があると一般化するには疑問がある。第3節より「少なくとも現時点では英語形容詞のカタカナ語の場合は名詞性を持っていない」ことが予測できた。本論文での考察により『英語形容詞は日本語に借入される時、「形容動詞の語幹」として「だ」と結合して述語となり、「な」

と結合して形容詞となり、「に」と結合して副詞となるのではないか』として「英語形容詞のカタカナ語の語彙範疇化について」の拙論を結びたい。

「貧乏」「空腹」「健康」「元気」などのように名詞性を持った英語形容詞のカタカナ語が今後出現するのかしないのかは不明であるが、出現する場合、それが古い時代に借入された英語形容詞の中からなのか、もしくは使用頻度の高い借入語の中からなのかは検証に値する今後の研究課題とする。

参考文献
影山太郎(1993)『文法と語形成』ひつじ書房
中島文雄(1987)『日本語の構造―日本語との対比』岩波書店
野中博雄(1999)「外来語の語彙範疇―英語形容詞の日本語語彙範疇化について」『桐生短期大学紀要』10：pp.117–123.
奥津敬一郎(1974)『生成日本文法論』大修館書店
大野 晋(1999)『日本語の文法を考える』岩波書店
時枝誠記(1950)『日本文法口語篇』岩波書店
上田博和(2004)「無活用動詞論―漢語外来語の属性概念表現」佐良木昌編『言語過程説の探求第1巻：時枝学説の継承と三浦理論の展開』pp.79–104．明石書店

辞典
『コンサイスカタカナ語辞典』第2版　三省堂編修所(2000)三省堂

学習指導要領の改訂と
英語授業の構造改革
世界のグローバル化と日本の言語施策

松土　清

要旨

　近年の流通経済のグローバル化の加速やインターネット利用者の急増が拍車をかけ、広域コミュニケーション・ツールとしての英語のニーズが急騰している。本論文では、アジア諸国の英語教育施策等を概観し、高等学校新学習指導要領に特化して、時代に即した英語教育構造改革の推進のあり方について論ずる。

キーワード　アジア諸国の英語教育、国家戦略としての英語、高等学校学習指導要領、英語授業の構造改革、大量インプット、アウトプットを引き出す授業

1. はじめに

　近年の流通経済のグローバル化の加速やインターネット利用者の急増が拍車をかけ、広域コミュニケーション・ツールとしての英語のニーズが世界中で急騰している。

　アジア諸国においても、英語のコミュニケーション・ツールとしての認識が確立され、学校内では積極的に学ばれ、そして学校外では積極的に使われている。シンガポール、インド、フィリピンなどの英語公用語国においてはずっと以前から英語は教育言語であるが、その他の英語国際語国でも早期の英語教育が実施されるようになった。アジア諸国においては、英語学習の目的自体が、かつての英米文化の理解や受容から離

れ、技術革新や経済発展など国家戦略の武器としての英語習得へと移行した。

日本における英語教育の潮流を学習指導要領の変遷に見ると、目標、科目設定、指導法、新出語数など、様々な紆余曲折を経て今日に至っていることがわかる。そのような背景の中で、今般の英語に関する改訂では小学校への外国語活動の導入、中学校の時間増、そして高等学校の科目再編成など、コミュニケーション・ツールとしての英語への重心移動がより鮮明となっており、世界の動向に合わせた、国策としての人材育成への意欲が感じられる改訂である。

本論文では、アジア諸国の英語教育施策等を概観し、平成25年度から年次進行で実施されている新高等学校学習指導要領に特化して、英語授業の構造改革のあり方について論ずる。

2. 日本の英語教育の新たな背景

2.1 世界語となった英語

長い間、国際共通語の在り方について、様々な学術的論議や政治・経済的論議があったことなどまるで嘘のように、ウインドウズの普及やネット世界の進展は、英語を民間レベルでの実質的な世界語に押し上げた。また、企業のさらなる多国籍化やインターネット利用者数の急増が世界中で英語の有用性に拍車をかけている。「インターネットの利用者は5年間で2倍になった。」とPingdomのモニタリング調査（2012年4月）がその結果を報じている。また、「インターネット利用者数が世界人口の3分の1に達した。」と国連の専門機関「国際電気通信連合（International Telecommunications Union, ITU）」が2012年10月に発表している。

このように、英語は多国間、多文化間コミュニケーションの最大、最強の道具となった。しかしながら、アメリカ人やイギリス人などのネイティブ・スピーカーの英語がそのままの形で、世界中に広まったということではない。多くのノンネイティブ・スピーカーが、英米文化から切

り離した場面で、それぞれの歴史的、社会的、文化的必然性に合わせて、異文化コミュニケーションの手段として英語を運用しているものであり、英語には過去とは全く異なる新しい国際的役割が与えられたものである。「世界の4人に1人が英語を使う」(David Crystal 2003)という推計の時代から、実質3人に1人が英語を使う時代へと急速に進んでいる。

2.2 アジア諸国の英語教育施策

1965年には、東南アジア諸国において英語を国際言語として振興するために、SEAMEO(東南アジア教育大臣機構)が組織され、バンコクに事務局が置かれた。また、1968年にはシンガポールにRELC(Regional English Language Centre)が設立され、各種セミナー等を実施することにより東南アジア諸国の英語学習の振興の中心的役割を果たしてもうすぐ半世紀に至る。

アジア諸国においては、かなり以前から英語教育に力を入れており、英語教育を小学校から開始している国が多い。また、教室内で英語を使うというのは当然の授業形態である。日本では大きな後れを取って、それも根強い反論を受けながら、今般初めて小学校に英語が導入されたことを考えると、日本人の英語認識の特異さは否定できない。明治の開国と同時に「いかに英書を正しく読むか」からスタートした日本の英語教育は、その後国家主義の台頭した大正時代や、敵性語として扱われた昭和前期、さらには極度に受験科目化した昭和後期など、様々な変遷を経て独自なスタイルが築き上げられてきた。

以下は、アジアのいくつかの国を抽出し、それらの国の英語教育施策のうち小学校における英語授業に特化した比較である。

インドでは、英語はヒンディー語とともに、連邦の公用語である。公立学校では小学校高学年から英語を教えるが、中間階級の多くの子弟は私立学校に通い早くから英語に接している。そこではヒンディー語の授業以外の全科目の教育言語は英語である。

シンガポールでは、以前は多民族による多言語国家であったが、国家

統一のための言語施策を強力に推進した。英語は第1公用語であるので、子ども達は小学校に入学する前から英語に触れている。英語は全ての学校の教育言語である。市街地と郊外で実施した現地調査（2012）によると子ども達は学校を離れても英語を使うことが多かった。

マレーシアでは、小学校入学時から英語は必修科目である。低学年から実用的なスピーキングとリスニングに重心を置いており、英語の授業以外にも算数や理科においては英語を教育言語としている。将来の進学先としてシンガポールは有力な選択肢である。

中国では、都市部の公立小学校を中心に英語は正課の教育課程に組み込まれている。近年において文法中心型からコミュニケーション重視型に授業が改善された。英語の授業は基本的に英語で行われている。2008年の北京オリンピック準備期間に強化した言語教育施策はその後の英語教育の改善に奏功した。

台湾では、教育部が2005年に小学校の正課に英語を導入した。また都市部における保護者の英語教育熱も高い。LL教室やCAIも活用し、進級とともに英語力が高まる仕組みが構築されている。日本の中高生との交流行事における台湾の中高生の英語を観察すると運用力と同時に豊富な語彙力に気づく。小学校の基礎の上に大量インプットが重ねられている。

韓国では、1997年から英語を小学校の必修科目としている。韓国では伝統的に教員の研修が熱心であるが、小学校教員の英語研修にも長い研修時間を課している。国内の多くの企業の採用試験にTOEICが課せられるなど社会全体に英語を重要視する空気が醸成されており、小学校の英語教育重視ともリンクしている。

2.3　英語を国家戦略の武器にした国、シンガポール

シンガポールの国土面積は東京23区とほぼ同じである。資源もほとんどなく、食料自給率も極めて低い輸入大国であり、現在でも生活の基本である水もマレーシアから供給を受けている。

シンガポールの民族構成は多様で複雑であり、言語学的、人類学的に

4大別した政府公表の資料によると、華人77%、マレー人15%、インド人7%、その他1%となっている。旧宗主国であるイギリスの影響も多く残しながら、イスラム系の区画やインド系の区画ありと生活文化の多様性を保有している。1965年にマレーシアから独立した当時の公用語はマレー語、北京語、タミル語、そして英語の4言語であった。

初代首相リー・クアン・ユーが開発独裁型の強い言語政策を推進し、1970年代後半に、全国民に対し共通言語としての英語の習得を義務づけ、1987年には英語教育を国家プロジェクトとして取り入れ、英語を学校教育用語とした。その後の発展の連鎖は次のとおりである。

「シンガポールのほとんどの人達が英語を使えるようになる。」→「世界中からたくさんの企業がシンガポールにやってきて、国内にたくさんの仕事が生まれた。」→「ネットによるグローバリズムが急速に広がり、ネット上での世界共通言語は事実上英語となった。」→「空港や港をアジア最高のレベルに整備し、外国企業に対する税制の緩和、接客マナーの向上など官民一体となった環境整備をした。」→「世界中からさらに人々が集るようになり、世界屈指の最先端都市を形成し、失業率は低く、人口は増加中である。」

このように、シンガポール政府は生き残りを賭けた国家戦略として、国語を英語にすることによって見事にその困難を乗り越えた。国民が英語を使えるようになったシンガポールは、世界の企業の拠点として、またアジアの経済、教育のハブとして、新たなる未来に大いなる活路を見出した。このシンガポールの急速な発展の原点は、先見の明を持った言語政策に他ならない。

2.4 グローバル時代の人材育成

日本は少子化に喘ぎ、世界は人口爆発に喘いでいるというパラドキシカルな現実がある。日本の総人口の減少とともに国内市場が縮小する中で、どうしても日本の企業は国外市場の開発を積極的に行うことにより活路を見いだしていくことが必要になる。

ビジネスの世界では、かつての国際化（internationalization）からグロー

バル化 (globalization) へと意識が移行し、経営用語としての多国籍企業 (multinational company) もグローバル企業 (global company) と峻別されている。世界を、国と国、あるいは民族と民族の集まりというイメージで捉えた「国際化」から、地球を1つの塊として見る「グローバル化」への移行をはっきりと認識することは、今日のビジネスの大前提である。

各種業界内では「ヒューマン・キャピタル戦略」が重要視され、英語を社内公用語にした会社、新卒採用者に一定のTOEIC得点を義務付けた会社、英語力の有無が人事考課に大きな影響のある会社等がメディアで取り上げられている。

「日本企業が人材の国際化に対応している度合いを測る指標(国際化指標)について」(経済産業省、平成21年4月)においては、求められる人材の筆頭に「外国語が話せて交渉できる人材」を置いており、次いで「ボーダレスなマネジメント能力を備えた人材」、「海外市場に精通した人材」、「イノベーションを生み出す高度な技術等を有した人材」となっている。

このような背景の中で、英語を学ぶ意味にも変化が生じてきている。一般教養としての英語から個人の生活文化を高める英語へ、受験科目としての英語からキャリア形成のための英語へ、知識としての英語から道具としての英語へと社会の要請が変化している。

さらに、日本のグローバル化を貿易構造から見ると、日本の輸出入の規模はアジアが最大であり、日本の企業が海外に派遣する要員数もアジア地区が圧倒的に最多である。また、日本人の海外旅行の行き先や日本を訪れる外国人の数の統計からもアジアとの関わりが益々大きくなっている。アジア諸国の人たちと英語でコミュニケーションがとれる人材の育成はまさに国家の急務である。

3. 日本の英語教育の構造改革

3.1 実技科目への重心移動

　世界の動向やアジア諸国の英語教育施策の現状を見ると、日本の英語教育の構造改革の必要性は誰の目にも明らかである。そしてその改革の求められる方向はまさしく実技科目への重心移動である。

　例えば楽器や球技をマスターしようとするときに、1つの技術を理解したからと言って次の段階に進むことはあり得ない。反復による習熟がない限り次の段階には進むことはない。英語に当てはめるなら、訳読による理解を目標とせず、反復によって使えるようになることを目標に置くことになる。そしてその反復のために有効なのは、現有の英語力に対して適正レベルの英語を大量インプットすることである。

　旧態依然とした文法訳読講義中心の日本式の英語教育は、長い時間をかけて確立されたがゆえに慣性が強く、その方向転換の容易ならぬことは多くの教師の実感するところである。今後その殻を破り、国家的プロジェクトとして日本の英語教育の方向転換を図るといっても、開発独裁型の政治的背景と歴史的条件が合致した前述のシンガポールの例のようなわけにはいかない。日本においては、公的な方法として最初に思い浮かび、また同時に法的拘束力もあるのが学習指導要領である。

3.2 学習指導要領

　学習指導要領による英語の授業の改善は、今後の国際社会における日本の国家戦略上の大きな生命線の1つであるといっても過言ではない。

　平成20年3月に告示され、小学校では平成23年4月から、中学校では平成24年4月から、そして高等学校では平成25年度入学生から実施された今般の学習指導要領の改訂は、もちろん前述のような背景を十分に勘案し、議論に議論を重ねて到達した1つの結論であろう。しかしながら、アジア諸国においてはずっと以前から強力な教育行政や英語教育施策が展開されてきている。例えば授業で扱う語彙数を旧指導要領の約2,000語程度から新指導要領では一気に3,000語程度に増やして

いるが、この改訂後の語彙数でさえ近隣諸国に比べると格段低い状況である。

　「アジア各国と日本の英語教科書比較」（教育再生懇談会会議資料 2008 年 5 月）によると、中学 3 年分の英語教科書に出現する異語数に関しては、韓国・台湾では日本の約 2 倍の語彙、中国では約 2～3 倍の語彙である。また、中学 3 年分のテキストの本文分量に関しては、韓国・台湾では日本の 2.5～3.5 倍、中国では 4～6 倍である。この現実を見ると、新しい学習指導要領の目指す方向の正当性については議論の余地もない。改訂された学習指導要領の趣旨を最大限に生かすべく、学校現場においては今までよりも大きく踏み込んだ取り組みが求められる。

　今般の学習指導要領改訂については、小学校に外国語活動が導入されたということで、日本の英語教育にとっては大きな転換点になる改訂である。英語の初学時期を早めたことの効果が中学校そして高校へと波及し、授業改善が連鎖していくことが期待される。

　中学校では、小学校との連携を図ることが学習指導要領に明記されたのと同時に、学習指導要領の内容の定着を確実に図ることもまた明記されている。授業時間は週 3 時間から 4 時間に増加した。

　高校に関しては、科目構成は一新され、「授業は英語で行うことを基本とする」と明記されている。文法事項については、必修の「コミュニケーション英語 I」においてすべての事項を取り扱うことになったことは大きな変更点である。

3.3　学習指導要領から読み取れるもの

　今回の学習指導要領からは、日本の高校を卒業したらこれくらいの英語力を持っているべきであるというメッセージが伝わってくる。それも 4 技能の統合を図る新科目を設定していることからも、コミュニケーション力の向上にかなりの重心が置かれている。この目的を達成するためには、教科書だけが変わり、旧態依然とした指導方法で授業を展開しただけでは意味がない。

　また、もう 1 つの特長は、言語はアウトプットすることで定着する

という理論で学習者の活動を重視している点にある。残念ながら今までの高校の授業では student-centered という考えは希薄であったことは否めない。生徒が発表する機会やペアワークを挿入することはあっても、そのような活動自体を中心に据えるケースは少なかった。新指導要領の趣旨を最大限に生かすためには、小学校では日常的である「生徒が主体の授業作り」を高校にもっと導入する必要がある。

3.4　コミュニケーション英語 I, II, III

　「コミュニケーション英語 I, II, III」は、旧要領の「英語 I, II」の延長線上で、4技能の統合をより明白に示している。高校の英語の教科書で扱う内容は通常難度の高いものが多く、今まで「リーダー」、「グラマー」、「ライティング」のようにスキルを分化して扱う合理性が優先されてきた。

　今般の改訂では、スキルを横断的に取り扱うことにより英語を立体的に捉えるというねらいが今まで以上に見え、実社会のコミュニケーション・スタイルに近く設定されたと言える。インプット一辺倒であった授業の中にアウトプット的要素を増やしていくことになるが、過渡期においては急速な変革を試みずに、年間計画の中で少しずつレッスン・スタイルを変えていくことにより円滑な移行が可能となるはずである。

3.5　「コミュニケーション英語基礎」の活用

　高校においては校種や学科により単位数が大幅に変わり、英語を学ぶ目的も多様であることが普通である。しかしながら、高校教科書になると一様に書き言葉の英語文章が急に増え、語彙数が増加する割にテキスト総量は少ない傾向にあり、高校に入ると急に英語が難しく感じられる。

　今までは「ブリッジ教材」を使うことなどにより、このギャップを埋める努力をしてきたが、その後に使用する高校教科書との断層を短期間に埋めることは困難であった。また、考慮すべき点として、高校入試の英語の得点分布に如実に表れるものであるが、入学生達の英語力には大

きな格差があるという実態がある。この入学時の英語力の実態に対して大学入試で問われる英語のレベルは高く、そのギャップを埋めるためには難度の高い教科書を早足で消化する以外はないという認識が根底にある。

　中学校で十分に学力がつかなかった生徒たちに、総復習的に学ばせる「コミュニケーション英語基礎」が導入されたのは、高校生の学力実態に合わせて何が何でも基礎基本だけは与えるという姿勢を感じさせるものである。しかしながら、科目履修順序の規定により、「コミュニケーションⅠ」は「コミュニケーション英語基礎」を履修した後に履修することが原則となる。必修科目「コミュニケーション英語Ⅰ」をどこに置くかという教務作業については、他の教科科目の配置等も考慮しながら慎重にする必要がある。

3.6 「英語表現」について

　「英語表現」の前身的存在の「オーラル・コミュニケーション」の取り扱いは校種により多様であった。普通科・専門教育学科では大学入試対策的な色彩が強い扱いが目立った。新指導要領の「英語表現」では、英語で発信する力をつけることを主目的とし、その発信力をグラマーやライティング・スキルが裏打ちする構成になっている。この方法で、計画的、持続的に授業を進めていく先に、生徒が「自分の考えをアウトプット」するというゴールが設定されている。高校の教師はこの点について十分な意識改革をして、文法訳読式の一方的な講義に傾く慣性を断ち切らなければならない。前述の国際競争力に繋がるような英語運用力を培うには大きな武器となる科目である。

4.　高校教室における諸課題

4.1　質の変化した入学生をどう受け止めるか

　高校の教師にとっては、科目の構成や教科書が変わることで自分の授業の展開方法を変えることに大きな関心が向くが、さらに大きな変化

は、小中学校で児童・生徒達が英語に触れる時間が増加したことによる英語力・関心・姿勢といった入学生達の質的変化である。小学校で素地を作り、中学校で基礎を養う、そしてその上に高校が来る。高校に入学してくる質の向上した生徒達をどう受け止め、どう伸ばしていくかという新しい課題がある。

　また、「言うは易く行うは難し。」が小中高の連携である。入学生が内定した時点で、中高の生徒指導主事達が一堂に会して、学校生活上配慮を要する生徒についての情報の受け渡しをするような機会は古くから確立されているが、小中高の教師が教科レベルでの交流を推進していくには時間的、予算的な余裕がないのが実情である。ほんの一握りの教師だけが小中学校に出前授業などの交流経験をするが、その経験から得たものは個人の範囲内に留まり、発展的に他の教師と共有することは困難である。そのような条件下で、高校の教師達は、最低限でも小学校の外国語活動で使われる「英語ノート」や近隣の中学校が採択している検定教科書に目を通しておくことは必須である。

4.2　授業を英語で行うことについて

　先ずはインプット一辺倒ではなく、生徒のアウトプットを引き出すことを想定しながら、授業を組み立てていくことが肝要である。今までの方法のままの授業を英語ですると、教師が授業時間中英語を話し通すことにもなりかねない。新しいスタイルの授業においては「伝達の方法」として英語を使う時間を増やしていくことによる成果が期待されているのである。芸術科や体育科などの実技科目の教師は常に生徒のモデルである。語学を実技と捉えた場合、英語教師がモデルとして英語を使うことは臨場感を高めるのみならず、生徒の動機付けとして大変有効であり、さらには教師自身が進化する大きなチャンスの１つでもある。もちろん英語を使うことは目的ではなく英語を学ばせる手段であることは常に念頭に置かれるべきである。

4.3 評価方法の改善について

　PDCA の重要さは学校経営に限るものではなく、各教科の授業にも当てはまる。学習評価は評価で終わっては意味がなく、その後の学習指導の改善につながらなければならない。学習指導要領の改訂に当たり、学習評価の方法についても改善を図っていく必要がある。

　平成 22 年 3 月の中央教育審議会初等中等教育分科会教育課程部会報告「児童生徒の学習評価の在り方について」においては、高等学校においても「目標に準拠した評価を着実に実施すること」が重視されている。

　「目標に準拠した評価」とは、当該教科・科目の目標や内容に照らしてその実現状況を捉えるものであり、生徒の学習状況を分析的に捉える観点別学習状況の評価と総括的に捉える評定とを、科目の目標と合致させる評価である。新学習指導要領における外国語科の評価の観点は、「コミュニケーションへの関心・意欲・態度」、「外国語表現の能力」、「外国語理解の能力」、「言語や文化についての知識・理解」である。

　上記の観点に照らすと、文法訳読式の記憶力だけを試すようなテストでは全く役に立たない。既習の単語力の範囲を大きく逸脱しない範囲の英文を読ませて概要や要点の理解度を問うような出題形式や、生徒の自発的なアウトプットを評価するような形式を積極的に取り入れるなど、試験の方法も大いに改善していかないと目標に準拠した評価に繋がらない。

5. 英語教育の構造改革の推進

5.1 大学入試との符号

　「英語を使えるようにする」という点において、旧指導要領と新指導要領の目標は一致している。そして高校の英語教師達は、英語を道具として使うことの有用性を自らの経験から誰よりも知っている集団である。にもかかわらず、授業となると必死で詰め込むスタイルになるのはなぜか。それは紛れもなく大学入試の存在である。

多くの英語教師達は、大学入試センター試験で問われる英語は学習指導要領と同一線上にあると承知している。しかしながら、各大学の二次試験の英語については、学習指導要領との乖離があると捉え、センター試験終了直後から二次対策講座を設けることが多い。

旧指導要領においても、多くの進学校では「オーラル・コミュニケーション」を避けて学校設定科目を組み込み、そこで実質的に受験対策の演習をしてきた実態があった。新しい指導要領の「コミュニケーション英語」に同様の事態が生じないようにするためには、各大学独自の英語問題の作成者は高等学校の指導要領を熟知していることが大前提である。中高合わせて学んだ3,000語と授業で学んだ英語操作力のレールの延長線上に受験英語があると実証的に伝えていくことが必要である。「落とす」試験から「とる」試験への変革の時に合わせ入試問題を新要領との符号という視点から総点検をする時である。

5.2　SELHi の実践から学ぶ

学習指導要領が改定されたからといって、現場教師はあらためて無から有を生み出すわけではない。今までの自分自身の教育実践のすべてが今後も有効に機能するはずである。また、同僚教師の実践や他校の研究の中にも大いに参考にすべきものがあるはずである。

平成14年度から推進されてきた文部科学省の SELHi（Super English Language High School）事業がその成果を挙げている。これは英語教育の先進事例となるような学校づくりを推進するため、英語教育を重点的に行う高等学校等を指定し、英語教育を重視したカリキュラムの開発、大学や中学校等との効果的な連携方策等についての実践研究を行うものであり、全国延べ169校で実施された。

それぞれの SELHi 指定校は特色のある研究課題を設定するが、事業全体の目標は、「読む・聞く・話す・書く」という4技能を駆使して自分の考えを発信できる英語力の育成にある。これはまさに新学習指導要領のねらいと合致しており、その研究成果は新指導要領への円滑な移行の鍵を多く含んでいる。全国の SELHi 校の研究成果が波及することに

より、授業改善は大きく前進するはずである。

　山梨県立甲府第一高等学校は、平成16年度から平成18年度までの3年間、文部科学省の指定を受け、「国際社会に生きる上で必要な発信力を段階的に高めるための指導法・教育課程の研究」を実施した。現在はPOST SELHi 校として、3年間の研究を発展的に生かしている。以下は甲府第一高校で立てた研究の4本柱である。

　① 3年間を見通した、発信力を高めるためのシラバスの研究
　　学校独自の「英語力シラバス」を「会話力、聴く力、語彙力、文法力、文章読解力、文章構成力」の6項目に分け、「学年別シラバス」でより具体的な方法を設定した。
　② 基礎的運用力を定着させ、段階的に発展させるための指導法の研究
　　インプットを増やしアウトプットを促す授業の実践を心がけ、和訳先渡し授業、ペアワーク Shadowing/Read and look up/Paraphrasing/Easy version の 活用 /Dialogue making/Chain reading/Last sentence dictation 等、効果がありそうなものはすべて積極的に取り入れた。
　③ 国際社会で生きるための実践的コミュニケーション能力の育成
　　オーセンティックな英語活用場面を設定し、Email 交換、SELHi 室（native speaker と自由に会話を楽しめる）の活用やイングリッシュ・セミナー、イングリッシュ・ワークショップ、英語暗唱大会、スピーチ・コンテスト等を開催した。
　④ 学校生活全体を通した異文化理解の促進

他教科の教師と連携し、ティーム・ティーチングを行うことにより、生徒の視野を広げ、人間的な成長に繋げていくことを目指した。

5.3　学校教育への理解

　学習指導要領が改訂されたり新しい制度が導入されたりすると、これだけお膳立てをしたのになぜ成果が挙がらない、教師は何をしているの

だと言わんばかりの意見をよく耳にする。教育を語るには、先ずは現場の実態の認識が不可欠である。

　学習指導要領がその趣旨に沿って機能していくためには、「教える教師」と「学ぶ生徒」という一種の契約関係が大前提なのである。しかしながら1つの教室の中には学習に対する姿勢が形成されていない生徒が何人もいるのが通例である。現場の教師達はこの契約関係以前の段階で多大な時間とエネルギーを使っている。

　また、教師は学級経営、分掌業務、部活動指導などの仕事を同時に背負っており、教科指導だけに集中できない環境にある。現場の教師の思いを代弁したり、現場の実情を伝えたりするものがあまりに少ないと実感する。教育政策の成否の鍵は最前線で実働する全国百万人を超える教師達が握っている。

5.4　教育行政ができること

　各都道府県あるいは市町村の教育委員会事務局は、文科省の意向の伝達、制度の整備、教育指導、また膨大な調査実施などで多忙を極めており、時間をかけて新しいものを創出する時間的余裕がないのが実情である。しかしながら、教育の改善については実質的に大きな力を持った組織であり、独自の制度を学校に指示することのできる機関である。例えば、前述のSELHiの研究成果の波及については、当該校の教師達による伝達講習を研修に組み込むこともできる。また人事計画の中でSELHi経験教師を指導教諭のような形で他校に配置替えしていくこともできる。

　また、1つの試案として、教育行政単位の大学区か中学区に1校程度、英語で教える小学校のデュアル・スクール（仮称）を設置し、放課後にコア科目をもう一度英語で復習したらどうだろうか。このような小規模のCLIL（教科学習と英語の語学学習を統合したアプローチ）は英語を教育過程全体の媒介言語とするイマージョン・プログラムよりもハードルが低く現実的であると考える。これは1つの例であるが、このような各自治体の創意工夫を凝らした独自の取り組みを支援することで、グ

ローバル化に対応できる人材を育成することも可能である。

6. おわりに

　グローバル化が急激に進行する世界で、その新時代の波を越えることのできる人材の育成が急務であることを述べた。その利益は当事者に留まらず国民全体に還元されるものである。世界の人口爆発に逆行して、日本では少子化が進行している。人材の総数減少というマイナスをプラスに転ずるためには質の向上しかない。そして、その質を形成する要件の中でも英語運用力は必須である。しかしながら、グローバル化と少子化の進行は予想外に急速でいまや時間的猶予がない。この事態を社会全体が認識し、社会全体で責任を分担するという意識の高揚が必要である。そのためには、行政がさらに積極的な施策を打ち出すこと、学校現場ではその具体化に努力すること、地域や保護者もその流れを理解し協力することが必要である。併せて、忘れてならないのがマスメディアである。世論形成を主導する大きな力を有するマスメディアの後方支援があれば大きな力となる。教室は社会のマイクロコズムである。社会全体が持てる力を結集して取り組んだとき、子供達は必ず変容する。

　教育には即効性を求められないし、短期の数値目標もなじまない。しかしながら、社会全体に後押しされながら、教師の意識が変われば授業が変わる。授業が変われば生徒達の質が変わる。新学習指導要領の導入を契機に英語の構造改革ができれば、それは国家戦略の武器となる。

参考文献・資料

David Crystal (2003) *English as a Global Language* Cambridge University Press
本名信行 (2006)『英語はアジアを結ぶ』玉川大学出版部
河添恵子 (2005)『アジア英語教育最前線』三修社
経済産業省 (2009)『企業の人材国際化指標について』
教育再生懇談会会議資料 (2008)「アジア各国と日本の英語教科書比較」

文部科学省(2009)『小学校学習指導要領』
文部科学省(2009)『中学校学習指導要領』
文部科学省(2009)『高等学校学習指導要領』
総務省(2012)『国際電気通信連合 2012 年世界国際電気通信会議の結果』
中央教育審議会初等中等教育分科会教育課程部会(2010)『児童生徒の学習評価の
　　在り方について』
山梨県立甲府第一高等学校(2006)『山梨県立甲府第一高等学校 SELHi 報告書』

シンハラ語における
無意志他動詞構文の主語について

宮岸哲也

要旨

　シンハラ語の無意志他動詞構文の主語としては、後置詞 atin を伴う名詞（atin 句名詞）、与格名詞、そして具格名詞の3つの形式が存在する。これらの中で動詞が非意図的動作主を要求すれば atin 句主語をとり、経験者を要求すれば与格主語をとり、起点を要求すれば具格主語をとる。そして、主語標示の違いによる無意志他動詞文の意味の違いについては、atin 句主語文は動作主の能動的行為により生じる非意図的事態、与格主語文は影響が主語に及ぶ事態、具格主語文は主語が起点や原因となって生じる事態を表す。また、動詞によっては、主語標示交替が可能なものと不可能なものがあり、主語標示交替の点から無意志動詞を分類すると、① atin 句主語のみ、②与格主語のみ、③具格主語のみ、④ atin 句主語と与格主語、⑤ atin 句主語と具格主語、⑥ atin 句主語と与格主語と具格主語の6タイプが存在する。本論文では、これらの6タイプに分類される無意志他動詞がどのようなものなのかを明らかにする。

キーワード　無意志他動詞、非意図的動作主、経験者、起点、主語標示交替

1.　はじめに

　シンハラ語[1]動詞は、語形変化により意志の有無を区別できる[2]。そ

して意志動詞の主語は主格で標示されるが、無意志動詞の主語は様々な形式で標示され、その中でも無意志他動詞の主語は、後置詞 atin[3] を伴う名詞と、与格、具格のそれぞれの名詞で標示される (Inman 1993: 38)。また、各々の形式の主語を持つ無意志他動詞文の意味と、主語標示交替については、先行研究 (Inman 1993, Henadeerage 2002, Chandralal 2010) でも断片的に述べられている。しかし、atin 句、与格、具格のそれぞれの主語について、Ⓐどのような法則性でどのような動詞と結びつくのか、Ⓑどのような主語標示交替が可能なのか、Ⓒ主語標示交替が可能な場合、どのようなニュアンスの違いが生じるのかの3点については、全体的に議論されていない。そこで、本論文ではこれらⒶⒷⒸの点について明らかにしたい。

2. 先行研究

シンハラ語無意志他動詞文の主語は、atin 句、与格、具格の3形式があり (Inman 1993: 38)、多くの無意志他動詞が atin 句主語のみを許容する (Inman 1993: 162)。また、kiyənəwa (言う)、kanəwa (食べる) など限られた動詞は、atin 句以外に与格の主語も許容する (Inman 1993: 162)。そして、atin 句主語文は動作主による何らかの行為 (意図的な時も有り得る) により、動詞の示す事態が生じることを表し、与格主語文は動詞の表す事態が主語の行為や意図によらず自ら生じることを表す (Inman 1993: 164)。なお具格主語文は、意志性を含み、話者の驚きを表す (Inman 1993: 170)。

上記の Inman (1993) の指摘の中で、atin 句主語文については (1) の例でもよく理解できる。つまり、ジョンが何か意図的にでも非意図的にでも身体を動かしていたら、偶然に腕や足が皿に当ってしまい、意図せずに皿を割ってしまったという事態である。

（1） joon atin　　　piⁿgaanə　　biⁿduṇa.　　　（Inman 1993: 162）
　　　ジョン［atin］　皿［対(格)］　割る［無意志・過去］
　　　（ジョンは皿を誤って割った）

　なお、atin 句主語文は、(2)のような可能表現や(3)のような謙遜表現にも用いられるが、このような表現は、Chandralal(2010: 159, 160)によると、無意志の解釈から派生したものではないらしい。本論文では、可能表現も謙遜表現も無意志の意味から派生したものと考えるが、その理由については 4.1 節で述べる。

（2） Kella atin　　maalu　　ageeṭə　　pihenəwa.　　（De Silva 1960: 101）
　　　少女［atin］　魚［対］　上手に　調理する［無意志・非過去］
　　　（少女は魚を旨く調理できる）

（3） man atin　dawəsəkəṭə　pitu　dahayak　witərə
　　　私［atin］1 日に　　　頁　　10　　　ぐらい
　　　liyəwenəwa.　　　　　　　　　　（Chandralal 2013: 160）
　　　書く［無意志・非過去］
　　　（私は 1 日に 10 頁ほど書くかもしれない）

　一方、与格主語文が、動詞の表す事態が主語の行為や意図によらず自ら生じることを表すという Inman(1993: 164) の指摘については、納得できない部分がある。確かに(4)が不適格なのは、ジョンの行為によって引き起こした結果のためであり、(1)のように atin 句主語をとらなければならないという理屈はわかる。しかし、そうであれば、与格主語を用いた(5)がなぜ適格なのかが、Inman(1993: 164) の指摘では説明できない。

（4） *joontə　　piⁿgaana　biⁿduṇa.　　　（Inman 1993: 162）
　　　ジョン［与］　皿［対］　割る［無意志・過去］
　　　（ジョンは誤って皿を割った）

(5) Ranjiṭǝ   pusaawǝ   pæægenǝwa. (Chandralal 2010: 106)
　　 ランジット［与］ 猫［対］ 踏む［無意志・非過去］
　　 （ランジットは誤って猫を踏んだ）

　次に、具格主語文が意志性を含み、話者の驚きを表すこと (Inman 1993: 170) については、(6) の例でも理解できる。しかし、どのような動詞が具格主語をとるのかについての説明がないので、この点での究明が必要であろう。

(6) mahatungen   ee   wæḍǝ   kerenne
　　 マハトゥン［具］ その 仕事［対］ する［無意志］
　　 næ̈.   (Inman 1993: 170)
　　 否定辞
　　 （マハトゥンは［話者の期待に反して］その仕事をしてない）

　最後に主語標示交替については、Inman (1993: 163) が atin 句と与格の主語交替が可能な (7) を示し、意志性の違いで両者の違いを説明している。確かに、結果として意志性の違いは認められるが、全ての無意志他動詞が意志性の違いを、atin 句と与格の主語交替で示せるわけではない。これは、先に挙げた (1) の atin 句主語文が、意志性を低めるために (4) の与格主語文にすることができないという事実からも理解できる。

(7) {andǝree atin   / andǝreeṭǝ}   wæli
　　 アンダレー［atin］ アンダレー［与］ 砂［対］
　　 kæwenǝwa.   (Inman 1993: 163)
　　 食べる［無意志・非過去］
　　 atin 句主語：アンダレーは（何か食物を意識して食べていると、
　　　　　　　　それに混じっていた）砂を（知らずに）食べてしまう。
　　 与格主語：アンダレーは知らず知らずのうちに砂を食べてしまう。

また、Henadeerage (2002: 15) では、atin 句と具格の主語交替が可能な(8)を示しているが、どちらも同じ意味を持つことが指摘されているだけで、双方の違いと主語交替が可能な条件については、言及していない。

(8) {amma atin / ammagen} Sinhalə kæᴂmə hoⁿdəṭə
　　　母［atin］　　母［具］　シンハラ料理［対］　よく
　　hᴂdenəwa.　　　　　　　　　　　(Henadeerage 2002: 15)
　　作る［無意志・非過去］
　　（母はいつもシンハラ料理を上手に作る）

以上、見てきたように、シンハラ語の無意志他動詞構文における主語の選択と交替の法則性については不明な点が多い。

3. 調査方法

前節で指摘した不明点を明らかにするために、先行研究 (Inman 1993, Henadeerage 2002, Chandralal 2010) で取り上げられた無意志他動詞文の用例を収集し、それぞれを atin 句、与格、具格の主語で標示した文123例からなる質問票を作成した。そして、それぞれについての正誤判断をシンハラ語母語話者（スリランカの大学で日本語を教えるシンハラ人教師と日本に留学しているシンハラ人の大学院生）8名にしてもらい、その結果について必要に応じて追加の質問を行った。

なお、分析の際には、ⓐ atin 句主語だけをとる他動詞文、ⓑ 与格主語だけをとる他動詞文、ⓒ 具格主語だけをとる他動詞文、ⓓ atin 句と与格だけの主語をとる他動詞文、ⓔ atin と具格だけの主語をとる他動詞文、ⓕ 与格と具格だけの主語をとる他動詞文、ⓖ atin 句と与格と具格のいずれの主語もとれる他動詞文の7タイプに分類を試みた。これによりⓐ～ⓒでは各々の主語形式をとる他動詞文の典型的特徴について、ⓓ～ⓖでは主語標示交替パターンとそれぞれの条件について、考察

するための必要なデータが得られる。

4. 調査結果と考察

4.1 atin 句主語だけをとる他動詞文

atin 句主語だけをとるという判断が大半を占めたのは (9) ～ (12) である。なお各例文の右側にある ( ) 中の atin は atin 句主語、与は与格主語、具は具格主語を示し、下線を引いたものは当該例文の主語標示、引いていないものは、それ以外の主語標示を示している。また、数字については、それぞれの主語標示を正しいと判断した人数を示している。

(9) <u>Ranjani atin</u>　　Sitawə　　tallu uṇa.
　　ランジャニ［atin］シータ［対］押す［無意志・過去］
　　　　　　　　　　　　　　　　　　（Henadeerage 2002: 54）
　　(<u>atin 8</u>, 与 1, 具 1)
　　（ランジャニはシータを誤って押してしまった）

(10) <u>Ranjit atin</u>　　gaha　　kæpenəwa.
　　ランジット［atin］木［対］切る［無意志・過去］
　　　　　　　　　　　　　　　　　　（Chandralal 2010: 108）
　　(<u>atin 7</u>, 与 1, 具 1)
　　（ランジットは木を無意識に切る）

(11) <u>Ranjit atin</u>　　minihaṭə　ægillen　ænuṇa.
　　ランジット［atin］男［与］指［具］突く［無意志・過去］
　　　　　　　　　　　　　　　　　　（Chandralal 2010: 153）
　　(<u>atin</u>8, 与 1, 具 2)
　　（ランジットは誤ってその男を指で突いてしまった）

(12) <u>miniha atin</u>　laməyəṭə　bænuṇa. (<u>atin 5</u>, 与 1, 具 1)
　　男［atin］子供［与］怒鳴る［無意志・過去］
　　（男は思わず子供を怒鳴ってしまった）

これらの例を見ると、(9)(10)の動詞は対格目的語をとり、(11)(12)の動詞は与格目的語をとっているが、いずれも動詞の意味としては、対象に対する働きかけや態度を表している。これらは全て動作主の行為による対象への影響が、動作主の意図によらず生じるものなので、本論文ではこれらの atin 句名詞を非意図的動作主と呼ぶことにする。

次に、atin 句主語文による可能と謙遜の表現について考える。(2)(3)の例は、それぞれ可能と謙遜の表現とされるが、(3)を謙遜表現としているのは、自分の能力を過小評価する文のためだと考えられる。Chandralal (2010: 159, 160) は、いずれの表現も無意志の解釈から派生したものではないとしている。しかし、主体の能力とは元々主体の意志とは関係なく備わるものなので、本論文では、atin 句主語文の可能・謙遜表現も無意志性から派生したものと考える。

ただ、ここで1つ問題となるのが (2)(3) の可能・謙遜を表す無意志他動詞文における atin 句主語の位置づけである。atin 句主語は本論文では非意図的動作主と位置づけているが、可能表現も atin 句主語文の1つとして認めると、atin 句主語は経験者にもなるとしなければならない。そうなると、次節で述べる経験者を表す与格主語との違いも問題になる。

実際に本論文で扱っている例文を見ると、atin 句主語による経験者と与格主語による経験者の間には違いが観察できる。つまり、(2)(3) の例のように atin 句主語は、対象に働きかける行為が能力的に可能だという主体としての経験者は表せても、(13)～(15) のような知覚、精神状態、所有の経験者は表せないのである。よって、可能・謙遜を表す atin 句主語文の主語は、このように限定的な経験者を表すのであって、経験者一般を表す与格主語とは区別できる。そして、可能・謙遜を表す atin 句主語文は、atin 句主語文の典型的な例とはならないとも言える。このことは、(3) の atin 句主語文が 4.4 節で挙げる (23) のように与格主語文に換えられることによっても裏付けられる。

(13) *<u>maa atin</u>　　pintuuraak　peenəwa.(atin 1，与 8，具 1)
　　　私［atin］　　絵［対］　　見える［無意志・非過去］
(14) *<u>laməya atin</u>　hiinəyə　matak uṇa.(atin 1，与 7，具 1)
　　　子供［atin］　夢［対］　思い出す［無意志・非過去］
(15) *<u>Chitra atin</u>　　kaarekak　tiyenəwa.(atin 0，与 8，具 2)
　　　チットラ［atin］　車［対］　　ある

　もう 1 つ注目すべき例は (16) で、これは (7) の atin 句主語文と同じであるが、Inman (1993: 163) は正文として扱っている。しかし、今回の調査では 8 人中 2 人の被験者しか正しいと判断していない。Inman (1993: 164–6) の説明では、atin 句主語文の場合は食べた行為は意識的でも砂を食べたことは無意識であり、与格主語文の場合は食べた行為自体が無意識だとしている。それにも関わらず、多くの被験者が (16) を非文としたのは、意志性の違いではなく、動作主と経験者の違いで判断したためではないかと考えられる。なぜなら、砂を食べてしまったことへの解釈は、動作主 (或いは加害者) というよりは経験者 (或いは被害者) のほうがより自然だからである。なお、動作主と経験者の違いから生じるニュアンスの違いは 4.4 節で詳しく述べる。

(16) *<u>andəree atin</u>　　wæli　　kæwenəwa.(atin 2，与 6，具 0)
　　　アンダレー［atin］　砂［対］　食べる［無意志・非過去］
　　　　　　　　　　　　　　　　　　　　　　　　(Inman 1993: 163)

4.2　与格主語だけをとる他動詞文

　与格主語だけをとる他動詞文は、前節で非文とされた (13) ～ (15) の atin 句主語を全て与格主語に換えた (17) ～ (19) である。これらの動詞は、知覚、精神状態、所有などの状態を表し、それぞれの主語はいずれも経験者である。また、前節の (9)(10) の atin 句主語を与格主語に換えると非文になるが、これらは、動作主としてしか解釈できないからである。

(17) maṭə　　pintuuraak　peenəwa.（与 8，atin 1，具 1）
　　　私［与］　絵［対］　　見える［無意志・非過去］
　　　　　　　　　　　　　　　　　　　　　（Chandralal 2010: 106）
　　　（私には絵が見える）

(18) laməyaṭə　　hiinəya　matak uṇa.（与 7，atin 1，具 1）
　　　子供［与］　夢［対］　思い出す［無意志・過去］
　　　　　　　　　　　　　　　　　　　　　（Henadeerage 2002: 54）
　　　（子供は急に夢を思い出した）

(19) Chitraṭə　　　kaarekak　tiyenəwa.（与 8，atin 0，具 2）
　　　チットラ［与］　車［対］　ある
　　　　　　　　　　　　　　　　　　　　　（Chandralal 2010: 106）
　　　（チットラは車を持っている）

4.3　具格主語だけをとる他動詞文

　今回の調査では、具格主語だけをとるという結果を明確に示す例はなかったが、(20)だけは具格主語が他の標示の主語よりも正しいという回答が多かった。この文の特徴は、3項動詞文であり、主語から与格名詞への対格名詞の移動が認められ、動詞が起点を必須的に要求していることである。なお、シンハラ語の具格は奪格と同じ形式で、基点としての基本的な意味を持つ。(20)の調査結果が出たのも、動作主としての意味よりも基点としての意味のほうがより相応しいと感じられたためだと考えられる。

(20) magen　lameaṭə　salli　　　yæwenəwa.（具 7，atin 4，与 2）
　　　私［具］　子供［与］　お金［対］　送る［無意志・非過去］
　　　（私は子供にお金を送ってしまう）

　逆に、具格主語だけを許容しない(21)を見てみると、文意に物の移動は認められず、主語を物が移動する基点として見なすことができない。

(21) *laməyagen puusawə pæguṇa.(具0, atin 8, 与 8)
　　 子供［具］猫［対］踏む［無意志・過去］

4.4　atin 句と与格だけの主語をとる他動詞文

　atin 句と与格の主語交替が可能な場合の文意の違いについて、Inman (1993: 163)は、(7)の atin 句主語文と与格主語文の比較で、意志性に違いがあることを示している。本論文では、(22)(23)のような例も atin 句と与格の双方の主語がとれる例として示せたが、これらの違いを意志性の違いだけで説明するのは難しい。まず、(22)は atin 句主語と与格主語のどちらも「子供が猫を踏んだ」という事態を表すが、atin 句主語のほうが意志性が高いという説明ではよくわからない。それよりも、atin 句主語が非意図的動作主で、与格主語が経験者であるという原理から説明すべきである。つまり atin 句主語は、非意図的でもその事態を引き起こした加害者である一方、与格主語は、その事態の影響を受けた被害者で、猫を踏んでしまった感触の気持ち悪さや、猫に噛み付かれたり引っ掻かれたりした肉体的苦痛を経験したことが考えられる。この考えは複数のシンハラ語母語話者にも確認している。また、(23)では atin 句主語を用いると煙草を吸う行為に焦点が当たる一方、与格主語を用いると喫煙の習慣の保有者に焦点が当てられる。

(22)　{laməya atin / laməyaṭə} puusawə pæguṇa.
　　　 子供［atin］　子供［与］　猫［対］　踏む［無意志・過去］
　　　　　　　　　　　　　　　　　　　　　　　（Henadeerage 2002: 42）

　　　(atin 8, 与 8, 具 0)
　　　(子供は猫を踏んだ)

(23)　{maa atin / maṭə}　dawəsəkəṭə　sigəraṭ　wissak
　　　 私［atin］　私［与］　1日に　　　煙草　　20本
　　　 witərə　pewenəwa.(atin 6, 与 8, 具 1)
　　　 ほど　　吸う［無意志・非過去］
　　　(私は1日に煙草を20本ぐらい吸う)

このように、atin 句と与格の双方の主語がとれる無意志他動詞の特徴としては、動詞のもたらす影響が、動作主に戻ってくるかどうかという再帰性と関係がある。具体的に見ると、(22)では猫を踏む感触の悪さや猫の反撃による負傷が、(23)では喫煙の常習性が、動作主が受ける再帰的な影響となっている。

4.5 atin 句と具格だけの主語をとる他動詞文

(24)〜(26)は今回の調査で、atin 句と具格の双方がとれると判断されたり、全体としてそのような傾向が見られたりした例である。これらのうち、(24)(25)の例文に共通する動詞の特徴としては、主語から他者への利益供与を意味することであるが、atin 句主語の場合は非意図的な動作主、具格主語の場合は起点、つまり行為により生じる事物の供給源になっている。(26)の動詞については、利益供与ではなく、対象の変化を生じさせる加害を意味するが、皿を割った主語を非意図的動作主として捉えれば atin 句主語をとり、原因＝起点として捉えれば具格主語をとる。

(24) {mahatun atin / mahatungen} ee wæḍə
　　　マハトゥン［atin］マハトゥン［具］その　仕事［対］
　　　kerenne　　　　næ. (atin 8, 具 8, 与 2)
　　　する［無意志］否定辞
　　　(マハトゥンはその仕事をしない)

(25) ee {laməya atin / laməyagen} demawpiyanwə
　　　その　子供［atin］　子供［具］　両親［対］
　　　rækenəwa. (atin 7, 具 7, 与 0)
　　　助ける［無意志・非過去］
　　　(その子供は両親を助ける)

(26) {miniha atin / minihagen} piⁿgaana biⁿduṇa.
　　　男［atin］　　男［具］　皿［対］　割る［無意志・過去］
　　　(atin 8, 具 4, 与 0)
　　　(男は皿を割った)

　なお、今回の調査の被験者の中には、atin 句主語文と具格主語文の意味的な違いは僅かであるが、前者は後者よりも丁寧であるという意見があった。これは、Henadeerage (2002: 15) では指摘されていなかった重要な指摘である。atin 句主語文に感じられる丁寧さは、atin 句主語文が謙遜表現にも用いられるという Chandralal (2010: 160) の指摘とも関連性があるかもしれない。また、具格主語文が丁寧に感じられないのは、具格主語の無意志他動詞文は話者の驚きを表すという Inman (1993: 170) の指摘と関係があるのかもしれない。ただ、この違いについて更に考察するためには、データを増やす必要がある。

4.6　与格と具格だけの主語をとる他動詞文

　今回の調査では、与格と具格だけの主語をとるような例は1つも見つからなかった。なお、次節で示すが、atin 句と与格と具格のいずれの主語もとれる動詞の例は多く見つかっており、与格と具格の主語がとれれば、基本的に atin 句主語もとれると考えられる。Inman (1993: 62) は、多くの無意志他動詞が atin 句主語のみをとると述べているが、このような無意志他動文の主語としての atin 句主語の優位性は、ここでも再認識できる。つまり、複数の形式の主語がとれる無意志他動詞では、必ず atin 句主語をとるが、与格主語や具格主語がとれない例があることは、それぞれ本節の 4.5 節と 4.4 節で示した通りである。

4.7　atin 句と与格と具格のいずれの主語もとれる他動詞文

　atin 句と与格と具格のいずれの主語もとれる他動詞として、確認できたのは (27) (28) の wiyədam wenəwa (浪費する) と liyəwenəwa ([無意識的に] 書く) である。これらの動詞文における3つの主語交替による文

のニュアンスの違いを母語話者に確認したところ、(27) においては、atin 句主語文は私のだらしなさ等で非意図的にお金を無駄遣いしてしまったこと、与格主語文はお金を無駄遣いしてしまう状況が私にもたらされたこと、具格主語文は私が原因でお金が無駄遣いされてしまった驚きを表している。また (28) においては、atin 句主語文は (3) の例でも示した通り自分の行為を謙遜して言うこと、与格主語文はそのような能力を有すること、具格主語文は予期せぬ結果への驚きをそれぞれ表している。

(27) {maa atin / matə / magen} mudal
　　　 私 [atin]　 私 [与]　 私 [具]　 お金 [対]
　　　 wiyədam uṇa. (atin 8, 与 8, 具 6)
　　　 浪費する [無意志・非過去]
　　　（私はお金を無駄遣いする）

(28) {man atin / matə / magen} dawəsəkəṭə pitu dahayak
　　　 私 [atin]　 私 [与]　 私 [具]　 一日に　 頁　 10
　　　 witərə liyəwenəwa. (atin 8, 与 7, 具 6)
　　　 ぐらい 書く [無意志・非過去]
　　　（私は一日に 10 頁ぐらい書く）

なお、この 2 つの動詞は意味的にはどのような共通性があるのだろうか。それは、消費も生産も、有から無へ、或いは無から有へという起点と終点が存在することである。そして、これらの動詞が具格主語をとれるのは、主語を基点として捉えることが可能で、また与格主語がとれるのは、終点で得られた影響を被る経験者として捉えられるからである。

また、(29) は、構文的には他動詞文であるが、意味的には自動詞である。そして、atin 句主語文は私の不注意で意図せずに失敗をしたこと、与格主語文は私が失敗という悪影響を受けたこと、具格主語文は私が原因で失敗が生じた驚きを表している。これらの文を他動詞として扱うか、自動詞として扱うかは意見が分かれるだろうが、自動詞として扱

うのであれば、(29)の具格主語文はInman (1993: 34)で述べられているような、無意志自動詞は対格か与格の主語しかとれないという説の例外となり注目できる。

(29) {man atin / matə / magen} loku warədak
　　　私［atin］私［与］　私［具］大きい　過ち［対］
　　　uṇa. (atin 8, 与8, 具8)
　　　なる［無意志・過去］(私は失敗した)

5. おわりに

　ここまでの議論を纏めると、シンハラ語の無意志他動詞は、基本的に非意図的動作主を要求すればatin句主語、経験者を要求すれば与格主語、起点を要求すれば具格主語をとる。そして、無意志他動詞文の主語標示交替パターンはatin句、与格、具格の各々1つしかとれない場合と、atin句と与格、atin句と具格、或いはatin句と与格と具格をとれる場合があり、与格と具格を主語としてとれるパターンはない。以上を図示すると図1になる。

　更に各々の主語標示交替パターンと動詞と主語の意味タイプについて纏めた表1を示す。なお、主語標示の違いによる無意志他動詞文の意味の違いも纏めると、atin句主語文は動作主の能動的行為により生じる非意図的事態、与格主語文は影響が主語に及ぶ事態、具格主語文は主語が起点や原因となり生じる事態を表す。

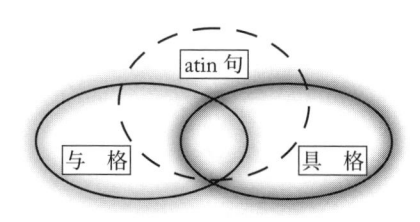

図1　シンハラ無意志他動詞の主語形式

表1 シンハラ語無意志他動詞文における主語交替パターンと動詞・主語の意味タイプ

主語標示交替パターン	無意志他動詞の意味タイプ	主語の意味タイプ
atin	働きかけ、態度	非意図的動作主
与格	知覚、精神状態、所有などの状態	経験者
具格	物を移動させる行為	起点
atin／与格	再帰性のある行為	非意図的動作主／経験者
atin／具格	利益許与、対象変化	非意図的動作主／起点
atin／与格／具格	消費、生産	非意図的動作主／経験者／起点

追記) 本論文は平成 24 年度安田女子大学学術研究助成費を受けて行った研究の成果の一部である。

謝辞

本論文の執筆に先立ち、ケラニア大学・サバラガムワ大学の先生方、日本の各大学院におられるスリランカ人留学生の方々に調査でご協力を頂いた。なお、本論文の文責は全て執筆者にある。

注

1. シンハラ語はスリランカの国語で、使用人口は約 1,400 万人である。インド・アーリア語族に属している。
2. 基本的に動詞語末が -anəwa、-inəwa であれば非過去意志、-uwa であれば過去意志、-enəwa であれば非過去無意志、-uṇa であれば過去無意志の動詞を表す。その他、不規則変化動詞もある。
3. atin は「手」を意味する名詞 ata の具格形が後置詞化したものである。この atin を伴う名詞を Inman (1993) では能格名詞 (ergative noun) と呼んでいるが、本論文では atin 句名詞と呼ぶ。

参考文献

Chandralal, Dileep (2010) *Sinhala*. Amsterdam: John Benjamins Publishing Company.
De Silva, M. W. S (1960) Verbal Categories in Spoken Sinhalese. *University of Ceylon*

Review 18. pp96–112. Colombo: University of Ceylon Press.

Gair, James (1990) Subject, case and INFL in Sinhala. In Mahindra K. Verma & Karavannur P. Mohanan (eds.) *Experiencer Subjects in South Aisan Languages*, pp13–41. Stanford: CSLI.

Henadeerage, Deepthi Kumara (2002) Topics in Sinhala Syntax. Ph. D. dissertation. Canberra: The Australian National University.

Inman, Michael Vincent (1993) Semantics and Pragmatics of Colloquial Sinhala Involitive Verbs. Ph. D. dissertation. Stanford, Calif.: Stanford University.

第 II 部

A Japan Fantasy in Virginia Woolf's "Friendships Gallery"[1]

Noriko Kubota

Abstract

"Friendships Gallery" written in 1907 is one of the earliest writings of Virginia Woolf (1882–1941). It was written as a biography of Violet Dickinson (1865–1948), who played a major role in Woolf's early life as her surrogate mother, tutor, mentor and a friend. It is composed of three chapters — the first two are a direct biography of Violet Dickinson, and Chapter Three, entitled "a story to make you sleep," was set in Tokyo, Japan.

Relatively little attention has been paid to this work, and the effect of Japan as a locale of the third chapter upon the whole story has rather escaped observation of critics. In this paper I would like to pay attention to Virginia Woolf's special interest in Japan represented in "Friendships Gallery." It is my intention to consider how Chapter Three, which initially appears independently detached from the first two chapters, is connected with the other chapters and what the role of Japan is in the whole work.

Keywords   Virginia Woolf, "Friendships Gallery", Japan, japonisme, fantasy

"Friendships Gallery" written in 1907[2] is one of the earliest writings of Virginia Woolf (1882–1941). It was composed as a biography of Violet Dickinson (1865–1948), who played a major role in Woolf's early life as her surrogate mother, tutor, mentor and a friend. "Friendships Gallery" was "typed with a violet typewriter ribbon and bound in violet leather with the title embossed in gilt on its cover" (Hawkes 1979: 272) and was presented to Violet Dickinson in August 1907. However, this heartfelt offering had been long forgotten and was miraculously found by chance among the books and papers of Violet Dickinson's brother, Oswald Eden, after his death in 1955. The original version is preserved in the Berg Collection in the Public Library, New York. It was once printed in *The Twentieth Century Literature* in 1979 with the introduction and notes by Ellen Hawkes, but it took more than a century until it was published in a book form: "Friendships Gallery" was contained in the sixth volume of *The Essays of Virginia Woolf* and came out in April 2011.

It cannot be said that "Friendships Gallery" was very mature work, with fragmentary passages in some parts. Virginia Woolf herself surely thought that it was not yet complete and expressed her intention to re-write it, asking Violet Dickinson several times to give it back to her.[3] According to Kirkpatrick, it is a typescript version "with holograph corrections and in other unidentified hands" (Kirkpatrick 1997: 422). But, despite its imperfection, it has a peculiar charm with the tracing of the flight of Woolf's copious mind.

The original version of "Friendships Gallery" is a short story of about fifty pages[4], and meant to be a biography of Violet Dickinson, as Virginia Woolf called it a "Life, or Myth" in her letter to Nelly Cecil dated 16 August 1907(*The Flight of the Mind* 304). It is composed of three chapters — the first two are a direct biography of Violet Dickinson. Chapter Three, entitled "a story to make you sleep," was set in Tokyo, Japan, and, interestingly, the name of Violet was not mentioned in this chapter.

Relatively little attention has been paid to this fascinating, early work. Occasionally it has been compared with *Orlando*, which was written more than twenty years later, to reveal Woolf's consistent inclination for biography throughout her writing career. Karin E.Westman defines this work as "the First *Orlando*" in her discussion of "Friendships Gallery" (Westman 2001: 39).[5] Also Adam Parkes sees this work as "a romantic biographical spoof about Violet Dickinson that anticipates the more extended experiment in *Orlando.*" (Parkes 1996: 164). Jane Marcus and Krystyna Colburn concern themselves with Woolf's lesbianism in "Friendships Gallery" Jane Marcus says that it was "one of many lesbian utopias" and Krystyna Colburn saw "a women's world" there (Colburn 2004: 75). However, the effect of Japan as a locale of the third chapter upon the whole story has rather escaped observation of critics. In this paper I would like to pay attention to the significant aspect of this work — Virginia Woolf's special interest in Japan represented in "Friendships Gallery" It is my intention to consider how Chapter Three, which initially appears independently detached from the first two chapters, is connected with the other chapters and what the role of Japan is in the whole work.

"Friendships Gallery" begins with Violet's birth and follows her progress in adult life as a society lady. What is conspicuous in the first two chapters is Violet's unconventionality, her incongruity with the outside world and her sense of uneasiness towards "Englishness." When she was born, she is described as follows;

> ...she was the cleverest child
> the noisiest child
> <and> the child with the finest lungs
> in the Parish.... ("FG" 275)

Furthermore, Violet grew up to be "as tall as the tallest hollyhock in the garden before she was eight;..."("FG" 276). These exceptional physical characteristics of Violet imply her incongruity with conventional society.

Chapter Two, which is entitled "The Magic Garden," deals with her conversation with a gardener. Violet is staying at Hatfield House where her friend Nelly, Lady Robert Cecil, lives. The narrator describes that Violet was "sitting on the most famous terrace in Europe, with the oldest oak trees in front of her, and the smoothest turf, and behind her the finest Elizabethan grey stone, …" ("FG" 285), and the reader easily recalls that Hatfield House used to be the abode of Queen Elizabeth I in her youth. "The oldest oak trees" evokes the figure of Orlando sitting under the oak tree and "the smoothest turf" reminds the reader of the turf, excluding women in *A Room of One's Own*. In that essay the turf of a Cambridge college, which had been smoothly mown for hundreds of years, was a symbol of male-oriented English society. Violet was at the very centre of English tradition, of English society, but Violet felt "discontent" ("FG" 285), staying in Hatfield House. In *Reading Virginia Woolf*, Julia Briggs spoke of Woolf's complicated attitude towards England and Englishness. She pointed out that the idea of England and Englishness can become "an embarrassment" for Woolf (Briggs 2006: 195). In this scene, Violet had the similar feeling, and then she encountered a gardener as unexpectedly as she may encounter "fauns." She "strode towards him, as though she had the precise place ready for him in her mind". ("FG" 286) They immediately began conversation;

> He explained the best way of treating roses, and how to lay on manure; he was dogmatic on the grafting of <u>Pyrus Japonica</u>, and

contradicted the lady flatly without apology on the matter of <u>Cyrus Asiatica</u>, remembering that he knew more than she did. ("FG" 286. Emphasis added.)

Here, while the gardener talks about the plants, he mentions two plant names; "Pyrus Japonica" and "Cyrus Asiatica." "Pyrus Japonica" meaning Japanese pear, is a real name and is also known as chaenomeles or Japanese quince, but Cyrus Asiatica is a fictitious name and it surely was invented to have a pun with "Pyrus Japonica" Although it is merely a conversation between the flower lovers, "Pyrus Japonica" and "Cyrus Asiatica" at the same time, retain a somewhat heterogeneous impression in this context. This scene implies that Violet, who had been surrounded by Englishness itself, encountered the heterogeneous outside world when she heard about "Pyrus Japonica" and "Cyrus Asiatica."

Especially, the word "Cyrus" reminds the reader of Cyrus the Great, a Persian king who ended the Babylonian captivity. During his reign over the thirty years in the 6th century, B.C., Cyrus the Great freed the slaves and was regarded as "The Liberator" in the Books of Isaiah and Ezra.[6] So it can be said that the paired words of "Pyrus Japonica" and "Cyrus Asiatica" referred by a gardener offered Violet a new vista, new potentiality. They were a kind of antithesis towards Englishness represented by Hatfield House, with its oldest oak trees and the smoothest turf, which made Violet discontent and uneasy.

The gardener himself serves as an important indication. He talks frankly and earnestly to Violet;

> In short he [the gardener] stood there for half an hour telling her of his wifes(sic) dyspepsia, how caustic is poison for tumours, how a drop warms the innards, how he would think over her words, and how if ever she came their way he would be proud to give her a cup of tea, "not spirits" he said with a wink and show her how to treat phylloxera with paraffin. ("FG" 286)

The passage is a vivid description of the humorous heart-to-heart conversation between two people beyond class barriers, but for that reason, it implies a violation of the class distinction for the people at that time. The gardener is described as follows;

> Freedom gleamed in his eyes while he spoke; and he waved his shears

towards the house as men waved bloodstained bayonettes once before the Bastille. ("FG" 286)

A gardener talking freely with "a real lady" ("FG" 286) is compared to people in one of the most decisive scenes of the French Revolution. Of course it is true that there is a comical exaggeration in the description of the enthusiastic gardener, but at the same time one cannot deny that Virginia Woolf is fully aware that there is a distinct subversive image of the gardener for the reader at the beginning of the twentieth century. The comparison of the gardener waving his large pair of shears, with people waving bloodstained swords at the symbolic venue of the French Revolution means that the conversation of people beyond the class barrier is itself a revolutionary act. "Pyrus Japonica" and "Cyrus Asiatica" mentioned in Chapter Two serve as a clash-like encounter with different cultures and also serve as both a destructive and constructive power because "Pyrus Japonica" and "Cyrus Asiatica" become a point of contact between two different cultures for Violet, who talks enjoyably with a gardener, however harsh and heterogeneous it might sound for conventional people.

Violet had felt "suffocated" ("FG" 287) with her environment, but after she met the gardener, she began to talk to people about what she had in mind, such as the drainage system of the house. In Chapter Two, Violet bought a cottage "with real drains, and real roses, and a place to sit out in and one's own china, and no ancestors" ("FG" 288). These may seem a trifle thing for the people around her, but only her friend Nelly understood the significance of the matter. It is notable that "the biographer" herself made a comment, stating that "[s]uch was the beginning of the great revolution which is making England a very different place from what it was." ("FG" 288) Thus, in the first two chapters, Violet's unconventionality, her sense of uneasiness towards Englishness, and her trial to have a breakthrough in to find an authentic manner of expression, were explored and the exploration was to continue in Chapter Three.

"The biographer" calls Chapter Three a kind of "Myth" ("FG" 292) set in Tokyo and subtitles it "a story to make you sleep." The story is written in the mode of a folk tale, beginning with a familiar "once upon a time" phrase, and "Tokio" is described as "the most beautiful city in the world" ("FG" 293). It is a fantasy story of "the two Sacred Princesses" who "came sailing over the sea on the back of a whale" ("FG" 295) and about a series of miracles which took place during their stay in Tokyo. Although the name of Violet is not mentioned in this chapter, the impact of unconventionality seen through the heroine in the previous chapters is all the more magnified here. Also on the Princesses finally leaving Tokyo, the image of Violet and her friend returning back to Britain after their stay in Japan is overlapped.

Violet Dickinson went on a world tour with Nelly Cecil, a friend of Violet, in the latter half of 1905 and they visited Japan during the journey.[7] They gave Virginia a "full report of their impressions" (Hawkes 1979: 271), and the third chapter was surely based on Violet Dickinson's actual visit to Japan in 1905. Virginia Woolf clearly had a keen interest and mentioned it variously in her letters. Woolf wrote to Violet Dickinson, saying that she had bought several "travelling books" for her in her letter to Violet in July 1905. In another letter to her, Woolf wrote, "I read that the Japanese bathe always 3 times a day: sometimes more often." (*The Flight of the Mind* 204). Again, Woolf wrote to Violet, saying;

> I feel that there words ought to be more durable than brass to travel all the way – where? Singapore, or Yokohama. ... Toby says you have all been received by the Mikado. Take care you don't get into Punch as an international joker.
> (*The Flight of the Mind* 208–9. Emphasis added.)[8]

Virginia Woolf also sent a letter to Nelly Cecil on board, saying;

> I am an authority upon Japan Now; I daresay I shall be given the Japanese books to do for the Times....I confess I should have felt more at my ease in Japan.
> (*The Flight of the Mind* 211–2. Emphasis added.)[9]

As far as Woolf's remaining letters are concerned, interestingly Japan seems almost the only country which caught Virginia Woolf's eye. In her letter to Violet and Nelly Cecil during that time, Woolf mentioned Japan several times through a series of playful remarks, but almost none about other countries where Violet might have visited. It may be because Japonisme[10] was in vogue in Britain from the late nineteenth century to the early twentieth century and people were familiar to things Japanese such as Ukiyoe prints and Japanese fans. We see Japanese fans in various pictures painted by the artists who were interested in Japonisme.[11] Liberty's Department Store was known as a fashionable shop which deals with goods from Asia including Japan and in one letter Woolf referred to

Liberty's.

Woolf said jokingly in the above-mentioned letter that she became such "an authority upon Japan" that the *Times* might ask her to write a review on books on Japan (*The Flight of the Mind* 211–2), [12] and in reality, she did review *The Call of the East*, essays on Japan and China, by Charlotte Lorrimer in the *TLS* on April 26, 1907, a few months before "Friendships Gallery" was presented to Violet Dickinson. It may indeed be plausible to say that *The Call of the East* by Charlotte Lorrimer offered another catalyst for Woolf to write a story based on Japan. When reviewing *The Call of the East* in 1907, Woolf noted a point of view which the author had been inspired by: Lorrimer was inspired by "a precious knowledge which is still current in the East"(Woolf, *TLS* April 26, 1907; pg. 131; Issue 276). Woolf paid attention to the author who watched a Japanese mother who had lost her child recently, noticing that she "arranged her lips in the set sweet smile which is to hide her sorrow." (Woolf, *TLS* 131). Here Woolf seemed to be particularly interested in the inner feelings hidden beneath the exterior.

In "Friendships Gallery," however, Woolf did not adopt a realistic representation of Japan, nor intended to make description of actual Japan as Lorrimer did. The vocabularies used as Japanese sentences did not sound Japanese or overall impression of the chapter was different from those which are intended to be truthful description of Japan. For example, "Tsai Gun Tsai gun," "Tsara Gun Tsara Gun" and "Tish Gun Tish Gun" were introduced as Japanese sentences to which Woolf added her translation("FG" 302). According to the author, they mean respectively that "Follow me, follow me," "Feed me, feed me," and "Comes sounding to the English Caw-Caw." ("FG" 302). Although the structure of the third sentence looks similar to the previous ones, Woolf gives utterly different meaning, which reveals that Woolf invented the Japanese–like phrases for fun. Similarly, Woolf also introduced "Rick-Shi"("FG" 294), "Rim-Shi-Ki," ("FG" 295), which mean, writes Woolf, interpreter, and "the Sin Sin" house ("FG" 296), but they were all deliberately invented to be incomprehensible Japanese. Thus the world represented in "Friendships Gallery" is meant not to be real Japan but to be something which could be called "Japan in her vision," or "A Japan Fantasy."

The "Japan Fantasy" goes on in the intentional penchant for a slapstick, burlesque style, and Japan is described as a society cut from the social restraints which England at her time was tied with. Violet, here Sacred Princess, a daughter of Emperor, finds her place. In the previous chapters, Violet's tall figure easily became an object of derision, and she obeyed patiently her godmother's advice to become a "Beacon of Godliness"("FG" 276). Here, the Sacred Princesses were totally free women and develop their own nature. Violet or the Princess was described to be "of the nature of a Giantess" ("FG" 295) as she "swallowed a magic seed when she was born so that nothing on earth could stop her growing;… moreover her powers were as marvelous as her height;" ("FG" 295).

In this chapter a series of strange things which almost nobody could have ever expected to happen occurred as though the narrator would like to pursue the most fanciful imagination to its extremity. For example, the narrator describes that "[there] was a great mountain grown in the middle of the city; and it had thousands and thousands of caves in it, and at the mouth of each there burnt a flame"("FG" 293). And people were anxious, thinking, "all the city will become before dawn one vast mountain, and snakes will run in and out of the flaming caves that were our homes." ("FG" 293) Again at the end of the story there is a passage as follows;

> Before one such blast they fled to the hill top; and looking fearfully into the bay beneath saw a vast wave with <a > curved back and silver ripples on it, rise from the floor of the sea to the summit; only it was no wave, but a monster. Out of his nostrils came two columns of stream, frizzling the air all round them, and his eyes were red caverns. Now they had just made up their minds to be devoured, when the two Princesses came down to the sea shore and bewitched the monster by making passes with certain magic wands called "Umbrellas".
> ("FG" 300)

Here the two Princesses bewitched and tamed the fearful Grendel-like monster of *Beowulf* with their umbrellas. The two Princesses, or Violet and her friend Nelly, became saviours in Japan. During the conversation with the gardener in Chapter Two, the paired phrases "Pyrus Japonica" and "Cyrus Asiatica" indicated a possible ground which was located antithetically against Europe. In Chapter Two, it was "the beginning of revolution" for Violet, who had felt discontent and suffocated, even to talk about drainage and to spend a real life in her own cottage. It should be noted that in Chapter Three, Violet was liberated and acted as a "Cyrus Asiatica" in Japan, beating and taming the monster and freeing people. Woolf created "a Japan Fantasy" in Chapter Three and in her vision Japan was described to be a country where "Cyrus Asiatica" lived, a country with infinite potentialities.

Woolf's interest in Japan runs throughout the whole work, beginning with allegorical use of "Pyrus Japonica" and "Cyrus Asiatica" and developing to her Japan Fantasy in Chapter Three. Japan in Woolf's vision serves as an antithetical ground in contrast to the land of Englishness.

Interestingly Woolf's attention to Japan continued to her later writing career and resulted into forming a new perception for Woolf. When Virginia and Leonard published *Two Stories* from the Hogarth Press as the first publication in 1917, the book was bound by Japanese paper. It was bound "in Japanese grass paper, some copies in dull blue, some in an overall red and white design" (Hussey 1995: 133) .

Figure 1. The Japanese pattern used for Virginia and Leonard Woolf's *Two Stories* (For the coloured version, please see the frontispiece page.)

The figure 1 is the "red and white design" of the cover of *Two Stories*. The pattern is called "Asa-no-Ha" (麻の葉) in Japanese, meaning "Leaves of Linen", one of the very popular Japanese patterns. The Woolf's choice of Japanese grass paper for the book binding of their first publication may be a mere incidental matter but still it was a significantly symbolic coincidence because the "Leaves of Linen" pattern implies the hope of sound growth as linens grow rapidly. [13]

In *Jacob's Room* (1922), the narrator refers to Japanese paper flowers, which were popular at that time in Britain. These Japanese paper flowers "opened touching on water" (*Jacob's Room* 81) and Woolf used the Japanese paper flowers to think over a paradox that the water flowers are, artificial as they are, more short-lived than the natural flowers themselves. Again in *The London Scene*, the paper Japanese water flowers are mentioned. In *To the Lighthouse,* some similarities with the Japanese way of thinking can be seen in Lily's process of achieving her vision. Taking Woolf's continued attention to Japan into consideration, Woolf's Japan Fantasy as seen in "Friendships Gallery" is surely a nurture-ground for Woolf's future perception.

Notes

1. This article is a revised edition of the paper which was presented in the 21th Annual Conference of the International Virginia Woolf Society, held at Glasgow University, UK in 2011. The title "Friendships Gallery" is abbreviated as "FG" in the citation of this paper.
2. There are different opinions about when "Friendships Gallery" was written. Mitchell A. Leaska, editor of *A passionate Apprentice: The Early Journals* 1897–1909, says that it was written in 1902 and revised in 1907. Leaska says that "Virginia responded to her with eagerness and affection, and wrote a prose piece called "Friendship's (sic) Gallery" at Fritham House, Lyndhurst, sometime in August-September of 1902." (163) and "[b]efore leaving for Sussex, Virginia sent Violet Dickinson the comic "Life" of her she had just "very hastily polished off."(367) It seems, however, more probable to speculate that it was written in 1907 as Ellen Hawkes states in her introduction to the work.
3. For example, in a letter of the 8th August 1907 to Nelly Cecil, Woolf said, "I cant(sic) remember now how bad it is; but I know it will have to be re-written in six months; and I shant do it; and I don't want immaturities, things torn out of time, preserved unless in some strong casket, with one key only." (*The Flight of the Mind* 304). Virginia Woolf entreated Violet Dickinson to give the work back to her, saying, "Do send it back here at once. Please never read, or quote or show – it puts me in a misery only to imagine it." (A letter to Violet, on 1 October 1907). In another letter to Violet, Woolf wrote, "Will you send me back the copy of my Life of you? I always forget it, and I want to have it, great work as it is!"(*The Flight of the Mind* 314)
4. 52 pages by Virginia Woolf's pagination.

5. Karin E. Westman, "The First *Orlando*: The Laugh of the Comic Spirit in Virginia Woolf's "Friendships Gallery," *Twentieth Century Literature*. March 22, 2001.
6. Isaiah 45:1–6 and Ezra 1:1–11 .
7. The note of the second volume of *The Letters of Virginia Woolf* says that "Lady Robert and Violet were planning to embark on a world-cruise to Vancouver and across the Pacific to Japan, returning home by the Suez Canal." (*The Flight of the Mind*. n.2 p.193)
8. Virginia Woolf's letter to Violet Dickinson dated 1 October, 1905.
9. Virginia Woolf's letter to Nelly Cecil dated 10 November, 1905.
10. Japonisme is a keen interest in Japanese art and also in things Japanese, and it swept Europe after Japan had opened its borders and resumed trading with other countries in 1854. Towards the end of the nineteenth century, not only artists but also ordinary people were attracted by Japanese prints called Ukiyo-e, Hokusai manga, porcelain, lacquer, textiles and furniture in Britain. The artists who were influenced by Japonisme were, to name a few, Monet, Renoir, Cezanne, Vincent van Gogh, Paul Gauguin, and Henri de Toulouse-Lautrec in France, James McNeill Whistler, Walter Crane and Aubrey Beardsley in Britain, and also Alphonse Mucha in the Czech Republic and Gustav Klimt in Austria. It can be said that an essential influence of Impressionist and Post-Impressionist paintings was Japanese art, in a number of ways. Above all, Van Gogh painted many pictures influenced by Japanese art such as "Japonesrie: Flowering Plum Tree (after Hiroshige)" and "The Courtesan (after Eisen)" (1887) and repeatedly mentioned Japan and Japanese art in his letters. He wrote to Theo, his brother, saying that "All my work is based to some extent on Japanese art" (Letter 640). In the twentieth century Britain, Duncan Grant painted pictures with a motif of Japonisme such as "Still Life, the Sharaku Scarf."and 'A Portrait of James Strachey.'
11. "La princess du pays de la porcelain" and "Symphony in White, No. 2: The Little White Girl" by James McNeill Whistler, "Lady with a Japanese Fan" by Maurice William Greiffenhagen and "One, Two, Buckle my Shoe" by Walter Crane are some of the examples.
12. It is an interesting fact that in those days a numerous books about Japan were written in English by Japanese people and were reviewed in many leading papers in Britain. For example, Kakuzo (Tenshin) Okakura published several influential books including *The Ideals of the East* (1903), *The Awakening of Japan* (1905) and *The Book of Tea* (1906). In 1905 when Virginia Woolf wrote this letter to Nelly, Yoshisaburo Okakura, younger brother of Kakuzo (Tenshin) published *The Japanese Spirit* with the introduction by George Meredith and the work was favourably reviewed in *The Times Literary Supplement* soon after the publication. Also, *The Russo-Japanese Conflict: Its Causes and Issues* by Kan-ichi Asakawa, *The Risen Sun* by Kencho Suyematsu were published in the same year and reviewed in *TLS*. *Hana*, a Japanese novel by Gensai Murai was translated by a Japanese and published in Britain in 1905.
13. In Japan the pattern is especially used for babies' clothes in the hope of their hap-

piness and well-being as the linen is thought to grow rapidly.

References

Briggs, Julia. (2006) *Reading Virginia Woolf.* Edinburgh: Edinburgh University Press.

Colburn, Krystyna. (2004) The Lesbian Intertext of Woolf's Short Fiction. In Kathryn N. Benzel and Ruth Hoberman eds. *Trespassing Boundaries: Virginia Woolf's Short Fiction.* New York: Palgrave Macmillan.

Hawkes, Ellen. (1979) Introduction to "Friendships Gallery." In Unpublished Virginia Woolf. *The Twentieth Century Literature.* Fall.

Hussey, Mark. (1995) *Virginia Woolf A to Z.* New York: Facts on File, Inc.

Kirkpatrick, B.J. and Stuart N. Clarke. 1997. *A Bibliography of Virginia Woolf.* Fourth Edition. Oxford: Clarendon Press.

Lorrimer, Charlotte. (1907) *The Call of the East.* London: Gay and Bird.

Parkes, Adam. (1996) *Modernism and the Theater of Censorship.* Oxford: Oxford University Press.

Westman, Karin E. March 22, (2001) The First *Orlando*: The Laugh of the Comic Spirit in Virginia Woolf's "Friendships Gallery." *Twentieth Century Literature.* 47, no. 1: 39–71.

Woolf, Virginia. April 26, (1907) Review of *The Call of the East. TLS,* Friday; pg. 131; Issue 276.

Woolf, Virginia. 1907. Fall (1979) "Friendships Gallery" in "Unpublished Virginia Woolf." *The Twentieth Century Literature*: 270–302. Also in *The Essays of Virginia Woolf,* Vol. 6. Stuart N. Clarke ed. London: Chatto & Windus, 2011.

Woolf, Virginia. (1922) *Jacob's Room.* London: Hogarth Press, 1965.

Woolf, Virginia. (1975) *The Flight of the Mind: The Letters of Virginia Woolf 1888–1912.* Eds. Nigel Nicolson and Joanne Trautmann, London: Hogarth Press.

Woolf, Virginia. (2006) *The London Scene: Six Essays on London Life.* New York: Ecco.

A Quest for Identity and an Epiphany about Love: *About Daddy*, a Partition Novel

Eiko Ohira

Abstract
Meena Arora Nayak's *About Daddy* (2000) is a story of Simran's quest for her identity, which is chained to the history of the Indo-Pakistani Partition because of her love for her father, in a way similar to the unnamed narrator in Amitav Ghosh's *The Shadow Lines* (1988) whose quest for identity is connected to modern Indian history through his father's cousin, Tridib, his "alter ego." Simran internalizes his father's guilt about India and is led to discover the suppressed story of his desire for his lost homeland and the epiphany of his love for India, much as the narrator of *The Shadow Lines* imagines Tridib's life in London during World War II and death in Dhaka in the riots of 1964 through his memories and those of people around him. Simran's father's guilt leaves his story untold, and this silenced story of guilt and love for his homeland crucially influences his daughter's identity formation. It causes her not only to be burdened with his guilt but also to relive the memories of his life in his homeland. Both Simran and the narrator of *The Shadow Line* try to discover the silenced stories of their beloved, however, unlike the imaginative narrator of *The Shadow Line*, Simran not only imagines her father's story, she is also doomed to experience her own guilt when he asks her to sprinkle his ashes on the border.

Keywords   India, partition, identity, epiphany, diaspora

1. A quest for identity

"I'm nothing. I'm not American, I'm not Hispanic, I'm not from Pakistan, I'm not Indian. What am I?" (*About Daddy* 12) This is the question that Simran, an Indian American protagonist in *About Daddy* (It will be described as "AD" from the next citation onwards.) asks her parents after she is called an enemy by Farzana, her schoolmate who had just migrated from Pakistan. Farzana's hostility causes Simran's identity crisis. Simran is forced to look into Farzana's image of the other, much as Calcutta is an "inverted image of the other", Dhaka, locked into an irreversible symmetry by the line", the "looking-glass border" in Amitav Ghosh's *The Shadow Lines* (1988:233).

Meena Arora Nayak's *About Daddy* (2000) is a story of Simran's quest for her identity, which is chained to the history of the Partition because of her love for her father, again in a way similar to the unnamed narrator in *The Shadow Lines* (1988) whose quest for identity is connected to modern Indian history through his father's cousin, Tridib, his "alter ego" (Urbashi Barat 2001: 130; A. N. Kaul 1995:302). Simran internalizes his father's guilt about India and is led to discover the suppressed story of his desire for his lost homeland, much as the narrator of *The Shadow Lines* imagines Tridib's life in London during World War II and death in Dhaka in the riots of 1964 through his memories and those of people around him. Simran's father's guilt leaves his story untold, and this silenced story of guilt and love for his homeland crucially influences his daughter's identity formation. It causes her not only to be burdened with his guilt but also to relive the memories of his life in his homeland. Both Simran and the narrator of *The Shadow Lines* try to discover the silenced stories of their beloved, however, unlike the imaginative narrator of *The Shadow Line*, Simran not only imagines her father's story, she is also doomed to experience her own guilt when he asks her to sprinkle his ashes on the border.

2. Daddy's silenced story of guilt

The story begins with Simran standing on the Indian side of the border to fulfill her father's dying wish. She remembers he told her, "Don't cremate me in India." ("AD" 1). He desires his soul to "feel the wound" he "helped inflict as long as it bleeds" ("AD" 1). His words of guilt toward his homeland are repeated again and again in Simran's mind.

How are her father's "bottomless...silent chasms" made visible, and how is his silenced story of guilt revealed to his daughter, causing her identity crisis? She is shocked when Farzana, a new girl from Pakistan calls her "enemy, with the contempt of a racial slur" ("AD" 11). Simran retaliates, but Farzana insists, "Indians are our enemies" ("AD" 11). She answers back "I'm not Indian, I'm American." But Farzana says, "No, you're not. You're Indian...." ("AD" 11). Back at home Simran ignores her mother's call, goes up to her room and puts "all the sheets and blankets and everything into trash bags to be given to the people in Bangladesh" ("AD" 11). Her mother tries to pacify her and asks what happened to her. Simran answers, "I hate it [the rain]. It's hurting all those people in the new country India made. I hate it. I hate you. I want to be Indian. Why don't you ever tell me I'm Indian? You're Indian, Daddy's Indian, then how I'm not?" ("AD" 12) Her parents are speechless, but Simran continues:

> 'I hate it. I'm nothing. I'm not American, I'm not Hispanic, I'm not from Pakistan, I'm not Indian. What am I?' 'Sure You're Indian.' My mother reached to touch my hair again. 'No, I'm not.' I jerked my head away. 'If I am, then how come you never talk to me about India, how come we never go there to visit, how come we don't speak the language or wear the clothes or talk about it? How come you never talk to me about India?....' ("AD" 12)

She knows she is Indian, but only because her parents are Indians. She has never considered being Indian as her own identity, because of her parents' silence, which is broken by her desperate appeal to them. Farzana's taunt locks her in a space of mirrors set facing each other, where she can neither deny being an Indian nor accept it.

Her father finally confesses what happened to him and what he did to his people in India, ignoring Simran's mother's appeal to stop:

> 'Because I love India here', he touched two fingers to his head, 'and here.' He touched the same fingers to his heart. 'But I hurt her. I hurt India. I hurt her very badly'. .....
>
> 'Because some Hindus and Muslims who didn't want to live together any more started killing each other, and the British, who ruled India at that time, divided her into two parts....So the people who lived on the wrong side had to leave their homes and go to the side they belonged to. But there were some bad people who couldn't wait for them to leave. They began killing them all' ....
>
> 'Did the Muslims hurt you, Daddy?' I touched his head.
>
> 'Yes. They killed my father, too.'...'Then Gajji [a gym teacher] was killed,' he said almost in whisper....A terrible fear rose up my spine. 'What did you do, Daddy?' I asked....'I killed a lot of people.' His

voice was cold and faraway as if he had entered the realm of the moon. 'I took Gajji's sword and hurt the Muslims in my neighbourhood.' ....

'No, don't.' My mother had moved to stand between Daddy and me as though by doing so she would prevent his words from reaching me. ...' I stood in the middle of the marketplace one day and hacked off innocent people who were only out to shop. I killed...' 'Enough!' My mother reached to cover his mouth with her hand as if to push the words back in. 'She's too young.' 'I hurt India,' Daddy continued, his voice muffled behind Mummy's hand. 'I killed people who loved me. I killed the trust between Hindus and Muslims so that they would never be able to live together in peace again. I helped divide them forever. I helped divide India. I tore her apart. And I left her bleeding and ran away and I can never go back.' ("AD" 13–14)

After hearing this story, Simran feels bound to his lost homeland. She is burdened with his traumatic past. She has not yet internalized his guilt but considers herself as one who has to protect him from invisible "relentless pursuers, from India whom he had hurt so much" ("AD" 15). India appears before her as "relentless pursuers" and "a nemesis" as well as "a victim" ("AD" 15). She understands her father is both a victim and an aggressor, but the crimes he committed are a terrible secret that should be locked away in her heart for ever. She is no longer watching a horror film, she is in it as a fighter to protect both him and herself. Thus Simran is bound to India because of her love for her father.

3. "I am my father's daughter"

India has often been represented as a female body, the "birth-sister" of Salim Sinai, or "Mother India, Bharat Mata" (*Midnight's Children* 1981:404), but in this text India appears not only as a divided nation but also "a nemesis" before a daughter of the Indian diaspora, a new image which undergoes further transformations as the story unfolds.

Interestingly, we see in this text an idea of cause and effect. Daddy as a little boy suffers from a near-fatal fever, and according to a holy man it is the effect of his mother's crime in a previous life, when she killed a beggar woman's little son. Simran sees a vision in which her father covers a crying little girl with "a ragged old quilt," saying, "This is a magic quilt. It makes pain disappear" ("AD" 23). This vision comes to her when she is in custody in India on charges of spying. Three officials try to extract a confession from her by incessant torture and Simran loses consciousness. The magic quilt she sees in her dream is the very thing her father's mother sewed and lay on her apparently dying son's form, chanting to a beggar "Leave him be. He doesn't belong to me. He is a beggar just like you. He has no one to feed him or love him…." ("AD" 25). This quilt, it seems, saved his life, and his mother makes her words come true, telling him to beg for his food for a year, wearing the quilt.

This episode strengthens the impression that penance for her father's crimes is Simran's fate, and the fatality unites the two. Simran replays the interrogation in her mind over and over in prison, and in the process her father's guilt and her innocence "become one"("AD" 31). And strangely enough, the crisis which started with Farzana's taunt in her sophomore year at high school seems to end while she is in custody. Nobody is chasing her father now because she (a surrogate for Daddy) is taken captive and interrogated in his homeland. She sympathized with his pain and guilt, and has been scared that invisible pursuers would take him from her. She watches over her father from outside, but now his crimes are fused with her innocence, and she sees them from within as her own guilt.

Now let us look more closely at how this relentless chase began. One day she went to Farzana's house to pick up some books and met her grandmother who had just come from Lahore. She saw the right sleeve of her shirt was empty. 'What happened to your grandmother's arm?' she asked Farzana. 'Someone cut it off a long time ago during the Partition riots back home,' she said. Simran panicked and rushed to her bathroom to vomit. All she could remember was seeing "Daddy standing in a street hacking at people with a sword over and over again, slicing off heads and arms…." ("AD" 35). She does all she can to protect her father from Farzana's grandmother's supposed vengeful pursuit. She even makes up a story of horror to tell a psychiatrist and leads him to suggest a transfer to another school, which guarantees that her father's identity will be safeguarded. Thus she eludes Farzana, but the "nightmare of her grandmother hounding Daddy"("AD" 37) "lay dormant in some fear-ridden space" in her mind" ("AD" 37).

Later, in Daddy's homeland, Simran learns about how he was loved and accepted not only by his family but also by Amjad's (his schoolmate's) Muslim family, who fostered him after his mother's death and his father's disappearance. The discovery of this story of his childhood and the days before the Indian Partition runs parallel with her mingling with the other women convicts while she is in custody. Sultana, a Muslim student who has been labeled as a terrorist because she killed some Hindu students, is one of them. Simran is deeply involved in her family's tragedy.

> I write about Daddy and Sultana, youth lost in blind rage and revenge. I write about India, the country my father lamented in his dreams and loved in his death. I write about myself, an unwilling participant forced into the midst of it all and now hopelessly involved. That night, lying under the blanket, I see Daddy's horrifying image replaced by Sultana's. ("AD" 112)

Innocent though Simran is, her father's guilt becomes her own through her days of imprisonment. How do her friendship with Sultana and Simran's sense of guilt lead her into the depth of Indian Muslims' lives? Simran makes a life-risking search for Sultana's brother and decides to stay with his family in Karim Gali, Muslim resident quarters which were attacked and set on fire by a Hindu group.

Why does Simran feel she should stay "amidst the terrorism and danger ("AD" 166)?" She says:

> 'Daddy,' I whisper, 'I know your guilt now.' I know that I cannot leave this country till I have delivered his ashes to the penance he craved. I also know I cannot abandon him to an eternity of that penance. I know I cannot leave now, because I am my father's daughter.
> ("AD" 163)

The phrase "I am my father's daughter," which is repeated over again after this, is the crucial step to regain her lost identity as an Indian. She identifies herself in this way for the first time when she visits Karim Gali and sees the victims of communal violence. Suddenly, she sees them as "inheritors of Daddy's legacy" ("AD" 160):

> These could have been the very same people in Lahore, the people Daddy massacred in his mindless rage. There are so many apologies I want to offer them, so many amends I want to make. How can I leave now? ("AD" 160)
> How does one apologize for the murder of loved ones, for the betrayal of one's own, for being the daughter of a man who poisoned the very soil meant to nurture? ("AD" 162)

She also says, "…because that's what Daddy created I want to help undo some of what he started. I want to stay here and renew the bonds he broke…. I want Daddy to stop weeping inside me….I want to help him find peace" ("AD" 166). Though India is still "a country that is foreign" ("AD" 171) to her, because Sultana and other convicts are kind to her, she sees the continuance of a spiritual bond from the days when her father lived in India.

"I am my father's daughter" ("AD" 172). When does this refrain end? Does Simran remain bound in this way? Let us look at a crucial scene during Shvrati, a Hindu festival in which Simran sees Kalida die trying to keep some sadhus from advancing to the road leading to the masjid. Kalida, a leader of CCPH (a peace organization) says, "If any Hindu crosses over to this road, he will have to cross over my body first—my body, a brahmin's body" ("AD" 289). And indeed they step on Kalida's body. Simran sees "Muslim youth pour out of the masjit waving staffs and swords…." ("AD" 289). And then, an explosion occurs. Simran sees grey smoke rise from the masjit and crumbling bricks. She feels pain in her fingers, tries to move her arm, and finds it sticky with blood. The bag which contains her father's ashes is torn open. "In a frenzy I begin to scoop Daddy's ashes from the ground into my lap—the ashes and the soil and the debris and bits of bone and flesh" ("AD" 290).

Simran attends the last rites for Kalida and sees Kalida's face "glows as if a sun is growing within him" ("AD" 291). "It is like the afterglow of an ecstasy, or a sudden flowering of an epiphany. In that instant, I am filled with such envy for Kalida, I lay my head on his chest and breathe in his death smell" ("AD" 291).

4. An epiphany about love and a lost object

What is revealed to Simran by Kalida's death? Let us look at the ending. Simran comes back to her home, and happens to watch the evening news, which shows "a clip of the masjid" like "an ancient ruin" ("AD" 292) on the screen. And Simran's monologue-like narrative follows:

> One time I remember I asked Daddy if he missed India. 'Like a lover,' he said, holding a hand over his heart as if to contain the broken pieces within.
>
> I remember the radiance on Kalida's face. How blind I have been. I saw Daddy suffer all his life and assumed it was his guilt that

consumed him. When all along, what he was really suffering from was the epiphany of love.... Perhaps in such a love affair, there is only a continuum—from Daddy's heartbreak to Kalida's consummation. That is why Daddy didn't let me annihilate his pain in the obliterating waters of the Ganga, but chose instead, to mingle with the soil of India, bloodied though it might be.

Realizing at last that I have delivered his soul not to peace, not to penance, but to ecstasy, I pull out my right hand from within the blanket. ("AD" 292–93)

In this epiphany, India is not only a victim and a nemesis but also the loved one to him. Now his desire is realized. What does his desire signify? Is it an ultimate hymn to India? How is the ecstasy of death in love related to Simran's subject formation? How does her identification as her father's daughter end?

Here let us examine how Simran experienced her father's death:

I didn't shed a single tear when he passed away. His pain and the promise I made him to alleviate it, weighed too heavily in my heart. My father may be dead to the world, but for me he still thrashes in the throes of death, my bereavement still awaits. ("AD" 78)

Simran can share his pain and guilt with him, but when she discovers his love affair with his homeland, she finds she can not follow him. At this moment her identification as her father's daughter seems to end. She could deliver his soul to ecstasy, which stopped the crying in her heart, to which she was bound at all times. Kalida is a key figure, who mediates Simran's awakening to her father's true story, that he was suffering not from his guilt but from the epiphany of his love for India. Simran sees on Kalida face a jouissance of death in love, which seems to project her father's own ecstasy. This is the sub-textual structure of desire in this text, desire for a lost object, the mother's body signified by Mother India.

This desire for the mother's body lurks underneath the surface narratives of many texts. In E. M. Forster's *A Passage to India* (1924) it lurks under the surface narrative of cross-cultural friendship. In *The Longest Journey* (1907) the mother figure is split between the two Mrs Elliotts: Agnes (Mrs Elliot as Rickie's wife), a fallen woman figure; and Mrs Elliott (Rickie's mother) a good mother figure, an ever-lasting earth figure with whom Ricki's dead body is to be fused. In *A Passage to India* the desire for the maternal body lurks underneath the narrative of triadic relationships among Mrs Moore, Aziz and Adela. Mrs Moore becomes the core of absence which signifies an original lost object, the mother's body as the object of not only Aziz's explicit desire—seen in his way of looking at her as the sacred—but also Adela's implicit desire for Mrs Moore—seen in her absolute reliance on Mrs Moore's power, her goodness and wisdom.

Githa Harihran's short story "The Remains of the Feast" (1992) deals with the theme of female subject formation in the context of mother-and-daughter fiction through the representation of a 90-year-old Brahmin woman (Rukmini) who violates a food taboo. We also find a desire for the mother's body in the representation of the blood which defiles Dracula's victims (*Dracula 1897*). It occurs, too, in the violation of incest taboo and the high caste widow's forbidden love affair with the untouchable youth in *The God of Small Things* (1997). Hariharan's *The Thousand Faces of Night* (1992) is also full of blood, its forbidden love affairs and polluting objects flowing out of bodies which blur "the boundary of the self's clean and proper body" (Kristeva, *Powers of Horror* 2000: 75). The desire for the maternal body is signified as a desire for the violation of a boundary which the maternal body does not respect. In *About Daddy*, we also find such polluting objects which threaten identity: in Daddy's ashes and Simran's blood mingled with the Indian soil, which is itself already long bloodied, and in Kalida's dead body and "his death smell" which Simran breathes.

About Daddy is, as the narrator says, about Daddy and about the India he "lamented in his dreams and loved in his death" ("AD" 112), but it is also about Simran and Sultana, who replaces Daddy because she has also lost her youth in "blind rage and revenge". Everything that happens to Simran and everyone she meets lead her to realize her father's epiphany of love for India ultimately, which enables her to accept his death in love, break the spell of her guilt-ridden identification with him, and release her from the role of caring wife-mother.

5. Simran's paranoiac sense of guilt

Simran and her father are bound as accomplices in his crimes like Siamese twins. At the moment Simran opens a Pandora's box, asking Daddy to tell his untold story, she is possessed by his fate and internalizes his "weeping," much like Adela in *A Passage to India* is possessed by her "echo" after

Marabar.

Bapsi Sidhwa's *Ice-Candy-Man* (1988) delineates how the titular figure, an aggressor, feels, but just a few Partition novels have dealt with the theme of betrayal and guilt. Simran's obsessive guilt reminds us of Adela's own. Adela's trifling action of striking the wall to start an echo in the Marabar cave is represented as a fatal deed, equivalent to Eve's rebellion against God, through Adela's paranoiac sense of guilt. After Marabar, Adela is obsessed with a sense of primary sin and degradation equivalent to Eve's. She is annoyed by the "echo" which she started in the cave. It chases her incessantly like a "ghost". Adela's desire to go back into the primeval desert represents both her sense of degradation and that of the whole human race.

Simran similarly feels she should stay in the midst of terrorism and danger, help Sultana's family, and renew the bonds Daddy broke, but Arun, a journalist insists the misguided people during the Partition should not be blamed for today's problems and maintains that Simran's guilt is "self-imposed" ("AD" 212) and self-destructive. Maybe he is right, her sacrificial deeds are too absurd, but this text represents memorably how one can be spell-bound by an absurd sense of guilt, though the representation of guilt as an "echo" in *A Passage to India* is much more impressive and subtly delineated.

6. The questions of Muslim minority and violence as a means to peace

In *About Daddy,* the combination of a daughter's quest for identity and a diaspora father's desire for his lost homeland, the main narrative a Siamese twin-like, almost incestuous father-and-daughter relationship, is uniquely structured among Partition novels. However, the questions of Muslim minorities in modern India and violence as a means to peace are raised, and are abandoned halfway, making it a lesser work than Forster's masterpiece.

References

Barat, Urbashi. (2001) Time in the Novel of Amtav Ghosh and Arundhati Roy: Technique as Meaning. *Indian writing in English: A Critical Response.* Ed. Syed Mashkoor Ali. New Delhi: Creative Books.

Forster, Edward Morgan. (1978a) *A Passage to India*. 1924; London: Hodder & Stoughton.
Forster, Edward Morgan. (1978b) *The Longest Journey*. 1907; London: Hodder & Stoughton.
Ghosh, Amitav. (1995) *The Shadow Lines*. 1988; NY: Oxford University Press.
Hariharan, Githa. (1996) *The Thousand Faces of Night*. 1992; London: The Women's Press.
Hariharan, Githa. (1993) The Remains of the Feast. *The Art of Dying and Other Stories*. Delhi: Penguin.
Kaul, A. N. (1995) A Reading of *The Shadow Lines*. *The Shadow Lines*: Educational Edition. 1988; NY: Oxford University Press.
Kristeva, Julia. (2000) *The Powers of Horror: An Essay on Abjection*. Trans. Jeanine Herman. NY: Columbia University Press.
Nayak, Meena Arora. (2000) *About Daddy*. Delhi: Penguin.
Roy, Arundhati. (1997) *The God of Small Things*. Delhi: IndiaInk Publishing Company.
Rushdie, Salman. (1995) *Midnight's Children*. 1981; London: Vintage.
Sidhwa, Bapsi. (1989) *Ice-Candy-Man*. 1988; New Delhi: Penguin.
Stoker, Bram. (1897) *Dracula*. 2003; London: Penguin.

An Analytical Study of *The Appeal* by John Grisham in Terms of Its Logic, Rationality, and Impact

Eiichi Akaho

Abstract

John Grisham is a lawyer, was once elected to the state House of Representative in Mississippi, and served until 1990. He started his writing as his hobby before he turned his career as a full-time writer. Most of his novels are based on his experience as a lawyer and as a law maker. The contour of *The Appeal* begins with a shocking verdict returned by a jury against a chemical company accused of dumping toxic wastes into the water supply of a small town causing the worst caner cluster in history. Carl Trudeau, an owner of the chemical company and a Wall Street predator, decided to purchase himself a seat on the Court. Through an intricate web of conspiracy and deceit, his group financed a young unsuspecting lawyer, Ron Fisk, manipulated him, marketed him, and molded him into a potential Mississippi Supreme Court justice. *The Appeal* became the number one New York Times Bestseller, although it wouldn't make a successful film. This novel makes it vague as to who is the main character through whom an author usually tells and/or appeals to the readers for his opinion and philosophy. It lacks in character development and logic in several ways. One of them is that Carl Trudeau, who seems to be a main character, did not conduct the political manipulation by his own initiative. Deliberation process of Ron Fisk who had to choose the decision against or for the verdict is irrational. The author, who knows both the law and politics from the inside, presented very well a powerful, timely and shocking story of political and legal intrigues. This novel built a remarkable degree of suspense into the all too familiar ploys.

Keywords John Grisham, *The Appeal*, judicial election, political and legal intrigues, toxic waste materials

1. Introduction

1.1 Background of John Grisham

John Grisham was born on February 8, 1955, in Jonesboro, Arkansas in the United States. When he was a child, he dreamed of being a baseball player. After realizing that he did not have a right talent as a professional baseball player, he turned his career majoring in accounting at Mississippi State University and then graduated from law school at Ole Mississippi in 1981. He practiced law about ten years specializing in criminal defense and personal injury litigation. He turned his career again by challenging a position in the state House of Representative, and served the state for seven years.

His first novel was *The Time to Kill*. This novel is based on his overheard experience as an attorney at the DeSoto County courthouse. He wrote this novel as a hobby while working at the state, and it was not easy for the book to be out in the pubic. He had to ask many publishers to bring out this novel, because publishers rejected his request one after another. It was Wynwood Press that accepted his request by giving it a modest 5,000 copy printing. His bitter experience to publish his first novel did not let him give up his novel composition. Eventually, his hobby turned out to be a full-time novelist, and triggered one of publishing's most marvelous success stories.

1.2 Outline of *The Appeal*

In a small town (Bowmore) in Mississippi there arose an incidence in which people started suffering from toxic water which was contaminated by the chemicals dumped by Krane Chemical which is owned by a billionaire called Carl Trudeau. Over hundred people died from cancers of kidney, liver, colon and leukemia. A local lawyer couple, Wes and Mary Paytons, felt sympathy for the victims and filed the trial to sue Krane Chemical. Paytons barrowed from the local bank a huge amount ($400,000) of money to sue Krane Chemical forcing them to accept a poor living status giving up the rich life. After seventy-one days of trial that included 530 hours of testimony from four dozen witnesses, a plaintiff of Payton's by the name of Jeannette Baker whose husband and five-year-old son died from cancer caused by the toxic chemicals drained to the ground water which was contaminated by Krane Chemical, finally won the trial and the local court announced that Krane Chemical should pay to Jeannette Baker the total of 41 million dollars including 38 million dollars for punitive damage and 3 million dollars for the damages of the wrongful death of her husband Pete Baker. This verdict meant the local court supported a liberal judge against the big corporation which is usually considered to be a supporter of the conservative party. The verdict was big news of the nation and most of big papers reported this event as epoch-making news in the front page. Due to this disadvantageous judgment, the stock value of Krane Chemical was going down and down the drain day by day, and Carl Trudeau lost, by paper, billions of dollars, at one point of the time. This judicial victory of Paytons created the following cardinal significance of the issues.

1.2.1 Other victims and their family members will file the sue against Krane Chemical and the company will loose billions of money if the verdict is not reversed.

1.2.2 Many other lawyers from all over the country will come to the small town in Mississippi and try to file the similar trial as to what Patrons did.

1.2.3 Krane Chemical will appeal the case to the state Supreme Court where one of important characters in the novel works as supreme court justice. Her name is Sheila McCarthy. She is considered to be liberal, and the political professional people expect that she will approve the so-called liberal verdict returned by the local court in Hattiesburg.

1.2.4 Senator Grott offered a help for Carl by introducing an election manipulator, who is Barry Rinehart and his group, Troy-Hogan. They picked up a young lawyer, Ron Fisk, to be a candidate to beat Sheila McCarthy.

1.2.5 Ron Fisk who is a so-called " a boy" bought by the powerful political broker to reverse the verdict in the state Supreme Court , was successfully elected, and reversed the verdict returned by the local court. He seems not to notice that he was used and tricked, although he wanted to find it out very hard.

The details of the above significant issues are described in the below. While Carl Trudeau was worried about his company's future, politically-influential man, Senator Grott, called at his office from Washington. Senator Grott wanted to save his company for his benefit and told Carl Trudeau that he could introduce Carl Trudeau a man so called "fixer, or election manipulator," and asked him if he can open the door to the fixer by the name of Barry Rinehart. Carl thought about it for a while and responded to him by saying "Yes, I will open the door." Billions of money is involved in this transaction and Carl Trudeau had to pay that amount of money and Senator Grott would get a substantial portion of it.

Troy-Hogan selected a candidate (a boy) to fight with Sheila McCarthy for a position in the state Supreme Court. They run so-called highly technical campaign using talented professionals in each field such as propaganda specialist, TV commercial advocate, poster designer, consultant, pollster and other specialists of the campaign. Ron Fist won the campaign and became a Supreme Court justice. He voted against upholding several large settlements in cases brought before the court on appeal. The Paytons expected he would do the same, when their case comes up for review.

There happened an unexpected accident at this point. That is, soon after Ron Fisk was elected his son was hit on the brain by a ball struck by a slugger and seriously injured by impact of a defective product. He was left permanently impaired due to the medical malpractice. This incidence of corporate responsibility apparently affected Ron and his family on a personal level. At the same time, because of this accident, Ron Fisk had to delay on his job in the Supreme Court including the vote for the crucial appeal for the Jeannette Baker's case against Krane Chemical. Other judges voted on time and it was four to four. Ron Fisk wavered and wavered in his judgment. He struggled with his voting responsibility, deluded himself and spent days and days bewilderingly. As far as the issue whether Ron Fisk noticed or not the fact that he was used and tricked by Troy-Hogan is concerned, the author seems not to render the clear-cut setting-up of this issue. However, it seems that he hit upon the trick.

Ron Fisk made no move to do what is right, and had come to relish his newly-established wealth and power. Finally he voted to reverse the verdict resulting in the victory of Carl Trudeau. In other words, he decided to support the big corporation and did not take any action for the incidence of his son. The reason why he did so is that he thought he looked silly if he would not have reversed the verdict. The final chapter is devoted in a nather eccentric way to the gorgeous show in the luxurious ship in Hudson River. The novel ended in applauding Carl Trudeau.

2. Results and discussion

2.1 Evaluation and criticism of *The Appeal*

The author mentioned after finishing the story in the back of the cover sheet outside of the novel itself that all characters in the novel are purely fictional, and there are not Cary County, no town of Bowmore, no Krane Chemical, and no products such as Pillamore 5, bichloronylon, no cartolyx. However, he admits that there is a lot of truth in this story. The competing interests fight for election seats on the bench are fairly common, he stated. He also mentioned that most of warring the factions is adequately described, the tactics are all too familiar, and the results are far off the mark.

It is fair to say that he decided to write this novel based on the true incidence which took place in a small town in the US. He was clever enough to avoid any nasty claims made by real persons or organizations by creating non-existing characters and organizations. The question is how much the story is based on the truth and what is his real intention to write this novel. These issues are discussed in the following section.

2.1.1 Comparison of two major characters competing the Supreme Court justice position

The final decision for the appeal was made by the supreme court of Mississippi, and the major characters and ploys were thrown in the novel to reach the surprising Supreme Court judgment. Table 1 summarizes and compares them. One of the major characters is 51 year-old Sheila McCarthy, who was currently serving as a Supreme Court justice earning $110,000. She is considered as most liberal of all. She is divorced once without a child. , and going with a boy friend, English professor. She is also interested in a handsome young clerk working in her office. Therefore, Troy-Hogan people judged her as a woman with some moral problem. Troy-Hogan viewed that she was against death penalty, soft for gay issue, soft for gun controls, and soft for crime. Her supporters include trial lawyer groups and people who had voluntarily stood for her campaign. As far as the campaign account is concerned, she has only $6,000 to start with.

Table 1. Comparisons of two major characters competing the supreme court position

NO	issue	Sheila McCarthy	Ron Fisk
1	marital status	divorced (no children)	married with three children
2	age	middle age (51)	young (39)
3	religion	not attentive	very attentive, Baptist, devout
4	job	supreme court justice (elected eight years ago)	unknown lawyer, junior partner in five men law firm which deals with defending lawsuits.
5	support	trial lawyers	church, big companies
6	where he/she lives	-	Brookhaven, Mississippi
7	race	-	white
8	party	said to be liberal	conservative
9	education	-	Ole Miss law school
10	affiliation	-	no affiliation with any trial lawyer group, American Rifle Association
11	bench experience	supreme court judge	no experience on the bench
12	glitches	-	no ethical glitches in law career
13	salary	$110,000 per year	$92,000 per year
14	specialty	-	work for insurance company, car wreck, arson, injured workers, liability claims
15	mortgage	none	everything
16	relationship in terms of suit and cases.	-	lost the cases in which McCarthy voted against Ron's firm
17	moral	questionable	squeaky-clean
18	death penalty	against	for
19	for crime	soft	severe
20	gun control	soft	against gun control
21	campaign account	$6,000 to start with	one million to start with and three million in total
22	gay issue (marriage between the same sex)	soft	against

Ron Fisk, on the other hand, is a 39 year-old young white local lawyer, serving with a salary of $92,000 as a junior partner in a five men law firm which deals with defending lawsuits. He is married and squeaky-clean man with three children, and a devout Baptist. He is conservative, has no ethical glitches in law career, and has no affiliation with any trial lawyer group. His legal experience involves works for insurance company, car wreck, arson, injured workers, and liability. He is against gun control and belongs to American Rifle Association. His campaign budget is million dollars to start with and estimated to be three million in total.

Troy-Hogan made a research on contrasts between them and found that Justice McCarthy had participated in three rulings cases involving Ron Fisk's firm. She ruled out each time over Fisk's firm files. One of the bitter experience of Ron Fisk encountered is that he had lost by 5 to 4 vote over a hotly disputed arson mess involving a warehouse. The conclusion of Troy-Hogan's research was that it is very likely that Ron Fisk had little use for only female justice in Mississippi.

There is a very clear cut differences between the two candidates. Most notable aspect of all is that Ron Fisk is a devoted conservative and Sheila McCarthy is well known liberal. Other contrasting and opposing features between them are that he is squeaky-clean while she has some problem in her moral, that he is a married devout Christian with three children while she is a divorced single without children and with little involvement in the church, and that he is not affiliated with any trial lawyer groups while many trial lawyer groups support her. In order to attract the attention of the reader and to make the novel successful it is important to make a good and vivid contrast between the two competing characters in any of the normal fiction. In this sense it is fair to say that the author earned a sizable credit in this work.

2.1.2 Disputing issues between the liberal party and the conservative party

This novel dealt heavily with the disputes between the two American competing parties. It is worthwhile to summarize their contrasts (Table 2). The conservative party supports death penalty, does not allow the marriage between the same sex, does not admit the abortion, is against gun control, and wants to seal the American border to prevent the illegal immigrants invading the nation. They want to keep the American way of life, rich and all-mighty.

Table 2. Comparisons of two major parties

NO	issues	liberal	conservative
1	marriage between the same sex	allow	do not allow
2	abortion	admit	do not admit
3	religion	free	very attentive
4	gun control	want to control	do not want to control
5	stem cell research	allow	do not allow
6	immigration	allow foreign people coming	seal American border
7	death penalty	do not support	support

The liberal party is soft in death penalty, permits the homo-sexual marriage, does not prohibit the abortion, is in favor of gun control, and shows an indulgent attitude toward the immigrants.

These opposing different aspects between the two major parties were cleverly used in order to reverse the verdict returned by the local court. This is, so-called "fix the verdict" and eventually resulted in saving the Carl Trudeau's Krane Chemical Corporation and associated enterprises. Troy-Hogan' sneaky maneuver was that to beat Sheila McCarthy in the up-coming election for the state Supreme Court justice would result in reversing the verdict. What they intended is that if they successfully select a candidate (Ron Fisk, in this case) to beat Sheila McCarthy and let him win the election, Ron Fisk will vote to reverse the verdict. The story was finalized to achieve the outcome that Troy-Hogan imagined to accomplish.

Although democracy is a preferred system of government, it is said that politicians threaten its sanctity by their greedy and venal nature (personal communication, 2013). It seems that one cannot ignore the ability to corrupt, especially when immense sums of money are in conflict with social/health issues. Liberals do not always understand the effects of these "ideals or tactics," and conservatives have been vilified by discussing the effects of these "ideals or tactics". Those who claim that they are in between the two extremists usually keep effective, well balanced measures to be taken.

2.1.3 Major and astounding issues in the US campaign and important and mysterious events in the story

The novel tells the reader the hidden and sneaky aspects of the US election campaign with respect to the tactics used, the amount of money involved, and the man power involvement. The novel involves surprising and mysterious incidences and events. It is worth –while to summarize those items, and they are shown in Table 3.

Table 3. Major and astounding issues in the US campaign and important and mysterious events in the story

NO	issues and events
1	To limit liability (e. g. to save Krane Chemical) in civil litigation is one of the Judicial Vision's major slogans to support big corporations in the US.
2	Tony Zachary and Barry Rinehart never mentioned to Ros Fisk that they wanted to save Krane Chemical.
3	Toney says that trial lawyers must be stopped.
4	What does this novel want to appeal? a) no ethical and philosophical appeal, b)just state the election manipulation. c) honest people (Paytons) were lost, and this is not normal style of the novel. d) the appeal of this novel is weak.
5	It is said that the story is mostly based on the true incidence in the United States, although the author modified the incidence and made up some of the stories. If we accept this fact, then it can be said that the author's intention to write this novel is just to disclose and divulge the dirty and surprising aspects of the judicial and political worlds in the US.
6	It is amazing to see that EPA (Environmental Protection Agency), one of the prestigious departments in the US, was bought by a big company like Krane Chemical.
7	The cancer rate in Bowmore is fifteen times the national average, and most people in the town is suffering from sickness and death caused by the dirty water more or less. But the verdict was reversed., contrary to the truth and the real fact. Therefore, one can say that the Supreme Court Justice is unreliable.
8	Ron Fist is an honest, family-oriented Christian with fine character. Considering this fact it is hard to accept the author's logic letting him reverse the verdict which is rational in many aspects.
9	Judicial Vision did not tell Ron Fisk that they selected him to save Krame Chemical. Their tactics is that they name Sheilla McCarthy as most liberal judge, and told Ros Fisk that they want him to fight with the liberal judge who they think that will support the local verdict to claim Krame Chemical for their dumping of the toxic chemicals. This is an indirect way to accomplish the task, which render a unique, interesting and mysterious plot (a true story in the US election?) to the novel.

Through the entire story, the author did not let Tony Zachary and Barry Rinehart tell Ron Fisk that they hired him to save Krane Chemical. The question is whether Ron Fisk noticed it or not. Ron Fisk is asking Tony Zachary many times who is paying the huge amount of the campaign money, while Tony did not tell him the truth. By asking the same questions many times and getting suspicious answers it is very likely that Ron Fisk noticed that some big company is supporting this campaign. But Ron Fisk never noticed the name of the company or the name of the company owner. This trick of the story gave the reader a thrilling feeling.

The next and most significant question is what the intention of the author to write this novel is. A far as I see this novel involves neither ethical, philosophical issues, nor humanistic proposals. It intends to deal with the disclosure of the real and dirty parts of the American judicial and political world. The honest people like Wes and Mary Paytons ended up with the loss in the Supreme Court, and the novel finishes itself with the applause of the profit-minded corporation. This is not a normal style of the novel and "the appeal" of this novel is weak.

The novel divulges many illegal transactions undergoing in the US. One of the most prestigious agencies like EPA (Environmental Protection Agency) was allured through the unacceptable deal to hide the illegal dumping of toxic chemical products discharged by Krane Chemical. We can vividly observe the violation of the rule and the system collapse of the US government as a fiction, although the real status may be somewhat different.

The cancer rate in Bowmore is fifteen times as many as the national average, and most people in the town are suffering from ailments caused by toxic water drained from the pit of Krane Chemical. Paytons and their plaintiff, Jeanette Bayker, won 42 million dollars by suing Krane Chemical, but they lost in the Supreme Court as a result of the reversal judge of the original verdict by the Mississippi Supreme Court. Ron Fisk is an honest, family-oriented Christian with fine character. Considering this fact it is hard to accept the author's logic to let him reverse the verdict which was judged based on the real fact and truth; in other words, it is a rational judge in many aspects.

Troy-Hogan did not tell Ron Fisk that they selected him to save

Krane Chemical. Their tactics are that they name Sheila McCarthy as most liberal judge who they thought would support the local verdict to claim Krane Chemical for their dumping toxic chemicals. This is an indirect way to accomplish the goal. This ploy is unique and interesting, and composes the mysterious plot of the novel.

In order to save Krane Chemical, a logical campaign slogan had to be posted, and at least it had to look rational. It is not acceptable as campaign propaganda if Ron Fisk says "I (Ron Fisk) stood for a position in the state Supreme Court Justice in order to save Krane Chemical by reversing the verdict made by the local court." A wise way to advocate the campaign is to switch this particular subject to the general subject by saying, "I (Ron Fisk) stood for in order to beat a liberal judge who is in favor of force against the liability in civil litigation among other hot issues to which we support from the conservative stand point".

2.1.4 Search and evaluation of the facts that this novel is based on the truth or the truth in part

The author mentioned that the novel involves a lot of truth. Literature search found the issue of "campaign finances and elected judges" written by French (2009). In August 2002, a West Virginia jury found a coal company, AT Massey Coal Company Inc., for fraudulent misrepresentation, concealment and tortuous interference with contractual relations. The plaintiffs were awarded the sum of 50 million dollars in compensatory and punitive damages. The State Trial Court then denied the coal company's post-trial motion challenging the verdict and the damages award in June 2004. West Virginia Trial Court found that the coal company had intentionally acted in utter disregard of the plaintiff's rights and ultimately destroyed its businesses because it concluded that it was in its financial interests to do so. The state of West Virginia held its 2004 judicial elections following the verdict and, but before the appeal. By knowing that the Supreme Court of Appeals of West Virginia would consider the appeal in the case, Mr. Don Blankenship, the coal company's chairman, decided to support an attorney, Brent Benjamin, who was campaigning the election against Justice McGraw, one of the incumbents who were seeking re-election. Mr. Blankenship contributed three million dollars to Mr. Benjamin's campaign. Mr. Benjamin was elected by fewer than 50,000 votes. Before the coal company filed the appeal, Mr. Carperton moved to disqualify the newly elected Justice Benjamin under the due process clause and the state's Code of Judicial Conduct based on the conflict caused by Mr. Blankenship's campaign involvement. Justice Benjamin denied the motion for his recusal indicating that he found nothing showing bias for or against any litigation. The Appeal Court on which he sat reversed the 50 million dollar verdict.

It is amazing to see that the very similar actual case and issue took place in the US. Readers should notice that there are several controversial issues in this novel, one of them is whether the Supreme Court judge should be or should not be elected. The author and/or, of course, his novel characters, should have stated their opinions clearly in the novel. French (2009) stated that the two United State's cases of "White and Caperton" demonstrate powerfully the question why they have elected judges. The judicial task remains the same irrespective of the mode of a judge's appointment. But the elected judge's burden of maintaining public confidence and avoiding concerns about impartiality and conflict of interest appears to be more difficult as well. This is not to say that the appointment process for unelected judges is perfect.

This novel has very little impact as a normal novel because the author failed to appeal anything. One of the novel's appeals should have involved the following. That is, the Supreme Court justice should not be elected. The Caperton case is a good example and the author should analyze the case and advocate his opinion through his characters by the skillful story telling.

2.1.5 Issues as to whether or not to elect the judge particularly for the Supreme Court and whether or not to recuse an elected judge from the case involving people who donated an exceptionally huge amount of money to put him/her on the bench

This novel does not advocate any philosophical, humanitarian, or ethical opinion. The question is what the author's real intention to write this novel is. The reader should have to guess his real or at least imaginable intention described in the novel. One of the significant issues in the story is whether or not the judges should be elected and the elected judges should disqualify themselves from cases involving people who spent exceptionally large sums of money to put them on the bench. *The New York Times* (2009) report on June 8, 2009 the following article with the title of "Justices tell Judges not to rule on major backers," The article initiates the issue by saying that the decision, the first to say that the Constitution's due process clause has a role to play in policing the role of money in judicial elections, ordered the chief justice of the West Virginia Supreme Court to recuse himself from a $50 million case against a coal company whose chief executive had spent $3 million to elect him. At that point of time the number of the states which elect at least some of their judges is thirty-nine. It is said that election campaigns have in those days grown increasingly expensive and nasty.

John and Maureen (2011) reviewed *The Appeal* and stated that the technicalities of working out the intrigues are crucial to his story, and they found that this story was able to keep the reader fully occupied.

2.1.6 The issue on Baker and Krane

It seems that the Baker and Krane case is a fiction version of the real case called "Pacific Gas and Electric (PG&E) vs. Erin Brockovich (2008)." The alleged case by Brockovich' firm took place in the Southern California town of Hinkley for the contamination of drinking water with hexavalent chromium.

Erin Brockovich was born in Lawrence Kansas, and is a legal clerk and environmental activist. A facility called the Hinkley Compressor Station, part of a natural gas pipeline connecting to the San Francisco Bay Area, was at the center of the case. PG&E used hexavalent chromium between 1952 and 1966 to fight corrosion in the cooling tower. The hexavalent chromium from the cooling towers was dissolved in the waste water which was discharged to unlined ponds at the site. The waste water percolated into the groundwater affected an area near the plant. The case was settled in 1966 for US $333 million, the largest settlement in the US judicial history in a direct action lawsuit. Brockovich's law firm received 133.6 million dollars for this settlement and Brockovich received two million dollars. Brokovich was involved in other settlements as well. She worked with one of related lawyers who accused Whitman Corporation for chromium contamination in Willits, California. Another lawsuit alleged contamination near PG&E's Kettleman Hills Compressor Station in Kings County, California which used the same pipeline as the Hinkley site.

2.1.7 Irrational and illogical portions or issues in the plot

Table 4 lists irrational and/or illogical portions of this novel. Ron Fisk got angry furiously when he found that Tony Zachary put on the TV the story which accused Sheila McCarthy of her nasty and greedy way of campaign without the previous approval from Ron Fisk. Ron Fisk got angry so much that he told Tony Zachary to fire him. But there is no understandable description and/or specific reason in which Ros wanted to fire him. Readers want to know the real reason why Ros got angry, why he wanted to fire Tony and why he finally did not fire Tony. This is very important plot of the novel. However, the author's description is very vague and unimpressive in the pertinent portion in the novel.

Table 4. Irrational, illogical parts or issues

NO	issue	description
1	Ros Fisk's anger to fire Tony	Ros Fisk called Tony Zachary and said that he did not like the AAATAV commercial which denounced Sheila McCarthy badly and that he was not told about it before it is broadcasted. And he said "you are fired." But there is no description in which he really fired Tony.
2	Clete Coney (a gambler and a drinker) did not quit.	He was asked to quit by receiving quitting money, and he agreed. But he was on the campaign list till the end of election.
3	injury of Ros's son	"What kind of impact does this event have in this novel?" This incidence should do something significant in this novel. He was permanently injured because of the defected product of the big corporation. Ron Fisk should act to accuse the big bat producing company and the big corporation in general of their dishonesty. However, he did not do anything of that sort, disappointing the related supporters.

Clete Coney, a gambler and a drinker, was also used by Troy-Hogan. He was given a substantial amount of money to stand for the Mississippi Supreme Court election, and he agreed to run for it. When the election came to close to the end, Coney was asked to quit the race, because Troy-Hogan did not want to have two opposing candidates against Sheila McCarthy. He agreed to quit providing that he receives a substantial amount of money. He received that promised money, but he remains in the election candidate list. This is a very misleading part of the srory and the author should have made it more precise and appellant or clear-cut in his intention.

Ron Fisk's son was seriously injured by the incidence caused by a defective bat strike produced by a big corporate (Table 4). This incidence should have something vey special role in this novel. Because it is a very serious accident and it took place at the very end of the story. A most reasonable plot following this incidence is that Ron Fisk should claim the big company to fight with the production of the defective bat. However, he did not act to blame the big company for their negligence. This is a very awkward way to write a novel. The readers of good conception are disappointed by the plot of this portion. The fact is that the author did not let Ron Fisk claim the big corporate despite the fact that his son was permanently disabled by the defective product made by a big corporate. This entire description is not logical and random in presentation and the significance of bringing up this story through the world-wide technical tactics is questionable.

2.1.8 Evaluation and criticism of the novel

The Appeal was praised very well in several media according to John Grisham (2008). The front pages of this publication reports several those praises. Beginning with *Los Angeles Times*, it quotes, "fascinating...filled with deadly accurate characterizations by an author who knows both the law and politics from the inside." Boston Globe says "This is a novel that could become its own era-defining classic. John Grisham holds up that same mirror to our age as Tom Wolf's 'The Bonfire of the Vanities'." "John Grisham is about as good a storyteller as we've got in the United States these days" is a comment by *New York Times Book Review*. Those critics praise the author for presenting the perversions of the political machine. However, one of the reviewers, Ari (2013), of *The Appeal* states that the book has all the drama but then it does not deliver anything. He also mentions that bad people get what they want and good people try but fail and that it is pointless if nothing special is going to happen. However, there is no doubt about the plotting and story-telling excellencies of John Grisham. This is well described by the Atlanta Constitution which says "Each book jacket should bear a warning to consumers: 'detrimental to sleep. You may read all night.'"

The value of this book is that it exposed an unethical surprising maneuver of the real political and judicial word in the US. This is amazing in a sense that even a judicial decision can be bought by money. The author claims that this election manipulation is not illegal by saying "as long as private money is allowed in judicial elections we will see competing interests fight for seats on the bench.'"

2.1.9 Review and rating by the readers who read *The Appeal*

In recent years, the Internet plays an important role not only on the social and political fields, but also on the professional and scientific fields. Goodreads (2012) is a comprehensive site of reviews, discussion and rating of all types of books. *The Appeal* is the number one *New York Times* best seller, and read by many readers. It was rated by 25,173 readers, and the rating details are shown in Table 5. The total number of ratings of three stars or less is 10,889, or 51%. It is surprisingly large in number considering the fact that the it is a very popular novel and praised in many media.

Table 5. Rating details by Goodreads on "*The Appeal*" by John Grisham

rating scale (number of stars)	number	%
5	3,335	15
4	6,862	32
3	7,866	37
2	2,358	11
1	665	3
total	25,173	100

It is interesting to observe the reviews of severe or bitter ratings and I would like to show synopsis of the reviews of the readers who rated by one star in Goodreads They say that *The Appeal* has the worst ending, of any book ever, that it is hard to understand the key point of the novel in which the poor lawyers who gave up everything for that case got nothing letting their lives completely over, that this book is not only cliché but also boring and lacks in any characters you like, that book lacks in a storyline, character development, excitement of any kind, and all other desirable elements of a novel, and that the author made Ron Fisk disappoint the reader because the reader expected him to see how he'd been manipulated and to turn the table on all of them.

On the other hand, there are, of course, praises and good ratings. They say that *The Appeal* is a powerful, timely and shocking story of political and legal intrigues in that we should not expect a happy ending all the time and if the author turned the book into happy ending the book would have been an absolute disaster by rendering us realty not fantasy, that it is comfortable to see how his Christian characters were reflective of the current Christian culture, that this is a very good book which also shows how to package and market a candidate - basically buying him/her a place on the docket, and that if you are any kind of political junkie you should read this book because it carries issue as much about political campaign as it does about jurisprudence.

There are several significant issues raised in this review of the readers of *The Appeal* as in the below.
A) The novel did not finish with happy ending. What is its significance? Does this unhappy ending affect the value of this novel?
B) The Supreme Court justice should be appointed but not elected like politicians because they can be bought out by big business and the one with the most money wins the race. And the readers wonder "Did the author address his opinion and/or persuade the reader guiding to what he believes on this subject?"
C) Poor lawyers got their verdict reversed without gaining anything. Mary Payton is a main character at least in the former part of the novel. Shouldn't the author do something good for her at the end or close to the end?
D) Ron Fisk seems to be a main character in the latter half of the novel. He did a good job in the election campaign, and the author well described the campaign manipulation and the political strategies in two competing parties. However, his final action to reverse the verdict and the deliberation process to reach the final vote are not logical and disappointing.

To begin with the first issue, the novel should not necessarily finish with happy ending. By ending like bad people win and good people lose, the author let the reader think what it is, what the author wants to tell us. This is a paradoxical way to write a novel. However, the reader has to be easy to read out the real intention of the author. A question is what the author wanted to tell the reader his real intention. There is no vivid description to guess the author's intention of that sort. All the way through the end the author made Carl Trudeau as a superman by calling him "great

Carl Trudeau." The author even let him say at the beginning "No one in this room is losing his job. Krane Chemical will survive this miscarriage of justice. I do not intend to lose this fight." If the author's real intention is the opposition against the election system for choosing the supreme court justice the author should have dealt with this point directly or indirectly while he did not. One way to do this is to let somebody or a new character say "As long as private money is allowed in judicial elections we will see competing interests fight for seats in the bench. One way to avoid this intrigue is to appoint the Supreme Court justice by non-partisan board" as he partly mentioned this at the end cover sheet which is not the inside of the novel. The other potential intention of the author includes an opposition of the misconduct of big corporation which sometimes do whatever they want for their benefit. This is a controversial and weighty issue in the novel but there is no clear description of this sort from the author's point of view. There are readers who want the author to have a suitable character to advocate the establishment of the law which prohibits or regulates the dumping of waste materials to the environment.

The second issue has something in common to the first issue. We wanted to see at least some plot in which two competing parties raise this issue and argue each other by proposing their doctrines and allegations.

The author did nothing nice for May Payton in the third issue. She is a looser till the end of the story. The author even let her write a give-up letter to the people in Bowmore. We wanted to see that she won't give up and says to the victims in Bowmore

> "We do not intend to lose this fight."
> "No one in this room is losing his/her job."
> "Paytons will survive this justice verdict."
> "I am not going to lose this game."

The final issue has something to do with character development and desirable plot establishment. If the author's intention is to finish the novel with unhappy ending, Ron Fisk's final decision to reverse the verdict can be acceptable.

3. Conclusions

I would like to propose the conclusions in an itemized manner.

3.1 This novel makes it vague as to who the main character is. Famous or not famous, all novels have the main character through whom an author tells and/or appeals to the readers his/her opinion, philosophy, ethics, humanitarian issue, or belief. Judging from the readers' reviews and based on my evaluation this novel does not have a main character. Carl Trudeau seems to be a main character. But if that is the case, one might say that the author is a novelist who is in favor of a rich man who uses a tremendous amount of money to beat the social and ethical righteousness. This is not a right way to write a novel. Therefore, this work is not qualified as an acceptable novel. It can be said that *The Appeal* is a peculiar novel, although it has been sold very well and praised by many media. It is hard to understand what the author's real intention and reason to write this novel is. Taken it granted that the author intentionally did not make a main character and wanted to advocate his intention through an irregular method, the author failed to accomplish the goal. Because there is no clear-cut evidence and/or description to notice that kind, of intention. A couple of the reviewers, John and Maureen (2011) state that John Grisham has given us a first-class legal thriller in which he is quite vocal in his opposition to the election of officials and judiciary within the law. This is only one favorite review which states understandable view point to praise this fiction. However, it is hard to notice that kind of phrases which describe "John Grisham's opposition to the election of officials and judiciary within the law."

A big fault, disadvantage or deficit of the plot is that the Great Carl Trudeau, who seems to be a main character, did not conduct the political manipulation by his own initiative. The novel should have written in the following way, which we call it the second version.

' Carl Trudeau decided to reverse the verdict by sending his man to the Mississippi Supreme Court justice through the manipulated election. Carl and his colleagues searched very hard who can handle this task by accepting their request. After strenuous search, he found Troy-Hogan. He also found that Senator Grott is the best person to negotiate this issue and to get contact with Troy-Hogan. Because his attendant discovered that the Senator Grott and Troy-Hogan have successfully worked together many times in a very intimate and sneaky way in the judicial election, Carl decided to call Senator Grott.

"Senator Grott, this is Carl Trudeau from New York, and how are you?"
"I am fine and nice to talk to you. How are you doing these days?"
"Very well, thank you. Well, I must to say that I have one thing I would like to ask your favor. This has something to do with judicial election."
"What is a matter with you?" Senator Grott replied.
"I understand that you know Barry Rinehart very well who handles election business. And I would like you to introduce him to me."
"Certainly I am pleased to introduce Barry to you. I will let him call you sometime tomorrow."
"Thank you very much Senator Grott." Car Trudeau gladly replied.

This second version clearly states that the Carl Trudeau's initiative which may make him a main character, although he is considered to be an arrogant and greedy individual. Then the author should let appear an individual or party who opposes the judicial election system. We might call such an individual or a party "election reformer." The election reformer can be an extremist, and he/she can appear less frequently in the novel and a short description of him/her opinion will do. At one point of the story, the author should have had a description in which the author let the election reformer argue and fight with the Trudeau group, and then let the election reformer gain victory over the Trudeau group.

3.2 Deliberation process of Ron Fisk who had to approve or reject the verdict returned by the local court.

Ron Fisk is a conservative individual in nature. Sheila McCarthy is said to be a liberal judge. Nothing wrong for them to compete with each other and there is no odd aspect bringing them in the story. However, the Baker and Krane case seems to have little to do with the competition of the two parties. The author described very well the intentional or so grossly negligent dumping by Krane Chemical of toxic chemicals which contaminated the ground water of Bowmore causing cancers whose rate was 15 times as large as the national average. Liberal or conservative, a thoughtful judge, if he/she is, should allege Krane Chemical for its punitive damages. Therefore, there is an irrationality or absurdity in the story to let Ron Fisk vote to reverse the verdict. Besides, his son was injured by the impact of a defective bat and permanently impaired by a medical malpractice. In other words, a matter of corporate responsibility affected him as a personal issue. In addition, Ron Fisk seems to notice the fact that he was used and tricked by Troy-Hogan, and apparently he was upset by the trick. Considering all those facts and his fine character, it is very much rational and logical to let him vote to approve the verdict. As a matter of the fact, he voted to reverse the verdict, surprisingly enough.

The credit can be given to the author, who knows both the law and politics from the inside, and presented very well a powerful, timely and shocking story of political and legal intrigues. The novel sounds like non-fiction and it depicts very accurately the tactics by which political candidates either can be propelled or ambushed and their campaigns can be subverted.

As was praised by many media, John Grisham is a good story teller and this novel could become era-defining classic. As is reviewed by New York Times (2008), this novel built a remarkable degree of suspense into the all too familiar ploys and Grisham delivered his savviest book in years, although it did not make a successful film.

Acknowledgements
I am grateful to my parent who raised me, trained me, and was patient enough to make me a professional individual who is able to accomplish his mission in writing this article.

References
Ali, A (2013) Goodreads (Feb 06, 13), http://www.goodreads.com/review/show/528121881, Accessed on March 31, 2013.
Brockovich, E (2013) Wikipedia (1 September 2013) http://www.wikipedia.org/, Accessed on March 31, 2013.
French, R S (2009) In Praise of Unelected Judges, *Public Policy Forum, Perth by the John Curtin Institute of Public Policy*, 1 July 2009.
Goodreads (2012) Wikipedia (Mar 1, 2012), http://www.goodreads.com/book/show/1248179.The_Appeal, Accessed on April 6, 2013.
Grisham, J (2008) *The Appeal*, Dell, New York.
John & Maureen (2011) *The Book Shelf*, My Book Blog (August 15, 2011), http://webcache.googleusercontent.com/search?q=cache:2dHiWBOrorsJ:https://

thebookshelfmybookblog.wordpress.com/2011/08/15/review-the-appeal/+the+appeal+grisham+review&cd=20&hl=ja&ct=clnk&gl=jp, Accessed on March 31, 2013.

Personal Communication (2013) with a native american who is familiar with *The Appeal*, April 4, 2013.

The New York Times (2008) Books of the Times: You Can't Win the Case, Buy an Election and Get Your Own Judge, January 28, 2008.

The New York Times (2009) Justices Tell Judges Not to Rule on Major Backers, June 8, 2009.

なぜ彼は引き金を引かなかったのか
『白鯨』第123章「マスケット銃」における
スターバックの逡巡[1]

髙橋　愛

要旨

　ハーマン・メルヴィルの『白鯨』においてスターバックは、白鯨への復讐というエイハブの腹案に唯一抵抗を示した人物である。本論文は、スターバックの人物像と彼の反乱の試みに注目し、『白鯨』の悲劇性について考察するものである。スターバックは、鯨捕りらしい剛胆さを持つが、経済合理性と家族への思いをもとに抑制した行動をとる。悲劇へと突き進むエイハブに抵抗する機会は第123章の「マスケット銃」で訪れるが、彼は逡巡するばかりで銃の引き金を引くことができなかった。彼が反乱を遂行できなかった理由として、彼が、エイハブが放出させる「何か」としか言いようのないものに魅了されたことがあげられる。その「何か」を解く鍵は、「ファルマコス」という悲劇的人物を表す概念にある。スターバックは、「ファルマコス」たるエイハブへの畏怖と敬意から彼を殺めることができず、ピークオッド号の航海を悲劇的なものに決定づけたと言える。

キーワード　ハーマン・メルヴィル、『白鯨』、男らしさ、ファルマコス

1. はじめに

　「『嵐が丘』、『リア王』とともに英語で書かれた三大悲劇の1つとも称される」(千石 2000: 635) という解説を持ちだすまでもなく、ハーマン・メルヴィルの『白鯨』が悲劇であることは言を俟たない。ピーク

オッド号の航海が悲劇に終わること、しかも、それが避けがたいものであることは、語り手のイシュメールが自らの捕鯨航海を1840年の大統領選と1842年の第1次アフガン戦争の間にはさまれた幕間狂言にたとえてみせたこと、船の名前がピューリタンによって全滅させられたアメリカ原住民の部族のものと同じであること、イライジャと名乗る男が契約後および乗船直前のイシュメールたちにつきまとって預言めいた言葉を投げかけることといった先触れにより、出航以前から示唆されている。またエイハブ自身も、モービィ・ディックと呼ばれる巨大な白鯨の追跡の最中に「この劇は脚本どおりにやることになっていて、変更不能なのだ」(Melville 1851: 418)と語り、その避けがたさを認めている。

『白鯨』に関して、物語の悲劇性と並んで言を俟たないこととして、「知的ごった煮」と称されるようなテキストの複層性がある。テキストの複層性は、ピークオッド号が演じる悲劇を語るうえで欠かせないものである。『白鯨』という物語の悲劇性とテキストの複層性について、テリー・イーグルトン(Eagleton 2003: 180)は、

> アメリカでは、ハーマン・メルヴィルが完全な災難で終わる偉大な悲劇作品を書きあげた。『白鯨』が散文で書かれなくてはならなかったのは、それが一般人の災厄を扱っているからだ。しかし、捕鯨士たちに彼らにふさわしい悲劇的威厳を授けるため、メルヴィルはリアリズムの拘束を破り、研ぎすまされたシェイクスピア的レトリックを駆使しながら悪魔的主人公を表現し、返す刀で、ブラバー銛やマッコウクジラの骨格構造について微に入り細を穿って描写した。

と述べている。

イーグルトンの指摘を踏まえてみても、逸脱やジャンルの横断を繰り広げつつ語られるピークオッド号の物語は、悲劇以外の何ものでもないということになるだろう。しかしながら、この悲劇は、エイハブの号令一下粛々と演じられたと言いきれるものではない。ピークオッド号に

は、エイハブが引きおこした熱狂に水をさし、筋書きを書きかえようと試みた人物がいる。それは一等航海士のスターバックである。エイハブに反発しながらも彼に強く引きつけられ、結局はモービィ・ディックに死を与えんという熱狂の渦にのみこまれていくスターバックは、『白鯨』という悲劇において少なからぬ役割を与えられているように思われる。

　スターバックはなぜ、悲劇へと突き進むエイハブの暴走を止められなかったのだろうか。もとい、彼はなぜエイハブの暴走を結局は受け入れたのだろうか。本論文では、スターバックの人物像と、第123章「マスケット銃」で語られるエイハブに対する彼のささやかすぎる抵抗に注目し、『白鯨』の悲劇性について考察してみたい。

2.　「いい人で、信心があついお人」

　『白鯨』でスターバックの名がはじめて言及されるのは、第21章「上船」においてである。その発言は甲板の物音に気づいた索具職人がおこなったもので、その際に「あの人はきびきびした一等航海士だ。いい人だ。それに信心があつい (He's a lively chief mate, that ; good man, and a pious)」(Melville 1851: 93)[2] と紹介される。さらに「真摯 (earnest)」(Melville 1851: 101)、「船乗りとしては格別に良心的 (uncommonly conscientious for a seaman)」(Melville 1851: 102) と述べられるところから、スターバックは、優れた人徳の持ち主だと言える。

　しかし、彼はただ人格者であるというだけではなく、捕鯨という生業に不可欠な剛胆さも持ち合わせている。ただし、スターバックの剛胆さあるいは勇気は、鯨捕りにありがちな向こう見ずな態度とは一線を画するものである。彼の勇気は、第26章「騎士と従者」において、

　　スターバックは好んで危険を求めるたぐいの人間ではなかった。この男にあっては、勇気はひとつの感情ではなく、自分にとってのひとつの有用な物件にほかならず、生死にかかわる肝要なばあいに

は、つねに手元にあって利用できる道具にほかならなかった。その
うえ、おそらく、スターバックの考えによれば、この捕鯨業におけ
る勇気とは、船につむ牛肉やパンとおなじく、重要な備蓄品のひと
つであって、いたずらに消費さるべきものではなかったのである。
それゆえ、スターバックは日没後にボートをおろして鯨を追うこと
はなかったし、あまり抵抗のはげしい鯨を深追いすることもなかっ
た。この危険な海にきて鯨を殺すのは自分が生きるためであって、
鯨が生きるために殺されにきているのではない、とスターバックは
かんがえるのだった。　　　　　　　　（Melville 1851: 102–103）

と述べられる。イシュメールによる説明からうかがえるように、スター
バックの勇気は、経済合理性に則って発揮されるものである。スター
バックにとって経済合理性が重要な指針となっていることは、

　　白鯨のゆがんだあぎとでも、死のあぎとでも、わたしはひるみませ
　　ん、エイハブ船長、それがちゃんとした商売の道理にかなっている
　　のならば、です。わたしがここにおりますのは、鯨をとるためでし
　　て、船長の復讐に手をかすためではありません。たとえあなたの復
　　讐がうまくいったとしても、鯨油にして何バレルになるでしょう
　　か、エイハブ船長？　ナンターケットの市場では、さしたるもうけ
　　にはなりませんよ。　　　　　　　　　（Melville 1851: 143）

という、第36章「後甲板」でおこなったエイハブに対する異議申し立
てにもはっきりとあらわれている。
　船乗りにありがちな向こうみずな勇気からスターバックを遠ざけてい
るのは、経済合理性のほかにもある。それは陸に残してきた家族の存在
である。家族が彼の勇気に及ぼす影響については、

　　外界の予兆と内心の予感をスターバックは敏感に感じとる。そして
　　時おり、それが鋼鉄の魂さえたわませることがあったが、何よりも

そのこころをたわませたのは、コッド岬においてきた若い妻や子どもにまつわる、はるかなる家庭の思い出であった。その思い出が、とくにこの男のような正直なこころの持ち主のばあいには、生来の剛毅一本の性質をたわませるように作用し、内心にひそむ潜在的な影響力にこころをひらかしめ、捕鯨業のように危険な生業においてはしばしば見られる、あの無謀な勇気の噴出を抑制するのであった。　　　　　　　　　　　　　　　　　　(Melville 1851: 102)

と述べられることから明らかである。[3] 経済合理性と家族という行動規範によって抑制された行動をとるスターバックは、ややもすると剛気に欠けるように、踏みこんだ言い方をすれば、船乗りとしての男らしさに欠けたところがあるように見えるかもしれない。しかし、スターバックの人物像については、「捕鯨業界のどこをさがしたって、あのスターバックくらい用心ぶかい男はいるもんじゃない」(Melville 1851: 102) と揶揄した二等航海士スタッブよろしく否定的な評価をくだしてしまう前に、19世紀のアメリカ捕鯨産業におけるジェンダー観や近代アメリカ社会に浸透していたジェンダー規範に目を向けておく必要がある。

　19世紀のアメリカ捕鯨業界をめぐる状況をジェンダーの観点から分析したマーガレット・S・クライトン (Creighton 1995, 1996) によると、捕鯨船の乗組員の文化は、メインマストを境にして対照を見せていたという。平水夫が占める前檣では活動領域の分離はなく、私的／女性的なものがほとんど排除されていた。他方、白人中産階級が多かったという高級船員[4]が住まう後檣では、個別の居住空間が用意され、陸と同じく、仕事場と憩いの場、すなわち、公的領域と私的領域の分離がなされていた。船内の私的領域のおかげで、捕鯨船の士官たちは、平水夫よりもずっと頻繁に陸に残してきた妻子に思いを馳せることができたというのである。[5] 19世紀のアメリカ社会において、感情は女性的なものであり男はその表出を抑制すべきとされていたこと[6]を考慮すれば、家族に対する感情によって行動を抑制するスターバックの態度は、捕鯨船の「騎士」としての威厳、すなわち、「鉄の男 (iron men)」[7] という言い回し

に象徴される命知らずの男らしさを損なうおそれがあるように思われる。しかし、航海士という彼の地位を踏まえ、さらに、自活し結婚して父となり家長として世帯の者を扶養する者こそが一人前の男であるという、植民地時代以来継承されてきた「アメリカ的な男らしさ（American manhood）」の概念[8]に目を向ければ、陸に残してきた家族への思いを船に持ち込み家族の幸福を思って行動することは、彼の男らしさを損なうものではなく、むしろ補強するものだと考えられる。したがって、経済合理性と家族を行動規範としながら捕鯨に従事するスターバックは、19世紀の中産階級の価値観に通じるアメリカ人としては立派(リスペクタブル)な男らしい男だと言える。

3. ささやかすぎる反抗

　ピークオッド号の乗組員のうち、モービィ・ディックに対して復讐を果たすというエイハブの偏執を押しとどめ航海の筋書きを変えようと試みたのは、スターバックだけであった。ところで、スターバックが立ち向かおうとしたエイハブとはどのような人物なのだろうか。

　エイハブが特異な人物であることは、モービィ・ディックによって奪われた脚の代わりに磨きあげられた抹香鯨のあご骨で作られた義足を装着するという、彼の身体の有り様によって象徴的に示されている。第51章「潮吹きの霊」で、「その片方の生きた足はいきいきとした響きをとどろかせていたのに、もう一方の死んだほうの足が立てるのはまるで棺桶を打つ音。この老人は生と死をまたにかけて歩いていたのだ」（Melville 1851: 192）と語られているように、エイハブは、自らの生身の足と死んだ鯨の骨でできた義足によって、文字どおり生と死をまたにかけている。相反する力を拮抗させるというエイハブの特異性は、身体ばかりでなくその内面にもみられる。彼が偏執狂となった経緯については、片脚が切断されてからの帰りの航海のなかで「引き裂かれた肉体が流す血と押しつぶされた魂が流す血がまじりあい、融合して」（Melville 1851: 156）狂気が形成されていったと語られるが、狂気が彼の内面を専

有してしまったわけではない。第41章「モービィ・ディック」において、

> エイハブの正真正銘の狂気がおさまったわけではなく、凝縮して小さくなっただけなのである。北欧の王者ヴァイキングのようなハドソン川はつねに水量を減ずることなく、キャッツキル山系の「高地(ハイランド)」の渓谷を流れるときには狭いながらも深い渓谷をうがって流れるのとおなじ理屈である。しかし、偏執狂が深い渓谷を流れるときにも、その膨大な狂気の水が一滴たりとも失われるわけではないように、その広漠たる狂気から、エイハブ生来のすぐれた知性が一滴たりともそこなわれるわけではなかった。エイハブは、かつては生きている主体だったが、いまや生きている道具になっていた。もしこのように激烈な比喩がゆるされるのならばだが、エイハブの局所的狂気は全体としての正気を襲って攻略し、その戦利品たる砲門のことごとくを狂気が目標とするものに集中したのである。その結果、エイハブは力を失うどころか、正気な手段によって筋のとおった目標を達成したときよりも千倍もの力をもって、そのただひとつの目標にむかって邁進するようになったのである。
>
> （Melville 1851: 157）

と述べられているように、生来の彼の知性は狂気によって損なわれることはなく、それどころかむしろ白鯨に復讐するという偏執的な目標を果たすために保持されている。いわばエイハブは、正気と狂気をまたいで立ち、精神においても相反するものを拮抗させているのである。[9] エイハブは、死や狂気に片足を踏み入れることで社会的な規律や規範から逸脱しているが、もう片方の足は生や正気の領域で踏みとどまっているため、彼が他者として排除されることはない。それどころか、外面においても内面においても相反するものを拮抗させるという特異性によって、彼は船員たちを圧倒し、求心力を獲得していると言える。そして彼が希求してやまないのは、モービィ・ディックという名の白鯨として具現化される、筋のとおらない「ボール紙の仮面」を突きやぶり、その背後に

ある「何だかよくわからんが、それでもなお筋のとおった何か (some unknown but still reasoning thing)」(Melville 1851: 140) をとらえることである。モービィ・ディックが現実界に踵を接し壁として現実界を封印するものだと考えれば、エイハブは、モービィ・ディックに死を与えて壁を突き破ることにより、現実界の深淵、すなわち、言語によって把握することのできない認識の枠組みの外側にある世界へ分け入ろうとした人物だと言える。[10]

　生と死や正気と狂気といった相反するものをまたにかけ社会的な規範から逸脱してしまっているエイハブに対して、スターバックは抵抗を試みることになるが、それは抵抗と呼ぶにはささやかすぎると言わざるをえない。スターバックがとる手段は、経済合理性や陸に残してきた家族への情にうったえる進言であるが、エイハブがそれを聞き入れることはない。スターバックがエイハブに抵抗する術は、「反乱でもおこさぬかぎり、スターバックはわしに反抗できぬ」(Melville 1851: 140) とエイハブが自ら述べているとおり、反乱という実力行使をおいてほかにないのである。しかし、「正直でこころ正しい人間 (an honest, upright man)」(Melville 1851: 386) のスターバックは、反乱という法を外れた手段にうったえることはない。

　ピークオッド号の航海において、スターバックが反乱を企てることが全くなかったというわけではない。反乱の試みは、物語も終盤間近となった第 123 章「マスケット銃」で描かれる。この章においてスターバックは、風向きが順風に変わったことを報告するために船長室に降りていったところ、かつて自分につきつけられたマスケット銃を目にし、心に芽生えてきた「邪悪な想念」(Melville 1851: 386) ——マスケット銃でエイハブを殺害すること——と生来の良心とのあいだでひたすら逡巡する。彼は銃を手に震えながら、

　　　この狂気の老人が乗組み全員を道づれに破滅へとむかうのを、だまって見ててもいいのだろうか？——そうだ、このまま手をこまねいて、もしこの船が悲惨なことになれば、エイハブは 30 人もの人

間の生命を故意にうばう人殺しということになる。それに、エイハブが自分の意地をとおすなら、この船が悲惨なことになることは目にみえている。そこでだ、もしこの瞬間に——エイハブをけしてしまえば、エイハブは罪を犯さずにすむわけだ。(Melville 1851: 387)

と語り、心に浮かんだ想念の正当性を論理的に導き出そうとする。しかし、その行為の非合法性に尻込みし、「それにしても、何か打つ手はないものか？合法的な手はないものか？——監禁状態にして強制送還する手は？」(Melville 1851: 387)と、法を犯すことなく正義をなす道を求めて自問する。しかし、強制送還という合法的手段はエイハブを猛り狂わせ、そうすることによって自らの精神の平衡が損なわれるおそれもあることに思いいたり、彼は、自分の身を安泰にしつつ航路を変える手段は船長を殺めること以外にはないのだと悟る。ところが、そう悟ってもなお、彼は覚悟を決められず、「もし天が稲妻をつかわして、これから人殺しになろうとしているこの男を、寝床のなかでシーツもろともに焼きつくしてしまうなら、天は人殺しということになるだろうか？——そして、わたしのばあいも人殺しだろうか、かりに——」(Melville 1851: 387)と語るばかりで、その逡巡を止めることができない。銃を手に立ちつくし神に進むべき道を請うたところで彼の口をついて出たのは、なぜか船長に対する報告の言葉であった。結局スターバックは、銃の引き金を引くことができずに引き下がるのである。

八木敏雄(1986: 87)は、スターバックの葛藤を浮き彫りにするという意味において「マスケット銃」という章が「なにも起こらないのに重要な章」だと指摘しているが、スターバックがただひたすらに逡巡するこの章は、ピークオッド号の運命を決定づけるという意味でも重要なものである。何も起こらなかったことで、すなわち、スターバックが彼に与えられた唯一の抵抗の機会に決然たる行動に出られなかったことで、ピークオッド号は悲劇へと大きく舵を切ったからである。第132章「交響楽」などでも描かれているように、エイハブが彼なりの人間性を表に出した機に乗じてスターバックが進言をおこなうことがあるものの、

モービィ・ディックの追跡劇の幕が途中でおろされることはない。結局スターバックは、「運命の手下 (the Fates' lieutenant)」(Melville 1851: 418) たるエイハブの手下として与えられた筋書きを演ずるほかなくなり、その役に甘んじることとなるのである。

4. なぜ彼は引き金を引かなかったのか？

「マスケット銃」において、スターバックは、「天使」との格闘の末に「邪悪な想念」を放棄し、結局は銃を元の位置に戻したとされる。しかし、彼が銃の引き金を引くことができなかったのは、殺人という行為そのものの罪深さを恐れて良心がとがめたからだけなのだろうか。彼がエイハブを殺めなかったのは、生来の善良さが悪意を駆逐したからというよりも、エイハブが持つなにがしかの力が彼の理性を圧倒したためであろう。

スターバックがエイハブに魅入られていることは、後甲板で彼が籠絡された際に、「わしのふくらんだ鼻の穴から何かが飛び出し、あいつの肺にはいっていきよった。もうスターバックはわしのものだ」(Melville 1851: 140) とエイハブが独白し、「わたしの意志とは無関係に、なんとも名づけようのない何か (the ineffable thing) が、私をあの人にしばりつけ、わたしには断ち切るすべのない綱でわたしを有無を言わさず引きずっていく」(Melville 1851: 144) と、さらに、「ああ、わたしには自分のみじめな役割がいやというほどよくわかる——わたしは反抗しながら服従し、なお悪いことに、憐憫をおぼえながらも憎んでいる！　わたしはあの人の目に、もしそれがわたしのものなら五体もなえてしまいそうなすさまじい悲しみの色を見る」(Melville 1851: 144) とスターバックも語っているところから明らかである。エイハブが放出させる「何か (something)」や「すさまじい悲しみの色 (some lurid woe)」こそ、スターバックの心をとらえ、マスケット銃の引き金を引くことをためらわせたものだと思われる。[11] エイハブについて「何か」あるいは「すさまじい悲しみの色」と言い表されるものとは、いったい何なのだろうか。

エイハブは、鯨の骨でできた義足を装着することで、生と死、そして正気と狂気をまたぐ存在となっていた。相反する力にまたがって立ち船員たちを圧倒する彼の姿から想起されるのは、「ファルマコス」と呼ばれる悲劇的人物である。「ファルマコス」とは、「動物的貧しさの極みにまで落とされたがゆえに、不思議にも神聖である人間」(Eagleton 2003: 280) のことである。「ファルマコス」についてイーグルトンは、

> 「ファルマコス」は神聖なのと同時に恐ろしいものであるから、そこには崇高の二重構造がみられる。崇高は言葉を超越した状態であるから言葉では表わせず、一方、スケープゴートは言葉以下だから、言説の網の目をすり抜け、言語化されない。それは言語から切り離され、それについて語るべきことはなにもない。つまり、人間の世界からその境界を越え、生と死の中間地帯に迷いこんだ猛烈に傷ついた生き物たちについては。象徴界からの訴えを拒絶した生き物たち、アブラハム、リア、オイディプス、アンティゴネーのような人物たちは、別の真実に命をかけて、ねばり強くコミットすることによって、革命的倫理を創始することができた。別の真実とはポジティブな体制を正当化するのでなく、自我の否定的側面を露呈させるもの、ジャック・ラカンの思想が「物」あるいは「現実(ザ・リアル)」の恐ろしい深淵と書き表わしたものであった。そうした人物は組織・機構が自らを機能させるために抑圧する真実を代表する。あらゆる社会集団のなかでも組織・機構に与するところがもっとも少ないから、彼らにはそれを変革する不思議な、そして、神聖な力がある。彼らは社会秩序の内的矛盾を擬人化し、自分の欠陥をとおしてその欠陥を象徴する。　　　　　　　　　　　(Eagleton 2003: 280)

と論じている。この議論を『白鯨』に照らしてみれば、エイハブがその目にたたえていた「すさまじい悲しみの色」とは、「ファルマコス」として、彼が人間の汚れや罪を背負わされていることをあらわすものだと言えないだろうか。「ファルマコス」たるエイハブにとって、モービィ・

ディックに対する復讐を果たすこと、すなわち、現実界を封印する壁をうがつことは、「別の真実」にコミットすることである。そして、スターバックをとらえた「なんとも名づけようのない何か」とは、「革命的倫理」を創始せんというエイハブの断固たる意志なのではないだろうか。

スターバックは、ピークオッド号の今次の航海の目的を知らされた時点で破滅的な最期を予期して船長に異を唱えはしたが、徹底的に歯向かうことはしなかった。その気になればエイハブを押しとどめることができたかもしれないのに、また、実力行使をする絶好の機会もあったというのに、スターバックがそうすることはなかったのである。

なぜスターバックはマスケット銃の引き金を引くことができなかったのだろうか。それは、汚辱にまみれることでたちあがる「ファルマコス」の神聖さと「革命的倫理」がうみだされる可能性をエイハブに見てとり、それを畏怖したからと言えるかもしれない。スターバックは、鯨捕りとしては十分に勇敢な人間ではあったが、その勇気はあくまで「この世に通例見られる理性をもたないものがそなえる恐怖 (the ordinary irrational horrors of the world)」 (Melville 1851: 103) が相手の時にふるわれるものであって、「より精神的なものゆえに、なおいっそう戦慄すべき恐怖 (those more terrific, because more spiritual terrors)」 (Melville 1851: 103) には抵抗ができないたぐいのものであった。そのことを思いおこせば、スターバックは、エイハブが「ファルマコス」としてその身に帯びているものに対して「精神的恐怖 (terror)」を感じて戦慄し、身動きができなくなったのであろう。

スターバックは、エイハブが「革命的倫理」なるもの——モービィ・ディックという壁／現実界を封印する壁を越えたところで生みだされるものゆえに言語化しえないもの——を創始する可能性に魅了されていたということも、彼が反乱をおこさなかった理由としてあげられるかもしれない。エイハブの試みにおいて「革命的倫理」が生みだされるには、モービィ・ディックと呼ばれる鯨の形で具現化される壁がぶち破られなければならない。「ファルマコス」たるエイハブは、この壁が破られる

よりも前に殺されるわけにはいかないのである。エイハブが放出させる魔力——スターバックにとっては「何か」としか言い表せない、「革命的倫理」の創出に対するエイハブの意志——に魅入られたからこそ、スターバックは、エイハブに手を貸さねばならないと、また、エイハブに引きずられていくしかないのだと感じ、破滅を防ぐ決定的瞬間にもなにもできずに悲劇的な終末を迎えることに甘んじたのである。

　スターバックはなぜ、マスケット銃の引き金を引かなかったのだろうか。そう問うならば、悲劇的人物の「ファルマコス」たるエイハブに対する畏怖と敬意があったからである。彼は抑制された勇気を持つ善良な男であったが、それゆえにピークオッド号の悲劇を決定づけたと言えよう。

注

1. 本論文は、新英米文学会例会（2010年11月20日、於早稲田奉仕園）における発表原稿に加筆修正を加えたものである。
2. 本論文において『白鯨』の訳文は八木敏雄のものを用いている。
3. スターバックの家族との結びつきは、エイハブによって導かれるピークオッド号の悲劇的な運命に対する抵抗という点からみても重要である。第132章「交響楽」において、エイハブがスターバックとの交感を求める瞬間があるが、偏執の世界を抜け出たエイハブが思いを馳せるものの1つは陸に残してきた妻であり、また、人間性を垣間見せたエイハブを捉えんとするスターバックが持ち出すのも家族である。
4. 森田勝昭 (1994: 103–106) によれば、後檣を占める船のエリート層（船長、士官、銛手）は捕鯨基地とその近郊の出身で、捕鯨者の家系の白人中産階級の者が中心であった。なお、『白鯨』においてスターバックの出自は「生まれはナンタケット、クェイカー教徒の家系である」(Melville 1851: 101) と述べられ、彼の階級に関する明確な記述はない。しかし、父も兄も鯨捕りであったとされていることも踏まえると、彼は、森田が示したような船のエリート層の人間と判断されよう。
5. 捕鯨船における領域の（不）分離については、Creighton (1995, 1996) を参照。
6. 19世紀アメリカの社会において感情あるいは情緒が女性的なものとされて

いたことについては、Faderman (1985) を参照。
7. 「鉄の男」と言い表される、屈強さや身体性に重きを置いた男らしさの理想像は、船乗りも含む労働者階級のサブカルチャーで長く見られたものである (Creighton & Noring 1996: ix-x)。
8. 植民地時代以来伝統的に見られた理想的な「男らしさ」については Lombard (2003) および Rotundo (1993) を参照。
9. エイハブが正気と狂気をまたいでいることは、「自分の手段は正気だが、その動機と目的が狂っているのだ」(Melville 1851: 151)、あるいは、「わしは悪魔にとりつかれているだけだ。わしは二重に狂った狂人だ！ わしの狂気は、おのれの狂気の正体を理解するときにのみおさまるたぐいの厄介な狂気だ！」(Melville 1851: 143) という、自らの狂気についての彼の分析に表れている。
10. 相反するものを拮抗させるエイハブの特異性については拙論 (髙橋 2008) を参照。
11. この「何か」については、第 39 章「夜直はじめ」においてスタッブが、夜半に義足の音を響かせて甲板を歩き回ることに対して呈した苦言を罵倒で返された時に感じたこと（第 29 章「エイハブ登場、つづいてスタッブ」）を思いおこしながら、「スターバックはあの晩おれが感じたのとおなじこと (something as I the other evening felt) を感じたみたいだな」(Melville 1851: 145) と述べている。

参考文献

Creighton, Margaret S. (1995) *Rites & Passages: The Experience of American Whaling*, 1830–1870, Cambridge: Cambridge University Press.

Creighton, Margaret S. (1996) *Davy Jone's Locker Room: Gender and the American Whaleman, 1830–1870. Iron Men, Wooden Women: Gender and Seafaring in the Atlantic World*, 1700–1920, Ed. Margaret S. Creighton and Lisa Noring, Baltimore: The Johns Hopkins University Press, pp.118–137.

Creighton, Margaret S. and Lisa Noring (1996), eds. *Iron Men, Wooder Women*, Baltimore: The Johns Hopkins University Press.

Eagleton, Terry. (2003) *Sweet Violence: The Idea of the Tragic*, reprinted ed., Malden, MA: Blackwell Publishing.（テリー・イーグルトン，森田典正訳，(2004)『甘美なる暴力 悲劇の思想』，大月書店）

Faderman, Lillian. (1985) *Surpassing the Love of Men: Romantic Friendship and Love between Women from the Renaissance to the Present*, London: The Women's Press.

Lombard, Anne S. (2003) *Making Manhood: Growing Up Male in Colonial New*

England, Cambridge, Mass: Harvard University Press.

Melville, Herman. (1851) *Moby-Dick*, Ed. Hershel Parker and Harrison Hayford, second ed., New York: W. W. Norton & Company.（メルヴィル，八木敏雄訳，（2004）『白鯨』，岩波書店）

森田勝昭．（1994）『鯨と捕鯨の文化史』，名古屋大学出版会．

Rotundo, E. Anthony. (1993) *American Manhood: Transformations in Masculinity from the Revolution to the Modern Era*, New York: Basic Books.

千石英世．（2000）「解説」，『白鯨』上，講談社，pp.635–650．

髙橋　愛．（2008）「恐怖から畏怖へ―『白鯨』における身体加工とジェンダー」，『F-GENS ジャーナル』，10 号，お茶の水女子大学 21 世紀 COE プログラム「ジェンダー研究のフロンティア」，pp.249–254．

八木敏雄．（1986）『『白鯨』解体』，研究社．

ワシントン・アーヴィングと
ウォルター・スコット
『スケッチ・ブック』はどのようにして生まれたか

瀧口美佳

要旨
　本論文では、ワシントン・アーヴィングが1817年夏父祖の国スコットランドを訪問し、かねてより敬愛するウォルター・スコットと面会の機会を得た事象を取り上げ、その邂逅の経緯を検証し、2人の語らいを通してアーヴィング文学の根幹が、スコットから授かった文学的知見や叡智に支えられていたという点について考察した。そしてその文学的示唆が、『スケッチ・ブック』の誕生や彼の文学的足跡にどのような影響を及ぼしたかについて検証した。この〈文学的巡礼〉とも呼ぶべき旅は、アーヴィングの独自の文学形成とその後の展開に深く寄与することとなった。またアーヴィングは『スケッチ・ブック』や『ブレイスブリッジ邸』で、イギリスの古き風俗風習を好んで取り上げているが、過ぎ去った時の流れに潜むロマンティズムを標榜する彼の文学にとって、広く文学を知り抜いているスコットとの邂逅は文学的観点から見ても最も意義深い事象であったといえよう。

キーワード　ワシントン・アーヴィング、ウォルター・スコット、スケッチ・ブック、アメリカ・ロマン派、アボッツフォード

1. はじめに

　アメリカ・ロマン派文壇の寵児と謳われたワシントン・アーヴィング (Washington Irving, 1783–1859) は、ヨーロッパ大陸の上質の文化及び

文学の影響を強く受けたアメリカ人作家の 1 人であったと目されている。ところが、日本に限らずアメリカにおいても、この作家をめぐる研究状況は同時代に活躍したアメリカ・ルネサンス期の文人の群、すなわちエマソン、ソロー、ホーソーン、そしてメルヴィルといった巨峰たちと比較すれば、研究量あるいは、その深さにおいても盛況とは言い難い。それはアーヴィングの文学活動が短編小説、歴史本、紀行文、そして伝記文学などの多岐にわたっているのも大きな理由の 1 つであると考えられる。

　アーヴィングの作家としての出発点が、1802 年に兄ピーターが発刊した『モーニング・クロニクル』(*The Morning Chronicle*) に掲載された「紳士ジョナサン・オールドスタイルの手紙」("Letters of Jonathan Oldstyle, Gent.")であったことは周知のことである。その後 2 年間のヨーロッパにおけるグランド・ツアーから帰国すると、兄ウィリアムと友人ジェイムズ・K・ポールディングと共に雑誌『サルマガンディ』(*Salmagundi*) を 20 回刊行して豊かな文才を披歴した。この雑誌は、ランスロット・ラングスタッフという架空の人物たちによって発行されているという形態をとってはいたが、アーヴィングのユーモアセンスが大いに発揮されていたことは一目了然であった。"Salmagundi"（寄せ集め）という名にふさわしく、この作品には喜劇的な要素や痛烈な風刺、さらにニューヨークの社交界についてのジョナサン・オールドスタイル風の叙述が含まれていた。

　またアーヴィングの初期の文学活動の代表作といえば、当時広い読者層に注目されたサミュエル・ミッチルの『ニューヨークの姿』(*A Picture of New York*, 1807) をパロディー化した『ニューヨーク史』(*A History of New York*, 1809) があげられる。この作品は出版後、1 年間で 2,000 ドル以上の収入を得るほどの成功を収め、アーヴィングは一躍アメリカ・ロマン派文壇における人気作家に躍り出て、確かな地歩を固めていったのである。

　その後 1815 年、家業である「アーヴィング商会」の国際的展開を目論み、兄ピーターのいるリヴァプールへと渡ったアーヴィングは、数ヶ

月間で帰国する予定を様々な事情により、1832年まで延ばすこととなった。

2. アボッツフォード邸訪問

　イギリスに渡ったアーヴィングは、不幸にして病床にあった兄ピーターに代わって「アーヴィング商会」の仕事に忙しくしていたが、次第に文学活動を再開するようになっていた。そして1817年の夏、仕事と観光を兼ねてスコットランドを旅する機会に恵まれた。当時のアーヴィングの置かれた状況に触れると、その年の4月に最愛の母セーラを亡くし、またアーヴィング商会が倒産に近い状況であったこと、さらに『ニューヨーク史』以後8年が経過していたものの、次の作品を出版できるまでには至っていないなど、順調とは言いがたいものであった。そのような状況におけるスコットランド旅行は、アーヴィングにとって、その後の文学的人生を決定づけることになったとも言える特筆すべき文学的巡礼である。文豪ウォルター・スコット (Walter Scott, 1771–1832) を、イギリス文壇では未だ無名に近い若いアメリカ人作家が訪れるわけであり、そもそもこの訪問の背後には、友人をはじめ周辺の人間の数年にわたる心強いサポートがあったことは、あまり知られていない。たとえば、その筆頭として挙げられるのは、アーヴィングの親友ヘンリー・ブルヴォートである。彼はニューヨークで最も裕福で有力な旧家の1つであるブルヴォート家の出であり、スコットがアーヴィングに興味を抱くきっかけを作ってくれた恩人なのである。すなわち、当時のイギリス及びヨーロッパ大陸では、未開に等しい新大陸アメリカの作家に興味を示すなど稀有な例でしかなかった。それゆえ、ブルヴォートの静かな功績は大きかったと言えよう。1813年4月エジンバラを旅行中であったブルヴォートは、スコットに『ニューヨーク史』の第2版を贈ると、スコットは、アーヴィング文学の表象するユーモアに対して大いに興味を示し、高く評価していたことが分かる。さらにアボッツフォード邸訪問に関して尽力してくれたもう1人が、当時世評の高かった詩人トマ

ス・キャンベルであった。彼はスコットランド出身の詩人で、彼が1810年に発表した作品にアーヴィングが序文を寄せたことから親しい交流が始まり、リヴァプールに渡って以来、親密な友情を結んでいた。そのキャンベルがしたためた紹介状を携え、スコットの住むアボッツフォード邸を訪れた時の様子が、1835年に出版された『クレヨンの雑録集』(*The Crayon Miscellany*) に収められている随想「アボッツフォード」("Abbotsford")で次のように述べられている。

> Before Scott had reached the gate he called out in a hearty tone, welcoming me to Abbotsford, and asking news of Campbell. Arrived at the door of the chaise he grasped me warmly by the hand: "Come drive down, drive down to the house, "he said.　　　　　(Irving 1978: 126)

スコットのまるで懐かしい友人をもてなすかのような、心からの歓迎ぶりに感動したアーヴィングは、短い時間で終えるつもりだったアボッツフォード邸訪問を、思いがけず4日間まで延ばすことになった。さらにはスコットの詩や小説に出てくる風景の中を共に散歩し、スコットの家族との団欒を楽しんだ。また馬車でスコットが幼少時に転地療養を行ったサンディー・ノウの農場やドライバラ寺院などへの遠出も経験した。このようなアボッツフォード邸での語らいなどから、アーヴィングの文学者としての後の方向が決定づけられたと言えるだろう。

> I left Abbotsford on Wednesday morning, and never left any place with more regret. The few days that I passed there were among the most delightful of my life, and worth as many years of ordinary existence.... I was with Scott from morning to night; rambling about the hills and streams, everyone of which would bring to his mind some old tale or picturesque remark. I was charmed with his family.　(Irving 1869: 248)

アーヴィングは兄ピーターへの手紙で「今までにこれほど去りがたい

気持ちになった場所はなく、アボッツフォードで過ごした数日は日常の何年分もの価値があった」とその感動を吐露した。一方スコットは、友人ジョン・リチャードソンへの手紙で次のように言及している。

> When you see Tom Campbell, tell him, with my best love, that I have to thank him for making me known to Mr. Washington Irving, who is one of the best and pleasantest acquaintances I have made this many a day. He stayed two or three days with me and I hope to see him again.
> (Grierson 1933: 532)

アーヴィングが非常に愉快な人物であったことや再会を望む旨を、2人の仲介してくれたトマス・キャンベルに伝えるようにと述べている。このようにアボッツフォード邸での4日間は、アーヴィングの人生において忘れられない滞在であったと同時に、長い思いやりに満ちた個人的な友情の始まりでもあったといえよう。

　また、スコットの代表的長編小説『アイヴァンホー』(*Ivanhoe*, 1819) に登場する女性「レベッカ」については次のような指摘がある。

> In addition, a specific influence of the younger writer on the older seems certain: a year or so after Irving's visit, Scott began Ivanhoe, which contains one of the most impressive of his many characterizations, that of the Jewish maiden Rebecca; it is likely that she was inspired by his American guest's description of Rebecca Gratz, a beautiful Philadelphia friend whom Irving had long known and admired.
> (McFarland 1979: 46)

マクファーランドは、この「レベッカ」とアーヴィングのフィラデルフィア時代の友人レベッカ・グラッツに共通性を見出し、アボッツフォードでの邂逅がアーヴィングにとって大きな意味を持っていただけでなく、スコットにも少なからず影響を与えていたと述べている。

3. スコットからの文学的影響

次にアーヴィングがスコットから受けた文学的影響と 1819 年から 20 年にかけて、英米両国で出版された短編集『スケッチ・ブック』(*The Sketch Book of Geoffrey Crayon, Gent.*) との関連性について述べてみたい。「アボッツフォード」の叙述から判断すると、アーヴィングはアボッツフォード邸でのスコットや彼の家族や従者、愛犬たちに囲まれた団欒を非常に気に入っていたようである。さらに、スコットはアーヴィングがアボッツフォード邸を去る際に、次のような助言を与えている。

> "They have kind hearts, "said he, "and that is the main point as to human happiness. They love one another, poor things, which is every thing in domestic life. The best wish I can make you my friend, "added he, laying his hand upon my shoulder, "is that when you return to your own country, you may get married and have a family of young bairns about you. If you are happy there they are to share your happiness—and if you are otherwise—there they are to comfort you."
>
> (Irving 1978: 165)

スコットは「家庭生活で一番大切なことは、お互いを大切に思いやる心であり、私が君（アーヴィング）に最も望むことは、故郷に帰ったら結婚し子どもに囲まれた家庭をもつことである。もし君が幸福なら家族は君の幸福を分かち合い、もしそうでないときは家族が慰めてくれるだろう」と述べた。明らかにスコットのこの発言に影響を受けたと思われる叙述が、『スケッチ・ブック』の短編「妻」("The Wife") に認められる。

> I was once congratulating a friend, who had around him a blooming family, knit together in the strongest affection. "I can wish you no better lot, "said he, with enthusiasm, "than to have a wife and children. If you are prosperous, there they are to share your prosperity; if otherwise,

there they are to comfort you." （Irving 1978: 22）

　語り手「私」(Geoffrey Crayon) が、友人レスリー夫妻について回想する中で「その友人は、咲きほこるような家族をもっていて、強い愛情で結ばれていた。彼は、妻や子どもと共に過ごすことほどすばらしいものはないのだ」と表現されている。これらの叙述には、かなりの共通性を見てとることができる。つまりジョフリー・クレヨンの吐露した結婚観には、スコットの影響が顕著に表れていると考えられるのではないだろうか。

　さらにアーヴィングは、スコットの言動だけでなく、アボッツフォード邸の日常的な光景にも強い印象を受けたようだ。それは、『スケッチ・ブック』の短編「クリスマス・イブ」("Christmas Eve") の次の場面にうかがえる。この短編は、1822年に発表された『ブレイスブリッジ邸』(Bracebridge Hall) の土台となる作品で、物語はヨークシャーのブレイスブリッジ邸が舞台となっている。作品中にブレイスブリッジ邸の愛犬たちについて、詳細な叙述がある。

> We were interrupted by the clamor of a troop of dogs of all sorts and sizes, "mongrel, puppy, whelp and hound, and curs of low degree," that, disturbed by the ring of the porter's bell and the rattling of the chaise, came bounding, open-mouthed, across the lawn.
> 　"—The little dogs and all,
> 　　Tray, Blanch, and Sweetheart, see, they bark at me!"
> cried Bracebridge, laughing. （Irving 1978: 161）

これは、アーヴィングがオリヴァー・ゴールドスミス (Oliver Goldsmith, 1730–1774) の『ウェイクフィールドの牧師』(The Vicar of Wakefield, 1766) とシェイクスピア (William Shakespeare, 1564–1616) の『リア王』(King Lear, 1604) の第3幕6場から引用した部分である。犬に関する箇所は「アボッツフォード」にも数多く記されており、その中か

ら上述の「クリスマス・イブ」に影響を与えたと思われるのが、次のアボッツフォード邸の番犬の様子である。

> The noise of the chaise had disturbed the quiet of the establishment. Out sallied the warder of the castle, a black greyhound, and, leaping on one of the blocks of stone began a furious barking. His alarum brought out the whole garrison of dogs:
> 　"Both mongrel, puppy, whelp and hound,
> 　And curs of low degree;"
> all open mouthed and vociferous.　　　　　（Irving 1978: 125–126）

「馬車の音がその屋敷の静寂を乱し、館の番犬である黒いグレイハウンドが飛び出し石塊の1つに跳び乗り、猛烈な勢いで吠え始めた。そのけたたましい声が、犬の守備隊全部を連れ出してきた。雑種も子犬も、幼犬そして猟犬も、そして劣等種の犬も、騒がしく吠えたてた」と表現されているスコットの飼い犬たちは、その後もたびたび「アボッツフォード」に登場している。

　以上、前出の2つの短編「妻」と「クリスマス・イブ」の叙述には、「アボッツフォード」との強い類似性が認められることが明らかである。つまりアボッツフォード邸で過ごした4日間の語らいの中にスコットから受けた影響が、『スケッチ・ブック』に顕著に表れていると考えることができるのではないだろうか。さらに、『スケッチ・ブック』の短編「船旅」（"The Voyage"）にスコットの影響が表れていると思われる部分がある。

> Ships, ships, I will descrie you
> Amidst the main,
> I will come and try you,
> What you are protecting,
> And projecting,

> What's your end and aim.
> One goes abroad for merchandise and trading,
> Another stays to keep his country from invading,
> A third is coming home with rich and wealthy lading.
> 　　Halloo! my fancie, whither wilt thou go?　　(Irving 1978: 11)

　上記の引用は「船旅」の冒頭部分であるが、スコットの『イギリスの吟遊詩人』(*English Minstrelsy*, 1810) の "Haloow, my Fancy" が引用されている。アーヴィングがスコットの詩を引用したことについて、『スケッチ・ブック』のオックスフォード・ワールド・クラッシックス版のエディターであるスーザン・マニングは、「スコットがウェイバリー・ノベルズで使用していた手法を、アーヴィングが取り入れた一種のエピグラムである」と分析している。従って『スケッチ・ブック』にスコットの影響を残したいというアーヴィングの明確な意図が、うかがえると考えてよいのではないだろうか。

　さらに、アボッツフォード邸でスコットと交わした文人同士としての語らいは、アーヴィングの文学作品に留まらず、その後の文学的な志向にまで影響を及ぼすこととなった。アーヴィングがアボッツフォード邸を訪れた後の執筆及び出版の状況は、『スケッチ・ブック』が2年後である1819年にアメリカで出版され、その翌年にイギリスで出版された。この時間的な流れから判断しても、アーヴィングがこの短編集に含まれる多くの作品を生み出したきっかけは、紛れもなくアボッツフォード邸でのスコットとの語らいの有意義な時間から生まれたものだったといえるであろう。

4.　文学的足跡における類似性

　『スケッチ・ブック』出版後、アーヴィングの経済状況および文人としての状況は好転したが、アーヴィングは1824年の『旅人の物語』(*Tales of a Traveler*) の出版後、4年ほど顕著な文学活動は控えていた。

その理由の1つとしては、『スケッチ・ブック』が好評であったのに対して、後続の2作品に対する評価が期待したほど良くなく、作家としての自信を無くしつつあったことも考えられる。そこで、アーヴィングはそれまでのスケッチ風の短編とは異なり、歴史文学のカテゴリーとなるコロンブスの生涯を題材にした『クリストファー・コロンブスの生涯と航海』(*The Life and Voyages of Christopher Columbus*, 1828) を出版した。また 1832 年に発刊した代表作の1つである『アルハンブラ物語』(*Tales of the Alhambra*) は、彼の作家としての地位を不動のものにしたといわれている。この作品はそれまでの『グラナダの征服記』(*Chronicle of the Conquest of Granada*, 1829) などとは趣が変わった、いわゆる「紀行文学」に分類されるものであった。

その後スペイン大使を経て帰国後、アーヴィングはスコットのアボッツフォード邸を模倣して建てたニューヨーク郊外の終の棲家「サニーサイド」で、積年の願望であった『ジョージ・ワシントン伝』(*Life of George Washington*, 1855–59) の執筆にとりかかり、伝記文学の領域に手を拡げることとなった。「サニーサイド」の構造様式は、規模や豪華さは劣るものの、河の近くを選んだロケーションなど細部に至るまでスコットのアボッツフォード邸の趣を感じさせる造りとなっている。

以上、アーヴィングの文学的足跡をたどってみたが、彼がエッセイから散文へと文学的カテゴリーを移し、その後歴史文学、紀行文学、そしてついに伝記文学にまで範囲を拡げることとなった経緯には、くり返すことになるが、ウォルター・スコットとの文学的類似性及びその影響がうかがえる。さらに両者の文学的類似性を検証するために、スコットの文学的足跡について述べたい。

スコットの本格的な文学活動は、詩や民謡の類から始まり、『最後の吟遊詩人の唄』(*The Lay of the Last Minstrel*, 1805)、『マーミオン』(*Marmion*, 1808)、そして『湖上の美人』(*The Lady of the Lake*, 1810) を出版するに及び、その人気は絶頂期を迎えた。しかしロマン派詩人ジョージ・ゴードン・バイロンの登場とともに、スコットは自分の詩の才能に限界を感じ、歴史小説の創作に専念したといわれている。代表作にはス

コットランドを舞台にした『ウェイバリー』(*Waverly*, 1814) やアーヴィングがアボッツフォード邸を訪問した際に執筆中であったと言われる『ロブ・ロイ』(*Rob Roy*, 1817)、そして『アイヴァンホー』が挙げられる。その後も多くの作品を生み出しながら、伝記文学の領域にも入っていき、晩年には『ナポレオン・ボナパルトの生涯』(*The Life of Napoleon Buonaparte*, 1827) を出版した。

　文学的足跡における端緒は、アーヴィングがエッセイ、スコットが詩というように異なるが、その後に散文、歴史小説、紀行文、最後に伝記というように文学的なカテゴリーを移していく執筆スタイルにおいてスコットの影響が強く表れているといえるのではないだろうか。

5. おわりに

　最後に、1815年5月故郷ニューヨークから短期滞在の予定でリヴァプールに向けて出発したワシントン・アーヴィングは、その後17年間に亘るイギリス及びヨーロッパ滞在の中で文学的成功を手に入れた。その契機となった事象が、ウォルター・スコットとの邂逅であったことは既述のとおりである。スコットとの語らいを振り返り、「アボッツフォード」の最後で次のように述べている。

> It was, as if I were admitted to a social communion with Shakespeare, for it was with one of a kindred, if not equal genius. Every night I retired with my mind filled with delightful recollections of the day, and every morning I rose with the certainty of new enjoyment. The days thus spent I shall ever look back to as among the very happiest of my life; for I was conscious at the time of being happy.　(Irving 1978: 165)

アーヴィングはこの4日間を「まるでシェイクスピアと社交的に親しく語り合うことを認められたかのようであり、これらの日々を人生で最も幸せな時として決して忘れないであろう」と表現し、感動の全てを凝

縮しているといっても過言ではない。

　1817年の夏の終わりに過ごしたアボッツフォード邸でのわずか4日間は、アーヴィングのその後の人生に大きな意義をもたらしたといえる。その文学的示唆により、彼はエッセイから散文へと文学スタイルを変える決意をし、同時にスコットの語る民話、騎士道物語、そしてドイツ民話にヒントを得て、その舞台をアメリカに移した「リップ・ヴァン・ウィンクル」("Rip Van Winkle")や「スリーピー・ホローの伝説」("The Legend of Sleepy Hollow")などを含む『スケッチ・ブック』を生み出すことにつながったと考えられるのではないだろうか。この作品中には、随所にスコットとの対話からの影響が顕著に表れているとともに、アーヴィングが『サルマガンディ』や『ニューヨーク史』で培った独自のユーモアセンスが光っていることも事実である。『スケッチ・ブック』以後は、アーヴィングの文学スタイルが短編から歴史文学へと移り、スペインで主に執筆した紀行文学と、その後の文学的足跡についてもスコットの文学的経緯と重なる部分も多く、スコットの影響、そしてアボッツフォード邸への訪問によって、アーヴィングが文学的叡智を手に入れたといえるだろう。

参考文献

Grierson, Herbert J. C. (ed.) (1933) *The letters of Sir Walter Scott*. London: Constable.

Irving, Pierre, M. (1869) *The Life and Letters of Washington Irving*. Philadelphia: J. B. Lippincott & Co..

Irving, Washington. (1978) *The Sketch Book of Geoffrey Crayon*, Gent. Ed. Haig, Judith Giblin. *Vol. 8* of *The Complete Works of Washington Irving*. Boston: Twayne.

Irving, Washington. (1979) *The Crayon Miscellany*. Ed. Terrell, Dahlia Kirby. *Vol. 22* of *The Complete Works of Washington Irving*. Boston: Twayne.

Jones, Jay Brian. (2007) *Washington Irving: an American Original*. New York: Arcade Publishing.

Manning, Susan. (ed.) (1996) *The Sketch Book of Geoffrey Crayon, Gent.*. New York: Oxford University Press.

松井優子(2007)『スコット―人と文学』勉誠出版
McFarland, Philip. (1979) *Sojourners*. New York: Atheneum.
齊藤　昇(2005)『ワシントン・アーヴィングとその時代』本の友社
Sutherland, John. (1995) *The Life of Walter Scott: A Critical Biography*. Oxford: Oxford University Press.
米本弘一(2007)『フィクションとしての歴史―ウォルター・スコットの語りの技法』英宝社

「キャンプ的感覚」で探究する
多元文化主義的ユートピア
『エンジェルズ・イン・アメリカ』と
エイズ危機下のニューヨーク

竹島達也

要旨

　本論文は、同性愛の劇作家トニー・クシュナーによる『エンジェルズ・イン・アメリカ』の第1部と第2部について、その演劇的スタイルと思想を分析し、舞台となっているエイズ危機下の1980年代のニューヨークとの相関関係を解明したものである。「国家的なテーマに関するゲイ・ファンタジア」という副題を持つ当作品は、スーザン・ソンタグが『反解釈』の中で提唱した「キャンプ的感覚」を各所に施し、実際の世界と空想の世界が錯綜し、エイズに翻弄され苦悩するゲイたちの過酷な現実と特異な心象風景がパノラマ的に展開する。そして、当作品の基本的なスタンスは、ウォルター・ベンヤミンの「進歩の代償としての歴史の廃墟」といった歴史観に基づくものである。本論文のエッセンスは、以上のような作品の本質に可能な限り踏み込み、それを多元文化主義的ユートピアとしてのニューヨークという枠組みと連動させることによって、新たな作品解釈を探究することにある。

キーワード　『エンジェルズ・イン・アメリカ』、エイズ危機下のニューヨーク、ゲイ・ファンタジア、「キャンプ的感覚」、ベンヤミン的歴史観

1.　はじめに

　『エンジェルズ・イン・アメリカ』(*Angels in America A Gay Fantasia on*

National Themes）は、今となっては 20 世紀のアメリカ演劇の名作の 1 つに数えられ、アメリカ演劇史の中でも非常に重要な位置を占めるに至っているのは衆目の一致する所である。『エンジェルズ・イン・アメリカ』の第 1 部である『至福千年紀が来る』(*Part One: Millennium Approaches*) は、1990 年代初頭、アメリカの中でも比較的リベラルな地域である西海岸のサンフランシスコやロサンジェルスでの公演を経て、イギリスに渡り、ロンドンのナショナル・シアター (the National Theater) で上演され、高い評価を得る。その後、アメリカでは、1993 年ブロードウェイのウォルター・カー劇場 (the Walter Kerr Theater) で初演を迎える。上演回数は、367 回を記録し (Broadway Database)、トニー賞、ピューリツァー賞、ニューヨーク劇評家協会賞といった主要な演劇賞を総なめにし、作者のトニー・クシュナー (Tony Kushner, 1956–) を一躍時代の寵児にした。

第 2 部である『ペレストロイカ』(*Part Two: Perestroika*) は、1993 年、ロンドンで第 1 部のリバイバル公演と共に上演され、ブロードウェイでも同年、ウォルター・カー劇場で初演を迎え、217 回の上演回数を記録し (Broadway Database)、1994 年度のトニー賞を受賞した。20 世紀後半のアメリカ演劇の代表作となった『エンジェルズ・イン・アメリカ』は、全米各地ばかりか、日本を含めた世界各国でも上演されている。そして、トニー賞の最優秀作品賞を受賞したトップ 5 の作品、また、ロンドンのナショナル・シアターによって 20 世紀を代表する 100 の劇作品にも選ばれている。

第 1 部『至福千年紀』。舞台は、1980 年代半ばで共和党レーガン政権の時代、エイズが蔓延し多くの犠牲者が出ているニューヨーク。ワスプのゲイ、プライアー (Prior) とユダヤ系のルイス (Louis) は、長年恋人関係にあった。しかし、プライアーがエイズを発症したため、ルイスは苦しみながらもプライアーから離れてゆく。他方、ユダヤ系でゲイでありながらアメリカの政界の黒幕として長年君臨してきたロイ・コーン (Roy Cohn) は、不正行為によって弁護士資格剥奪の危機に直面し、若い弁護士でモルモン教徒のジョー (Joe) を司法省に送ることによって、自らの

苦境を打開しようとする。しかし、ロイもエイズに感染していることが発覚する。

　ロイの片腕とも言えるジョーは、モルモン教徒の妻ハーパー(Harper)に、同性愛者であることを気づかれ、自分に正直に生きようと決意して同じ裁判所に勤務しているルイスに惹かれてゆく。ハーパーは、夫との結婚生活への不満から精神安定剤を濫用し、幻覚の世界へと入ってゆく。一方、ルイスに捨てられたプライアーは、エイズの症状が悪化する過程で不思議な夢を見るようになり、遂には天使が自分の部屋に舞い降りるまでになる。

　第2部『ペレストロイカ』。プライアーは、アメリカの天使から人類の代表とも言える預言者になるよう要求され、天国に行く。天国でプライアーは、チェルノブイリの原子力発電所の爆発によって集合した各大陸の天使たちに会うものの、人類の苦境を打開できないことを悟り、人間として生きることを決意して地上に戻る。そして、モルモン教のビジターセンターで、ジョーとの夫婦生活が破綻したハーパーや、息子ジョーを心配してソルトレイク・シティーからやって来たハンナと知り合う。

　ロイ・コーンは、エイズの症状が悪化し、黒人のゲイの看護師ベリーズ(Belize)に看取られて、病院で死んでゆく。ジョーとルイスは、一度は性愛に溺れるものの、プライアーを忘れられないルイスは、ジョーと別れる。そして、最終的には、ハーパーはジョーと別れ1人でサンフランシスコへ旅立ち、プライアーもルイスと復縁することはない。4年後、セントラル・パークのベセズダ噴水の前に、プライアー、ルイス、ハンナ、ベリーズが集まり、東西冷戦の終結を契機に始まる劇的な世界の変化と新しい世界の構築について語る。最後には、エイズにかかりながらも生き続けているプライアーが、ゲイたちがエイズの時代を生き抜き、世界が前向きに発展することを望み、幕となる。

　以上が『エンジェルズ・イン・アメリカ』第1部並びに第2部の梗概であるが、本論文においては、『エンジェルズ・イン・アメリカ』とその主たる舞台になっているニューヨークとの相関関係を本質的なレベ

ルにおいて探究することを主目的とする[1]。最初に、エイズ危機に見舞われた1980年代のニューヨークとゲイたちの置かれた苦境について概観した後で、『エンジェルズ・イン・アメリカ』が、その世界を「キャンプ性」とも言える独自の特性や感性によってどのように表現しているかを分析する。次に、作品とその舞台になっているニューヨークとの関係を、ゲイのコミュニティーとゲイの演劇文化という視点から捉え直してみる。さらに、ドイツの歴史哲学者ウォルター・ベンヤミン（Walter Benjamin, 1892–1940）の歴史観をベースに、多元文化主義的ユートピアの建設というキーワードを加えることによって、本論文のテーマの解明をより精緻なものにしてゆきたい。

2. エイズ危機に見舞われた1980年代のニューヨーク

ニューヨークは、アメリカにおいて世界に開かれた玄関口として、サンフランシスコと並び称されるほどの全米最大級のゲイ・コミュニティーを擁しているものの、歴史的にアイルランド系やイタリア系が多いために、カトリック教会勢力による同性愛に対する強い反発から、1980年代の初めにおいてもセクシュアリティーに起因する差別を撤廃する動きが本格化することはなかった（Kaiser 1997: 270）。それに加えて、1980年10月、共和党のロナルド・レーガンが、圧倒的な国民の支持を得て、大統領に当選する。

保守的な傾向が強く、クシュナーがヒトラーのナチスと同一視する（Pacheco 1998: 54）レーガン政権の登場が象徴的に示しているように、1980年代は、ゲイの解放運動が活性化した1970年代とは対照的に、ゲイの受難の時代となる。ニューヨークにおいても、1980年11月、マンハッタンにおける最大のゲイ・コミュニティーが存在するグリニッチ・ヴィレッジで、ゲイを標的にした銃乱射事件が起きた。これは、ホモフォービアによる殺傷事件であり、2名が殺害され、6名が負傷した（Kaiser 1997: 274–275）。

そして、1981年夏、ニューヨーク市とサンフランシスコの湾岸地域

において、カポジ肉腫にかかった、主として40歳以下のゲイの若者たちについての現場の医師による40件以上にのぼる報告があった。これがエイズ危機の始まりであり、ガエタン・デューガス（Gaetan Dugas）という名前のカナダ人の客室乗務員が、発生源を意味する「患者ゼロ」（"Patient Zero"）であった。

ニューヨークには、アメリカの他のどの都市と比べてもはるかに多くのエイズ患者がおり、1983年までに、1261名ものニューヨーク市民がエイズと診断され、そのうちの41パーセントもが死亡した（Kaiser 1997: 300）。にもかかわらず、ニューヨーク・タイムズも当時のニューヨーク市長、エドワード・コッチ（Edward I. Koch, 1924–）もなかなかエイズを重大な危機と認識せず、また、レーガン政権に至っては、無関心極まりなく、多くのエイズによる死者が出るまではその重い腰を上げることはなかったのである。その結果、ビル・クリントンによる大統領選挙運動の初め（1992年）までに、全米で23万人のアメリカ人がエイズと診断され、そのうち少なくとも15万人が死亡した。その数は、朝鮮戦争とヴェトナム戦争で戦死した米兵の数よりも多い（Kaiser 1997: 330）。

3. 「キャンプ的感覚」で捉えるエイズ危機

『エンジェルズ・イン・アメリカ』においても、エイズは、プライアーやロイ・コーンの身体を蝕み、人間が本来持っている免疫が機能せず、2人は健康であれば特に問題がないような細菌やウィルスにすぐに感染してしまう。彼らは、発熱や激痛、そして呼吸困難に絶えず見舞われ、生と死の間を行き来する。エイズに苦しむプライアーの口からも、1986年の段階でエイズが流行し、友人の半数が既に死亡し、自分もまだ31歳にしかなっていない（Kushner 1995: 181）という発言が出てくる。そのような極限状態に陥った登場人物は、幻想や妄想を抱き、天使や幽霊のような超現実的なものを頻繁に見るまでになっている。

しかし、『エンジェルズ・イン・アメリカ』は、エイズに見舞われている1980年代半ばのニューヨークの危機的な状態を、直截的にそして

感傷的には描いてはいない。エイズに苦しむ同性愛者たちを中心に据え、その苦境を、時には、感傷的に、時には、激しい怒りを込めて取り上げた、『アズ・イズ』(*As Is*, 1985)や『ノーマル・ハート』(*The Normal Heart*, 1985)といった先行作品とは、かなり異質なスタンスで、エイズに苦しむ同性愛者たちの世界を表現していると言えるのである。

『エンジェルズ・イン・アメリカ』が本質的に備えている独自性や異質性を解明する上で、重要なキー概念となる感覚は、アメリカの批評家スーザン・ソンタグ(Susan Sontag, 1933–2004)が『反解釈』(*Against Interpretation*, 1961)の中で展開した〈キャンプ〉という感覚であると言えるのではなかろうか。

ソンタグは、「〈キャンプ〉についてのノート」の中で次のように述べている。

> …キャンプの本質は、不自然なものを愛好するところに—人工と誇張を好むところに—ある。　　　　　　　　　　（ソンタグ 2010: 431）

> …つまりキャンプとは、誇張されたもの、〈外れた〉もの、ありのままでないものを好むことなのだ。　　　　　　（ソンタグ 2010: 437）

> キャンプとは、真面目に提示されはするが、「ひどすぎる」ために、完全に真面目には受け取れない芸術のことである。
> 　　　　　　　　　　　　　　　　　　　　　　（ソンタグ 2010: 446）

> キャンプは世界の喜劇的ヴィジョンを提出する。…喜劇は、標準以下の参加ないしディタッチメントの経験である。
> 　　　　　　　　　　　　　　　　　　　　　　（ソンタグ 2010: 454）

そして、『エンジェルズ・イン・アメリカ』の作品世界と「キャンプ的な感覚」との密接な相関関係については、ビグズビーも、作品のキャンプ的であると解釈できる諸特徴を列挙し、観客に真面目に考えさせな

い真面目な劇、そして、祝祭的な劇であると見なしている（Bigsby 1999: 113）。

　プライアーは、自らの想像の世界の中で、かつてそうであったようにドラッグ・クイーンの衣装と化粧で現れ、第 2 部では、ニューヨークを代表するようなドラッグ・クイーンの派手で陽気な葬式の場面まで登場する。エイズにかかった人々が次々に死んでゆくニューヨークの過酷な現実は、プライアーの苦悩やロイ・コーンの壮絶な死と相まって、観客に暗澹たる思いを抱かせることは間違いない。しかし、プライアーが遭遇する天使とその卑猥とも言えるやり取り、マンハッタンのセント・ヴィンセント病院の診療室に突然現れる燃え上がる聖書、そして五大陸の天使たちが一堂に会する天国などが、エイズ劇といった狭隘な世界をはるかに超越した、喜劇的で、誇張された、きわめて不自然な世界を提供する。

　幕切れに位置し、第 1 部のクライマックスとも言える、プライアーの部屋に天使が飛来し、天からのメッセージを伝える場面でも、プライアーは強烈な性欲に駆られている。また、クシュナーはブレヒト流の異化効果を狙って、天使が天井からピアノ線によって吊られていることがはっきりわかるように仕向けられている。さらに、第 2 部では、再度天使が飛来する際には、プライアーとの空中での激しい性交の場面まで登場する始末である。

　エイズ危機の時代に人類の代表に選ばれたプライアーと天使との邂逅は、本来ならば、厳粛な場面となることを多くの観客が予想するところだが、その予想は見事なまでに裏切られるのである。このように見てくると、『エンジェルズ・イン・アメリカ』は、「ひどすぎる」ために、完全に真面目に受け取れない芸術であり（ソンタグ 2010: 446）、異化効果を観客が覚える喜劇的ともいえる場面が多用され、標準以下の参加ないしディタッチメントの経験（ソンタグ 2010: 434）を観客にさせるゆえに、キャンプ的な感覚がきわめて濃厚だと言えるのである。

　エイズによる受難の時代を迎えた同性愛者たちにとってのニューヨークは、現実には、第 1 部の 3 幕における、ハンナが迷い込んだ廃墟と

化したサウス・ブロンクス(the South Bronx)が象徴するような世紀末的な絶望に満ちた世界と称しても決して過言ではない。サウス・ブロンクスは、貧困と犯罪が渦巻く全米最悪のスラム街の1つであり、1970年代以降保険金目当ての建物の放火が頻発し、まさに廃墟と化していた。ハンナがそこで出会ったホームレスの女性は、ノストラダムスの大予言について言及し、人類が様々な愚行を重ねた末に行き着く墓場を暗示する。

しかし、『エンジェルズ・イン・アメリカ』は、エイズに苦しむプライアーの幻想や妄想の世界をその内奥に至るまで深く掘り下げ、そこにおいてキャンプ的感覚を最大限に活用することによって、現実とはまったく異質とも言える世界を築き上げている。この魔術的とも形容できる世界では、天使や幽霊が跳梁跋扈し、現実とファンタジーとの世界との境界が消滅する。観客は、エイズという疫病の流行によって引き起こされた過酷な現実に没入することなく、キャンプ的な感覚によって生じる一種の祝祭空間を目の当たりにすることによって、半ばファンタジーの世界と化した1980年代半ばのニューヨークを体感することができるのである。

4. ゲイ文化の聖地としてのニューヨーク

『エンジェルズ・イン・アメリカ』の舞台になっている1980年代後半のニューヨークは、先述したように、「ゲイの都」とも呼べる側面が強く、作品中にもマンハッタンを中心としたゲイに密接に関連する場所が登場する。セントラル・パークの南部に位置し、小規模な森林地帯になっているランブル(the Ramble)は、ゲイの出会いの場所として知られる。ランブルで、ルイスはプライアーを見捨てた罪悪感を晴らすために行きずりの男を求め、ジョーも自己のセクシュアリティーに忠実になろうとすると、ランブルに自然と足が向いてしまうのである。そして、ジョーはランブルの中にある公衆電話から、深夜、ソルト・レイク・シティーにいる母親に電話し、自らのセクシュアリティーについて告白す

る。この場面は、ジョーがハーパーとの夫婦生活を破綻させ、自分の母親までも巻き込む騒動へとつながり、劇を動かす点で、非常に重要な意味を持つ。

　第2部においても、ジョーとルイスがしばらく同棲した後、海岸で今後の身の振り方について話し合う場面があるが、その海岸は、ロング・アイランドの東南に位置し、大西洋に面するジョーンズ・ビーチ (Jones Beach) というゲイたちが集まる海岸である。その他にも、ルイスは、ジョーとの会話の中で、ニューヨーク近郊にあるゲイのコミュニティーとして知られるファイアー・アイランド (Fire Island) やゲイたちの専用浴場の1つである聖マークのバス (the St. Mark's Baths) についても言及する。『エンジェルズ・イン・アメリカ』の基本的な地理的枠組みは、ゲイの登場人物たちの生活圏や行動範囲をベースにしたゲイのコミュニティーとしてのニューヨークであると言っても過言ではない。

　『エンジェルズ・イン・アメリカ』は、同性愛の劇作家クシュナーがゲイを巡る根元的な問題を扱っているだけではなく、同性愛文化のアイコンを各所に配置することによって、アメリカのゲイ文化ひいては同性愛文化との連帯を紡ぎ出そうとしている。第1部の冒頭付近で、ロイ・コーンは、『ラ・カージュ・オ・フォール』(*La Cage aux Folles*, 1983) の素晴らしさをジョーに話しているが、『ラ・カージュ・オ・フォール』は、ゲイのカップルを初めて本格的に取り上げたブロードウェイのミュージカルである。

　また、プライアーが長年飼ってきた猫は、シーバ (Sheba) という名前が付けられ、プライアーがエイズを発症した際に家を出てしまい、プライアーは「愛しのシーバよ、帰っておいで」と叫ぶ。これは、アメリカの同性愛の劇作家ウィリアム・インジ (William Inge, 1913–1973) の代表作『愛しのシーバよ、帰れ』(*Come Back, Little Sheba*, 1950) のパロディーであり、実際のシーバは猫ではなく犬である。更に、同じくアメリカの同性愛の劇作家テネシー・ウィリアムズ (Tennessee Williams, 1911–1983) の代表作『欲望という名の電車』(*A Streetcar Named Desire*, 1947) の登場人物であるステラ (Stella) やその主人公ブランチ (Blanche) の実家で

あったプランテーションの名称であるベル・リーブ（Belle Reeve）が、第1部のプライアーとベリーズとの会話の中で使用される。

　そして、第2部の終盤では、天国から帰還したプライアーが、『欲望という名の電車』の幕切れの名台詞、"I have always depended on the kindness of strangers."（Kushner 1995: 271）を口にする。この科白の意味するところは、一義的には、プライアーがエイズにかかりながらも生きてゆこうと決意することになったことで、自分を支え続けてくれたニューヨークの人々の親切に対する感謝の念を表したものである。また、この科白は、同時に、『エンジェルズ・イン・アメリカ』自体が歴史的に先行するゲイ文化の蓄積の上に成り立っていることを意識したクシュナー自身の、今までのゲイ文化の担い手に対する敬愛と畏敬の念の表明であるとも解釈できるのではなかろうか。『エンジェルズ・イン・アメリカ』には、ゲイ同士の時代を超えた連帯と協働の精神が結実し、その双方が共振・共鳴するようになる装置が各所に施されていると見なすことができるのである。そして、それは、作品自体が今までとは違った次元の新しい時代のゲイ文化のアイコンになることに寄与しているのである。

　『エンジェルズ・イン・アメリカ』は、物理的には「ゲイの都」である1980年代のニューヨークというロカールを舞台にしていると同時に、ニューヨークの演劇文化の枠組みの中での、他のゲイ文化との間テクスト性という一種の相互作用を通じて、ゲイ演劇の聖地とも言えるニューヨークを前景化しようとしているのである。

5. 多元文化主義的ユートピア構築を目指して

　『エンジェルズ・イン・アメリカ』というタイトルは、コロンビア大学で中世の歴史を研究し、天使に強い興味を持っていたクシュナーが、天使が寝室の天井を突き破って入ってくる夢を見た際に直観的に思い浮かんだものである。そのような事情もあり、作品の中には、アメリカの天使のほかに、他の大陸の天使たちも登場するが、その天使のベースと

なっているものは、ドイツの画家ポール・クレー（Paul Klee, 1879–1940）の「新しい天使」と題された絵であり、その絵についてのベンヤミンの解釈である。

　ベンヤミンは、クレーの天使の絵について次のように述べている。

> …楽園から嵐が吹きつけていて、それが彼の翼にはらまれ、あまりの激しさに天使はもはや翼を閉じることができない。この嵐が彼を、背を向けている未来の方へ引き留めがたく押し流してゆき、その間にも彼の眼前では、瓦礫の山が積み上がって天にも届かんばかりである。私たちが進歩と呼んでいるもの、それがこの嵐なのだ。
> 　　　　　　　　　　　　　　　　　（ベンヤミン 2011: 653）

　この記述は、ベンヤミンの歴史観が典型的に表れている部分である。クシュナーは、ルイジアナ時代に親交を結んだキンバリー・フリン（Kimberly T. Flynn）を通じて知るに至ったベンヤミンの思想（Kushner 1995: 286）から大きな影響を受けているのである。そのベンヤミンの歴史観とは、「進歩の代償としての歴史の廃墟」（Fisher 2001: 54）といった考え方で、人間の歴史上における進歩には、様々な悲劇が必然的に伴い、その荒廃した地点における人間の絶え間ない奮闘努力が未来を築き上げるというものである。

　『エンジェルズ・イン・アメリカ』では、特に第 2 部において、旧ソビエト連邦のゴルバチョフ書記長による「建て直し」を意味する改革であるペレストロイカというタイトルが典型的に表しているように、西暦 2000 年という新たな千年紀を迎える際に、エイズ危機やチェルノブイリの原発事故のような人類にとっての大きな試練とそれらをいかに乗り越えるかが焦点となっている。

　クシュナーが自ら述べていることからも明らかなように、変化というものは極めて困難ではあるが、不可能というわけではなく、第 1 部とは違って、第 2 部『ペレストロイカ』には変化は成し遂げられるという希望がある（Pacheco 1998: 60）。第 1 部の幕切れにおける天使の飛来

が意味するところは、オープン・エンディング的な要素が大きく、あくまでも変化の可能性は曖昧なものになっている。しかし、第2部における天国の場面では、人類の代表となったプライアーは、神が人類を見捨て未来に希望が持てないことがよくわかっているにもかかわらず、天国にとどまることを望まず、地上に帰って可能な限り生きることを選択する。そして、このような『エンジェルズ・イン・アメリカ』の骨格を形成するとも言える展開は、まさにベンヤミンの歴史観とその根本において通底し、エイズに苦しみ続けたプライアーは、歴史の生き証人となるべく、地上へと戻るのである。また、第2部では、モルモン教の受難の歴史も語られているが、ニューヨーク州から西部ソルト・レイク・シティーへと迫害されながら約束の地を求め続けたモルモン教徒たちの旅路もまた、『エンジェルズ・イン・アメリカ』の基本的な歴史観と共通する。

　第2部のエピローグは、セントラル・パークの中心よりやや南側に位置するベセズダの噴水が舞台となっている。「国家的テーマについてのゲイ・ファンタジア」という副題を持つ『エンジェルズ・イン・アメリカ』の最終場面を飾るにふさわしく、ベセズダの噴水の天使像(*the Angel of the Waters*, 1873)は、レズビアンの女性彫刻家エマ・ステビンズ(Emma Stebbins, 1815–1882)が南北戦争の戦死者を追悼するために建造したものである。つまり、同性愛と国家の歴史という要素がこの天使像には、濃縮されているのである。また、ベセズダの噴水は、ユダヤ人の国家であった古代イスラエルに存在したと言われる、病に苦しむ人々の身体や精神を癒した同名の噴水をモデルにしたものである。ベセズダの天使像と噴水は、作品中でプライアーが解説しているように、死者を追悼するものの、死のない世界を暗示し、その天使の翼は、石や鉄でできた非常に重いものではあるが、飛行の際のエンジンとなるのである(Kushner 1995: 279)。

　『エンジェルズ・イン・アメリカ』の最後でベセズダの噴水に集まった登場人物たちは、人種、エスニシティー、宗教、ジェンダー、セクシュアリティーの点において実に多様性に富んでいる。プライアーはワ

スプのゲイであり、ルイスはユダヤ系のゲイ、ハンナはヘテロセクシュアルの女性のモルモン教徒、ベリーズは黒人のゲイである。そして、プライアーは、エイズの新薬であるAZTの投薬が功を奏し、まだ生きている。

このエピローグは、エピローグでありながらも、『エンジェルズ・イン・アメリカ』の全体の中において非常に重要な意味を持ち、ベンヤミンの歴史観に基盤を置いた作品のテーマを集約的に表している。『エンジェルズ・イン・アメリカ』は、エイズによって再び受難の時代を迎えたゲイたちが、大きな歴史のうねりの中で、差別や無関心に直面しながらも前向きに生きてゆくことを声高に訴えている。プライアーは、エイズと闘病するゲイの代表として、たとえエイズによって命を落とすことになる者がいたとしても、今までのようにその死は恥じたり、隠匿されるべきものでは決してないと宣言するのである (Kushner 1995: 280)。

クシュナーが、多様性に富んだ背景を持ち、相互に人間関係を結ぶに至った登場人物を配置したことは、アメリカに新しい時代のユートピアを建設する目標と密接に関連してくる。第2部において、ジュディー・ガーランド (Judy Garland, 1922–1969) が主演した『オズの魔法使い』(*The Wizard of Oz*, 1939) の歌の一部が歌われる場面が出てくる。ジュディー・ガーランドは、ゲイたちにとって偶像視されるカリスマ的な存在であり、1969年6月の彼女の葬儀が、ゲイ解放運動の嚆矢となるストーン・ウォール暴動の引き金になったことは広く知られている (Kaiser 1997: 192–202)。また、『エンジェルズ・イン・アメリカ』は各所にゲイ文化のアイコンが散りばめられ、作品中でプライアーとロイ・コーンが中心的な役割を果たすことからも、作品の大きな基調は、ゲイのユートピアの建設を目指していることは間違いのないことである。クシュナーは、基本的にはゲイの理想郷の建設を目指しているのだが、ベセズダの噴水の場面で、3人のゲイの中に、ヘテロセクシュアルでモルモン教徒の女性であるハンナを投入し、ハンナが彼らと人間関係を結ぶことによって、はるかに多様なマイノリティー連合による多元文化主義的なユートピアの建設を志向しているのである。

そして、そのユートピアの象徴的な存在になるのが、ベセズダの噴水である。ベセズダの噴水は、ニューヨークの厳冬期である2月には、パイプの中の水は凍りつき、噴水から水が流れ出ることはない。しかし、冬が終わり春が来れば、再び水が流れ出すのである。この事実は、一度枯渇した旧イスラエルに存在したベセズダの噴水が、至福千年紀に再び水をたたえ、人々の再生に寄与するという伝承とリンクする。ニューヨーク、マンハッタンのほぼ中心に位置するベセズダの噴水と天使像は、1980年代の保守的なレーガン政権の影響下においてエイズによって壊滅的な打撃を受けたゲイたちの再生と東西冷戦終結後の新しい時代のユートピア建設に向けての果敢な飛躍を象徴的に表し、ニューヨークを、クシュナーが『エンジェルズ・イン・アメリカ』の中で説くベンヤミン流の「進歩」について、アメリカひいては世界に発信するキー・ステーションとするのである。

注

1. *The Cambridge Companion to the Literature of New York* において、『エンジェルズ・イン・アメリカ』とニューヨークとの相関関係について、14章の "Staging lesbian and gay New York" で取り上げられている (211) ものの、紹介の域を超えていない。
2. 『エンジェルズ・イン・アメリカ』第1部並びに第2部の本文の邦訳は、すべて拙訳である。

参考文献

ヴォルター・ベンヤミン (2011)『ベンヤミン・コレクション 1―近代の意味』浅井健二郎編訳、筑摩書房

Bernstein, Robin. (2010) Staging lesbian and gay New York. *The Cambridge Companion to the Literature of New York.* Cambridge: Cambridge University Press.

Bigsby, Christopher. (1999) *Contemporary American Playwrights.* Cambridge: Cambridge University Press.

Burns, Ric. (2003) *New York: An Illustrated History.* New York: Knopf.

Chauncey, George. (1994) *Gay New York: Gender, Urban Culture, and the Making of the*

Gay Male World 1890–1940. New York: Basic Books.

Cunningham, Michael. (1998) Thinking about Fabulousness. *Tony Kushner in Conversation*. Ed. Robert Vorlicky. Ann Arbor: University Press of Michigan. 62–76.

Fisher, James. (2001) *The Theater of Tony Kushner: Living Past Hope*. New York and London: Routledge.

Jackson, Kenneth T., ed. (1995) *The Encyclopedia of New York City*. New Haven and London: Yale University Press.

Kaiser, Charles. (1997) *The Gay Metropolis: The Landmark History of Gay Life in America since World War Two*. New York: Harcourt Brace.

Kushner, Tony. (1995) *Angels in America: A Gay Fantasia on National Themes*. New York: TCG.

Leer, David Van. (1995) *The Queening of America: Gay Culture in Straight Society*. New York and London: Routledge.

Miller, Carl. (1996) *Stages of Desire: Gay Theatre's Hidden History*. New York and London: Cassell.

Pacheco, Patrick R. (1998) Thinking about Fabulousness. *Tony Kushner in Conversation*. Ed. Robert Vorlicky. Ann Arbor: University Press of Michigan. 51–61.

スーザン・ソンタグ(2010)『反解釈』高橋康也他訳、筑摩書房

Internet Broadway Database (http://www.ibdb.com/)

ハーレム・ルネサンスにおける
プリミティヴィズムとネグロフィリア
『新しい黒人(ニューニグロ)』とアーロン・ダグラス

中地 幸

要旨

ハーレム・ルネッサンスの金字塔といえるアレン・ロック編纂の『新しい黒人』において「黒人性」および「アフリカ」がどのように特徴づけられているかを検証し、アーロン・ダグラスの芸術を考察することにより、アフリカン・アメリカン・モダニズム文学と芸術における「プリミティヴィズム」と「ネグロフィリア」の特殊な役割を明らかにする。

キーワード　プリミティヴィズム、ネグロフィリア、『新しい黒人(ニューニグロ)』、アーロン・ダグラス、アフリカン・アメリカン・モダニズム

1. はじめに

1920年代から1930年代にかけての西洋モダニズム芸術はアール・デコによって特徴づけられる。アール・デコは「速さと新しさ、異国性と官能性を表象する」(ウッド 2005: 10) 様式として、1920年代初頭までにアール・ヌーヴォーと入れ替わった。アール・ヌーヴォーが流れるような曲線や自然のモチーフを使ったいわば反工業的で反近代的な美の様式だとすれば、アール・デコは産業主義の躍動感を直線的幾何学模様で表象した大量生産的で工業主義的な近代装飾芸術様式であった。1925年にパリで開かれた現代産業装飾国際博覧会は、アール・デコを時代の最先端デザインとして提示することに成功したと言われている[1]。

アール・デコの波はアメリカにも押し寄せた。ニューヨークでは 1927 年にアール・デコ様式のクライスラー・ビルが着工されており、ニューヨークの摩天楼の多くは 1930 年代までに建設されている。1920 年代のアメリカは「ジャズ・エイジ」と呼ばれ、その名称通りアフリカ系アメリカ人文化が主流文化と混淆し、商品化された時代でもあった。そもそもフランスにおいて、アール・デコ装飾芸術は、「プリミティヴィズム（原始主義）」や「ネグロフィリア（黒人びいき）」など異国的（エキゾチック）な要素を備えた「帝国主義の意匠」といわれるが[2]、非西洋芸術への傾斜はアメリカのアール・デコにも顕著に見られる。しかし、アメリカにおいて、黒人は単なる植民地的他者ではなかった。すでに奴隷制の時代を通して、アメリカには、「アンクルトム」や「サンボ」、「マミー」、「ジェザベル」、「サファイア」といった人種差別的な黒人のステレオタイプが流通していた[3]。

このようなステレオタイプに対しアフリカ系アメリカ人が強く抵抗を示し、黒人イメージの再構築をはかったのが、ハーレム・ルネサンスと呼ばれる 1920 年代のアフリカ系アメリカ人によるモダニズム芸術運動である。その金字塔とも言われる『新しい黒人（ニューニグロ）』において、哲学者アレン・ロックは「古い黒人」とは全く違った精神を持つ「新しい黒人」の出現を「新しい精神が大衆の中に目覚めた」（Locke 1925b: 3）と言って、高らかに謳いあげた。ロックの巻頭エッセイ「新しい黒人」は、ハーレム・ルネサンスの思想的マニフェストと考えられる。

しかしハーレム・ルネサンスについて、ネーサン・ハギンズは、それが白人によって主導されたものであったと批判した（Huggins 1991: 85）。またデヴィッド・レバリング・ルイスは、「ハーレム・ルネサンスは、やや強いられた現象であり、人種関係を改善するという最大の目的のために公民権運動の指導者たちにより組織的に推進され方向づけられた文化ナショナリズムと言えるものだった」（Lewis 1979: xxviii）とそれが純粋な内発的芸術運動でなかったことを指摘している。さらにヘンリー・ルイス・ゲイツ・ジュニアは、ハーレム・ルネッサンスはオーラルな伝統に基づいた黒人美学を白人中産階級的なものへと変容させたと

して、その欠点をあげている (Gates Jr. 1987: xxiii)。確かにハーレム・ルネッサンスには白人パトロンの影響が強かったことは否めない。『ハーヴェイ・グラフィック』の編集長ポール・ケロッグ、ハーレムの「ゴッドマザー」シャーロット・メイソン、写真家で作家のカール・ヴァン・ヴェクテン、バーンズ・コレクションのアルバート・C・バーンズ、ハーモン基金のウィリアム・E・ハーモンなどの白人たちが発言力を持っていたことは確かであり、西洋アール・デコ芸術の特徴ともいえるプリミティヴィズムやネグロフィリアも顕著に見られる[4]。

しかしハーレム・ルネッサンスが外部的力によってのみ方向づけられたとする見解は、その内部的力を見損なう危険性を伴う。本論文では、ハーレム・ルネッサンスのダイナミズムを明らかにするために、ハーレム・ルネサンス研究の中で最も論争を巻き起こす問題の1つである黒人による黒人のためのプリミティヴィズムとネグロフィリアについて考察していきたい。いったいアフリカ系アメリカ人芸術家の「ブラック・デコ」[5]とは何だったのか。この点を『新しい黒人』に焦点をあて考察し、その上でハーレム・ルネッサンスを代表する芸術家アーロン・ダグラスの芸術作品について論じていきたい思う。

2. 『新しい黒人』における「黒人性」

20世紀初頭のアメリカでは、1896年のプレッシー対ファーガソン裁判の判決によって出された「分離すれども平等」という考えのもと、公共施設や交通機関での黒人分離を当然とするジム・クロウ法が運用されていた。このような差別的状況を甘んじて受け入れてきた黒人指導者ブッカー・T・ワシントン[6]をW・E・Bデュボイスは『黒人の魂』において痛裂に批判し[7]、新しい公民権運動の旗手としてハーレムに登場した。1909年、デュボイスはNAACP（全国黒人地位向上協会）を設立し、1910年にはその機関誌として文芸雑誌『クライシス』（図1）を創刊している[8]。『クライシス』は、『メッセンジャー』や『オポチュニティ』（図2）といった雑誌とともに、ハーレム・ルネサンスの礎を築く

役割を果たした。

『クライシス』の趣旨を受け継いだ『新しい黒人』は、1925年3月に「新しい黒人」特集号を出版した雑誌『サーヴェイ・グラフィック』を1冊の本に組み直したものである[9]。『新しい黒人』は、随筆、評論、小説、詩、音楽、美術他、書誌情報など網羅的に扱ったアンソロジーであり、その全般的な装飾はドイツ人画家ヴィーノルド・ライスが担当し、アフリカ的イメージや幾何学模様ほか、アフリカ美術の写真が本の随所に挿入された。また口絵としてライス画の「ブラウン・マドンナ」が置かれた（図3）。「ブラウン・マドンナ」は奴隷制時代のステレオタイプとは違う新しい黒人女性を表象した[10]。

『新しい黒人』の巻頭エッセイにおけるロックの主張は、1) 芸術において黒人は真剣に探求される対象となるべきである、2) 新しい黒人はアメリカの新しい民主主義の基軸となるべきである、3) アメリカ黒人は世界中に散らばった黒人と結束し、アフリカの将来的発展のために尽力すべきである、という3点にまとめることができる。3点目はデュボイスの主張とも通じる。デュボイスは「アメリカ黒人に先導され、世界の黒人たちは知り合い、情を等しくし、話し合うために、お互いに手を伸ばしあう」(DuBois 1925: 412) とアメリカ黒人を中心とした世界の黒人の結束の可能性を語った。

このような「黒人性」に重きを置いた考え方は、『新しい黒人』の黒人文学論や芸術論にも共通するものである。「黒人の若者は語る」においてロックはアメリカ黒人特有の経験（奴隷制や差別経験）や人種への愛着をアフリカ系アメリカ人文学の特徴であると述べている (Lock 1925c: 47–53)。またアルバート・C・バーンズは「黒人芸術とアメリカ」において、黒人は感情的な豊かさを祖先から受け継いでいるので豊かな芸術を作ることができると主張する (Barnes 1925: 19–28)。さらに J. A. ロジャーズは「アメリカにおけるジャズ」において、ジャズをアメリカ黒人の「精神」と定義している (Roger 1925: 216–24)。そのほか、ウィリアム・スタンレー・ブレイスウェイトやアーサー・ハフ・フォーセットが黒人文学論を寄せているが (Braithwaite 1925: 29–44, Fauset 1925:

238-44)、彼らも抑圧された経験や生まれつきの芸術的感覚を「黒人らしさ」と捉え、黒人伝統に基づいた芸術作品の創造の必要性を主張している。

　文学作品の中では、ラングストン・ヒューズの「黒人、川を語る」が『新しい黒人』のイデオロギーを表現した詩として注目に値するだろう。

　　私は川を知っている
　　私は世界と同じくらい古く、人間の血脈の血の流れよりも古い川を
　　知っている
　　私の魂は川のように深くなった
　　私は文明の夜明けにユーフラテス川で水浴びをした
　　私はコンゴ川の近くに小屋を建て、そこで川が私を寝かしつけた
　　私はナイル川を見わたし、そこにピラミッドを立てた

　　私はエイブラハム・リンカーンがニューオーリンズに下ったときに
　　ミシシッピ川の歌声を聴いた
　　私は川の泥色が日没で黄金に変わるのを見た

　　私は川を知っている
　　古く、濁れる川を
　　私の魂は川のように深くなった　　　　　（Hughes 1925: 141）

　ヒューズはこの詩において時空を超えた「私」という普遍的な黒人存在を作り出し、その「私」をエジプトやチグリス・ユーフラテス文明の創造者として描きだし、さらにそれをミシシッピ川の流れるアメリカ南部で労働を強いられた黒人奴隷と結び付けた。つまりヒューズはアフリカ文化の継承者としてアメリカ黒人を位置づけ、アメリカ黒人を中心としたブラック・ナショナリズムを抒情的に謳いあげたのである。この詩に表現されるように、ハーレム・ルネサンスは「黒人性」に国際的な色彩を与えようとする意志に貫かれていた。アール・デコの越境的様式さ

ながら、「黒人」とは、「非西洋」と「西洋」、「過去」と「現在」、「プリミティブなもの」と「モダンなもの」を結びつける重要な精神的媒体であり、世界を接合するキーワード的存在として提示されたのである。

3. 「二重の意識」と異化される「アフリカ」

　しかし常に原始性と結び付けられる「黒人性」はハーレム・ルネサンスの黒人指導者たちにとって悩ましい問題であったことも事実である。デュボイスは『黒人の魂』において、「アメリカ人であることと、黒人であること——2つの魂、2つの思想、2つの折り合わない熱望」(DuBois 1903: 5)を「二重の意識」と呼び、アメリカ黒人の歴史はこの二重の自己を統一しようする熱望の歴史であると述べた。「黒人性」は、アメリカ黒人に「苦痛に満ちた自意識、病的といっていいような人間観、また自身にとって致命的である精神的な躊躇」(DuBois 1903: 164)をもたらすものとデュボイスは考えていた。

　このような懊悩は、『新しい黒人』においては、カウンティ・カレンの「遺産」という詩の中にも見出すことができる。詩の第1節においてカレンはアフリカを賛美する。

　　　アフリカは私にとって何だろう
　　　赤銅の太陽と緋色の海、
　　　ジャングルの星とジャングルの道、
　　　赤褐色の強い男たちと堂々たる黒い
　　　女たちの股から私は生まれたのだ
　　　エデンの鳥が鳴くのはいつだろうか　　　　　(Cullen 1925: 250)

　アフリカは原始の自然が残された、人間が原罪をおかす前の「エデン」である。赤のイメージがその原始性を強烈に印象づける。またアフリカは「香しき森と菩提樹の木」の土地とユートピア化される。しかし、詩の後半ではアフリカの異端性が強調されるにいたる。

僕の改宗には高い代価がついた
僕は、謙遜の説教者
イエス・キリストに属する
異教の神々は無関係だ——
奇妙で、奇異な異教の神々を
黒人たちは棒切れや
粘土や、脆い石の破片から作り出す
自分たちの姿に似せて　　　　　　　　　　　（Cullen 1925: 252）

　カレンにとってアフリカとは、キリスト教者としての自己の存在を危機に陥れるものであり、一種の脅迫観念でさえある。ここでアフリカ人は棒切れや石で作った奇妙な神々を偶像視する野蛮な民族として捉えられている。異端なアフリカの血を引き継いでいることに対するカレンの不安は、デュボイスが抱えた不安とも通じるといえるだろう。アフリカの「原始性」は彼が「完全」なアメリカ人になることを邪魔するのである。
　しかしながら、全体を通して『新しい黒人』は悲観的ではない。興味深いのは、『新しい黒人』の第2部の中におさめられた「黒人のアメリカニズム」という文化人類学者メルヴィル・J・ハースコヴィッツの随筆である (Herskovits 1925: 353-60)。ハースコヴィッツはアメリカ黒人が、文化的にアフリカ人ではなくアメリカ人であるということを強調している。つまりここで「アフリカ」はアメリカ黒人から完全に切り離されている[11]。この主張はロックの「先祖の芸術の遺産」にも表れている (Locke 1925a: 254-67)。ここでロックは、アメリカ黒人芸術はアフリカ芸術とは違っていると強調する。すなわちアメリカ黒人芸術とアフリカ芸術に、精神的、感情的類似性があるとみなすのは全くの誤解であり、アフリカ芸術へのアメリカ黒人のリアクションは西洋人のそれと全く同じであると述べている。しかしアフリカ芸術はヨーロッパの現代アートにぬきさしならぬ影響を与えており、そうしたヨーロッパの芸術家の作品は新しいアメリカ黒人芸術家のインスピレーションとなり、ま

た模範となるべきである、とロックは主張するのである。そうすることにより、アメリカ黒人芸術家は、黒人のステレオタイプを打ち崩し、黒人表象の新しいスタイルを見つけていくだろうとロックは考える。

　このように『新しい黒人』において「黒人性」は強調されるものの、「アフリカ」は遠く、離れたものとして、異化される。基本的には、黒人はアメリカに連れてこられた時にアフリカ文化を失ったという考え方が取られるのである[12]。こうして内的不安を取り除いた上で、彼らが問題とするのは「新しい黒人」すなわち「黒人のアメリカ人」のアイデンティティの確立であった。ロックはアフリカ芸術を全く異質なものと捉えながらも、それが新しい黒人モダニズムの機動力として役に立つと考えていた。つまりイメージとしての「アフリカ」や「黒人性」は有効なものとされ、ヨーロッパ経由のアール・デコの「ネグロフィリア」と「プリミティヴィズム」は、アメリカ黒人にとっても新しい意味構築のトポスを提供すると考えられたのである。

4.　ダグラスのアメリカン・ニュー・プリミティヴィズム

　さてここで目をハーレム・ルネサンスの視覚芸術のほうに向けていきたい。ライスの「ブラウン・マドンナ」が示すように「混血」が「新しい黒人」の表象に使われたのは、黒人と同時にアメリカ人（白人）であろうとする「新しい黒人」たちの欲望の視覚的表現と考えられるが、ハーレム・ルネサンスの芸術家たちは単純化されたラインを使うブラック・デコにもおおいに興味を示した。しかも、ブラック・デコを促進したのは単に白人たちではない。アフリカ系アメリカ人芸術家たちがブラック・デコに自己表現の新しい可能性を見たのである。本論文ではこの例として、ハーレム・ルネッサンスを代表するアフリカ系アメリカ人芸術家アーロン・ダグラスを取りあげて考えたい。

　ダグラスは 1899 年にカンザス州トピカに生まれた[13]。1922 年にネブラスカ大学の芸術学部を卒業し、カンザスシティのリンカーン高校で教師の職を得るが、1925 年にはニューヨークに移住し、以後、『新しい黒

人』ほか、ハーレム・ルネッサンスの代表的な雑誌である『クライシス』や『オポチュニティ』、『ファイヤー』、『サーヴェイ・グラフィック』の表紙や挿絵、またジェームズ・ウェルドン・ジョンソン、クロード・マッケイ、ラングストン・ヒューズ、カウンティ・カレン、ウォーレス・サーマン、カール・ヴァン・ヴェクテンなどの作家たちの作品の表紙絵や広告を描き、ハーレム・ルネッサンスの文芸運動を視覚的側面から支えた。1929年にはテネシー州の名門黒人大学フィスク大学の図書館の壁画を手掛け、その後フィスク大学の教員として迎えられ、芸術学科の主任として1966年に退職するまでアフリカ系アメリカ人学生の教育にたずさわった。彼の巨大な油絵は現在フィスク大学、及びハーレムにあるニューヨーク公立図書館の読書室の壁に掛けられている。ダグラスは1979年に80歳の生涯を終えた。

「私は新しく、モダンなものを作りたかった。アメリカに旋風を引き起こしていたアール・デコなどの芸術にふさわしい何かを作りたかった。それでキュビスムや事物との数理的関係を強調したような直線を多く使うという考えに至ったのである」とダグラスは述べているが（Driskell 2007: 89–90）、注目すべき点は彼がヨーロッパ芸術、とりわけ「アール・デコ」様式に強い興味を示していたことである。ロックの理想と同様、ダグラスが求めたのは、ヨーロッパにおけるプリミティヴィズムのアメリカ的応用、すなわち「アメリカン・ニュー・プリミティヴィズム」（Goeser 2007: 25）の確立であった。この意味において、ダグラスの芸術が、彼の師匠であるドイツ人画家ヴィーノルド・ライスの模倣に始まったことは驚くにあたらない。

ライスはオハイオ州シンシナティの鉄道駅の壁画の作者として知られているが[14]、アメリカのモダニズム芸術運動で重要な役割を果たした人物である[15]。1886年にドイツのカールスルーエに生まれ、ミュンヘンの応用芸術学校でアートを勉強した。ミュンヘンでは、カンディンスキーが中心となった青騎士の母体でもあるミュンヘン新芸術家協会が1901年に発足しており、おそらくライスはその影響下にあったと思われる。1913年にアメリカに移民として渡り、旅をしながらブラックフッ

ト族などアメリカ先住民の肖像画を描いた。またホテルやレストランの内装や外装のデザインの仕事をした。1915年には『モダン・アート・コレクター』という雑誌の創刊にも関わっている。1920年にはメキシコに足を延ばし、アステカ・インディアンを描いた。またハーレム・ルネッサンスの雑誌にも挿絵や肖像画を描くようになった。ダグラスにアフリカ的モチーフを基盤にアメリカ黒人解釈のデザインを発展させるよう指導したのはライスだという (Goeser 2007: 26)。

　ダグラスはライスから、アール・デコ、キュビスム、フォービスムといった西洋芸術様式を十二分に吸収したようだが、それ以上に、ダグラスはライスの模倣といってもおかしくないほど類似した作品を作り出した。例えば1925年の『ハーヴェイ・グラフィック』誌はライスの「ハーレムの夜明け」(図4) を掲載しているが、左右にビルがそびえたち、中心に層をなした日輪が広がる風景は、1934年にダグラスが描いた壁画「ニグロの生の諸相—塔の歌」(図5) の構図と類似している。またダグラスのトレードマークは黒いシルエットだが、このシルエット手法がライスゆずりであることは、1923年に刊行されたイギリス人作家ルフェリン・ポーイズの『エボニーとアイヴォリー』のためにライスが描いた表紙絵からも明らかである (図6)。1926年の『オポチュニティ』の表紙においてダグラスは、グラデーションで人物などの輪郭をとるライスの手法を応用している (図7)。またダグラスの作品のアシンメトリーな構図はライスから学んだものといえるだろう。ハーレム・ルネッサンスのイメージを強烈に提示するダグラスの芸術は、決してオリジナルなものとは言い難いのである。

　しかしながら、ダグラスの芸術が単にライスの作品の模倣に終わらなかった点は、奇しくも、壁画というライス譲りの分野において発揮されている[16]。ダグラスの芸術がいわゆるアール・デコ芸術と異なる点は、人物たちに託される感情の表現、そしてまたその絵画が歴史的な物語を担っている点といえるだろう。ジェームズ・A・ポーターはダグラスの人物像を想像上のエキゾティシズムとして痛烈に批判したが (Porter 1969: 114)、注意したいのはダグラスが使う人物たちの輪郭である。19

世紀の人種差別主義者の描く典型的な黒人シルエットを使う現代アフリカ系アメリカ人アーティスト、キャラ・ウォーカーの作品のシルエットと比べれば一目瞭然だが、ダグラスは、大胆に単純化された形を使い、新しいタイプのシルエットを作り出している (Goeser 2007: 21)。ライスにおいては、黒人たちは細い胴体や長く細い手足の持ち主であり、どこかエキゾチックな存在だが、ダグラスの描く黒人たちは1920年代のものはライスに近いものの、1930年代になると次第に強く、雄々しくなっていく。とりわけ壁画に描かれるのは尊厳ある黒人像である。つまりダグラスは、ライスに倣いながらも、黒人をエキゾチックな他者として見るアール・デコ様式を無批判に受け入れたわけではなかった。様式に従い、黒人を装飾として図象化しながら、同時にその姿に尊厳ある主体性を与える努力をしたのである。ここではイメージの置換が巧妙に行われているといえる。

またダグラスの作品を特徴づけるものには、民族的記憶へのこだわりがあるといえるだろう。アール・デコ芸術は基本的には都市型で未来志向であるが、ダグラスの壁画は、アフリカ系アメリカ人の奴隷制の過去を模索している。スフィンクスといったエジプトの神話的イメージ、また逃亡奴隷が逃亡の際に道しるべにしたと言われる北極星のイメージを使い、アフリカ系アメリカ人の奴隷制における苦難の歴史を神話化し物語化しているのである。また都市イメージと黒人を組み合わせるアール・デコの手法を使い、ダグラスは過去から現在、そして未来への時間的流れを表現することに成功している（図8）。高くそびえ立つ高層ビルは、ダグラスにおいては、「人種的地位向上」のメタファーでもある。さらに壁画では「コミュニティ」が強調されている。複数の人物たちは喜びや苦しみを分かち合う「同士」として描かれる。

アール・デコ装飾には、アフリカ、中米、中国、日本といった広範囲な非西欧世界からの造形が取り入れられており、それが西洋芸術に取り入れられる際には常にハイブリッドな特質を帯びた。ダグラスの試みはその範囲にとどまるものではあるが、その表象の中で行われた様々な転向、とりわけ政治的転向が視覚的に行われていることは見逃してはなら

ないだろう。ブラック・デコという西洋の美術形式を用いながら、ダグラスはその帝国主義的イデオロギーを反転させた。反植民地主義、ブラック・ナショナリズム、そして公民権運動時代に炸裂するブラック・パワーへの希求は、確実にここに表現されているのである。ダグラスの作品は、雑誌や壁画など、集団によって共有される空間に置かれたことにより、20世紀のアフリカ系アメリカ文化を構築し先導する役割を果たしたともいえる。さらに壁画芸術においてダグラスはアフリカ系アメリカ人によるアメリカの国家叙事詩を完成させたのである。それは20世紀アメリカの「ブラック・ヒストリー」であった。

5. むすびにかえて

ハーレム・ルネッサンスはダグラスのみならず、多くのアフリカ系アメリカ人芸術家に支えられた。アーチボールト・モトレイ、パーマー・ヘイデン、サージェント・クロード・ジョンソン、ロイス・メイルー・ジョーンズ、リチャード・ブルース・ヌージェント、チャールズ・オルストン、オーガスタ・サヴェッジ、そしてジェーコブ・ローレンスやロメア・ビアデンなどがモダニズムのアフリカ系アメリカ人芸術を模索した[17]。ハーレム・ルネサンスは一枚岩の運動ではなく対抗的文化の融合と衝突により、時にその境界線を危うくしながら進化を遂げたといえる。

ところで、アール・デコが「共産主義かファシズムのいずれかの表明」（ヒリアー 1986: 86）として権力への賛美の形式に加担していくのは1930年代であるが[18]、ハーレム・ルネサンスの文学者および芸術家たちの多くが1930年代には共産主義へと傾いていくのは決して偶然ではなかったのかもしれない[19]。この点は1930年代の連邦政府によるニューディール政策の中の公共芸術政策との関連を踏まえた上で、また別の機会に稿を改めて論じていきたい。

注

1. この点は天野知香『装飾・芸術―19–20世紀のフランスにおける「芸術」の位相』(ブリュッケ、2001年)の第一部を参照。なおアール・ヌーヴォー、アール・デコに関する全般的な情報は、海野弘『アール・ヌーボーの世界』(中央文庫、2001年)、海野弘『アール・デコの時代』(中央文庫、2005年)、千足伸行監修『アール・ヌーヴォーとアール・デコ 甦る黄金時代』(小学館、2001年)、およびイギリス、ヴィクトリア・アルバート美術館のウエブサイトの "Art Deco" ⟨http://www.vam.ac.uk/page/a/art-deco/⟩ を参考にした。

2. 天野知香「アールデコの位相―装飾芸術／ブラック・デコ／モダン・ガール」『アール・デコ―きらめくモダンの夢』15–28頁参照。1931年パリで開催された植民地博覧会によるブラック・デコは明確に可視化されたという。

3. Deborah Gray White の *Ar'n't I a Woman: Female Slaves in the Plantation* (New York: Norton, 1999) にはアフリカ系アメリカ人女性のステレオタイプが奴隷制の中で形成され、利用されたことが書かれている。また人種ステレオタイプについては Kenneth W. Goings, *Mammy and Uncle Mose: Black Collectibles and American Stereotyping* (Bloomington: Indiana University Press, 1994) が詳しい。

4. この点は Amy Helene Kirchke, *Aaron Douglas: Art, Race and the Harlem Renaissance* (Jackson: University Press of Mississippi, 1995) の第3章が詳しい。

5. 「ブラック・デコ」は美術批評家ロザリンド・クラウスがジャコメッティのプリミティヴィズムについて論じる上で用いた用語である。Rosalind E. Krauss, *The Originality of the Avvant-Garde and Other Modern Myths* (Cambridge: MIT Press, 1986), 48頁を参照。また天野知香は「時代の兆候―アールデコとその周辺」でこの用語を説明した上で、アフリカ性を喚起するモダンな様式と定義している。なおアールデコとアメリカ黒人という題材で常に取り上げられるジョセフィン・ベイカーは、本論文ではあえて取りあつかわなかったが、「黒いヴィーナス」ジョセフィン・ベイカーはその舞台だけでなく、フランス人画家ポール・コランのポスターおよび版画集において図版化されたことによりフランスのアール・デコ文化には欠かせない存在となっている。

6. Washinton のアトランタでのスピーチは自伝 *Up from the Slavery* の第14章に収められている。なおこのスピーチにより Washington が1895年の Frederick Douglas の死後、最も強い黒人指導者となったと Kevin K. Gaines は *Uplifting the Race: Black Leadership, Politics, and Cuture in the Twentieth Century* (Chapel Hill: University of North Carolina P, 1996) に書いている (39)。

7. W. E. B. DuBois, *The Souls of Black Folk* (1903. New York: Penguin, 1989) の第3章 "Or Mr. Booker T. Washington and Others" において DuBois の Washignton

への批判は展開されている。
8. 『クライシス』についての情報は、Sondra Kathryn Wilson, "Introduction." *The Crisis Reader*. Ed. Sondra Kathryn Wilson. New York: Modern Library, 1999) を参考にした。
9. 『サーヴェイ・グラフィック』の黒人特集はロックが編集したが、4万部もの売り上げを記録したという。『新しい黒人』への組み直しについては Martha Lane Nadell, *Enter the New Negro: Images of Race in American Culture* (Cambridge: Harvard University Press, 2004) が詳しい。
10. 「ブラウン・マドンナ」のような「混血女性」がハーレム・ルネッサンス芸術で頻繁に使われたことの意味は Cherene Sherrard-Johnson, *Portraits of the New Negro Woman: Visual and Literary Culture in the Harlem Renaissance* (New Brunswick: Rutgers University Press, 2007) を参照。
11. しかしながら Herskovits は1941年に出版した *The Myth of the Negro Past* においてはアメリカ黒人はアフリカの過去の文化を持っていないという考えには否定的で、むしろそれを受け継いでるという論を展開している。
12. この考えは Herskovits が *The Myth of the Negro Past* を出版するときまでにはほぼ常識となっていたようだが、ここにはハーレム・ルネサンス運動における作為もあるかもしれない。
13. Douglas についての情報は、Stephanie Fox Knappe による "Chronology" in *Aaron Douglas: African American Modernist* (Ed. Susan Earle. New Haven: Yale University Press, 2007), 207–34 および Amy Helene Kirchke, *Aaron Douglas: Art, Race and the Harlem Renaissance* (Jackson: University Press of Mississippi, 1995) を参考にした。
14. ライスの壁画は1933年にオープンしたシンシナティ・ユニオン駅に飾られていたが、現在は鉄道が閉鎖されたため、鉄道駅は美術館(シンシナティ・ミュージアム・センター)へと変わっているが、ライスの壁画はそのまま展示されている。詳しくは美術館サイト〈http://www.cincymuseum.org〉を参照。
15. ライスについては、Alastair Duncan, *American Art Deco* (New York: Thams and Hudson, 1986)、および C. Ford Peatross, "Winold Reiss: A Pioneer of Modern American Design." *Queen City Heritage* (Summer–Fall 1993): 38–57 を参考にした。
16. なおメキシコでは1920年代に壁画運動がディエゴ・リベラらを中心に起こっており民主運動と関わりを見せていた。ダグラスは壁画に取り組むことにより、リベラのような役割を果たしたといえる。
17. アフリカ系アメリカ人美術史については、Shanon F. Patton, *African American*

Art (Oxford: Oxford University Press, 1998)、Samuella Lewis, *African American Art and Artists* (Berkeley: University of California Press, 2003)、Celeste-Marie Bernier, *African American Visual Arts* (Edinburgh: Edinburgh University Press, 2008)を参照。

18. 宮本陽一郎「アメリカのアール・デコ―即興、機械、摩天楼」『アール・デコ展―きらめくモダンの夢』46 頁を参照。
19. William J. Maxwell, *New Negro, Old Left: African American Writing and Communism between the Wars* (New York: Columbia University Press, 1999) が示唆に富む。

参考文献

天野知香．(2001)『装飾・芸術―19-20 世紀のフランスにおける「芸術」の位相』ブリュッケ

天野知香．(2005)「アールデコの位相―装飾芸術/ブラック・デコ/モダン・ガール」『アール・デコ―きらめくモダンの夢』展覧会カタログ　天野知香監修　東京都美術館、福岡市美術館、サントリー・ミュージアム、15-28.

天野知香．(2009)「時代の兆候―アール・デコとその周辺」『ドレスタディ』56 号、京都服飾文化財団

Barnes, Albert C. (1925) Negro Art and America. *The New Negro*. Reprint. Ed. Alain Locke. New York: Simon and Schuster, 1997. 19–28.

Bernier, Celeste-Marie. (2008) *African American Visual Arts*. Edinburgh: Edinburgh University Press.

Braithwaite, William Stanley. (1925) The Negro in American Literature. *The New Negro*, 29–44.

Cullen, Countee. (1925) Heritage. *The New Negro*. 250–53.

Driskell, David C. (2007) Some Observations on Aaron Douglas as Tastemaker in the Renaissance Movement. *Aaron Douglas: African American Modernist*. Ed. Susan Earle. New Heaven: Yale University Press, 89–90.

DuBois, W. E. B. (1903) *The Souls of Black Folk*. Reprint. New York: Penguin, 1989.

DuBois, W. E. B. (1925) The Negro Mind Reaches Out. *The New Negro*, 385–414.

Duncan, Alastair. (1986) *American Art Deco*. New York: Thames and Hudson.

Fauset, Arthur Huff. (1925) American Negro Folk Literature. *The New Negro*, 238–44.

Gaines, Kevin K. (1996) *Uplifting the Race: Black Leadership, Politics, and Culture in the Twentieth Century*. Chapel Hill: University of North Carolina Press.

Gates, Jr., Henry Louis (1987) *Figures in Black: Words, Signs, and the Racial Self*. New York: Oxford University Press.

Goeser, Caroline. (2007) *Picturing the New Negro: Harlem Renaissance Print Culture and Modern Black Identity*. Lawrence: University Press of Kansas.

Goings, Kenneth W. (1994) *Mammy and Uncle Mose: Black Collectibles and American Stereotyping*. Bloomington: Indiana Univesity Press.

ヒリアー、ベヴィス(1986)『アールデコ』西澤信弥訳　パルコ出版

Herskovits, Melville J. (1925) The Negro Americanism. *The New Negro*, 353–60.

Herskovits, Melville J. (1941) *The Myth of the Negro Past*. Reprint. Beacon Press, 1990.

Huggins, Nathan. (1991) *Harlem Renaissance*. New York: Oxford University Press.

Hughes, Languston. (1925) The Negro Speaks of Rivers. *The New Negro*, 141.

Kirchke, Amy Helene. (1995) *Aaron Douglas: Art, Race and the Harlem Renaissance*. Jackson: University Press of Mississippi.

Knappe, Stephanie Fox. (2007) Chronology. *Aaron Douglas: African American Modernist*. Ed. Susan Earle. New Heaven: Yale University Press, 207–34.

Krauss, Rosalind E. (1986) *The Originality of the Avant-Garde and Other Modernist Myths*. Cambridge: MIT Press.

Lewis, David Levering. (1979) *When Harlem Was in Vogue*. New York: Penguin.

Lewis, Samuella. (2003) *African American Art and Artists*. Berkeley: University of California Press.

Locke, Alain. (1925a) The Legacy of the Ancestral Arts. *The New Negro*, 254–67.

Locke, Alain. (1925b) The New Negro. *The New Negro*, 3–25.

Locke, Alain. (1925c) Negro Youth Speaks. *The New Negro*, 47–53.

Maxwell, William J. (1999) *New Negro, Old Left: African American Writing and Communism between the Wars*. New York: Columbia University Press.

宮本陽一郎(2005)「アメリカのアール・デコ―即興、機械、摩天楼」『アール・デコ展―きらめくモダンの夢』展覧会カタログ　天野知香監修　東京都美術館、福岡市美術館、サントリー・ミュージアム、39–46.

Nadell, Martha Lane. (2004) *Enter the New Negros: Images of Race in American Culture*. Cambridge: Harvard University Press.

Patton, Shanon F. (1998) *African American Art*. Oxford: Oxford University Press.

Peatross, C. Ford. (1993) Winold Reiss: A Pioneer of Modern American Design. *Queen City Heritage*: 38–57.

Roger, J. A. Jazz at Home. (1925) *The New Negro*, 216–24.

Porter, James A. (1942) *Modern Negro Art*. Reprint. New York: Arno Press, 1969.

千足伸行監修. (2001)『アール・ヌーヴォーとアール・デコ　甦る黄金時代』小学館

Sherrand-Johnson, Cherene. (2007) *Portraits of the New Negro Woman: Visual and*

Literary Culture in the Harlem Renaissance. New Brunswick: Rutgers University Press.
海野　弘．(2001)『アール・ヌーボーの世界』中央公論新社
海野　弘．(2005)『アール・デコの時代』中央公論新社
Washington, Booker T. (1901) *Up from the Slavery: An Autobiography*. Reprint. New York: Penguin, 1986.
White, Deborah Gray. (1999) *Ar'n't I a Woman: Female Slaves in the Plantation*. New York: Norton.
Wilson, Sondra Kathryn. (1999) Introduction. *The Crisis Reader*. Ed. Sondra Kathryn Wilson. New York: Modern Library.
ウッド、ギレーヌ．(2005)「序」『アール・デコ―きらめくモダンの夢』展覧会カタログ　天野知香監修　東京都美術館、福岡市美術館、サントリー・ミュージアム、9–13.

346　中地　幸

図1　アーロン・ダグラス「黒人女性の担う重荷」『クライシス』表紙（1927年9月）イェール大学所蔵。
Aaron Douglas, *Burden of Black Womanhood*, cover, *The Crisis* (September 1927). Yale Collection of American Literature, Beinecke Rare Book and Manuscript Library, Yale University.

図2　ヴィーノルド・ライス『オポチュニティ』表紙（1925年2月）
Winold Reiss, cover, *Opportunity* (February, 1925). Reproduced with the permission from the Reiss Partnership.

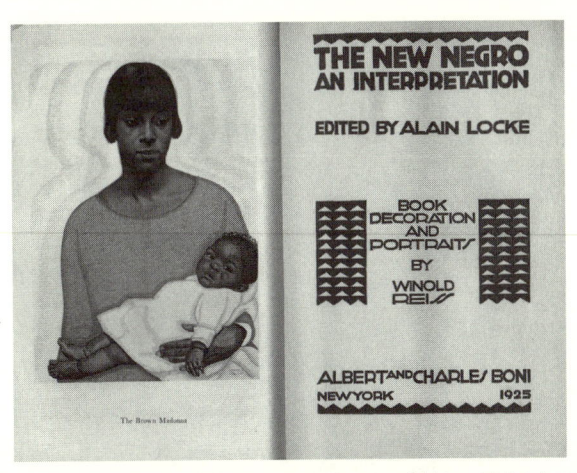

ハーレム・ルネサンスにおけるプリミティヴィズムとネグロフィリア　347

図3　ヴィーノルド・ライス「ブラウン・マドンナ」『新しい黒人』(アレン・ロック編、1925年)
Winold Reiss, "Brown Madonna" *The New Negro* (1925). Reproduced with the permission from the Reiss Partnership.

図4　ヴィーノルド・ライス「ハーレムの夜明け」(1925年)
Winold Reiss. "Dawn in Harlem." 19 3/4 X 14 3/4 inches, ink and wash on paper, ca 1925 Reproduced with the permission of the Reiss Partnership.

図5 アーロン・ダグラス「ニグロの生の諸相―塔の歌」(1934 年)ニューヨーク公共図書館ショーンバーグ黒人文化研究センター所蔵。

(カラー版は口絵参照)

Aaron Douglas, *Aspects of Negro Life: Song of the Towers*, 1934. Oil on canvas.©Art & Artifacts Division, Schomburg Center for Research in Black Culture, The New York Public Library.

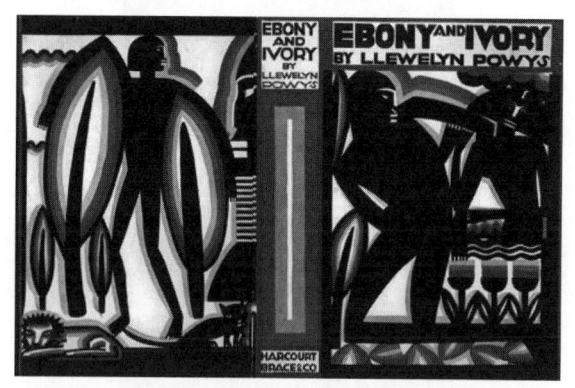

図6 ヴィーノルド・ライス『エボニーとアイヴォリー』表紙(レウェリン・ポーイーズ著、1923 年)

Winold Reiss. Cover, *Ebony and Ivory* (1923). Reproduced with the permission from the Reiss Partnership.

ハーレム・ルネサンスにおけるプリミティヴィズムとネグロフィリア 349

図7 アーロン・ダグラス『オポチュニティ』表紙（1926年2月）イエール大学所蔵。
Aaron Douglas, Cover, *Opportunity* (February, 1926). Yale Collection of American Literature, Beinecke Rare Book and Manuscript Library, Yale University.

図8 アーロン・ダグラス「シカゴの創立」（1933年）カンザス大学スペンサー美術館所蔵。（カラー版は口絵参照）
Aaron Douglas, *The Founding of Chicago*, 1933. Spencer Museum of Art, The University of Kansas, Museum purchase: R. Charles and Mary Margaret Clevenger Fund, 2006. 0027

サッコ＝ヴァンゼッティ事件を語る
シンクレアの『ボストン』とドス・パソスの『USA』

花田　愛

要旨

　アプトン・シンクレアの『ボストン』とジョン・ドス・パソスの『USA』は共にサッコ＝ヴァンゼッティ事件を語る作品である。シンクレアの『ボストン』は、実証主義的手法で裁判記録を読み解き、フィクショナルな語りで時代の傾向や土地に根づく精神をも描き込む。因果的説明とフィクションの両方が相互依存的に共存できるスタイルで、恣意的に作り込まれた〈事実〉の形成過程を再現し、一連の事件そのものがフィクションであることを暴く。一方、ドス・パソスの『USA』は、因果律を手放し無秩序を許容することによって旧来の枠組みに分類されることのない独自のスタイルを生み出し、事件で分断されてしまったアメリカの集合的な歴史を群衆の側の言葉で語ることに成功している。事実とフィクションを区別するということ自体が問い直されるようになった現代において、この 2 つの作品が挑んだ新しい歴史の語り方には大いなる可能性が秘められている。

キーワード　サッコ＝ヴァンゼッティ事件、歴史、フィクション、アメリカ文学

1.　はじめに

　1920 年 4 月 15 日、マサチューセッツ州の古都ボストンの南にあるサウスブレントリーで、製靴会社の現金を運んでいた会計係と警備員が強

盗団に襲われ死亡する。2人のイタリア移民ニコラ・サッコとバルトロメオ・ヴァンゼッティがこの事件の容疑者として逮捕され、有罪判決を受け電気椅子による死刑の宣告を受ける。全世界の著名人や知識人たちがその判決に異を唱えた[1]が、6年以上にもわたる赦免運動もむなしく2人は1927年8月23日に処刑されてしまう。

ヴァンゼッティの声明[2]が示している通り、彼らの命に代わる「勝利」は様々な反響を世に巻き起こす。死刑直後から追悼の詩や戯曲、小説など多くの作品が執筆された。文学以外の芸術分野においても数々の作品が残されている。例えば、画家ベン・シャーンは23点から成る作品群「サッコとヴァンゼッティ」シリーズを描いている。また、映画『死刑台のメロディー』がイタリアとフランスにより合同制作され、音楽の分野でも様々なアーティストが彼らを追悼する歌やオペラ、ミュージカルなどを残している。

2人が刑死してから50年後の1977年、マサチューセッツ州知事マイケル・デュカキスが、裁判は不公正であり、両人とその家族、その子孫から一切の汚名と不名誉が取り除かれると宣言した後も、この事件に関わる作品が生み出され続けている。1999年にはウィリアム・ブレナンによる『ぼろの上着と杖』が出版され、2006年にはピーター・ミラー監督によるドキュメンタリー映画『サッコとヴァンゼッティ』が制作されている。多くの出来事が、忘却されていくにつれて「同時代の記憶」から「歴史的過去」へと徐々に移り変わっていく運命にある中で、サッコ＝ヴァンゼッティ事件を記憶に留めようとする試みが現代においても受け継がれている。

本論文では、こういった数々の試みの嚆矢となった2つの作品に注目する。サッコとヴァンゼッティが刑死したまさにその年にこの事件を語ることを決意した2人の作家がいる。アプトン・シンクレアとジョン・ドス・パソスである[3]。彼らが残した作品『ボストン』と3部作『USA』を検証することで、それぞれがサッコ＝ヴァンゼッティ事件を語るということにどのように取り組んでいるのかを明らかにし、今を生きる私たちが現在と過去を語るためのヒントを探っていきたい。

2. 歴史を語るということ ── 歴史と文学の関係性

　「歴史」という意味を表す英語の history という語は、「調査(inquiry)」や「語り(narrative)」といった意味を持つラテン語の historia に由来すると言われる[4]。過去の出来事を調査して語るという意味合いを与えられた history という語の成り立ちからしても、歴史と物語は本来、不可分なものであった。ところが、小説が飛躍的発展を遂げ歴史小説が流行をみせた 19 世紀、西欧の諸地域では歴史記述をナショナル・ヒストリーへ取り込もうとする動きが加速する。時を同じくして、近代歴史学が事実とフィクションを選別する作業を開始する。歴史記述とは事実だけを実証的に提示することであり、文学的な物語の記述とは異なると主張し、厳密な資料操作に基づく文献史学の方法を追究し始める。近代科学の一領域として晴れてその仲間入りを果たした歴史学は、文学と決別することとなる。対する文学の側は、フィクションの持つ創造性や柔軟性に重きを置き、日常生活からかけ離れた美学を称賛するようになる。文学批評の分野で新批評が広がりを見せた 1940 年代以降には、文学を取り巻く社会的・歴史的背景からテクストを切り離し、自己完結的な作品の言葉や構造を分析することによってそこに文学性を見出し、文学の自律性を謳う流れが主流となる。

　しかし、この文学の文学らしさを追究し学問領域として純化しようとする流れが徐々に滞り始めると、独立性を維持してきた作品をさまざまな体系の中で読み込んでいく作業が進められるようになる。構造主義による言語論的展開以降、内向きだった作品への解釈が多方向に、あるいは多層的に外に開かれるようになり、やがて文学研究における歴史への関心が高まり、ついには文学と歴史学の新しい関係性を見出すニューヒストリシズムが登場する。

　歴史学の領域からも緩やかにではあるが、歩み寄りが見られ始めるようになる。「歴史上の事実は純粋なかたちで存在するものではなく、また、存在し得ないものであるゆえ、決して〈純粋に〉私たちへ現われては来ない。つまり、いつも記録者の心を通して屈折してしまうものなの

だ」(Carr 1961: 22) と述べたのは、近代の歴史学のあり方に疑問を投げかけ、新たな現代の歴史学の立場を表した歴史家E・H・カーである。

そして今日、事実とフィクションとを区別するということ自体が問い直されるようになったポストモダンの知的状況下において、少なくとも文学の分野では事実かフィクションかという旧い二項対立を飛び越えていく用意が整ってきたように思われる[5]。

こうした背景を踏まえた上で、歴史を語るフィクショナルな枠組みの1つとしてシンクレアやドス・パソスの作品を取り上げるとき、それぞれの作品が旧い二項対立をはるかに超越し、新しい歴史の語り方に挑んでいることに気づかされるのである。

3. シンクレアの『ボストン』
——因果的説明とフィクションの共存関係

『ジャングル』、『石油！』と共にアプトン・シンクレアの3大小説の1つとも言われる『ボストン』は、上流階級出身の貴婦人コルネリア・ソーンウェルを主人公とする設定で展開する。彼女の3人の娘たちはすでに成長し、それぞれ社会的に成功した夫と結婚している。60歳になるコルネリアは夫の死をきっかけに家出をする。置き手紙を残してこっそり家を出た彼女は、ノース・プリマスの町でイタリア移民の家に下宿し、職を探し始める。やがて綱工場で袋縫いの仕事に就くことになる彼女は、生まれて初めて単純労働に携わり、自分とは異なる階級の世界を知るようになる。下宿先のブリニ家との暮らしにも溶け込み、同じく下宿人であったバルトロメオ・ヴァンゼッティと意気投合するのである。

著者シンクレアは、この一風変わった作品を「序章」のなかで「現代歴史小説」(Sinclair 2009: xxxv) と形容する。現代と歴史という一見、両立しない概念を連結させたオクシモロン（矛盾撞着語法）とも言えるこのスタイルを選んだ意図はどこにあったのであろうか。この「序章」においてシンクレア自身が、サッコとヴァンゼッティに関する事件、及びそ

れと並行して取り扱われる実業界や金融界の話はこの時代のボストン史の一部であると述べる (Sinclair 2009: xxxv)。実際にサッコ゠ヴァンゼッティ救済委員会にも加わっていたシンクレアは、2人の死後、3,900頁にもおよぶデダムでの裁判記録を参考にしながら本作を執筆し[6]、事件の研究に従事していた12人に原稿をチェックしてもらったことを告白している (Sinclair 2009: xxxvi)。事件に関わる部分とボストンの金融史についてはきわめて実証的に忠実に再現しようとした著者の姿勢が窺われる。

その一方で、シンクレアは自身の旧友で60歳になるときに家出したコルネリアという実在の女性を主人公にしたが、彼女とサッコ゠ヴァンゼッティ事件との関わりは一切なかったことを断わっている (Sinclair 2009: xxxvii)[7]。また、ソーンウェル家を取り巻く銀行業のメロドラマに登場するのは架空の人物であると述べ (Sinclair 2009: xxxv)、実証的な歴史記述にこだわりつつも、そのなかにフィクションを織り交ぜていると言明する。しかし現代に生きる私たちは、いかなる方向からも自由にテクストに入り込むことができる。シンクレアが意識していた事実とフィクションの融合というスタイルは、作者本人の意図はさておき、果たしてどのような体系をうち建てているのだろうか。

ところで、この作品の中でも特に実際の裁判記録を意識しながら記述されていると思われる部分は、サッコとヴァンゼッティが逮捕されてから法廷に舞台を移す第9章以降である。ここで、著者は証人による証言の曖昧性や物的証拠の不当性を立証していく作業に徹している。この作業は、プリマスとデダムでの両方の審理のみならず、その後の裁判のやり直し請求などにおいても繰り返し行われている。

製靴会社の帳簿係メアリー・スプレインは、当時、建物の2階の窓から事件を目撃した1人として証言台に立った。彼女は予審でサッコを3回見分した上で「私の持ち合わせた機会ではその男だという資格はないと思います」(Sinclair 2009: 383) と供述していた。というのも、スプレインが容疑者の乗っていた自動車を目撃できたのは、銃声が鳴り響き騒然とした現場で、時間にしてほんの1〜2秒の間であった。とこ

ろが、実際の証人尋問において彼女は予審の供述を翻し、強盗の容姿をサッコのそれとそっくりに、また驚くほど詳細に「黒い髪、黒い眉毛、こけた頬、きれいに髭を剃った気味悪いほど蒼白い顔」(Sinclair 2009: 383) をしていたと供述する。明らかに信憑性の薄い証言であるにもかかわらず、検察の巧みな尋問によって被告に不利な証言が展開されていくのである。

またローラ・アンドルーズという女性は、犯罪事件に先立つ4時間近く前に自動車を停めていた2人の男に話しかけ、そのうちの1人がサッコだったという証言をした。しかし、被告側の証人ハリー・カアランスキーは、アンドルーズが「お上は私をつかまえていってあの人たちを再認させたいのよ。でも私はあの人たちのことはちっとも知らない。会ったことはないし、再認なんかできないわ。」(Sinclair 2009: 385) と話しているのを聞いたと証言する。これに対して、セーヤー判事がすかさず「君はその女をとらえて虚偽を陳述させようとする、お上を代表するその人物が誰であるかを摘発しようと試みたかね？」(Sinclair 2009: 385) と詰問する。これにカアランスキーは「はい、それは少しも思いつきませんでした。私は良くわきまえてなかったものですから。ちっとも…。」(Sinclair 2009: 385) と答えるのがやっとだった。被告側の証人が核心を突く証言をすると、それを判事が朝三暮四とも思える方法でずらしていくのである。

こういった数々の証言を検証していく中で、読者はある共通した尋問の傾向が浮かび上がってくることに気がつくであろう。それは、多くの証人が「暗示法の犠牲」(Sinclair 2009: 383) になっているということである。もともと証人自身の記憶は曖昧であるのに、効果的な議論や尋問によって、さも〈事実〉であるかのごとき幻想を与えうる証拠を生み出しているのである。裁判記録という原資料に書かれた〈事実〉を蒐集し、並べ、分析し、そこから透けて見える共通性が作品の中に書き込まれているのである。このことは、〈事実〉に忠実でありながら、なおかつその〈事実〉にいかなる順序、いかなる文脈で発言を許すかを決めているのは人間であるということを強烈に知らしめていることにもなる。

また、物的証拠の検証についても同じような傾向が見てとれる。致命弾はサッコの所持していたピストルから発砲されたものではないという鑑定結果が出ていた。州警察署長プロクター警部は審理において婉曲的に「私の意見では、あのピストルによって発射されることはあり得ます」(Sinclair 2009: 402) という答え方をする[8]。語りは次のように続く。

> 言葉のトリックではないか。証人はその致命弾がそのピストルから発射された「かも知れない」と意味している。ところが地方検事は陪審官に向かって、証人の言葉は、それは「間違いなく」そのピストルから発射されたのであって、世界中の他のどのピストルからも発射されたはずはない、というまったく別の意味をもつものとして説明している。　　　　　　　　　　　　(Sinclair 2009: 402)

このように、『ボストン』では検察や判事の審理の進め方が核心的な問答には行き着かず、言葉というものが常に彼らによってごまかしの材料となってしまうことを明らかにしている。すなわちこれは、事実を追求すべきはずの裁判がいかに虚偽の証言や操作されたトリックで塗り固められていくかを再現しているものであり、本来最も実証主義的に事実を調査すべき法廷がフィクショナルなものへと化していく過程を、堂々と同じ手法で、つまり因果的説明によって辿っていくのである。

更に、作品は裁判記録などの原資料には残されていない、この事件に関わる人物たちの動機や傾向性を探っていく。例えば、ヴァンゼッティが法廷で次第にやり込められていってしまう要因の1つを彼の内面的性格に見出す。フィクショナルな登場人物コルネリアの眼を通して描かれるヴァンゼッティは、貧しき者へ寄り添う心を持ち (Sinclair 2009: 40–3; 80)、自らの損得を考えずに正しいことを貫く (Sinclair 2009: 80–2)。人情家 (Sinclair 2009: 76) で、読書家の一面 (Sinclair 2009: 89) もある。その反面、無政府主義や社会主義の思想についての話になると激しく議論する様子 (Sinclair 2009: 53–4; 60–2; 100–1) も頻繁に描写される。

一方、セーヤー判事を外国人嫌いにした要因を、同時代の「赤恐怖」に怯えるアメリカの風潮と共に、ボストンという土地が持つ風土や脈々とそこに息づく精神に見出す。例えば、赤へのヒステリーを背景にアメリカが無政府主義者や反逆の疑いのある外国人を掃討していく様子は、時代の気運に色づけされながら描かれる。例えば、探偵機関が要注意人物を探す様子は馬が餌を探して飼葉桶をむさぼる比喩が使われる（Sinclair 2009: 195）。また、「赤」と見なされた人々が「ソヴィエトの箱舟」と呼ばれた政府の輸送艦ビュフォードでロシアへ強制送還されると、「自分なら石の船に鉛の帆をかけて送り出すものを」（Sinclair 2009: 195）などという政治家もあちこちに現れる。こういった気運を、戦争終結から 1 年後のアメリカに充満した「クリスマス気分」（Sinclair 2009: 195）と形容する。

　さらに、貴族階級が支配するボストンという土地では、移民や労働者階級の人間は理解されにくい立場にあったことが説明される。上流階級であるコルネリアの家族が引き起こす内輪もめや家族会議の様子はほとんどすべてその血統を意識した、異なる階級や人種に対する偏見に満ちたものであり、まるでこれからこの土地で起こるサッコ＝ヴァンゼッティ事件がフレームアップとなることを予想させるかのようである。また、コルネリアが初めて非戦論者として演説をすることになる 20 世紀クラブという団体は、「誰がどこから来て何の話をしても、それが世界の改革に関係のある話なら、何でも歓迎」（Sinclair 2009: 134）される「世界に 2 つとない、自由主義的な老人たちの集団」（Sinclair 2009: 134）だが、実際のところ「これほど外見の紛らわしい場所はなかった。立派な羽毛が必ずしも立派な鳥だとは限らない。褪せた黒い絹を着て、縁がほつれた傘を手にした、目の前の老婦人は、ひょっとしたら北ミシガン半島の銅山の持ち主かもしれないし、あるいは、イースト・ボストンの街区を 6 つも所有している人間かもしれない」（Sinclair 2009: 134）のである。改革や自由主義といっても一筋縄ではいかない、まさにボストンの諸相を縮図にしたようなクラブである。

　一方、ニュー・イングランドで連綿と受け継がれてきたソローやエマ

ソンの超絶主義の精神も、ボストンでは諸刃の剣となる。サッコとヴァンゼッティが逮捕されたことを手紙で知ったコルネリアが共にイタリア湖水地方を訪れていた記者のピエール・レオンと無政府主義について議論する場面がある。ここで「私たちニュー・イングランドっ子はそういう［無政府主義的］信条で育てられてきました。私たちはそれを超絶主義と呼んでいますが。」(Sinclair 2009: 232) というコルネリアに対して、ピエールは「アナーキストの書店でソローの『市民の反抗』の本を置いてないところはありません。」(Sinclair 2009: 232) と答える。これは、無政府主義と超絶主義の思想に類似性を見出す素地がニュー・イングランドに根づいていることを深く認識させる記述である。

　しかし、ボストンではなじみ深いこの思想によって、サッコとヴァンゼッティの行為は簡単に〈反逆的行為〉と見なされることになる。後に彼らの逮捕の要因の1つともなった兵役逃れのためのメキシコへの逃亡は、次のように説明される。

　　ヴァンゼッティもサッコも決してメキシコへ逃げてゆく必要はなかったのだ。イタリア国民として2人とも徴兵へ取られるはずはなかったのである。…(中略)…彼らは思想においては徴兵忌避者となったのだったが、超絶主義の本場であるニュー・イングランドでは実際の徴兵忌避者と同じことであった。　　(Sinclair 2009: 138)

つまり、倫理的には理想主義・個人主義の立場にある超絶主義が反体制的側面を持ち合わせていることをよく知っているボストンは、彼らの行為が反逆的であると決めつける素地を備えていたという解釈である。作品全編を通じて散りばめられているこういった記述は、史実を記録してある原資料よりも、その背後にあるボストンという土地柄やそこに住まい営みを維持してきた人たちの生の雰囲気に基づいて書かれていると考えられる。

　富山太佳夫は、歴史を記述するスタイルの中でも評伝小説というジャンルに注目し、「人々の認める何らかの整合性がそこにある限り、その

ような動機や目的を精神分析学的に、あるいは時代の言説の傾向性から推定して、対象となる人物の行動やその人物に関わる事実と出来事を説明することができる」(富山 2002: 35)と述べ、『チーズとうじ虫』や『マルタン・ゲールの帰還』といった著作を「文化の周縁部分に生きるしかなかった人々の評伝」(富山 2002: 35)と呼ぶ。『ボストン』は、まさにアメリカ社会の中で周縁に生きるしかなかった人間たちの評伝である。膨大な量のデッダムの裁判記録を丹念に読み解き、残された証言、証拠、記録と向き合いながら、裁判の経緯を圧倒的な筆致で描き出している。そして、同時代の実社会においてごまかされ、ずらされ、恣意的に作り込まれてしまった〈事実〉の形成過程を、作品の中で再現することによって、その表面を覆っていたメッキを私たち読者の前で剥がしてみせる。裁判の過程そのものがいわばフィクションであったことを作品の中で暴露しているのである。

4. ドス・パソスの『USA』
——因果律を追究しない民衆史

シンクレアの『ボストン』に遅れること10年、ドス・パソスの3部作『USA』が世に出る。この作品は、それまでのドス・パソスの作品群の中でも最も歴史とフィクションの関係性を自意識的に探究している作品とも言える。「集団小説」とも言えるスタイルを構築した『マンハッタン乗換駅』(*Manhattan Transfer*) は、『USA』ほど歴史の再構築に意識的ではない。一方、『USA』以降の作品は、より因果律に基づいた歴史に重きを置くようになる。ドス・パソスが、サッコ＝ヴァンゼッティ事件の抗議デモに参加して警察に拘束された時にこの作品の着想を得たことは様々なエッセイや伝記で述べられている[9]が、この事件そのものを『USA』はどのように描いているのだろうか。

ドス・パソスは自身のことを「歴史の建築家」(Dos Passos 1988: 147)、「二流の歴史家」(Dos Passos 1988: 115)と称し、自らの主著を「同時代の年代記」(Dos Passos 1988: 238)と呼んでいるが、『USA』は実際、

一般的な近代小説のスタイルとは異なるドス・パソス独自の体裁を持つ。4つのモード、すなわち、自然主義的なタッチで多数の登場人物の行く末が語られていく「ナラティヴ」、新聞の記事や広告のキャッチコピー、当時の流行歌のフレーズなどがコラージュされた「ニューズリール」、アメリカの代表的な偉人たちの歴史が語られる「伝記」、そして自伝的で自己言及的なエクリチュール「カメラ・アイ」が不規則に混在しながら展開していく。

　ドス・パソスによって描かれるサッコ゠ヴァンゼッティ事件は、シンクレアのそれとまったく異なる。最も違う点は、事件が直接扱われている箇所が作品全体に占める割合である。『ボストン』ではソーンウェル家の内輪もめやボストン金融界のいざこざ以外のすべてがこの事件と関わっているのに対し、『USA』では数えるほどのページ数にしかならない。メアリー・フレンチが事件の抗議デモに加わる「ナラティヴ」(Dos Passos 1996: 1147–55) と、その直後に続く「ニューズリール 66」、「カメラ・アイ 49」と「カメラ・アイ 50」に留まる。しかし、たとえその分量は少なくとも、事件に関わる部分は紛れもなくこの3部作のクライマックスである。他の場面では各モードが直接的に交錯することはほとんどないのに、「カメラ・アイ 49」で殺人事件の現場であり、アメリカ建国の始まりともなったプリマスを辿るルポルタージュが展開されると、労働運動に奔走するメアリー・フレンチの「ナラティヴ」が続く。彼女が救済委員会のメンバーとなって死刑反対のデモに加わり留置所に入れられると、それに呼応するかのように「ニューズリール 66」と「カメラ・アイ 50」が事件に関連したエクリチュールを展開する。

　「ニューズリール 66」に貼り付けられた新聞やパンフレットの切り抜き、いわば断片化された原資料の集合体の中には「サッコとヴァンゼッティは死ぬ運命にある」(Dos Passos 1996: 1156) という一節がコラージュされ、その最後にはサッコが息子に宛てた手紙の一部分が貼り付けられる。

　「カメラ・アイ 50」は、ボストンでの助命運動の敗北と2人の死刑執行、もはや1つの国家ではなくなってしまったアメリカが描かれてい

るが、ここで最も注目すべきことは、それまでの 1 人称の語りであった「カメラ・アイ」が 2 人称の語り we へと変化している点である。この we とは、2 つに分断されたアメリカにおいてサッコとヴァンゼッティを救おうと闘う側の人々を指す。そして、「われわれの国アメリカはあいつらに打ち負かされてしまった　あいつらは建国の父たちが話していた清らかな言葉をひっくりかえし汚らわしく濁ったものにしてしまった」(Dos Passos 1996: 1157) とその敗北を嘆く。この 2 人称への語りの変化は、事件がただ個人の問題ではなく、アメリカ全体の問題であり、そこに明確な対立関係が生じたことを示唆している。それまでは声にならなかった群衆の声を we は自ら〈われわれ〉と呼び、語りはじめるのである。まさに群衆の歴史が紡がれはじめる瞬間である[10]。

　しかし、敗北者となった we は歴史を語るために、汚されてしまったからといって言葉そのものを諦めて手放してしまう選択はしない。「カメラ・アイ 51」は「われわれには対抗するものとして言葉しかない」(Dos Passos 1996: 1210) という 1 節で締めくくられている。また、最後の「ナラティヴ」はメアリー・フレンチに託される。知人が自殺を図ったことを知って友人のエイダが動転して電話をかけてくる。しかし、同志の 1 人が殺されたことで頭がいっぱいのメアリーはエイダの電話を切り、書類を集めて委員会の会議へと急ぐのである。「ナラティヴ」は、そしてその他の 3 つのモードを含めた『USA』は、言葉が堕落してしまったこと嘆きつつもなお、言葉の持つ力を信じ、闘い続ける道を選択するのである。それは、このテクストに終着点はなく開かれたままの状態となっていることを意味している。批評家バーバラ・フォーレイは、小説という形式、特にリアリズム小説や物語形式が、本質的にブルジョア的な圧力を持っている要因の 1 つに、ナラティヴが閉ざされた結末に向かっていく過程において矛盾を解消するという「傾向」を持ち合わせていることを挙げている (Foley 1993: 261)。「カメラ・アイ」の we が嘆く「ひっくりかえされてしまった言葉」、そのなかに、近代文学が作り出した因果律を追い求める小説や物語形式が含まれるとすれば、〈われわれ〉は歴史を紡ぐための言葉として、そういった操作された言

葉を容認するわけにはいかないのである。

5. おわりに

　シンクレアの『ボストン』でヴァンゼッティは入植者が初めてアメリカの地を踏んだプリマス・ロックを訪れ、熱く正義を語る。建国の父たちの清らかな言葉が汚されてしまったプリマスで、イタリアからやってきた移民のサッコとヴァンゼッティは死の判決を受ける。同時代にこの事件を生の記憶として持った2人のアメリカ人作家は、それぞれ違ったやり方でこの事件を語り継ぐことに成功した。シンクレアは『ボストン』において〈事実〉と思われてきた裁判がフィクションであったことを、裁判が取ったのと同じ因果的な説明により証明してみせ、同時に、フィクションの持つ想像力を借りて、原資料だけでは読み取ることができない時代の傾向や土地に根づく精神を描き込み、因果的説明とフィクションの両方が相互依存的に共存できるスタイルを作り上げた。ドス・パソスは、因果律そのものを手放し、旧来の仕組みに回収されることのない群衆の言葉で歴史を語ることを試みた。不連続で、断片的で、無秩序な、開かれたままのテクストは、言葉による闘いを続ける決意を示している[11]。

　1927年5月、ドス・パソスはシンクレアにサッコとヴァンゼッティを救うための協力を申し出る手紙を書き送っている (Dos Passos 1973: 371)。2人は近しい友人になることはなかったが、お互いの思考や作品を尊敬していたという。この2人の作家が〈サッコ＝ヴァンゼッティ事件〉を語ろうとした文学的試みには、共に歴史かフィクションかという二項対立をはるかに超越し、新しい歴史の語り方を切り開く可能性が秘められている。

注

1. ジョン・ドス・パソスやアプトン・シンクレアを筆頭に、ドロシー・パーカー、エドナ・セント・ヴィンセント・ミレイ、キャサリン・アン・ポーターらが抗議デモに参加し、ロマン・ロラン、H・G・ウェルズ、アルバート・アインシュタイン、アンリ・バルビュス、アナトール・フランス、ジョン・デューイらも判決に反対する声明を出した。当時のイタリアの首相ムッソリーニも米大統領に抗議し、日本からも草野心平が抗議文を送っている。
2. 死刑判決の後にヴァンゼッティが、その受難を彼らの「勝利」であると告げた以下の声明は、多くの知識人や芸術家たちにインスピレーションを与えた。「この事件がなかったら、…(中略)…現在私たちが偶然にも成し遂げた、人間が許し合い、正義を貫き、互いに理解し合うための仕事を、私たちは一生かかってもやり遂げられなかっただろう。…(中略)…この最後の瞬間こそ私たちのものだ。この受難こそ私たちの勝利だ。」(Sacco and Vanzetti 1997: lv)
3. シンクレアは、『ボストン』を「書こうとした決心は 1927 年 8 月 22 日午後 9 時 30 分(太平洋沿岸時間)になされた。それはある新聞社から、サッコとヴァンゼッティが亡くなったという電話を受け取った時であった」(Sinclair 2009: xxxv) と告白している。また、ドス・パソスは、1927 年に 3 部作の 1 作目『北緯 42 度線』の執筆が開始されたことを明言している (Dos Passos 1973: 383; 1988: 235)。
4. *Oxford English Dictionary* の "history" の項目、および *Oxford Latin Dictionary* の "historia" の項目を参照のこと。この語が持つ文化的意味合いや用法の詳しい変遷については、Williams (1983) の "history" の項目を参照のこと。
5. 近代歴史学と文学の関係性については兵藤 (2002) を参照のこと。
6. 一方でシンクレアは、プリマス法廷の裁判記録は入手できなかった (Sinclair 2009: xxxvi) とも述べている。
7. Hapke (2001: 178-9) は、コルネリアの人物造形は、実在の人物で救済委員会の主要メンバーであった Gertrude L. Winslow と Glendower Evans を融合させたものだと述べる。
8. デッダムでの裁判の後、プロクター警部は良心の呵責から「ほかならぬその致命弾は、紛れもなくサッコが所有していたピストルから発射されたものであったと確言するよう検事から幾度も頼まれた」(Sinclair 2009: 401) ことを激白した宣誓供述書を作る。弁護団は、この宣誓供述書に基づいて裁判のやり直しを求めるが、判事はこれを却下する。
9. Browder 1998: 41; Dos Passos 1973: 435; Dos Passos 1988: 235; Ludington 1998: 263-4; Pizer 1988: 24 を参照のこと。

10. 宮本（1996: 416-33）は、「ポピュラス」が身体を獲得し美学的表象を与えられていると論じる。
11. 上西（1996: 376）は、『USA』が断片的で雑多なテクストが無秩序に集合する、その多様性の大きさがこの作品のエネルギーとなっていると述べる。

参考文献

Browder, Laura. (1998) *Rousing the Nation: Radical Culture in Depression America*. Amherst: University of Massachusetts Press.
Carr, E. H. (1961) *What is History?* London: Penguin Books.（E・H・カー　清水幾太郎訳（1997）『歴史とは何か』岩波新書）
Dos Passos, John. (1973) *The Fourteenth Chronicle: Letters and Diaries of John Dos Passos*. ed. Townsend Ludington. Boston: Gambit.
Dos Passos, John. (1988) *John Dos Passos: The Major Nonfictional Prose*. ed. Donald Pizer. Detroit: Wayne State University Press.
Dos Passos, John. (1996) *U. S. A.* New York: Library of America.
Foley, Barbara. (1993) *Radical Representations: Politics and Form in U.S. Proletarian Fiction*, 1929-1941. Durham: Duke University Press.
Hapke, Laura. (2001) *Labor's Text: The Worker in American Fiction*. New Brunswick: Rutgers University Press.
"historia." *Oxford Latin Dictionary*. 2003ed.
"history." *Oxford English Dictionary*. 2nd ed. (1989)
兵藤裕己編（2002）『岩波講座　文学9　フィクションか歴史か』岩波書店
Ludington, Townsend. (1998) *John Dos Passos: A Twentieth Century Odyssey*. New York: Carroll.
宮本陽一郎（1996）「マシン・エイジのヒストリオグラフィ―ジョン・ドスパソス『ビッグ・マネー』におけるアヴァンガルドと民衆史」渡辺利雄編『読み直すアメリカ文学』pp.416-33．研究社
Pizer, Donald. (1988) *Dos Passos' U.S.A.: A Critical Study*. Charlottesville: University Press of Virginia.
Sacco, Nicola and Bartolomeo Vanzetti. (1997) *The Letters of Sacco and Vanzetti*. New York: Penguin Books.
Sinclair, Upton. (2009) *Boston*. Cambridge Mass: Linnaean.
富山太佳夫（2002）「歴史記述はどこまで文学か」兵藤裕己編『岩波講座　文学9　フィクションか歴史か』pp.17-40．岩波書店
上西哲雄（1996）「歴史を語るテクスト―ドスパソスのジャンル」渡辺利雄編『読み直すアメリカ文学』pp.367-80．研究社

渡辺利雄編(1996)『読み直すアメリカ文学』研究社
Williams, Raymond. history. (1983) *Keywords: A Vocabulary of Culture and Society*. London: Fontana Paperbacks.(レイモンド・ウィリアムズ　椎名美智・武田ちあき・越智博美・松井優子訳(2008)『完訳　キーワード辞典』平凡社)

フォークナー世界と「過去」

依藤道夫

要旨

　ウィリアム・フォークナーは、ミシシッピー州の申し子である。同州は、南部的特性の色濃い地方であり、かつては、奴隷制に基づく保守的農園体制を維持していた。南北戦争後も、人種差別は残った。フォークナー及び彼の作品は、彼の家系を含む深南部の風土や歴史に深く根差している。彼は、南北戦争や自家の歴史、曾祖父、黒人問題、貧乏白人などの諸テーマを扱った。

　フォークナー文学は、ミシシッピーや深南部の「過去」と深く絡み合った遡及性(そきゅうせい)の強い世界なのである。一見特殊に写るフォークナー世界と「過去」の問題は、実は、History の原義に即し、古典の王道にかなっているのである。

キーワード　ミシシッピー、農園体制(プランテーション)、奴隷制度、南北戦争、曾祖父フォークナー大佐

1. ミシシッピー川と農園体制

　ウィリアム・フォークナー(William Faulkner, 1897–1962)は、ミシシッピー(Mississippi)州の申し子である。ミシシッピー川に育まれたミシシッピー州の大地は極めて肥沃でありながら、同州は今日でさえ全米最貧州の1つである。それは、奴隷制度(Slavery)という負の過去を背負い、南北戦争(1861–65)における南部敗北の象徴的存在の1つとも

なっている。そして今日もなお、とりわけ北部的、ニューイングランド的視点からは、後進性色濃い土地柄とみなされがちである。南部諸州の誇る南部騎士道的、南部紳士的精神は、決して K. K. K. 的とは言わないまでも、白人保守層主体の古色蒼然たる思想風土との絡みで説明されることがある。

　元々、チカソー族 (the Chickasaws) やチョクトー族 (the Choctaws) が長年蟠踞していたミシシッピー地方は、1830 年代の合衆国中央政府による彼らインディアンのオクラホマ (Oklahoma) 等への強制移住による排除に始まる歴史を持つ。以来、入植して来たアングロ・サクソン主体の白人たちは、インディアンたちの狩猟中心の前有史時代的な社会体系に代わる農業を基盤とする新体系を樹立してゆく。

　地道な土着的農業社会に概して適応し難い自立心強く、剽悍なインディアンたちに対して、アフリカや西インド諸島から移入された黒人奴隷たちは、湿気の多い熱暑に強く、忍耐強く従順な気質を有していた。白人開拓者たちの一部は農園主 (Planter) となって、こうした黒人たちの利点を生かし、彼らを最大限活用することによって、農園体制 (Plantation) を構築していったのである。遅れてやって来た者たちを含めて、地主にも小規模自営農にも、また職人や商人、教師や弁護士、役人や牧師などの中間層白人にもなれなかった小作の白人たち、いわゆる貧乏白人 (Poor White) は、農園体制の中で農園主に雇われ、黒人奴隷たちの監督官になったり、文字通り小作の農業者や諸農園を転々とする移動季節労働者となったりして、それぞれの生存を計った。

　貧乏白人たちは、黒人層に微妙に優越する地位に置かれることにより得られる奇妙な人種的誇りを糧とし、生き甲斐として暮らしていたとも言える。ちょうどサトペン農園 (Sutpen's Hundred) のウォッシュ・ジョーンズ (Wash Jones) のように…。

　最上位に立つ農園主たちは、そのようにして貧乏白人たちの不満を押さえつつ、彼ら主体の農園体制を維持したともいえよう。

2. 黒人たちの状況の推移

　南部特有のミシシッピーの農本主義的階級制度は、南北戦争によって破壊される。しかしそれは一掃されはしなかった。結局は、その残滓以上のものが維持され続けたのである。解放された奴隷たちの多くが、北部の工業地帯に流入していったことも、事実である。が、南部に残留したそれ以上にはるかに多くの黒人たちは、農地所有者になることもかなわず、元の農園に留まり、相変わらず元の主人たちの下で小作人として生きてゆく他に道はなかったのである。つまり、売買される奴隷の身分からは名目的には解放されたが、人生や生活の実質は余り変わらず、依然として社会の底辺に位置づけられ、経済的にも自立など望むべくもなかったわけである。村や町の居住区も、人種により区分けされ、死後の墓地までもそうだった。この不自然かつ不条理な状態は、21世紀の今日まで続いている。

　黒人たちの悲惨な境遇が改善され始めるのは、第二次世界大戦中の大勢の黒人兵たちの犠牲や 1960 年代の公民権運動、マーティン・ルーサー・キング牧師（Martin Luther King, Jr., 1929–68）らによる改革運動やジョン・F. ケネディ（John F. Kennedy, 1917–63）政権による改善の努力などによってである。しかも、キング師暗殺、ケネディ兄弟暗殺などの恐ろしい犠牲も伴なった結果なのである。

　初の黒人大統領バラク・オバマ氏（Barack Obama, 1961–）の登場は、斜めに見れば、合衆国の世界に対するリーマン・ショック（"Lehman Shock"）への中和剤のようなにおいもしないではないが、オバマ氏自身、極めて優秀な指導者であることに異論はなく、白人層の人種面での意識改革を大いに促すことになったことは否めない。

3. フォークナーと深南部の過去

　『アブサロム！アブサロム！』（*Absalom! Absalom!*, 1936）や「デルタの秋」（"Delta Autumn", *Story* 誌。1942）、『墓場への侵入者』（*Intruder in the*

Dust, 1948)等の中でアメリカの黒人と白人が融合できるのは長年月を経た先のことであり、まだまだ待たねばならぬ、と述べたフォークナーは、とうに泉下の人であるとはいえ、黒人大統領の一足飛びの出現に最も驚いた一人だったのではなかろうか。それは、確かに、さすがのフォークナーの予想をもはるかに超える事態の早過ぎる実現だった。

そのフォークナーと彼の文学は、上述した深南部(the Deep South)、ミシシッピーの風土や歴史により生み出されたといえる。そうした歴史には、彼自身の家系や南北戦争が密接に絡んでいた。多くの深南部人もそうであろうが、フォークナーにも物心ついた幼時から深南部やミシシッピーの過去や歴史が沁み込んでいたのである。

4. フォークナーと外界

これまた少なからぬ深南部の若者たちがそうであったろうが、フォークナー青年も、ミシシッピー圏の外へ出ようと試みたことがあった。故郷の先輩のフィル・ストーン(Phil Stone, 1893–1967)の働きかけや失恋の痛手もあったとはいえ、第一次世界大戦の頃、彼フォークナーは、ストーンの学ぶコネティカット州ニュー・ヘイヴン(New Haven)のイェール大学(Yale University)そばのストーンの下宿に同宿した。ストーンのイェールの文学仲間に接したり、大学近くにあったウィンチェスター連発銃器会社(Winchester Repeating Arms Company)でアルバイトをしたりした。また、カナダのトロント(Toronto)の英国空軍に入隊して、飛行訓練を受けたが、休戦(1918年11月)の成立により、結局ヨーロッパの戦場には赴かぬまま、除隊している。更に、1921年、ニューヨーク(New York)のエリザベス・プロール(Elizabeth Prall)の書店で働いたりもした。1925年には、ニューオーリンズ(New Orleans)中心部のホテルに長期滞在していた有名作家シャーウッド・アンダーソン(Sherwood Anderson, 1876–1941)の教えを乞いたいと、そのホテルのすぐ近くに友人の画家ウィリアム・スプラットリング(William Spratling)と下宿したりもした。アンダーソンの妻となったエリザベス・プロールとの縁もあ

り、フォークナーは、この高名な作家と知り合え、彼の支援で最初の長編小説『兵士の報酬』(1926) の出版にこぎつけることが出来た。しかし、フォークナーは、結局、故郷に戻る。1930 年代にフランス等のヨーロッパ旅行も試みたが、彼が外界に住み着くことは生涯を通じてなかった（晩年、バージニア大学のあるシャーロッツヴィル［Charlottesville］に一時居住したことはある）。外界にあこがれても、故郷のミシシッピーに引き戻される、戻ってしまう、そうした彼の意識構造は、彼自身の体質は無論のこととして、彼の家系や生い立ち、曾祖父の存在、南北戦争などに深く根ざしていたのである。そして彼の創作家としての時間的ベクトルは、未来へ一歩進んでもまた二歩、三歩、いや、九歩も十歩も過去に遡行するというものであった。

5. フォークナー作品と深南部の歴史

　フォークナー作品における過去への遡及性というテーマに関しては、最も人口に膾炙している短編小説「エミリーのバラ」("A Rose for Emily", *Forum*, 1930) や意識の流れ (Stream of Consciousness) の手法を駆使した問題作、長編小説『響きと怒り』(*The Sound and the Fury*, 1929) などがまず思い浮かぶ。両作とも過去の出来事をベースに、回想やフラッシュ・バックの技法なども用いながら、登場人物たちを描写し、過去の経緯がいかにして現在を紡ぎ出しているのかを明らかにしようとしている。そしてそれは、現在の事態を過去に照射してみるというよりはむしろ、過去の累積が恰も噴火口内の溶岩が盛り上がり、噴き出してこぼれ、あふれ出るように、出現 (emerge) し、固まって現在を成してゆくという恰好である。

　フォークナーは、『サートリス』(*Sartoris*, 1929)、『征服されざる者』(*The Unvanquished*, 1938)、『アブサロム！アブサロム！』(*Absalom! Absalom!*) などの諸作品で南北戦争を扱った。また、『サートリス』や『響きと怒り』、『征服されざる者』などで、自家の歴史や曾祖父ウィリアム・クラーク・フォークナー大佐 (Colonel William Clark Falkner,

1825–89) の事績などを語った (作品中ではジョン・サートリス [John Sartoris] 大佐として描かれている)。更に、「あの夕陽」("That Evening Sun", *American Mercury*, 1931) や『墓場への侵入者』(*Intruder in the Dust*) などで黒人問題、人種問題を、「ウォッシュ」("Wash", *Harper's Magazine*, 1934) や「納屋は燃える」("Barn Burning", *Harper's Magazine*, 1939)、スノープス三部作 (Snopes Trilogy) などで貧乏白人を取り上げた。フォークナーの故郷オックスフォード (Oxford) の歴史は、『尼僧への鎮魂歌』(*Requiem for a Nun*, 1951) などにも詳しい (作品中ではジェファーソン [Jefferson] として描かれる)。いずれのテーマや問題も、深南部やミシシッピー州の過去や歴史と密接に関係している。

　南北戦争、彼自身の家系を含むミシシッピーの過去、人種問題や階級問題など深南部の歴史は、フォークナーと彼の文学において一丁目一番地であり、ミシシッピー川がミシシッピー・デルタを広域に潤すように、ミシシッピーの歴史が彼の精神と文学を満たし、支え続けたように思える。

6. フォークナーの普遍性

　フォークナーは、家族、一族や先輩のフィル・ストーンらから北部ミシシッピーやフォークナー家の過去について、幼時から聞かされていた。とりわけ彼と同名の曾祖父ウィリアムの存在は、彼にとり大きかった。子供のフォークナーが学校の先生から将来何になりたいかと問われ、「ひいおじいさんのような偉い作家になりたい」と答えたことはよく知られている (ちなみに、曽祖父は裸一貫、刻苦勉励して農園主、軍人、法律家、実業家、政治家になるとともに、『メンフィスの白バラ』(*The White Rose of Memphis*, 1881) に代表されるロマンス作家としても活動した)。

　フォークナーは、自らも愛車を走らせて、南北戦争の古戦場を巡ったといわれている。奴隷時代からフォークナー家に仕えたマミー・キャロライン・バー (Mummy Caroline Barr) の小振りの墓は、今もオックス

フォードの町はずれのセント・ピーターズ共同墓地（St. Peter's Cemetery）に白人たちの墓石に混じって存在する。特例的扱いだが、フォークナーが自分たち兄弟（彼は四人兄弟の長男）を育て上げた彼女マミー（"Mammy Callie"）を作品中でディルシー（Dilsey）として生き生きと描写したのは、彼の彼女への愛着の深さと人種問題への深いこだわりの故であったろう。

　ともかく、ミシシッピーの過去や歴史は、フォークナーに単に作品の材料を供給するのみならず、その背後にある精神や文化、南部人の間の深い絆などを付与していたのである。奴隷制度や敗戦、貧困や社会の後進性など過去の多くの負の遺産を抱える深南部ミシシッピーではあるが、むしろそのことこそがフォークナーを苦悩させ、思索させ、かつ大成させもしたのではあるまいか。フォークナーの描き上げた南部の精神や魂は、増々普遍化されて、その永続性や不滅性を深め、世界中の読者に多大のインパクトを与えた。そうした彼の文学は、過去への遡及性に富みながらも、その工夫を凝らした技法ともども、未来、即ち後の世に鮮やかな光を投げかけた。彼の後に続いた20世紀のアメリカ文人たちのみならず、他の諸外国の文人たちにも未来志向の大きな影響を与え続けたのである。南米コロンビアのガルシア・マルケス（Gabriel Jose García Márquez, 1928–）や中国の莫言（1955–）、日本の熊野出身の中上健次（1946–1992）などもそうした人々なのである。

7. History（Historie）とフォークナー

　「歴史」を意味する History（＜Histoire［仏］）という語は、元来、「物語」の意味も有している。物語と歴史は、同根なのである。それは例えば、文学史を遡った伝承や神話の段階を考えてみれば、うなずけることである。物事を単純化していうならば、一見奇抜で特殊に思えるフォークナー及びフォークナー文学と「過去」の問題は、実は History（Histoire）の本来の定義に即し、古典的文学（物語）の王道にかなうものとみなすこともできる。それゆえにこそ、彼の作品世界が多くの読者の

みならず、多くの創作家たちの琴線に触れ、彼らの創作意欲も掻き立てて来ているのであろう。

第 III 部

Exploiting the Oncogenic MYC Pathway Activation in Targeting Triple-Negative Breast Cancer: Utility of CDK Inhibition Revisited

Dai Horiuchi

Abstract

Estrogen, progesterone and HER2 receptor negative "triple-negative" breast cancers encompass the most clinically challenging sub-type, for which there currently exists no targeted therapeutic strategy. We find that triple-negative tumors exhibit elevated MYC expression, as well as altered expression of MYC regulatory genes, resulting in increased activity of the MYC network. In primary human breast tumors, MYC signaling did not predict response to neo-adjuvant chemotherapy, but was associated with poor prognosis. We exploit the increased MYC expression found in triple-negative breast cancers by employing a synthetic-lethal approach dependent on cyclin-dependent kinase (CDK) inhibition. CDK inhibition effectively induced tumor regression in triple-negative tumor xenografts. The pro-apoptotic BCL-2 family member BIM becomes up-regulated following CDK inhibition and contributes to this synthetic-lethal mechanism. The results indicate that aggressive breast tumors with elevated MYC expression are uniquely sensitive to CDK inhibitors.

Keywords Triple-negative breast cancer, MYC oncogene, Cyclin-dependent kinase, Personalized cancer treatment

1. Introduction

Clinically relevant biomarkers used to guide the use of targeted therapeutics for breast cancer include the overexpression of the human epidermal growth factor receptor 2 (HER2) and the expression of the estrogen (ER) and progesterone receptors (PR). For breast tumors that are positive for these receptors ("receptor positive"), a number of targeted therapeutic strategies have been successfully developed in the past decades.

These include the use of small molecule kinase inhibitors, treatment with inhibitory monoclonal antibodies and anti-hormonal therapies. Unfortunately, no such biomarker to predict response to selective therapeutics has been established for the most challenging receptor "triple-negative" subtype of breast cancer (Bauer et al. 2007; Carey et al. 2006; Liedtke et al. 2008).

Gene expression profiling of human primary breast tumors has identified several distinct molecular subtypes including "luminal A and B", "HER2$^+$", "basal-like", and "normal-like" (Perou et al. 2000; Sorlie et al. 2001). Approximately 70% of triple-negative tumors belong to the basal subtype (Bertucci et al. 2008), which often exhibits aggressive characteristics such as poor differentiation, a higher rate of proliferation and increased metastatic capability (Livasy et al. 2006; Sarrio et al. 2008). In clinical studies, patients with triple-negative tumors have been found to respond to neo-adjuvant chemotherapy with equal or better efficacy than those with receptor-positive tumors (Carey et al. 2007; Liedtke et al. 2008), presumably due to the higher mitotic index observed in triple-negative tumors. However, a complete pathological response is rarely achieved in patients with triple-negative tumors, who have a tendency to experience early relapse and a diminished 5-year disease-free survival (Bauer et al. 2007; Dent et al. 2007). The molecular events that occur in triple-negative breast cancer have not been elucidated and therefore, the mechanism for the poor prognosis of this subtype remains unclear.

Several studies have suggested that the MYC proto-oncogene may play an important function in aggressive breast cancers. MYC is a basic helix-loop-helix zipper (bHLHZ) motif –containing transcription factor whose activity is tightly regulated by its direct binding to another bHLHZ protein MAX. MYC activation can lead to transcriptional or repression of specific genes. (Eilers and Eisenman 2008). The global transcriptional influence of MYC is also mediated through a MYC regulatory network whereby MYC activity is precisely controlled by the activity of multiple competingrepressive MAX binding partners (i.e. MAD, MGA, MXD4, and MNT) (Cowling and Cole 2006; Grandori et al. 2000). MYC plays roles in multiple signaling pathways including those involved in cell growth, cell proliferation, metabolism, microRNA regulation, cell death and cell survival (Dang 1999; Eilers and Eisenman 2008; Meyer and Penn 2008). Furthermore, MYC signaling has recently been shown to be upregulated in high-grade mammary tumors with presumptive cancer stem cell properties (Ben-Porath et al. 2008; Wong et al. 2008).

The genomic locus, 8q24, which harbors the MYC oncogene, is amongst the most frequently amplified region in breast cancers of various sub-types (Jain et al. 2001). More recent studies have identified a MYC transcriptional gene signature associated with the basal molecular subtype (Alles et al. 2009; Chandriani et al. 2009; Gatza et al. 2010). Other studies have examined staining of primary breast tumor tissues for MYC protein expression and did not find a clear connection between MYC overexpression and patient outcome (Bland et al. 1995; Naidu et al. 2002). Thus, evaluating the contribution of MYC signaling to triple-negative breast cancer would open up new mechanistic insights and potentially new therapeutic approaches to treat this aggressive tumor type.

A number of outstanding questions about the relevance of MYC signaling in triple-negative breast cancer remain unresolved. Is MYC expression alone altered in triple-negative tumors or is the expression of other MYC signaling components (i.e. competing MAX binding proteins) also changed? Furthermore, does MYC signaling alter response to conventional chemotherapeutics that are routinely used to treat triple-negative breast cancer? Finally, if MYC signaling is up-regulated in triple-negative tumors, can one take advantage of this feature to develop new targeted therapeutics? In this study, we employ several complementary approaches to address these questions.

Synthetic lethal approach has been proposed as a treatment strategy against cancers that lack obvious "druggable" targets (Reinhardt et al. 2009). As an example, small molecule inhibition of poly (ADP-ribose) polymerase (PARP) in patients with BRCA1/2 mutations has provided a proof of concept for exploiting synthetic-lethality in the clinic (Fong et al. 2009; Tutt et al. 2010). Our previous work found a synthetic-lethal interaction between MYC overexpression and inhibition of the mitotic cyclin-dependent kinase 1 (CDK1) by using transgenic MYC-driven models of lymphoma and liver cancer (Goga et al. 2007). However, whether this synthetic-lethal approach has utility in treating triple-negative breast cancers remains unknown.

In this study, we investigated whether exploiting a synthetic-lethal approach dependent on elevated MYC signaling is effective in treating triple-negative breast cancer. To gain a comprehensive understanding for the role of MYC in triple-negative breast cancer, in the current study we combine gene expression and protein analysis from patient tumors with functional studies in cell lines and tumor models. Here, we examine the efficacy of a CDK inhibitor currently in clinical development against triple-negative breast cancer and investigate the mechanism of synthetic-lethality.

2. Results

2.1 MYC expression is disproportionally elevated in triple-negative breast cancer

We sought to understand whether MYC signaling is an important oncogenic event in triple-negative breast tumors. The Investigation of Serial Studies to Predict Your Therapeutic Response with Imaging and Molecular Analysis (I-SPY TRIAL) is an NCI-sponsored multi-institutional study of Stage II and III breast cancer patients to identify diagnostic markers, validate hypothesis, and develop new treatment strategies against breast cancer (Barker et al. 2009; Esserman et al. 2012; Jones 2010). This clinical trial collects extensive clinical annotation and global mRNA expression from primary tumor samples. Using mRNA expression data from 146 primary patient tumor samples for which hormone receptor and HER2 expression were available, we found that MYC mRNA levels are significantly elevated in triple-negative tumors (Fig. 1A). We next examined MYC protein and phospho-MYC (T58/S62) expression in 208 independent primary breast tumor samples from a separate cohort using reverse-phase quantitative protein arrays. The 66 triple-negative tumors expressed significantly elevated MYC protein (Fig. 1B) and phospho-MYC (not shown) compared to the 142 tumors that were receptor-positive. MYC phosphorylation at these sites has been shown to enhance MYC transcriptional activity as well as alter protein stability (Chang et al. 2000; Sears et al. 2000; Seo et al. 2008). Finally, using previously published mRNA expression profiling data (Neve et al. 2006), we examined whether MYC expression in 48 established human breast cell lines correlated with the receptor status. These 48 human breast cell lines have been shown to accurately model aspects of breast cancer biology (Neve et al. 2006) and have been extensively used for mechanistic studies. Compared with the cell lines that are not triple-negative, triple-negative cell lines had substantially elevated MYC mRNA (Fig. 1C). Taken together, these three independent data sets confirm the association between elevated MYC expression and triple-negative tumors.

2.2 MYC signaling is up-regulated in triple-negative tumors

To evaluate MYC activity in primary tumors, we applied a previously validated MYC transcriptional gene signature (Chandriani et al. 2009), which is comprised of 352 genes, to the I-SPY data set. We ordered the patient tumor samples by the Pearson correlation to the MYC gene expression signature (Fig. 2A) and tumors were divided into high, medium and low correlation groups (see Materials and methods). Triple-negative breast tumors were significantly enriched in the high MYC gene expression group ($p < 0.001$, Fig. 2A). These results indicate that a disproportionate number of primary triple-negative breast tumors exhibit elevated MYC function. A MYC gene signature has previously been correlated with a basal molecular sub-type of breast cancer (Alles et al. 2009; Chandriani et al. 2009; Gatza et al. 2010), which encompasses 70% of triple-negative cancers. Whether MYC signaling is also increased in other molecular sub-types of human breast cancer remains unclear. We therefore examined the MYC gene signature across different molecular sub-types of breast cancer in the I-SPY data set. Consistent with prior studies, we found that a high MYC gene signature correlated most strongly with the basal sub-type; however, we also observed that the luminal B molecular sub-type had significantly higher MYC signature than luminal A or HER2 sub-types (Fig. 2B). While most luminal B tumors express hormone receptors, this sub-type is often associated with increased tumor proliferation and worse outcome than luminal A (Voduc et al. 2010). Our results indicate that along with basal, the luminal B molecular sub-type is also associated with increased MYC signaling, which may, at least in part, explain the worse outcome for this tumor-type (Cheang et al. 2009).

2.3 Up-regulation of MYC signaling is associated with poor prognosis

We next examined the clinical outcome of patients based on their MYC gene signature in the neo-adjuvant I-SPY TRIAL. We found that an increased MYC gene signature was associated with significantly shortened disease-free survival with a median follow-up of 3.9 years ($p = 0.005$, Fig. 3A). Surprisingly, we found that the response of primary tumors at the time of surgery, immediately following the completion of conventional neo-adjuvant chemotherapy, did not differ based on MYC signature scores (Fig. 3B). To further examine the association between MYC signaling and response to neo-adjuvant chemotherapy, we divided the total patient population into two categories. One group was composed of those patients who exhibited either complete response or minimal residual cancer burden (RCB 0-I) (Symmans et al. 2007)) after conventional chemotherapy. The other group was composed of those with substantial residual disease (RCB II-III). For patients who had a dramatic response to neo-adjuvant chemotherapy (RCB 0/I), increased MYC signaling did not significantly alter prognosis (Fig. 3C). In contrast, for those patients whose tumors had only minimal response to neoadjuvant chemotherapy (RCB II/III), an increased MYC signature was associated with early disease recurrence (Fig. 3D, $p < 0.001$).

2.4 Triple-negative breast cells with elevated MYC expression are sensitive to CDK inhibition

Given the poor outcome of patients that have tumors with elevated MYC activity, we sought to identify a therapeutic strategy that could target these tumors. Synthetic-lethality between MYC-overexpression and the inhibition of the mitotic kinase cyclin-dependent kinase 1 (CDK1) has previously been observed in engineered cells and transgenic mouse models (Goga et al. 2007). However, this synthetic lethality has not been examined in human cancer, including breast cancer. Purvalanol A, an experimental small molecule CDK inhibitor that has higher specificity toward CDK1 (Gray et al. 1998), induced apoptosis in lymphoma cells and hepatocytes engineered to overexpress MYC (Goga et al. 2007). Importantly, CDK1 inhibition has been found to have little effect on the viability of control cells or normal mouse tissues at the concentrations used (Goga et al. 2007).

We reasoned that triple-negative breast cancer cells that have arisen to overexpress MYC might also be sensitive to a synthetic-lethal interaction with CDK inhibition. To model our observations from the I-SPY clinical samples, we tested a panel of triple-negative cell lines with elevated MYC expression and a panel of receptor-positive lines that were expected to have lower MYC expression based on previously published mRNA data (Neve et al. 2006) for their sensitivity to CDK inhibitors (Fig. 4A). In these experiments, we tested two CDK inhibitors: purvanol A, and another CDK inhibitor dinaciclib (SCH-727965, MERCK) (Parry et al., 2010) that is currently in phase II clinical trials against various tumor types (Dickson and Schwartz 2009). iDinaciclib nhibits CDK 1, 2, 5, and 9 at concentrations of 1–5 nM, which can be readily achieved *in vivo*, and exhibits improved pharmacokinetic (PK) and pharmacodynamic (PD) properties, compared to other CDK inhibitors previously evaluated in clinical trials.

Breast cell lines were treated with purvalanol A (10µM) or dinaciclib (10nM), respectively, and were subjected to a Promega CellTiter cell viability assay. These chosen concentrations induce cell cycle arrest without causing cell death in non-tumorigenic human epithelial as well as fibroblast cells (Fig. 4A and (Goga et al. 2007)). Human epithelial cells engineered to overexpress MYC (RPE-MYC) undergo cell death when treated with purvalanol A, whereas those with endogenous levels of MYC expression (RPE-NEO) do not, serving as positive and negative controls, respectively (Fig. 4A and (Goga et al. 2007)). Dinaciclib exhibited >1,000 fold higher potency compared with purvalanol A in inducing apoptosis in epithelial cells engineered to over-express MYC but not in control RPE-NEO cells (Fig. 4A). In breast cell lines, CDK inhibitor treatment induced substantial cell death in each of the 5 triple-negative cell lines tested (range 25–65%), whereas most of the receptor-positive lines showed resistance to such treatment (Fig. 4A). One receptor-positive line, SKBR3, was sensitive to these inhibitors (eliciting> 25% cell death); however, this may be due to an increased MYC expression found in these cells (Fig. 4A), which was not predicted from previously published mRNA profiling data (Neve et al. 2006).

Although these small molecule CDK inhibitors are selective for either CDK1 (purvalanol A) or for a few CDKs (dinaciclib), it is possible that other non-CDK kinases may also be inhibited and thus may contribute to the overall cell death phenotypes. To address this issue of specificity and further investigate synthetic-lethality between MYC overexpression and CDK inhibition, we performed siRNA experiments to knock-down specific CDKs in a panel of triple-negative as well as receptor-positive cell lines (Fig. 4B). We found that the treatment of all three triple-negative cell lines with CDK1 siRNA for 72 hours resulted in a significant amount of cell death, while the viability of receptor-positive lines was only modestly affected (Fig. 4B). Interestingly, we found that CDK2 siRNA could also induce cell death, but to a lesser extent in two of the triple-negative lines and in one of the receptor-positive lines, which is in agreement with recent observations that CDK2 function may be essential for the viability of certain cancer types (Molenaar et al. 2009). The higher potency of cell killing induced by dinaciclib may be, in part, due to its ability to inhibit both CDK1 and CDK2 (Parry et al. 2010). Unexpectedly, we found that CDK1 siRNA tresatment dramatically increased CDK2 protein expression in all of the three triple-negative lines, and one of the receptor-positive cell lines; whereas CDK2 siRNA did not alter CDK1 protein expression (Fig. 4B). It remains to be determined whether this CDK2 up-regulation indicates a compensatory mechanism within the cell cycle encountering the loss of the only mitotic CDK.

We next asked whether the observed CDK inhibition-induced cell death in cells with elevated MYC expression is dependent on their MYC status. To address this question, we first used an RNAi approach to knock-down MYC protein expression. We found that pre-treatment of RPE-MYC cells with MYC-specific siRNA significantly reduced the extent of CDK inhibition-dependent cell death (Fig. 4C). Similarly, the sensitivities of three triple-negative cell lines treated with MYC siRNA prior to the addition of purvalanol A were greatly reduced (Fig. 4D). We next used a lentiviral transduction method to overexpress MYC in receptor-positive cells to examine whether MYC-overexpression alone is sufficient to render these otherwise resistant cells sensitive to CDK inhibition. We found that purvalanol A treatment of T47D and HCC1428 cells engineered to overexpress MYC resulted in significantly increased cell death (Fig. 4E). Thus, these results suggest that elevated MYC expression is necessary and it increases the sensitivity of breast cancer cells to CDK inhibitors. Interestingly, whereas MYC RNAi demonstrated a dramatic decrease in MYC protein expression (Fig. 4D), it did not appreciably alter cell viability (not shown).

2.5 CDK inhibition induces *in vivo* tumor regression in mouse xenograft models of triple-negative breast cancer

A stringent test of any therapeutic strategy is the ability to inhibit or regress *in vivo* tumor growth. Using xenograft transplant models of breast cancer, we examined the *in vivo* efficacy of inhibiting CDKs in human triple-negative tumors with elevated MYC expression. We focused on dinaciclib due to its higher potency and improved pharmacokinetic properties compared with purvalanol A. We attempted to generate tumor xenografts of three triple-negative and three receptor-positive human breast cancer cell lines. Tumor cells were transplanted into Balb/c Nu/Nu mice and were allowed to form measurable tumors (200–250 mm^3 in volume). Two triple-negative cell lines with elevated MYC expression, MDA-MB-231 and HCC3153, Formed tumors with high penetrance and were used for subsequent studies. Our attempts to grow tumors of receptor-positive cells were not successful either due to the inability to form tumors or because only small sporadic tumors, despite our efforts to increase tumor engraftment by using Matrigel.

The triple-negative tumor-bearing mice were then treated twice weekly for two weeks with dinaciclib (50 mg/kg/dose IP) or vehicle control. The mice treated with diluent experienced a 120–150% increase in growth of tumors during the experimental period. In contrast, dinaciclib treated mice had a dramatic response with ~ 50% tumor regression (Figs. 5A and 5B). In an independent experiment, we also examined the effects of dinaciclib on the established MDA-MB-231 and HCC3153 xenografts 24 hours post treatment. We found a dramatic decrease in the overall phosphorylation levels of presumptive CDK substrates that have the consensus CDK motif as well as in the phosphorylation of a validated CDK1 substrate protein phosphatase 1-alpha (PP1-alpha) (T320) (Blethrow et al. 2008; Dohadwala et al. 1994) in primary tumors (Figs. 5C). This was accompanied by the induction of apoptosis as demonstrated by PARP cleavage in tumor tissues (Figs. 5C). Similar marked reduction in the phosphorylation of CDK substrates and increased PARP activation were also observed for the third triple-negative tumor xenograft (SUM149PT) not shown), which exhibited only limited penetrance in tumor formation. Taken together, these results demonstrate that small molecule inhibition of CDKs represents a novel and feasible treatment strategy against human triple-negative breast cancers.

2.6 BIM up-regulation mediates CDK inhibition-dependent cell death

We next sought to understand the mechanism that underlies the synthetic-lethal interaction between elevated MYC expression and CDK inhibition in epithelial cells. We previously reported that CDK-inhibition-induced apoptosis was independent of p53 but required activation of the mitochondrial intrinsic apoptotic pathway (Goga et al. 2007). We therefore reasoned that inhibition of CDKs might either increase the activity of pro-apoptotic BCL-2 family members or decrease the activity of pro-survival factors. To test this hypothesis, we examined the protein expression of components of the mitochondrial intrinsic pathway in matched RPE cells engineered to overexpress MYC (RPE-MYC) or control cells (RPE-NEO). RPE cells have modest levels of endogenous MYC expression (Fig. 4A), which makes them a suitable model to study their response to MYC overexpression. We found that a pro-apoptotic BH3-only member BIM was substantially up-regulated in RPE-MYC cells (Fig. 6A) as has been previously observed in other cell types engineered to overexpress MYC (Egle et al. 2004; Hemann et al. 2005). BIM up-regulation was also observed in a non-tumoigenic triple-negative breast cell line (MCF10A) engineered to overexpress MYC (not shown). Surprisingly, BIM was dramatically further up-regulated after RPE-MYC cells were treated with Purvalanol A, whereas BIM protein levels remained undetectable in RPE-NEO cells throughout the time-course (Fig. 6A). BIM up-regulation in RPE-MYC cells coincided with the cleavage of PARP, an event that indicated induction of apoptosis (Fig. 6A). Protein quantification revealed that the extent of BIM protein up-regulation in this particular cell line was 2.2-fold (Fig. 6B). This level of BIM up-regulation is likely to be significant, because BIM up-regulation induces apoptosis unless its activity is concomitantly suppressed by overexpression of anti-apoptotic BCL-2 family members (O'Connor et al. 1998). Quantitative PCR (TaqMan) analysis showed up-regulation of BIM mRNA (~ 2.5-fold) following treatment of RPE-MYC cells with purvalanol A (Fig. 6C). These results suggest that BIM up-regulation following CDK inhibition is due, in part, to increased BIM mRNA levels. BIM mRNA also increased in RPE-NEO cells following purvalanol A treatment but remained substantially lower than the levels observed in RPE-MYC cells (Fig. 6C). Interestingly, we found that dinaciclib treatment of RPE-MYC cells resulted in the up-regulation of not only the BIM-EL isoform found with Purvalanol A treatment, but also the shorter isoforms BIM-L and BIM-S (Fig. 6D), which have been shown to be significantly more potent in inducing apoptosis (O'Connor et al. 1998). This may, at least in part, explain the higher potency associated with dinaciclib compared with that of purvalanol A (Fig. 4A).

We postulated that the cell death observed in MYC overexpressing cells after CDK inhibition is dependent on a threshold level of BIM, which is not reached in RPE-NEO cells. To test this hypothesis, we asked whether BIM is necessary for cell death induced by CDK inhibition in the context of MYC overexpression. Pre-treatment of RPE-MYC cells with BIM-specific siRNAs protected the cells from Purvalanol A induced cell death (Fig. 6E). These findings establish BIM as a major contributor to CDK inhibitor-induced apoptosis. We next tested triple-negative breast cell lines with endogenously elevated MYC expression and observed similar BIM up-regulation upon CDK inhibitor treatment (Figs. 6F and 6G). To determine if BIM was required for the induction of cell death in these cells following CDK inhibitor treatment, we generated stable cell lines expressing a control or BIM shRNA (Fig. 6H). We found that BIM depletion attenuates cell death following Purvalanol A treatment (Fig. 6I). These results indicate that the mechanism of CDK inhibitor-induced apoptosis in triple-negative cells with elevated MYC expression involves BIM up-regulation.

In addition to the pro-apoptotic BCL-2 family member BIM, we found that all of the three pro-survival BCL-2 family members, BCL-2, BCL-xL, and MCL-1, were also up-regulated in RPE-MYC cells compared to RPE-NEO cells in the absence of Purvalanol A (not shown). This is consistent with the hypothesis that cancers that have evolved to sustain high MYC expression have reached a balance between pro- and anti-apoptotic factors to limit spontaneous apoptosis (Hemann et al. 2005; Lowe et al. 2004). This is also consistent with previous observation that co-overexpression of MYC and BCL-2 occurs in high-grade human breast tumors (Sierra et al. 1999). In our study, however, the expression levels of these pro-survival members did not change appreciably upon CDK inhibition (not shown). Thus, treatment of tumors with elevated MYC expression, such as triple-negative breast cancers, with CDK inhibitors may tip the balance in favor of apoptosis by increasing BIM expression.

3. Discussion

There is an urgent need to develop targeted therapeutic strategies against triple-negative breast cancer. To identify these therapeutic targets, a better understanding of the biology of triple-negative breast cancer is needed. In this study, we investigated the biology of triple-negative cancers and identified that MYC signaling is elevated in these tumors.

Several studies have shown that the basal breast cancer sub-type exhibits enrichment for a MYC transcriptional gene signature (Alles et al. 2009; Chandriani et al. 2009; Gatza et al. 2010). However, basal breast tumors account for only ~70% of triple-negative tumors, and the importance of MYC signaling in the remaining 30% has previously been unknown. In clinical practice, tumors are routinely evaluated for ER, PR and HER2 receptor status and thus the pathological determination of the triple-negative subtype is more relevant for deciding on a course of treatment. We found that 33 of 36 triple-negative tumors (92%) in the I-SPY TRAIL had a high or intermediate MYC gene signature score (Fig. 24) that correlated with worse outcome (Fig. 3A and 3D).The present study also demonstrates, for the first time, that MYC signaling is associated with diminished disease-free survival in patients whose tumors exhibited poor response to neoadjuvant chemotherapy (Fig. 3D).

To determine whether elevated MYC signaling can be exploited to treat triple-negative breast cancer, we assessed the utility of a synthetic lethal approach between MYC up-regulation and CDK inhibition. Small molecule inhibition of CDK activity was effective in inducing significant cell death in triple-negative cell lines with elevated MYC expression as well as in mouse xenograft models. We found that the mechanism of such cell death included the up-regulation of the pro-apoptotic BCL-2 family member BIM. Thus, this study represents a significant step forward in identifying apoptotic mechanisms for treating triple-negative breast cancers.

Although prior studies have focused on the many biological functions of MYC, how this information could be translated into developing novel ways to treat breast cancer remains unclear. In an emerging era of personalized medicine, it is crucial to identify what specific patient populations would most benefit from a given treatment strategy. We found that, for patients who experienced a limited tumor response to conventional neoadjuvant chemotherapy, disease-free survival was strongly influenced by MYC expression. Insights into components of MYC signaling, therefore, will provide potential targets that could be exploited as new therapies for this subset of breast cancer patients. However, despite up-regulation of MYC signaling in a variety of human cancers, the potential utility of direct MYC inhibition remains unclear. For instance, MYC knock-down via RNAi has not been found to diminish the viability of cultured tumor-derived cells (Guan et al. 2007), consistent with our observations in this study with breast cancer cells. On the other hand, inhibition of MYC-MAX dimerization using an experimental compound, 10058-F4, led to the induction of apoptosis in cultured human leukemia cells (Huang et al., 2006). Furthermore, *in vivo* inhibition of MYC transcriptional activity using a conditional dominant-negative mutant induced cell death and caused tumor regression in a KRAS-initiated mouse lung tumor model (Soucek et al. 2008). Whether the differences among these observations are due to the methods employed (i.e., knocking-down MYC protein expression versus inhibition of its transcriptional activity) or to the extent that each cancer type depends on deregulated MYC activity requires further investigation.

An alternative approach to directly inhibiting MYC is to employ a MYC-dependent synthetic-lethal strategy. We previously identified a form of synthetic-lethal interaction between MYC-overexpression and CDK1 inhibition using engineered cell lines as well as *in vivo* model systems (Goga et al. 2007). More recent reports have shown that the RNAi-mediated or small molecule inhibition of two additional cell cycle kinases,

CDK2 and aurora kinase B, respectively, have synthetic-lethal interactions with MYC-overexpression in certain cancer cell types (Molenaar et al. 2009; Yang et al. 2010). Another study has also reported that agonist-mediated activation of a TRAIL (Tumor Necrosis Factor Related Apoptosis Inducing Ligand) receptor (DR5) induces MYC-dependent synthetic lethality (Wang et al. 2004). These distinct forms of synthetic-lethality appear to require fundamentally different cellular mechanisms of cell death, including different requirements for an intact p53 tumor suppressor pathway (Goga et al. 2007; Molenaar et al. 2009; Wang et al. 2004; Yang et al. 2010). For example, 44–82% of primary basal breast tumors either lack p53 or harbor p53 mutant alleles (Carey et al. 2006; Sorlie et al. 2001). Therefore, CDK1-MYC synthetic lethality, which is p53-independent (Goga et al. 2007), may be particularly useful in treating these tumors.

The idea of targeting cell cycle kinases to selectively kill tumor cells, which often exhibit higher proliferation rates than non-tumorigenic cells, is appealing and has indeed led to the clinical development of a number of small-molecule CDK inhibitors (Malumbres et al. 2008; Shapiro 2006). However, there have been a number of issues associated with their clinical development. Previous generations of CDK inhibitors generally suffered from low *in vivo* potency and poor PK/PD properties. More recent, third-generation CDK inhibitors, including dinaciclib, exhibit significantly improved PK/PD properties, and offer greater promise for *in vivo* use. Indeed, dinaciclib was well tolerated in Phase I trials and is currently being evaluated in Phase II trials against various tumor types (Dickson and Schwartz 2009; Parry et al. 2010). Prior clinical studies have also suffered from a lack of understanding of which tumor types are the most likely to be responsive to CDK inhibitors (Malumbres et al. 2008). Therefore, selection of patient cohorts based on molecular targets, such as MYC over-expression, may improve the therapeutic potential of CDK inhibitors in clinical trials.

In the present study, we found that CDK inhibition increases BIM protein levels not only in the model cells engineered to overexpress MYC but also in a panel of patient-derived triple-negative breast cancer cell lines with elevated MYC expression. Elevated BIM plays a direct role in CDK inhibition-induced cell death. Prior studies have found that BIM isoforms can be regulated at both the transcriptional and post-translational levels. Protein expression of the shortest isoform Bim-S is sufficient to potently induce apoptosis (O'Connor et al. 1998). By contrast, the activity of the longest isoform BIM-EL can also be modulated by distinct phosphorylation mechanisms that can either stabilize the protein or induce its degradation via the proteasomal pathway (Hubner et al. 2008). In our studies we found that both isoforms can be upregulated in epithelial cells following CDK inhibitor treatment.

Previous reports have shown that BIM expression is elevated upon MYC overexpression (Egle et al. 2004; Hemann et al. 2005). Having uncovered that CDK inhibition triggers induction of BIM expression, we became interested in studying the relationship between the protein expression levels of MYC and BIM in a panel of untreated breast cancer cell lines. We did not find a correlation between MYC and BIM expression in these cells regardless of their molecular subtypes or receptor status (not shown). Therefore, in a given cellular context, it is likely that the relative increase in BIM activity in response to CDK inhibition, not the absolute basal level of BIM expression determines whether or not apoptosis can be initiated (Fig. 7). Thus, the protein stoichiometry among BIM and anti-apoptotic BCL-2 family members such as BCL-2, BCL-xL, and MCL-1 is likely to dictate if apoptosis is triggered. In this respect, a combinatorial approach of CDK inhibition with inhibition of anti-apoptotic BCL-2 family members would be predicted to have a synergistic effect in inducing cell death in MYC overexpressing triple-negative tumors. Indeed, a number of BH3 mimetics (Chonghaile and Letai 2008), namely, ABT-737/263 (Oltersdorf et al. 2005) and obatoclax (Nguyen et al. 2007), are currently under development for clinical use.

In conclusion, we have shown utility for small molecule CDK inhibitors in the treatment of triple-negative breast tumors with elevated MYC expression. It is likely that CDK inhibitors will be effective not only against MYC-overexpressing triple-negative tumors but also for aggressive receptor-positive tumors with elevated MYC expression (i.e. luminal B). Methods for immuno-histochemical analysis on paraffin-embedded primary tumor biopsies for MYC protein expression have been previously described (Gurel et al. 2008; Ruzinova et al. 2010). In addition, gene expression profiling methods on primary breast tumors are becoming available for use in the clinic (Van't Veer et al. 2002). Such technologies could be applied to assess whether MYC signaling is elevated in patient tumor samples (Alles et al. 2009; Chandriani et al. 2009; Gatza et al. 2010). Thus, these detection methods for MYC activity have the potential to be translated for routine use in the clinic. Considering the lack of established targeted therapeutics against triple-negative tumors, we propose that MYC status will prove useful as a predictive biomarker of response to

CDK inhibitors for the treatment of triple-negative breast cancers.

Figure legends

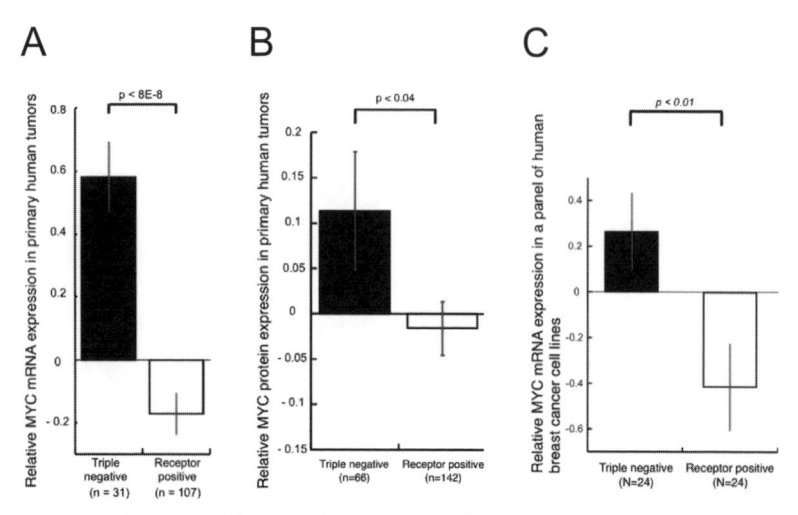

Figure 1. Elevated MYC expression in human triple-negative cancers.
(A) Increased MYC mRNA expression in triple-negative versus receptor-positive primary breast tumors collected through the I-SPY TRIAL ($p < 0.0001$). (B) Increased MYC protein expression in triple-negative primary tumors. Shown is an independent cohort of 208 patients for which quantitative reverse-phase protein arrays were performed. (C) Relative expression of MYC mRNA in a panel of established human breast cell lines (Neve et al. 2006). The error bars represent means +/- S.E.M. p-values were calculated by two-tailed t-test.

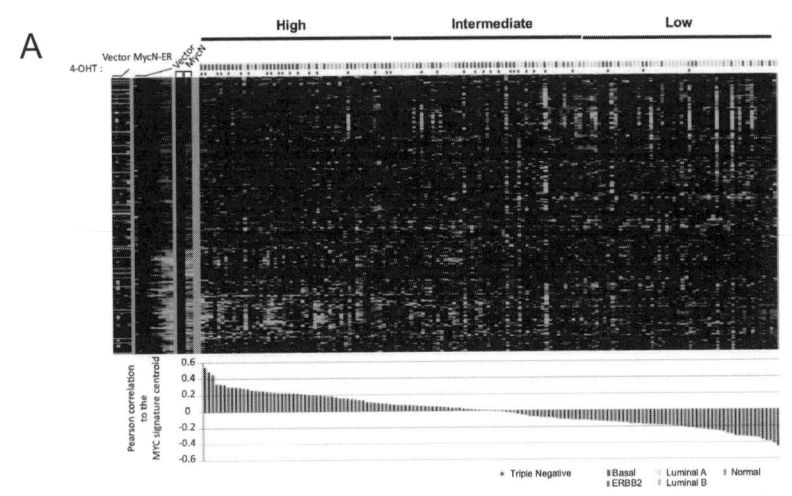

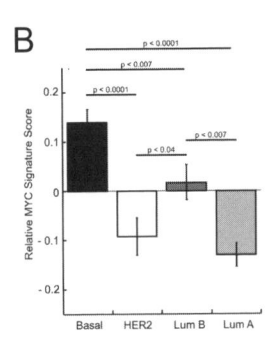

Figure 2. Elevated MYC signaling in human triple-negative breast cancers.
(A) 149 primary tumors ordered by each tumor's Pearson correlation to a 352 gene MYC Signature Centroid. Triple-negative tumors are enriched for the high MYC gene signature ($p < 0.005$; Fisher's Exact Test). Triple negative tumor samples are indicated with a red dot, while molecular sub-types are indicated with colored bars. (B) Correlation between MYC gene expression signature and breast cancer molecular subtypes. Relative MYC gene expression was based on each tumor's Pearson correlation to the MYC gene signature. Student two-tailed t-test is shown for each comparison. (C) Expression of multiple genes within the MYC signaling pathway are altered in triple-negative breast cancers. Schema shows various MAX-interacting genes that are deregulated and can positively or negatively modulate MYC transcriptional activity. Genes are shaded green if expression is suppressed in triple-negative versus receptor-positive tumors, and red if expression is increased in triple-negative tumors. MAX $p = 0.02$; MYC $p < 0.0001$; MYCN $p = 0.06$; MXD4 $p = 0.03$ (two-tailed t-test).

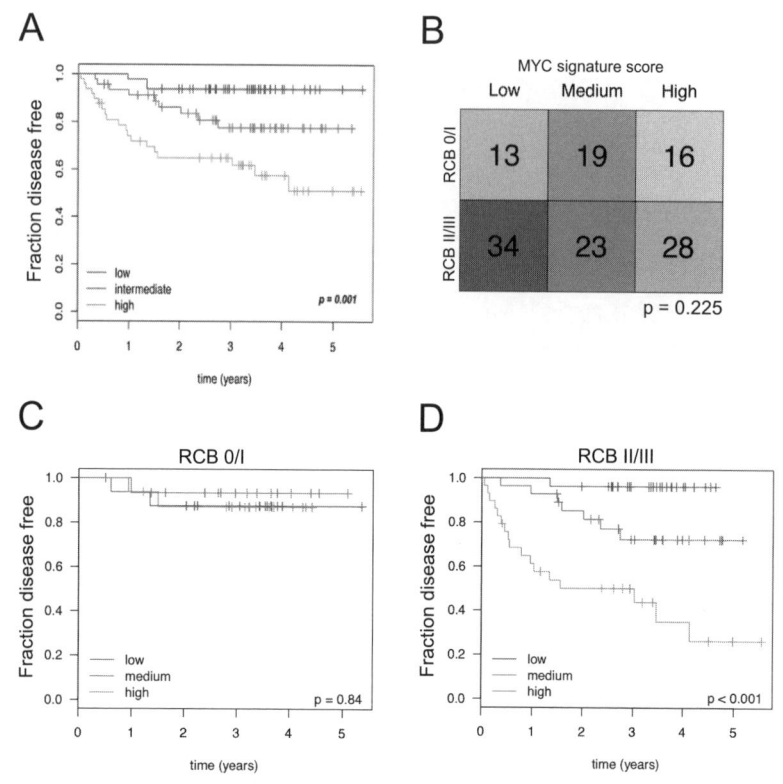

Figure 3. Elevated MYC signaling is associated with poor outcome.
(A) Patients with higher MYC-pathway activation are at increased overall risk of breast cancer recurrence. I-SPY TRIAL patients (n = 149) were divided into tertiles based on the relative expression of the genes in the MYC signature in their pretreatment biopsy samples. Differences in risk of disease recurrence between these groups were assessed using a Cox proportional hazards model and Wald's test. (B) MYC-pathway activation is not significantly correlated with tumor burden following neo-adjuvant chemotherapy. I-SPY TRIAL patients with gene-expression data and for which residual disease burden (RCB 0-III) (Symmans et al. 2007) was determined at the time of surgery (n = 133) were divided into tertiles based on their relative expression of the genes in the MYC signature in their pretreatment biopsy samples. The association between residual tumor burden and MYC-pathway activation tertile was assessed using Fisher's Exact Test. (C) Recurrence by MYC signature in RCB 0/I patients. (D) Recurrence by MYC signature in RCB II/III patients. (E) Multivariate analysis considering receptor status and MYC pathway activation as a continuous variable.

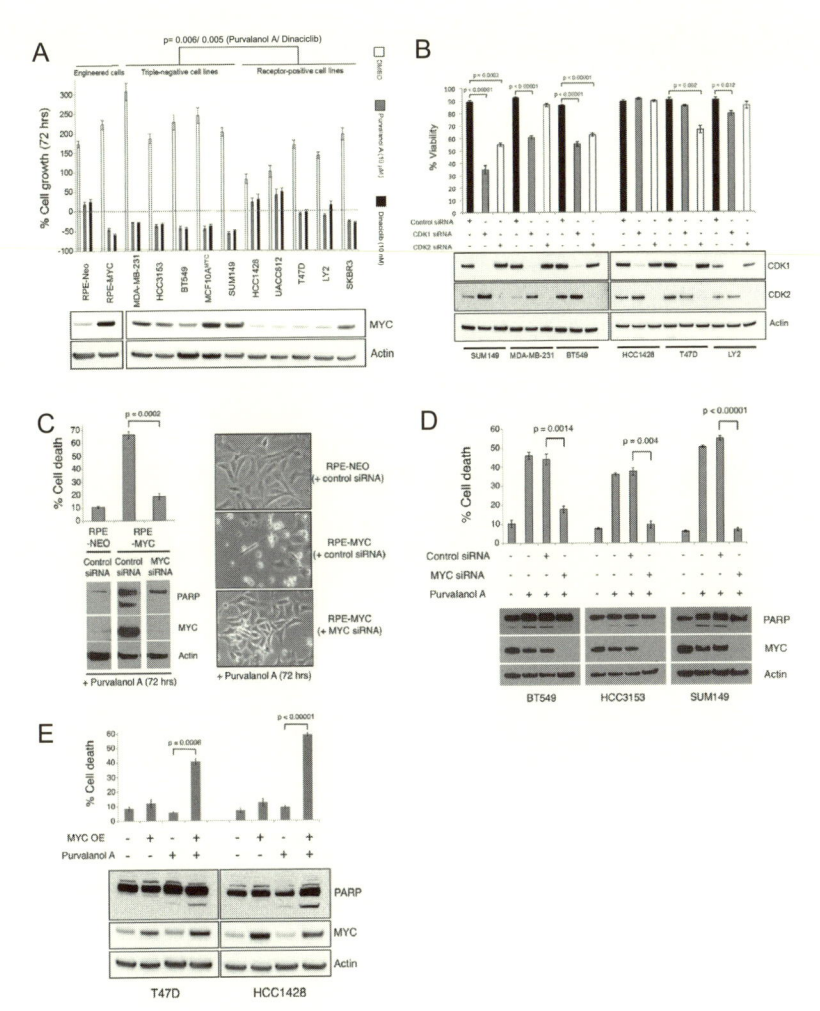

Figure 4. Elevated MYC expression sensitizes triple-negative cancers to CDK inhibition.
(A) A panel of triple-negative as well as receptor-positive breast cells, together with a matched pair of non-tumorigenic model epithelial cells (RPE cells) engineered to overexpress MYC, were treated with CDK inhibitors purvalanol A (10 µM) or dinaciclib (10 nM) for 72 hours and subjected to a CellTiter cell viability assay (Promega). Dashed line indicates the relative starting cell number at the time of adding CDK inhibitors (Time-0). Positive numbers indicate cell growth and negative numbers indicate cell death. *P*-values were calculated by two-tailed t-test for comparisons of cell lines treated with each of the two inhibitors. (B) Cell cycle profiles of three triple-negative cell lines and three receptor-positive cell lines after treatment with purvalanol A

(10 µM) or dinaciclib (10 nM) for 72 hours. The percentage of cells in G1 and G2-M phases of the cell cycle, as determined by DNA content based on propidium iodide staining is indicated. (C) A panel of triple-negative as well as receptor-positive breast cancer cells were treated with siRNA against CDK1 or CDK2 for 72 hours and assessed for cell viability. (D) MYC-dependency of cell death induced by CDK inhibition in RPE cells. RPE-MYC cells were first treated with either MYC siRNA or control non-specific siRNA for 24 hours, then treated with purvalanol A for 72 hours. The collected cells were analyzed for cell viability by Guava ViaCount assay and for PARP activation by western blotting. (E) siRNA mediated MYC knock-down rescues triple-negative cells from undergoing apoptosis upon purvalanol A treatment. MYC knock-down attenuates purvalanol A-dependent PARP activation in triple-negative cells. (F) Receptor-positive cell lines, T47D and HCC1428, engineered to overexpress MYC undergo cell death accompanied by PARP cleavage following 72 hours of purvalanol A treatment. The experiments were repeated at least 3 times in triplicate. The error bars represent means +/- S.E.M. *P*-values were calculated by two-tailed t-test.

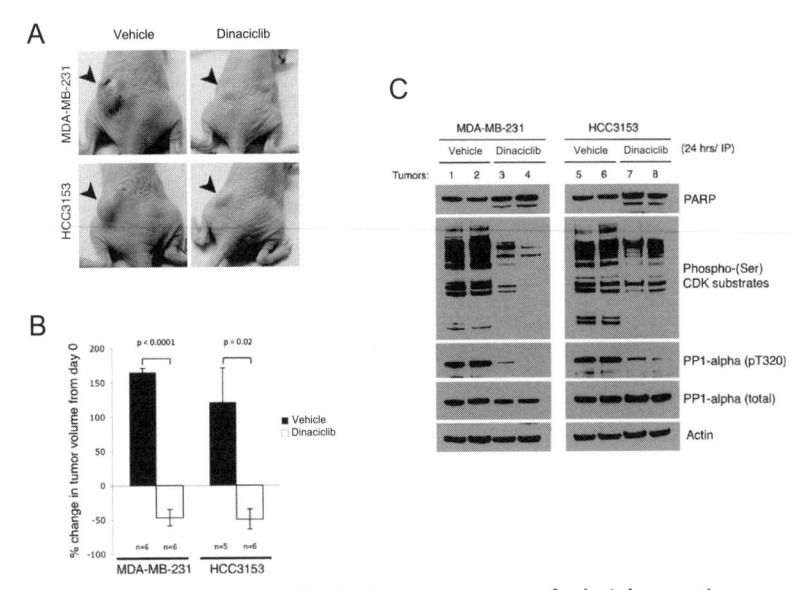

Figure 5. CDK inhibition is effective in treating xenografted triple-negative tumors in mice.
(A) CDK inhibition induces tumor regression in mouse xenograft models of triple-negative breast cancer. Representative photos of tumors after two-weeks of treatment with either vehicle alone or with dinaciclib (50mg/kg IP twice weekly) are shown. (B) Regression of triple-negative tumors in nude mice treated with the CDK inhibitor dinaciclib dina(50mg/kg IP twice weekly) for 2 weeks. Each treatment group per tumor cell type contained the indicated number of mice. The error bars represent means +/- S.E.M. *P*-values were calculated by two-tailed t-test. (C) PARP activation as well as marked reduction in the Serine-phosphorylation of presumptive CDK substrates occurs in tumors within 24 hours of dinaciclib administration. This antibody recognizes amino acid sequences that contain phosphorylated CDK consensus epitope, which is (K/R)(phosphorylated-S)(PX)(K/R) where X can be any amino acid. Two independent tumor samples for each treatment (vehicle or dinaciclib) are shown per cell line. Mean +/- S.E.M are shown.

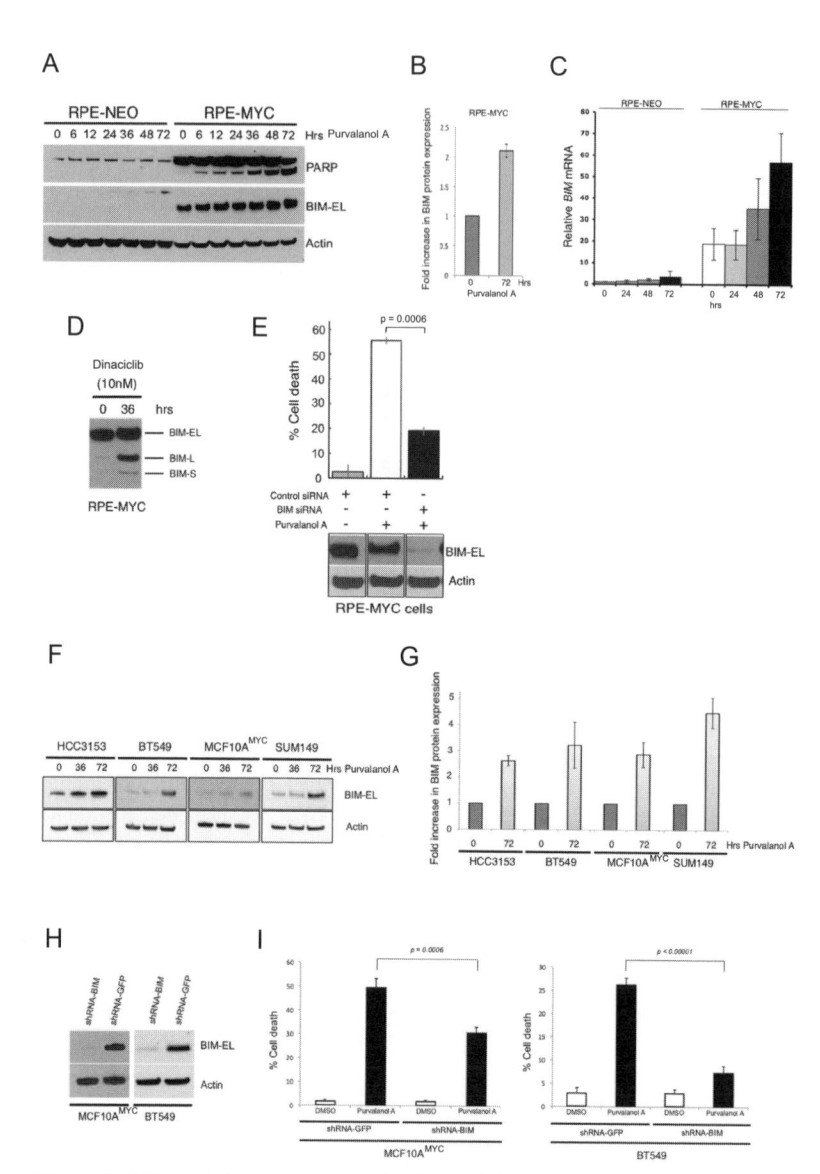

Figure 6. BIM contributes to the mechanisms of CDK inhibition-induced cell death in cells with elevated MYC expression.

(A) RPE cells, with or without constitutive MYC overexpression, were treated with 10μM purvalanol A for 72 hours and were tested for the expression of BIM as well as for an apoptosis indicator PARP and loading control β-Actin. The results shown are representatives of at least 5 independent experiments. (B) Relative fold change in BIM protein expression in RPE-MYC cells treated with Purvalanol A for 72 hrs. The

Purvalanol A time-course experiments were repeated at least 5 times and BIM protein up-regulation was quantified as described in Experimental Procedures. (C) Increased BIM mRNA expression following Purvalanol A treatment. BIM mRNA levels were quantified by qPCR in RPE cells with or without constitutive MYC over-expression. (D) BIM up-regulation in RPE-MYC cells treated with dinaciclib for 36 hours. (E) RPE-MYC cells were transfected with either a pool of specific BIM siRNAs or a pool of control non-targeting siRNAs and cell viability was determined following treatment with 10μM purvalanol A for 72 hours. (F) Up-regulation of BIM protein expression in a panel of triple-negative cells. Several triple-negative cell lines were tested for BIM protein expression following treatment with 10μM purvalanol A for 72 hours. (G) Quantification of BIM up-regulation. Shown are the means from at least 3 independent experiments that yielded the following S.E.Ms, respectively: +/- 0.2 (HCC3153), +/- 0.88 (BT549), +/- 0.48 (MCF10A^{MYC}), and +/- 0.57 (SUM149PT). (H) shRNA-mediated BIM knock-down in two triple-negative cell lines, MCF10A^{MYC} and BT549 cells. shRNA against GFP was used as negative control. (I) BIM knock-down diminishes cell death of MCF10A^{MYC} and BT549 cells following purvalanol A treatment. The experiments were repeated at least 3 times in triplicate. Error bars represent means +/- S.E.M. P-values were calculated by two-tailed t-test.

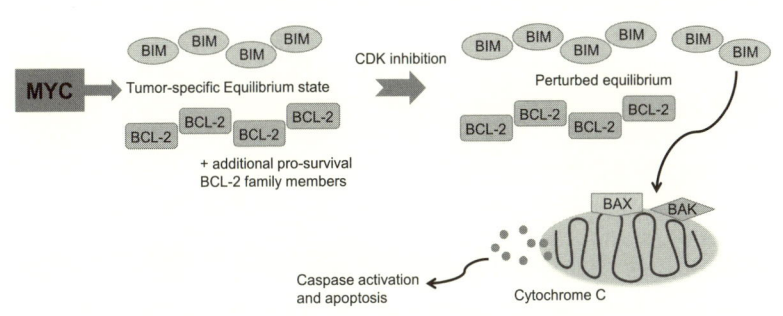

Figure 7. A model of CDK inhibition-induced cell death in MYC-overexpressing breast cancer cells.
Homeostatic conditions reached between pro-apoptotic BIM and anti-apoptotic BCL-2 family members in the presence of elevated MYC expression favors tumor cell growth. CDK inhibition results in the up-regulation of BIM, perturbing this homeostasis, which results in mitochondrial Cytochrome C release and the activation of caspases resulting in cell death.

4. Materials and methods

4.1 I-SPY Trial.

Expression microarray results were available for 149 tumors prior to treatment. Eleven tumors could not be designated as triple negative or not triple negative, owing to a lack of staining for one or more receptor types, leaving 138 available for analysis. Details of the I-SPY Trial protocol and characteristics of enrolled patients will be described elsewhere (Esserman et al. 2012). All patients included in our analysis had pre-treatment core biopsies for which gene-expression measurements had been determined using Agilent 44K microarrays (catalog #G4112F). Microarray hybridization was performed as per manufacturer, the background was subtracted and Lowess normalized log2 ratio of Cy3 and Cy5 intensity values were calculated. For MYC mRNA levels, a MYC-specific probe (A_32_P60687) was compared across the 146 samples for which receptor status was known. Patients enrolled in the trial received conventional neo-adjuvant chemotherapy that included: doxorubicin and cyclophosphamide and/or paclitaxel per the I-SPY protocol prior to definitive surgical resection. The extent of residual disease was quantified using residual cancer burden (RCB) and reported by RCB Class (RCB 0-III) (Symmans et al., 2007).

Bioinformatics and analysis of the I-SPY data.

Expression of the MYC signature (Chandriani et al. 2009) in the I-SPY dataset was examined by first converting the platform-specific probe identifiers in both studies to UNIGENE cluster identifiers (Build 2009 version). Data from multiple probes mapping to the same UNIGENE cluster IDs were averaged. The MYC pathway activity refers to the MYC gene signature score centroid that was calculated as described (Chandriani et al. 2009). The Pearson correlation of each tumor's expression profile of these genes to the MYC Signature centroid was determined. The tumors were then ordered, from high to low, by the Pearson correlation value. Tumors that lacked conclusive receptor status information were excluded from analysis. The remaining tumors were divided into tertiles representing three groups with high, intermediate or low correlation to the MYC signature centroid. Recurrence-free survival was analyzed using Cox Proportional Hazards models that were evaluated using Wald's Test. This analysis was performed using the survival package (version 2.35–7:Terry and Thomas) in the R Environment for Statistical Computing (version

2.10.0 :Team). Associations between categorical variables were evaluated using Fisher's Exact Test. This analysis was performed using the stats package in the R Environment for Statistical Computing (version 2.10.0;(Team)).

4.2 Reverse-Phase Protein Array Analysis of MYC and Phospho-MYC expression.

Protein was extracted from the human tumors and reverse-phase protein lysate microarray was done as described previously (Hennessy et al. 2007; Hu et al. 2007; Liang et al. 2007; Tibes et al. 2006).

4.3 Cell culture.

The propagation of human breast cell lines used in this study and their global mRNA expression profiling has been previously described (Neve et al. 2006). Engineered human epithelial cell lines RPE-NEO and RPE-MYC cells were previously described (Goga et al. 2007). The MYC-overexpressing versions of the receptor-positive cell lines T47D and HCC1428 were established by infecting the cells with the lentivirus prepared using pLVX-AcGFP-N1 plasmid with a full length human MYC cDNA cloned into the EcoRI-XhoI sites.

4.4 Cell viability assays.

Promega CellTiter (MTT) cell viability assay shown in Fig. 4A was performed in 96-well plates, using TECAN Safire2 plate reader that runs Magellan software, according to the manufacture's instruction. Each cell line was plated onto 10 wells per experiment and the assay was repeated at least 5 times. For the rest of the cell viability experiments described throughout this manuscript, a flow cytometry-based Guava ViaCount viability assay (Millipore) was performed according to the manufacture's instruction.

4.5 Cell cycle analysis.

Cell lines were treated with DMSO, purvalanol A (10 µM), or dinaciclib (10 nM) for 72 hours. Following treatment, cells were fixed in 70% ethanol and stained with propidium iodide to measure DNA content. Samples were analyzed on a LSRII flow cytometer. Cell populations were gated to exclude cell debris and doublets and cell cycle distribution of live cells was determined using Flowjo analysis software.

4.6 Protein lysate preparation and western blotting analysis.

Cultured cells were washed with ice-cold phosphate buffered saline (PBS) and harvested directly into radioimmunoprecipitation assay (RIPA) buffer (50mM Tris, 150mM NaCl, 0.5% sodium-deoxycholate, 1% NP40, 0.1% SDS, 2mM EDTA, pH 7.5) containing COMPLETE protease inhibitor cocktail (Roche) and phosphatase inhibitors (Santa Cruz Biotechnology). Isolated tumor tissues were first washed in ice-cold PBS and homogenized on ice using Tissue Tearor (Biospec Products, Inc.) in RIPA buffer containing protease inhibitors and phosphatase inhibitors. Protein concentrations were determined by performing DC Protein Assay (Bio-Rad) using bovine serum albumin (BSA) as standard. The following antibodies were used for western analyses: MYC (Epitomics), β-Actin (Sigma), PARP (Cell Signaling), BIM (Assay Designs), Puma (Cell Signaling), Bid (R&D Systems), Bax (Cell Signaling), Bak (Santa Cruz), BCL-2 (Cell Signaling), BCL-xl (Santa Cruz), MCL-1 (Abcam), Phospho-(Ser) CDK substrates (Cell Signaling), PP1-alpha (Epitomics), PP1-alpha (pT320) (Epitomics). CDK1 (Santa Cruz), CDK2 (Santa Cruz).

4.7 Determination of relative protein expression levels.

Bio-Rad VersaDoc Imaging System (4000 MP) was used to quantify protein expression. BIM up-regulation at the protein level was determined by normalizing pre-saturated BIM signals to those of β-Actin. To determine the relative MYC protein expression levels across a panel of breast cell lines, the MYC signals acquired through anti-MYC western blotting were normalized against total fluorescence from the Ponceau S stained bands as previously described (Nijjar et al. 2005).

4.8 Small molecule CDK inhibitors.

Purvalanol A was purchased from Sigma and was reconstituted in 100% DMSO. Unless otherwise indicated, it was used at a concentration (10 µM), previously shown to induce cell cycle arrest in various mammalian cell lines (Goga et al. 2007; Gray et al. 1998). Dinaciclib was provided by the Drug Synthesis and Chemistry Branch, Developmental Therapeutics Program, Division of Cancer Treatment and Diagnosis, National Cancer Institute (Bethesda, MD) nand MERCK. Dinaciclib was reconstituted either in 100% DMSO for cell culture use or in 20% hydroxypropyl beta cyclodextrin (HPBCD) for mouse studies.

4.9 Mouse xenograft studies.

For all the breast cancer cell lines used in this study, 1×10^7 cells in 200μl PBS or combined with Matrigel were subcutaneously injected into immuno-deficient female mice (Balb/c Nude/Nude) aged 6–8 weeks. The tumors were allowed to grow for 3–4 weeks (with the tumors reaching approximately 200–250 mm^3 in volume) before the animals were treated with either dinaciclib at 50mg/kg or vehicle alone (20% HPBCD) via intraperitoneal (IP) injection.

4.10 siRNA/shRNA experiments.

Unless otherwise noted, siRNA against human CDK1, CDK2, MYC, and BIM (BCL2L11), respectively, and a pool of non-targeting control siRNA (siGENOME SMART pool siRNA) were purchased from Dharmacon and used according to the manufacture's protocol. For the MYC knock-down experiments described in Fig. 4D, the liposomal siRNA preparations against human MYC and luciferase (negative control), respectively, were provided by Alnylam Pharmaceuticals, Inc. (Cambridge, MA). The retroviral shRNA constructs used in this study are pMKO shRNA Bim (Addgene plasmid 17235) (Schmelzle et al. 2007) and pMKO shRNA GFP (Addgene plasmid 10675) (Masutomi et al. 2005), which were purchased from Addgene.

4.11 Analysis of *BIM* mRNA levels using quantitative PCR.

RPE cells, with or without constitutive MYC over-expression, were treated with purvalanol A for 0, 24, 48 and 72 hours. Total RNA was isolated from cells using mirVana (Ambion), and digested with DNaseI to remove contaminating DNA (Ambion). cDNA was prepared from 1μg of total RNA using Superscript II reverse transcriptase kit (Invitrogen). Real-time PCR was performed using probes specific for human *BIM* and *β-ACTIN* purchased from ABI, according to the manufacturer instructions. Samples were run in triplicate on a Bio-Rad Real-Time Thermal Cycler. Variation of *BIM* expression was calculated using the ΔΔCT method (Livak and Schmittgen 2001) with *β-ACTIN* mRNA as an internal control.

Acknowledgements

The author acknowledges that this article is an edited version of the original primary report previously published in *Journal of Experimental Medicine* (Horiuchi et al. 2012), and thus thanks the original co-authors for their contributions and The Rockefeller University Press for permission for the reuse of the published materials. During the course of the study, the author was supported by a Post-doctoral Fellowship Award and an Innovative, Developmental, and Exploratory Award from California Breast Cancer Research Program (15FB-0006, 171B-0024), and is currently supported by a K99/R00 Pathway to Independence Award from the U.S. National Institute of Health/National Cancer Institute (1K99CA175700).

References

Alles, M.C., M. Gardiner-Garden, D.J. Nott, Y. Wang, J.A. Foekens, R.L. Sutherland, E.A. Musgrove, and C.J. Ormandy. (2009) Meta-analysis and gene set enrichment relative to er status reveal elevated activity of MYC and E2F in the "basal" breast cancer subgroup. *PLoS One.* 4: e4710.

Barker, A.D., C.C. Sigman, G.J. Kelloff, N.M. Hylton, D.A. Berry, and L.J. Esserman. (2009) I-SPY 2: an adaptive breast cancer trial design in the setting of neoadjuvant chemotherapy. *Clin Pharmacol Ther.* 86: 97–100.

Bauer, K.R., M. Brown, R.D. Cress, C.A. Parise, and V. Caggiano. (2007) Descriptive analysis of estrogen receptor (ER)-negative, progesterone receptor (PR)-negative, and HER2-negative invasive breast cancer, the so-called triple-negative phenotype: a population-based study from the California cancer Registry. *Cancer.* 109: 1721–8.

Ben-Porath, I., M.W. Thomson, V.J. Carey, R. Ge, G.W. Bell, A. Regev, and R.A. Weinberg. (2008) An embryonic stem cell-like gene expression signature in poorly differentiated aggressive human tumors. *Nat Genet.* 40: 499–507.

Bertucci, F., P. Finetti, N. Cervera, B. Esterni, F. Hermitte, P. Viens, and D. Birnbaum. (2008) How basal are triple-negative breast cancers? *Int J Cancer.* 123: 236–40.

Bland, K.I., M.M. Konstadoulakis, M.P. Vezeridis, and H.J. Wanebo. (1995) Oncogene protein co-expression. Value of Ha-ras, c-myc, c-fos, and p53 as prognostic discriminants for breast carcinoma. *Ann Surg.* 221: 706–18; discussion 718–20.

Blethrow, J.D., J.S. Glavy, D.O. Morgan, and K.M. Shokat. (2008) Covalent capture of kinase-specific phosphopeptides reveals Cdk1-cyclin B substrates. *Proc Natl Acad Sci U S A.* 105: 1442–7.

Carey, L.A., E.C. Dees, L. Sawyer, L. Gatti, D.T. Moore, F. Collichio, D.W. Ollila, C.I. Sartor, M.L. Graham, and C.M. Perou. (2007) The triple negative paradox: primary tumor chemosensitivity of breast cancer subtypes. *Clin Cancer Res.* 13: 2329–34.

Carey, L.A., C.M. Perou, C.A. Livasy, L.G. Dressler, D. Cowan, K. Conway, G. Karaca, M.A. Troester, C.K. Tse, S. Edmiston, S.L. Deming, J. Geradts, M.C. Cheang, T.O. Nielsen, P.G. Moorman, H.S. Earp, and R.C. Millikan. (2006) Race, breast cancer subtypes, and survival in the Carolina Breast Cancer Study. *JAMA.* 295: 2492–502.

Chandriani, S., E. Frengen, V.H. Cowling, S.A. Pendergrass, C.M. Perou, M.L. Whitfield, and M.D. Cole. (2009) A core MYC gene expression signature is prominent in basal-like breast cancer but only partially overlaps the core serum response. *PLoS One.* 4: e6693.

Chang, D.W., G.F. Claassen, S.R. Hann, and M.D. Cole. (2000) The c-Myc transactivation domain is a direct modulator of apoptotic versus proliferative signals. *Mol Cell Biol.* 20: 4309–19.

Cheang, M.C., S.K. Chia, D. Voduc, D. Gao, S. Leung, J. Snider, M. Watson, S. Davies, P.S. Bernard, J.S. Parker, C.M. Perou, M.J. Ellis, and T.O. Nielsen. (2009) Ki67 index, HER2 status, and prognosis of patients with luminal B breast cancer. *J Natl Cancer Inst.* 101: 736–50.

Chonghaile, T.N., and A. Letai. (2008) Mimicking the BH3 domain to kill cancer cells. *Oncogene.* 27 Suppl 1: S149–57.

Cowling, V.H., and M.D. Cole. (2006) Mechanism of transcriptional activation by the Myc oncoproteins. *Semin Cancer Biol.* 16: 242–52.

Dang, C.V. (1999) c-Myc target genes involved in cell growth, apoptosis, and metabolism. *Mol Cell Biol.* 19: 1–11.

Dent, R., M. Trudeau, K.I. Pritchard, W.M. Hanna, H.K. Kahn, C.A. Sawka, L.A. Lickley, E. Rawlinson, P. Sun, and S.A. Narod. (2007) Triple-negative breast cancer: clinical features and patterns of recurrence. *Clin Cancer Res.* 13: 4429–34.

Dickson, M.A., and G.K. Schwartz. (2009) Development of cell-cycle inhibitors for cancer therapy. *Curr Oncol.* 16: 36–43.

Dohadwala, M., E.F. da Cruz e Silva, F.L. Hall, R.T. Williams, D.A. Carbonaro-Hall, A.C. Nairn, P. Greengard, and N. Berndt. (1994) Phosphorylation and inactivation of protein phosphatase 1 by cyclin-dependent kinases. *Proc Natl Acad Sci U S A.* 91: 6408–12.

Egle, A., A.W. Harris, P. Bouillet, and S. Cory. (2004) Bim is a suppressor of Myc-induced mouse B cell leukemia. *Proc Natl Acad Sci U S A.* 101: 6164–9.

Eilers, M., and R.N. Eisenman. (2008) Myc's broad reach. *Genes Dev.* 22: 2755–66.

Esserman, L.J., D.A. Berry, A. Demichele, L. Carey, S.E. Davis, M. Buxton, C. Hudis, J.W. Gray, C. Perou, C. Yau, C. Livasy, H. Krontiras, L. Montgomery, D. Tripathy, C. Lehman, M.C. Liu, O.I. Olopade, H.S. Rugo, J.T. Carpenter, L. Dressler, D. Chhieng, B. Singh, C. Mies, J. Rabban, Y.Y. Chen, D. Giri, L. van 't Veer, and N. Hylton. (2012) Pathologic Complete Response Predicts Recurrence-Free Survival More Effectively by Cancer Subset: Results From the I-SPY 1 TRIAL–CALGB 150007/150012, ACRIN 6657. *J Clin Oncol.*

Fong, P.C., D.S. Boss, T.A. Yap, A. Tutt, P. Wu, M. Mergui-Roelvink, P. Mortimer, H. Swaisland, A. Lau, M.J. O'Connor, A. Ashworth, J. Carmichael, S.B. Kaye, J.H. Schellens, and J.S. de Bono. (2009) Inhibition of poly(ADP-ribose) polymerase in tumors from BRCA mutation carriers. *N Engl J Med.* 361: 123–34.

Gatza, M.L., J.E. Lucas, W.T. Barry, J.W. Kim, Q. Wang, M.D. Crawford, M.B. Datto, M. Kelley, B. Mathey-Prevot, A. Potti, and J.R. Nevins. (2010) A pathway-based classification of human breast cancer. *Proc Natl Acad Sci U S A.* 107: 6994–9.

Goga, A., D. Yang, A.D. Tward, D.O. Morgan, and J.M. Bishop. (2007) Inhibition of CDK1 as a potential therapy for tumors over-expressing MYC. *Nat Med.* 13: 820–7.

Grandori, C., S.M. Cowley, L.P. James, and R.N. Eisenman. (2000) The Myc/Max/Mad network and the transcriptional control of cell behavior. *Annu Rev Cell Dev Biol.* 16: 653–99.

Gray, N.S., L. Wodicka, A.M. Thunnissen, T.C. Norman, S. Kwon, F.H. Espinoza, D.O. Morgan, G. Barnes, S. LeClerc, L. Meijer, S.H. Kim, D.J. Lockhart, and P.G. Schultz. (1998) Exploiting chemical libraries, structure, and genomics in the search for kinase inhibitors. *Science.* 281: 533–8.

Guan, Y., W.L. Kuo, J.L. Stilwell, H. Takano, A.V. Lapuk, J. Fridlyand, J.H. Mao, M. Yu, M.A. Miller, J.L. Santos, S.E. Kalloger, J.W. Carlson, D.G. Ginzinger, S.E. Celniker, G.B. Mills, D.G. Huntsman, and J.W. Gray. (2007) Amplification of PVT1 contributes to the pathophysiology of ovarian and breast cancer. *Clin Cancer Res.* 13: 5745–55.

Gurel, B., T. Iwata, C.M. Koh, R.B. Jenkins, F. Lan, C. Van Dang, J.L. Hicks, J. Morgan, T.C. Cornish, S. Sutcliffe, W.B. Isaacs, J. Luo, and A.M. De Marzo. (2008) Nuclear MYC protein overexpression is an early alteration in human prostate carcinogenesis. *Mod Pathol.* 21: 1156–67.

Hemann, M.T., A. Bric, J. Teruya-Feldstein, A. Herbst, J.A. Nilsson, C. Cordon-Cardo, J.L. Cleveland, W.P. Tansey, and S.W. Lowe. (2005) Evasion of the p53 tumour surveillance network by tumour-derived MYC mutants. *Nature.* 436: 807–11.

Hennessy, B.T., Y. Lu, E. Poradosu, Q. Yu, S. Yu, H. Hall, M.S. Carey, M. Ravoori, A.M. Gonzalez-Angulo, R. Birch, I.C. Henderson, V. Kundra, and G.B. Mills. (2007) Pharmacodynamic markers of perifosine efficacy. *Clin Cancer Res.* 13: 7421–31.

Horiuchi, D., L. Kusdra, N.E. Huskey, S. Chandriani, M.E. Lenburg, A.M. Gonzalez-Angulo, K.J. Creasman, A.V. Bazarov, J.W. Smyth, S.E. Davis, P. Yaswen, G.B. Mills, L.J. Esserman, and A. Goga. (2012) MYC pathway activation in triple-negative breast cancer is synthetic lethal with CDK inhibition. *J Exp Med.* 209: 679–96.

Hu, J., X. He, K.A. Baggerly, K.R. Coombes, B.T. Hennessy, and G.B. Mills. (2007) Non-parametric quantification of protein lysate arrays. *Bioinformatics.* 23: 1986–94.

Huang, M.J., Y.C. Cheng, C.R. Liu, S. Lin, and H.E. Liu. (2006) A small-molecule c-Myc inhibitor, 10058-F4, induces cell-cycle arrest, apoptosis, and myeloid differentiation of human acute myeloid leukemia. *Exp Hematol.* 34: 1480–9.

Hubner, A., T. Barrett, R.A. Flavell, and R.J. Davis. (2008) Multisite phosphorylation regulates Bim stability and apoptotic activity. *Mol Cell.* 30: 415–25.

Jain, A.N., K. Chin, A.L. Borresen-Dale, B.K. Erikstein, P. Eynstein Lonning, R. Kaaresen, and J.W. Gray. (2001) Quantitative analysis of chromosomal CGH in human breast tumors associates copy number abnormalities with p53 status and patient survival. *Proc Natl Acad Sci U S A.* 98: 7952–7.

Jones, D. (2010) Adaptive trials receive boost. *Nat Rev Drug Discov.* 9: 345–8.

Liang, J., S.H. Shao, Z.X. Xu, B. Hennessy, Z. Ding, M. Larrea, S. Kondo, D.J.

Dumont, J.U. Gutterman, C.L. Walker, J.M. Slingerland, and G.B. Mills. (2007) The energy sensing LKB1-AMPK pathway regulates p27(kip1) phosphorylation mediating the decision to enter autophagy or apoptosis. *Nat Cell Biol*. 9: 218–24.

Liedtke, C., C. Mazouni, K.R. Hess, F. Andre, A. Tordai, J.A. Mejia, W.F. Symmans, A.M. Gonzalez-Angulo, B. Hennessy, M. Green, M. Cristofanilli, G.N. Hortobagyi, and L. Pusztai. (2008) Response to neoadjuvant therapy and long-term survival in patients with triple-negative breast cancer. *J Clin Oncol*. 26: 1275–81.

Livak, K.J., and T.D. Schmittgen. (2001) Analysis of relative gene expression data using real-time quantitative PCR and the 2(-Delta Delta C(T)) Method. *Methods*. 25: 402–8.

Livasy, C.A., G. Karaca, R. Nanda, M.S. Tretiakova, O.I. Olopade, D.T. Moore, and C.M. Perou. (2006) Phenotypic evaluation of the basal-like subtype of invasive breast carcinoma. *Mod Pathol*. 19: 264–71.

Lowe, S.W., E. Cepero, and G. Evan. (2004) Intrinsic tumour suppression. *Nature*. 432: 307–15.

Malumbres, M., P. Pevarello, M. Barbacid, and J.R. Bischoff. (2008) CDK inhibitors in cancer therapy: what is next? *Trends Pharmacol Sci*. 29: 16–21.

Masutomi, K., R. Possemato, J.M. Wong, J.L. Currier, Z. Tothova, J.B. Manola, S. Ganesan, P.M. Lansdorp, K. Collins, and W.C. Hahn. (2005) The telomerase reverse transcriptase regulates chromatin state and DNA damage responses. *Proc Natl Acad Sci U S A*. 102: 8222–7.

Meyer, N., and L.Z. Penn. (2008) Reflecting on 25 years with MYC. *Nat Rev Cancer*. 8: 976–90.

Molenaar, J.J., M.E. Ebus, D. Geerts, J. Koster, F. Lamers, L.J. Valentijn, E.M. Westerhout, R. Versteeg, and H.N. Caron. (2009) Inactivation of CDK2 is synthetically lethal to MYCN over-expressing cancer cells. *Proc Natl Acad Sci U S A*. 106: 12968–73.

Naidu, R., N.A. Wahab, M. Yadav, and M.K. Kutty. (2002) Protein expression and molecular analysis of c-myc gene in primary breast carcinomas using immunohistochemistry and differential polymerase chain reaction. *Int J Mol Med*. 9: 189–96.

Neve, R.M., K. Chin, J. Fridlyand, J. Yeh, F.L. Baehner, T. Fevr, L. Clark, N. Bayani, J.P. Coppe, F. Tong, T. Speed, P.T. Spellman, S. DeVries, A. Lapuk, N.J. Wang, W.L. Kuo, J.L. Stilwell, D. Pinkel, D.G. Albertson, F.M. Waldman, F. McCormick, R.B. Dickson, M.D. Johnson, M. Lippman, S. Ethier, A. Gazdar, and J.W. Gray. (2006) A collection of breast cancer cell lines for the study of functionally distinct cancer subtypes. *Cancer Cell*. 10: 515–27.

Nguyen, M., R.C. Marcellus, A. Roulston, M. Watson, L. Serfass, S.R. Murthy Madiraju, D. Goulet, J. Viallet, L. Belec, X. Billot, S. Acoca, E. Purisima, A. Wiegmans, L. Cluse, R.W. Johnstone, P. Beauparlant, and G.C. Shore. (2007) Small molecule obatoclax (GX15–070) antagonizes MCL-1 and overcomes MCL-1-mediated resistance to apoptosis. *Proc Natl Acad Sci U S A*. 104: 19512–7.

Nijjar, T., E. Bassett, J. Garbe, Y. Takenaka, M.R. Stampfer, D. Gilley, and P. Yaswen.

(2005) Accumulation and altered localization of telomere-associated protein TRF2 in immortally transformed and tumor-derived human breast cells. *Oncogene.* 24: 3369–76.

O'Connor, L., A. Strasser, L.A. O'Reilly, G. Hausmann, J.M. Adams, S. Cory, and D.C. Huang. (1998) Bim: a novel member of the Bcl-2 family that promotes apoptosis. *Embo J.* 17: 384–95.

Oltersdorf, T., S.W. Elmore, A.R. Shoemaker, R.C. Armstrong, D.J. Augeri, B.A. Belli, M. Bruncko, T.L. Deckwerth, J. Dinges, P.J. Hajduk, M.K. Joseph, S. Kitada, S.J. Korsmeyer, A.R. Kunzer, A. Letai, C. Li, M.J. Mitten, D.G. Nettesheim, S. Ng, P.M. Nimmer, J.M. O'Connor, A. Oleksijew, A.M. Petros, J.C. Reed, W. Shen, S.K. Tahir, C.B. Thompson, K.J. Tomaselli, B. Wang, M.D. Wendt, H. Zhang, S.W. Fesik, and S.H. Rosenberg. (2005) An inhibitor of Bcl-2 family proteins induces regression of solid tumours. *Nature.* 435: 677–81.

Parry, D., T. Guzi, F. Shanahan, N. Davis, D. Prabhavalkar, D. Wiswell, W. Seghezzi, K. Paruch, M.P. Dwyer, R. Doll, A. Nomeir, W. Windsor, T. Fischmann, Y. Wang, M. Oft, T. Chen, P. Kirschmeier, and E.M. Lees. (2010) Dinaciclib (SCH 727965), a novel and potent cyclin-dependent kinase inhibitor. *Mol Cancer Ther.* 9: 2344–53.

Perou, C.M., T. Sorlie, M.B. Eisen, M. van de Rijn, S.S. Jeffrey, C.A. Rees, J.R. Pollack, D.T. Ross, H. Johnsen, L.A. Akslen, O. Fluge, A. Pergamenschikov, C. Williams, S.X. Zhu, P.E. Lonning, A.L. Borresen-Dale, P.O. Brown, and D. Botstein. (2000) Molecular portraits of human breast tumours. *Nature.* 406: 747–52.

Reinhardt, H.C., H. Jiang, M.T. Hemann, and M.B. Yaffe. (2009) Exploiting synthetic lethal interactions for targeted cancer therapy. *Cell Cycle.* 8: 3112–9.

Ruzinova, M.B., T. Caron, and S.J. Rodig. (2010) Altered subcellular localization of c-Myc protein identifies aggressive B-cell lymphomas harboring a c-MYC translocation. *Am J Surg Pathol.* 34: 882–91.

Sarrio, D., S.M. Rodriguez-Pinilla, D. Hardisson, A. Cano, G. Moreno-Bueno, and J. Palacios. (2008) Epithelial-mesenchymal transition in breast cancer relates to the basal-like phenotype. *Cancer Res.* 68: 989–97.

Schmelzle, T., A.A. Mailleux, M. Overholtzer, J.S. Carroll, N.L. Solimini, E.S. Lightcap, O.P. Veiby, and J.S. Brugge. (2007) Functional role and oncogene-regulated expression of the BH3-only factor Bmf in mammary epithelial anoikis and morphogenesis. *Proc Natl Acad Sci U S A.* 104: 3787–92.

Sears, R., F. Nuckolls, E. Haura, Y. Taya, K. Tamai, and J.R. Nevins. (2000) Multiple Ras-dependent phosphorylation pathways regulate Myc protein stability. *Genes Dev.* 14: 2501–14.

Seo, H.R., J. Kim, S. Bae, J.W. Soh, and Y.S. Lee. (2008) Cdk5-mediated phosphorylation of c-Myc on Ser-62 is essential in transcriptional activation of cyclin B1 by cyclin G1. *J Biol Chem.* 283: 15601–10.

Shapiro, G.I. (2006) Cyclin-dependent kinase pathways as targets for cancer treatment. *J Clin Oncol.* 24: 1770–83.

Sierra, A., X. Castellsague, A. Escobedo, A. Moreno, T. Drudis, and A. Fabra. (1999) Synergistic cooperation between c-Myc and Bcl-2 in lymph node progression of

T1 human breast carcinomas. *Breast Cancer Res Treat.* 54: 39–45.

Sorlie, T., C.M. Perou, R. Tibshirani, T. Aas, S. Geisler, H. Johnsen, T. Hastie, M.B. Eisen, M. van de Rijn, S.S. Jeffrey, T. Thorsen, H. Quist, J.C. Matese, P.O. Brown, D. Botstein, P. Eystein Lonning, and A.L. Borresen-Dale. (2001) Gene expression patterns of breast carcinomas distinguish tumor subclasses with clinical implications. *Proc Natl Acad Sci U S A.* 98: 10869–74.

Soucek, L., J. Whitfield, C.P. Martins, A.J. Finch, D.J. Murphy, N.M. Sodir, A.N. Karnezis, L.B. Swigart, S. Nasi, and G.I. Evan. (2008) Modelling Myc inhibition as a cancer therapy. *Nature.* 455: 679–83.

Symmans, W.F., F. Peintinger, C. Hatzis, R. Rajan, H. Kuerer, V. Valero, L. Assad, A. Poniecka, B. Hennessy, M. Green, A.U. Buzdar, S.E. Singletary, G.N. Hortobagyi, and L. Pusztai. (2007) Measurement of residual breast cancer burden to predict survival after neoadjuvant chemotherapy. *J Clin Oncol.* 25: 4414–22.

Team, R.D.C. R: A language and environment for stastical computing. *R Foundation for Stastical Computing, Vienna, Austria.*

Terry, T., and L. Thomas. Survival: Survival analysis, including penalised likelihood. . R package version 2.35–7.

Tibes, R., Y. Qiu, Y. Lu, B. Hennessy, M. Andreeff, G.B. Mills, and S.M. Kornblau. (2006) Reverse phase protein array: validation of a novel proteomic technology and utility for analysis of primary leukemia specimens and hematopoietic stem cells. *Mol Cancer Ther.* 5: 2512–21.

Tutt, A., M. Robson, J.E. Garber, S.M. Domchek, M.W. Audeh, J.N. Weitzel, M. Friedlander, B. Arun, N. Loman, R.K. Schmutzler, A. Wardley, G. Mitchell, H. Earl, M. Wickens, and J. Carmichael. (2010) Oral poly(ADP-ribose) polymerase inhibitor olaparib in patients with BRCA1 or BRCA2 mutations and advanced breast cancer: a proof-of-concept trial. *Lancet.* 376: 235–44.

Van't Veer, L.J., H. Dai, M.J. van de Vijver, Y.D. He, A.A. Hart, M. Mao, H.L. Peterse, K. van der Kooy, M.J. Marton, A.T. Witteveen, G.J. Schreiber, R.M. Kerkhoven, C. Roberts, P.S. Linsley, R. Bernards, and S.H. Friend. (2002) Gene expression profiling predicts clinical outcome of breast cancer. *Nature.* 415: 530–6.

Voduc, K.D., M.C. Cheang, S. Tyldesley, K. Gelmon, T.O. Nielsen, and H. Kennecke. (2010) Breast cancer subtypes and the risk of local and regional relapse. *J Clin Oncol.* 28: 1684–91.

Wang, Y., I.H. Engels, D.A. Knee, M. Nasoff, Q.L. Deveraux, and K.C. Quon. (2004) Synthetic lethal targeting of MYC by activation of the DR5 death receptor pathway. *Cancer Cell.* 5: 501–12.

Wong, D.J., H. Liu, T.W. Ridky, D. Cassarino, E. Segal, and H.Y. Chang. (2008) Module map of stem cell genes guides creation of epithelial cancer stem cells. *Cell Stem Cell.* 2: 333–44.

Yang, D., H. Liu, A. Goga, S. Kim, M. Yuneva, and J.M. Bishop. (2010) Therapeutic potential of a synthetic lethal interaction between the MYC proto-oncogene and inhibition of aurora-B kinase. *Proc Natl Acad Sci U S A.* 107: 13836–41.

福島第一原子力発電所から放出された
セシウム137土壌沈着密度分布図の作成

沢野伸浩

要旨

　2011年3月11日に発生した東日本大震災と引き続き発生した津波より福島第一原子力発電所が被災し、炉心溶融を含む深刻な事故が発生した。放出された放射性物質は風とともに拡散し、関東圏を含む東日本一帯の地域が放射性物質により汚染する結果となった。今後、長期間の汚染モニタリング調査が必須となるが、その指標物質として半減期が30.1年と比較的長いセシウム137が上げられる。セシウム137の土壌沈着量は、米国核安全保障局（NNSA）が事故直後の2011年3月17日より計測を開始し、計測値等を記録した詳細なデータを同年10月21日より公開した。このデータをdisjunctive krigingを用いて内挿することで「面的」なデータに変換し、汚染濃度を場所毎の汚染濃度をより正しく推定するために等高線入りの「濃度分布図」を作成すると同時に、実際に地上で実際に測られた値との比較・検証を行った。

キーワード　福島第一原子力発電所事故、汚染地図、セシウム137、土壌沈着密度、disjunctive kriging

1. チェルノブイリ原発事故と居住制限

　1986年4月26日にウクライナ共和国プリピャチのチェルノブイリ原子力発電所4号炉が非常用電源系の実験運転中に制御不能状態に陥り、爆発事故を起こし放射性物質が飛散する同時に深刻な土壌汚染を引き起

こした。チェルノブイリ原子力発電所事故後、放射能に汚染された地域は、セシウム 137 の土壌沈着密度により、一定の基準を設定した上でその範囲と対応が決められたことが今中 (1998) などにより、詳しく報告されている。その基準は、事故時に存在していたソビエト連邦が崩壊し、ベラルーシ、ウクライナ、ロシアの 3 か国に現在分かれているが、若干の用語の相当等はみられるものの基本的には、いずれもセシウム 137 の土壌沈着密度を基に以下のように決められた。

第 1 ゾーン：緊急避難ゾーン (原則、原子力関連要員等を除き一般民の居住は不可能：1,480kBq/m^2 以上
第 2 ゾーン：移住義務ゾーン (原則、この範囲内の住民の居住は認められず、国家が責任を持って住民を移住させるとしたゾーン)：555kBq/m^2 以上 1,480kBq/m^2 未満
第 3 ゾーン：移住権利ゾーン (原則、住民が希望すれば移住が認められるゾーン)：185kBq/m^2 以上 555kBq/m^2 未満
第 4 ゾーン：放射線管理ゾーン (厳重な放射線管理を必要としつつ、居住は可能とされたゾーン)：37kBq/m^2 以上 185kBq/m^2 未満

今中 (2013) には、事故があったチェルノブイリ原発周辺の比較的最近の情報が記載されており、それによれば基本的に第 1 ゾーンおよび第 2 ゾーン内での居住は今日でも認められていない。しかしベラルーシの一部の村では、主として経済的な理由から「集団帰還」が行われている状況が報告されている。いずれにしても、チェルノブイリ周辺の地域ではセシウム 137 の土壌沈着密度 555kBq/m^2 を基準に居住の可否が判断されている事実を認識する必要があるだろう。

この基準がどのような経緯で決められたかについては、それを明確に示す資料は見あたらない。しかし、元々、チェルノブイリ原発事故が起こった当時、放射能の計測に Bq (ベクレル) といった MKS 単位系は使われておらず、Ci (キューリー) が用いられていた。1Ci = 37kBq である

ため、40Ci/km^2 = 1,480kBq/m^2、15Ci/km^2 = 555kBq/m^2 であり、汚染現場での計測のやりやすさやセシウム 137 は長期間にわたり安定して環境中に存在すること、さらに空間線量との相関が高いこと等からこの基準が設定されたものと推測できる。

一方、日本の場合、事故当初（2011 年 4 月 21 日まで）福島第一原発から半径 20km の同心円の内部が「計画的避難区域」とされたが、その後、空間線量が 20mSv/年を超える地域とされた。従って、チェルノブイリ原発事故の際のような、長期間安定的に存在するセシウム 137 の土壌沈着密度のデータを基に計画範囲や区域を決めるといった方法はとられていない。さらに、チェルノブイリ原発事故の際の「ゾーン」に相当する「区域」の具体的な指定については、それを「地図上に示す」という方法ではなく、日本の場合は「地名で示す」ことにより行われており、2013 年 3 月 31 日時点での「避難指示解除準備地域」は、例えば、「葛尾村大字落合字関下の全ての区域」というような表現により行われている[1]。

2. 米国エネルギー省核安全保障局による放射能データ測定と公開

福島第一原子力発電所での事故発生直後より米国エネルギー省（DoE: Department of Energy）、核安全保障局（NNSA: National Nuclear Safety Administration）は、福島県を中心に航空機によるモニタリング調査の準備を開始した。米国時間 2011 年 3 月 14 日に 33 名の専門家と約 7 トンの専用機材を積載した C-17 専用機を日本に派遣し、同機は日本時間で 16 日午前 1 時 55 分に横田基地に到着、3 月 17 日から福島第一原子力発電所（以下、「福島第一」）上空を含む計測を開始した。計測は地上における空間線量に加え、大気濃度、土壌含有濃度、専用測定装置による地上計測、航空機による広域的な土壌沈着密度測定が行われ、土壌含有濃度については、Ba-140、Ce-144、Cs-134、Cs-136、Cs-137、I-131、I-132、Mo-99、Sr-89、Sr-90、Sr-Total、Te-129m、Te-132 の合計 13

項目で測定が行われている (Lyons and Colton, 2012)。

　日本においては、事故直後から「緊急時迅速放射能影響予測ネットワークシステム (SPEEDI)」による放射能の拡散予測が行われ、その結果を公開しなかった政府の対応が批判されたが、NNSA による航空機測定結果については、3月17日の結果が18日に、18日の結果が19日といった具合に測定直後とのデータが日本政府に提供されており、SPEEDI によるシミュレーションとは比較にならない精度の高い情報が実際には存在していた。この件について、2012年7月10日に行われた参議院予算委員会で取り上げられることとなり、当時の枝野幸男経済産業大臣が参議院予算委員会で陳謝の答弁を行っている。

　一方、2011年10月21日より、米国政府は日本で行われた放射能測定結果について、エネルギー省のホームページを通して公開する措置を取った[2]。実際の公開は2段階で行われ、最初の公開から約半年後の2012年7月6日からは、パスワードの登録が必要とされるものの、さらに詳しいデータの公開が行われ今日に至っている[3]。

　米国より約1年遅れて日本政府は2012年9月12日より（航空機測定については、10月1日より）測定データの公開を文部科学省のホームページより開始した[4]。米国が公開しているデータが全ての測定結果をほぼそのまま、いわゆる「生データ」の状態で公開しているのに対し、文部科学省のデータ公開は、航空機測定のデータについて見ると、実際に公開されているのは、測定結果を逆距離加重法 (IDW: Inverse Distance Weight Method) により内挿（補間）した結果であり、米国が公開したデータとは質的に大幅に異なったものとなっている。

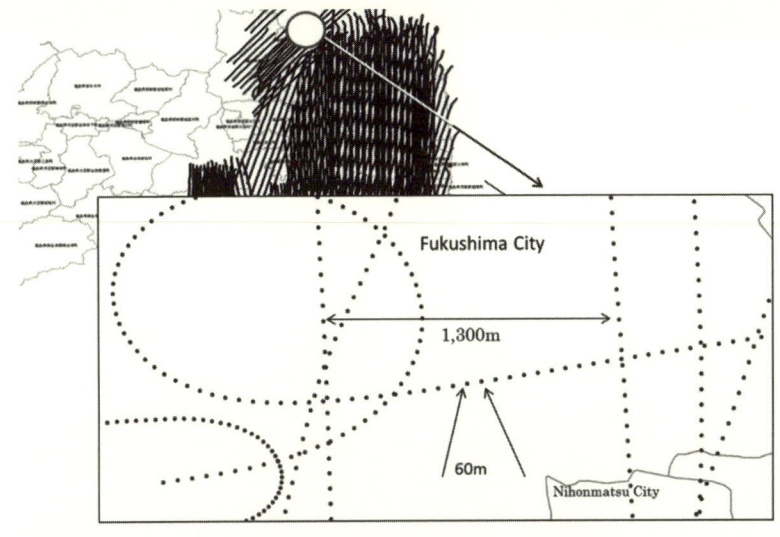

図1 NNSAによる航空機モニタリング調査

3. NNSA モニタリング調査

　NNSA による航空機モニタリング調査は、2011 年 3 月 17 日より 5 月 28 日までの 2 ヶ月以上に及び、その範囲は福島第一原発を中心にほぼ 80km の範囲と一部、さらに首都圏を含む関東地方一帯に及ぶ。

　図 1 は、NNSA によって公開されたデータの一部をそのまま地図上に点として既存地図上に重ねたものである。この図に示したとおり、データを取得した飛行経路の間隔は、600〜1300m 程度、データサンプリングの間隔は 60m 程度なっている。また、飛行高度は、地上から約 300m であった。

　これら、位置と値のわかる点データを使って「面 (surface)」を作り出す手法を一般に「内挿」や「補間」と呼ぶ。内挿には原理的に、ある数学的な関数をそのまま点データに適用する手法と、あらかじめ何らかの空間的な偏りや特性を内挿に反映させ、確率論的に行うものとの 2 種類が存在する。そして、文部科学省が現在「航空機測定データ」として公開している IDW による内挿結果は前者の典型例で、後者は一般に

「空間統計(学)的手法」、英語では kriging と呼ばれている。前者は、比較的少ないパラメータの設定で面的な分布をよく反映させることができることが知られている。しかし、IDW の場合は未知の点の値を推定する際、既知の点の値と未知の点との距離を使った一種の平均の計算を行うため、予測値は必ず推定に使われる未知の点群が持つ値の最大値と最小値の範囲内に収まることになる。従って、その未知の点の本当の値が内挿計算を行う空間内の最小値と最大値の間に収まらない場合、内挿された結果は不自然なものとなる。一般に、IDW による内挿結果を空間的な分布として見た場合、「(値の大きい)尾根や(値の小さい)谷を維持できない」といった欠点が存在することが知られ、この問題は内挿値から等値線を発生させ、「ある値以上の範囲」を特定するような場合、「致命的」なものとなる。

　図2は、文部科学省が「航空機測定データ」として公開しているIDW による内挿値群から数学的な表面モデル(サーフェス)を作成し、それを元に福島県三春町およびその周辺を対象に $20kBq/m^2$ 間隔の等値線を発生させたものである。一方、図3は NNSA の不均一な元データを disjunctive kriging により内挿し、図2同様に $20kBq/m^2$ 間隔の等値線を発生させたものである。

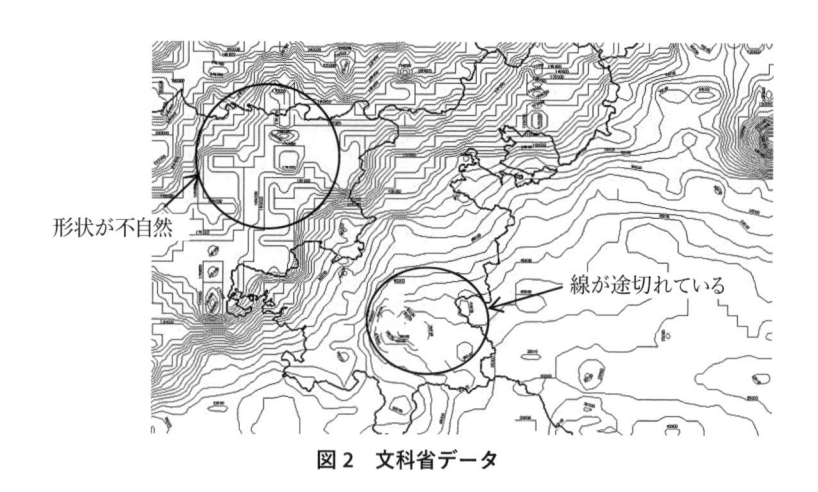

図2　文科省データ

図3　NNSAデータ(ほとんど全ての等値線が閉曲線を構成)

　これら図2と図3を比較してみると明らかなとおり、濃度値そのものの空間的な分布について大きな差は見られない。しかし、ある濃度値に着目し、その範囲を特定するための等値線を決定しなければならないような場合、IDWによる内挿には問題が多いことがわかる。すなわち、もし、今回文部科学省が公開しているデータを使って、例えば、チェルノブイリ原発事故時のように555kBq/m^2以上の範囲を特定しようとした場合、その境界線が途切れ途切れになったり、IDWによる内挿の欠点である「尾根・谷が維持できない」と問題により不自然な形状になったりするため、何らかの修正が必要となるなど、そのままでの利用が困難なためである。

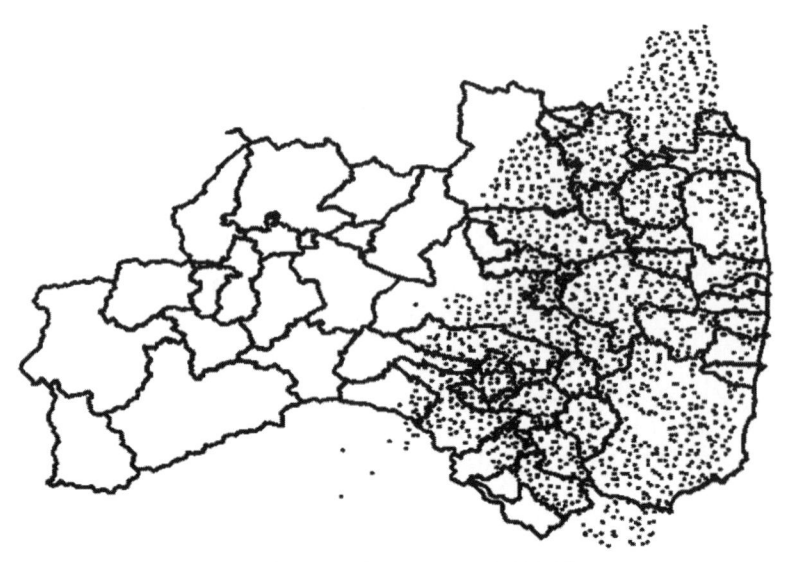

図4 比較のために抽出を行った文科省データ

4. 内挿精度の検証

　NNSA が公開しているデータ、文部科学省が公開しているデータのいずれも直接地表面のセシウム 137 の沈着量を測定しているものではなく、NaI と呼ばれる計測器を航空機に搭載し、そこでカウントされた放射線量を地表の値に換算したものであるため誤差の混入は避けられない。文部科学省は、航空機測定のデータは IDW による内挿値を公開する一方で、地表で測られた値についてはそのままの状態で測定点とそれに対応した値を公開している。そこでこのデータと、①文部科学省が公開している IDW による内挿結果、② NNSA のデータを disjunctive kriging により内挿した結果、③ NNSA のデータを IDW で内挿した結果の3つと比較し、どれがセシウム 137 の現実の土壌沈着密度を最も精度良く反映しているかについて、その検証を行った。

　検証の手法は、①〜③のデータはいずれも内挿により作成されたラスター形式のデータである。そこで各ラスターを構成するピクセルに絶対的な緯度経度に相当する座標値を与え（実際にはラスターおよび比較す

るための地上データの計測点の両方の座標値をあらかじめ日本9系の平面直角座標系に変換することで距離の座標に統一)、地上に計測点が存在するピクセルの値を抽出することで、地上測定点とその地点に最も近い(あるいは、その測定地点をラスターデータのピクセル内部に持つ)値との対照表を作成し、相互に比較を行った。

また、データの抽出は、元々、文部科学省の地上測定データは福島県内を中心に合計 2,200 点ほど存在する。しかし、その一部は NNSA の飛行範囲外にあり、また、$10kBq/m^2$ 未満の値のデータについては、地上のバックグランドの放射能の影響を相対的に強く受けている可能性が高いため、これらを除外し、実際の比較は図4に示す 1,586 点について相関係数、RMS(二乗平均平方根)誤差を求めることより行った。その結果を表1に示す。

表 1 相関係数と RMS 誤差

	①文科省 IDW	② NNSA_DJK	③ NNSA_IDW
相関係数	0.819	0.866	0.858
RMS 誤差	0.352	0.359	0.280

DJK: disjunctive kriging

5. チェルノブイリ原発事故との比較

まず、相関係数で見た場合、②の NNSA のデータを disjunctive kriging により内挿した結果が最も値が大きく、RMS 誤差で見た場合、③の値が最も小さくなった。これらはいずれも「大差」というほどのことはないが、「文部科学省が測定した地上のデータ」と「NNSA のデータを disjunctive kriging により内挿した結果」や「NNSA のデータを IDW で内挿した結果」の方が「文部科学省が自身で内挿により作成した結果」と比較して、いずれも精度が高い結果が得られたことは注目に値する。ただし、この結果は元々の値の分布が数値の大きい方により大きな偏りが見られる点に注意が必要である。加えて、RMS 誤差はその特性上、数値の大きい方により大きな差が生じやすいため、相対的な「あて

はまり」は良くても誤差を評価する際、元となるデータの分布形状等に十分な注意が必要なことは言うまでもない。さらに、単なる誤差の大小だけではなく、内挿された結果の空間的な「滑らかさ」なども加味した評価を行う必要がある。

図5にNNSAが公開したデータを元にdisjunctive krigingで作成したチェルノブイリ原発事故で住民の避難対策や移住政策に使われた基準と同じ範囲を示した。ただし、この図ではチェルノブイリ原発事故で「放射能管理区域」に指定された範囲はNNSAのデータからでは値が小さすぎるため内挿することができず、その3倍の値である111kBq/m^{2}以上の範囲を示している。また、表2にゾーン毎の面積の概算を示した。

6. 考察

今中(2013)は、チェルノブイリ原発事故と福島第一原子力発電所事故の放射能の総排出量を比較し、後者は前者の2〜4割程度、と評価した。チェルノブイリ原発事故は、その詳細は明らかではないものの、規模の小さな核爆発を伴う巨大な「火災」であったと考えられるのに対し、福島第一原子力発電所事故はいずれの事故炉も冷却水の喪失とそれに伴う熱暴走により、原子炉と環境を隔てている「防護壁」の崩壊や、水素爆発による放射性物質の飛散であり、事故の性格は大きく異なっている。さらに、事故後の気象が放射性物質の拡散と極めて強く関係していることも明らかであり、両者を一概に比較することはできない。しかし、放射能による汚染面積は、表2の「チェルノブイリ／福島」の欄に示したとおり、ごく大雑把にはチェルノブイリ原発事故は、福島第一原子力発電所事故の約10倍程度規模を持つことがわかる。一方、表2に示した福島第一原発の面積の数値には海域が参入されていないため、仮に総排出量の半分が海域に拡散したとすると、放射能の総排出量について今中の予測は、かなりの確率で正しいものと推測できる。すなわち、今回、我々が直面した福島第一原子力発電所事故の規模を放射能の放出量やその汚染範囲で見た場合、チェルノブイリ原発事故の「半分程

度」との認識を持つ必要があると言えよう。

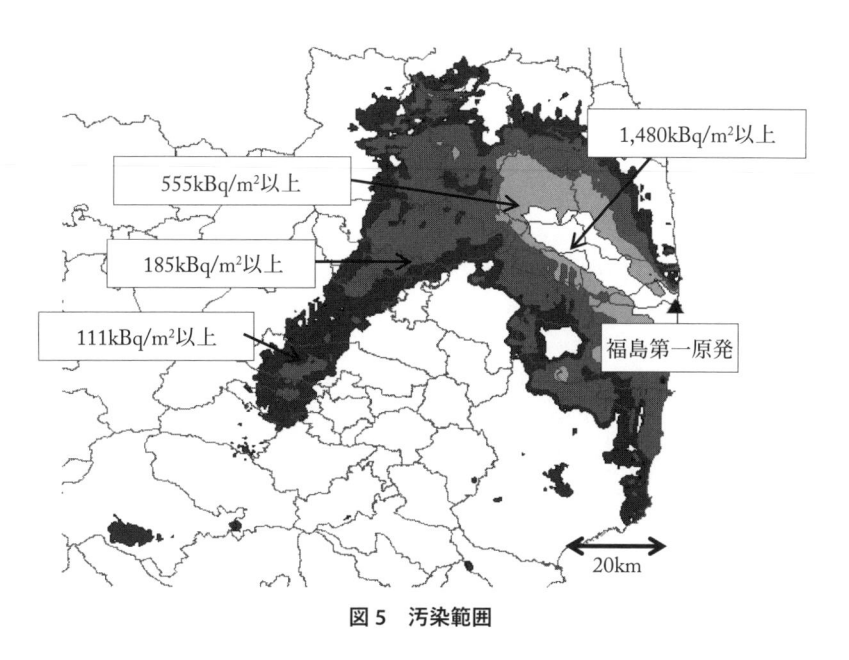

図5 汚染範囲

表2 福島第一・チェルノブイリとの汚染面積比較

	Contamination Area (ha)		
濃度	>185KBq/m^2	>555KBq/m^2	>1,480KBq/m^2
チェルノブイリ	1,912,000	720,000	310,000
福島	217,262	76,790	27,243
チェルノブイリ/福島	8.8	9.4	11.4

7. 結語

　福島の被災現地では、今まさに除染作業が行われ、その復興に向けた努力が続けられている。その試みにとって、できる限り精度の高い地表面での汚染レベル、すなわち安定的な放射性物質の土壌沈着密度の把握が不可欠であることは論を待たない。そのために、文部科学省は航空機モニタリング結果を IDW による内挿値でなく、その実測値を一刻も早

く公開し、できる限り精度の高い地表面の汚染地図の作成を可能にするとともに、今度の対策立案に対して、データをより有効に活用できるような方策を講ずるべきである。

注
1. 首相官邸ホームページ（みなさまの安全確保）
   http://www.kantei.go.jp/saigai/pdf/20130307siji_katurao.pdf
2. 米国核安全保障局ホームページ
   http://explore.data.gov/Geography-and-Environment/US-DOE-NNSA-Response-to-2011-Fukushima-Incident-Fi/kxp6-xc7d
3. パスワード付き米国核安全保障局ホームページ
   http://www.nnsaresponsedata.net
4. 放射性物質の分布状況等調査データベース
   http://radb.jaea.go.jp/mapdb/top.html

参考文献

Craig Lyons and David Colton. (2012). *Aerial Measuring System Japan, Health Physics*, Vol. 102, No. 25, pp.509–515

今中哲二（編著）(1998).『チェルノブイリ事故による放射能災害　国際共同研究報告書』技術と人間

今中哲二 (2013).『放射能汚染と災厄―終わりなきチェルノブイリ原発事故の記録』明石書店

執筆者一覧（A list of contributors）

2014 年 2 月 28 日現在（As of 28th February, 2014）

都留文科大学文学部英文学科専任教員及び名誉教授（五十音順）
Department of English, Tsuru University

（The order of the Japanese syllabary）

今井　隆*（Takashi Imai）教授（Professor）
大平栄子（Eiko Ohira）教授（Professor）
奥脇奈津美（Natsumi Okuwaki）准教授（Associate Professor）
竹島達也（Tatsuya Takeshima）教授（Professor）
中地　幸（Sachi Nakachi）教授（Professor）
福島佐江子*（Saeko Fukushima）教授（Professor）
松土　清（Kiyoshi Matsudo）特任教授（Adjunct Professor）

窪田憲子（Noriko Kubota）名誉教授（Professor Emerita）
依藤道夫（Michio Yorifuji）名誉教授（Professor Emeritus）

（* 編集代表者）

都留文科大学文学部英文学科卒業生（卒業年順）
Graduates, Department of English, Tsuru University

（The order of the graduated year）

赤穂榮一（Eiichi Akaho）神戸学院大学名誉教授（Professor Emeritus, Kobe Gakuin University）1966 年卒業（Graduated in 1966）

内藤　徹 (Toru Naito) 仁愛女子短期大学 (仁愛大学兼任) 教授 (Professor, Jin-ai Women's College (Jin-ai University)) 1969 年卒業 (Graduated in 1969)

野中博雄 (Hiroo Nonaka) 桐生大学教授 (Professor, Kiryu University) 1975 年卒業 (Graduated in 1975)

竹村雅史 (Masashi Takemura) 北星学園大学短期大学部教授 (Professor, Hokusei Gakuen University Junior College) 1979 年卒業 (Graduated in 1979)

沢野伸浩 (Nobuhiro Sawano) 金沢星稜大学女子短期大学部教授 (Professor, Kanazawa Seiryo University, Women's College Department) 1984 年卒業 (Graduated in 1984)

斎藤伸治 (Shinji Saito) 岩手大学教授 (Professor, Iwate University) 1984 年卒業 (Graduated in 1984)

宮岸哲也 (Tetsuya Miyagishi) 安田女子大学准教授 (Associate Professor, Yasuda Women's University) 1987 年卒業 (Graduated in 1987)

澤崎宏一 (Koichi Sawasaki) 静岡県立大学准教授 (Associate Professor, University of Shizuoka) 1989 年卒業 (Graduated in 1989)

松岡幹就 (Mikinari Matsuoka) 山梨大学大学院准教授 (Associate Professor, University of Yamanashi) 1991 年卒業 (Graduated in 1991)

上原義正 (Yoshimasa Uehara) 日本大学非常勤講師 (Part-time Lecturer, Nihon University) 1994 年卒業 (Graduated in 1994)

山田昌史 (Masashi Yamada) 島根県立大学准教授 (Associate Professor,

University of Shimane) 1995 年卒業 (Graduated in 1995)

髙橋　愛 (Ai Takahashi) 徳山工業高等専門学校准教授 (Associate Professor, Tokuyama College of Technology) 1997 年卒業 (Graduated in 1997)

堀内　大 (Dai Horiuchi) カリフォルニア大学サンフランシスコ校ポストドクトラルフェロー (Postdoctoral Fellow, University of California, San Francisco) 1997 年卒業 (Graduated in 1997)

寺川かおり (Kaori Terakawa) 獨協大学非常勤講師 (Part-time Lecturer, Dokkyo University) 1999 年卒業 (Graduated in 1999)

瀧口美佳 (Mika Takiguchi) 立正大学非常勤講師 (Part-time Lecturer, Rissho University) 1999 年卒業 (Graduated in 1999)

花田　愛 (Ai Hanada) 関東学院大学非常勤講師 (Part-time Lecturer, Kanto Gakuin University) 2000 年早期卒業 (Early Graduated in 2000)

安原和也 (Kazuya Yasuhara) 名城大学准教授 (Associate Professor, Meijo University) 2002 年卒業 (Graduated in 2002)

言語学、文学そしてその彼方へ
――都留文科大学英文学科創設 50 周年記念研究論文集

Linguistics, Literature and Beyond: A Collection of Research Papers Celebrating the 50th Anniversary of the Foundation of the Department of English, Tsuru University

Edited by the Editorial Committee for the Research Papers Celebrating the 50th Anniversary of the Foundation of the Department of English, Tsuru University

発行	2014 年 3 月 15 日　初版 1 刷
定価	20000 円＋税
編者	© 都留文科大学英文学科創設 50 周年記念研究論文集編集委員会
発行者	松本功
装丁者	萱島雄太
印刷所	三美印刷株式会社
製本所	株式会社 星共社
発行所	株式会社 ひつじ書房

〒 112-0011 東京都文京区千石 2-1-2 大和ビル 2 階
Tel.03-5319-4916　Fax.03-5319-4917
郵便振替 00120-8-142852
toiawase@hituzi.co.jp　http://www.hituzi.co.jp/

ISBN978-4-89476-682-2

造本には充分注意しておりますが、落丁・乱丁などがございましたら、小社かお買上げ書店にておとりかえいたします。ご意見、ご感想など、小社までお寄せ下されば幸いです。

ひつじ研究叢書（言語編）第 96 巻
日本語文法体系新論—派生文法の原理と動詞体系の歴史
清瀬義三郎則府著　定価 7,400 円＋税

日本語の膠着言語としての性質に着目し、用言の活用が無い文法「派生文法」を提唱。派生文法の原理を説き、現代語全般、文論をも含めた文法論を詳述、史的研究もとりあげる。

ひつじ研究叢書(言語編) 第109巻
複雑述語研究の現在
岸本秀樹・由本陽子編　定価 6,800 円+税

ミニマリズムや生成語彙論、事象構造論など近年の言語理論の発展により言語に対する知見を深める可能性を秘める「複雑述語」に関する最先端の研究成果を著した論文を集成した。

ひつじ研究叢書(言語編) 第111巻
現代日本語ムード・テンス・アスペクト論
工藤真由美著　定価 7,200 円＋税

日本語のバリエーションとして標準語と諸方言を位置づけた上で、〈叙述文の述語〉の中核をなす〈ムード・テンス・アスペクト〉を中心に、その多様なあり様について考察。

日本語複文構文の研究

益岡隆志・大島資生・橋本修・堀江薫・前田直子・丸山岳彦編　定価 9,800 円＋税

「連用複文・連体複文編」、「文法史編」、「コーパス言語学・語用論編」、「言語類型論・対照言語学編」の 4 部構成で日本語の複文の総合的な研究をめざす大著。

複合動詞研究の最先端―謎の解明に向けて
影山太郎編　定価 8,600 円＋税
日本語にみられる「晴れ渡る」といった複合動詞が、どのような仕組みで、どういった歴史があるのか、また外国語の場合はどうか。これらの謎に若手からベテランの研究者が挑む。